MURDER BY DECEPTION

A Matt Berkeley Novel

by

WILLIAM KERR

Murder by Deception   William Kerr

Murder by Deception is a work of fiction.
Names, characters, places (other than governmental
or other such locations open to public access)
and incidents are the products of the author's imagination
or are used fictitiously. Any resemblance to actual events,
locales or persons, living or dead, is entirely coincidental.

Published 2019 by
Amazon Kindle Direct Publishing

Copyright © 2019 by William Kerr

ISBN: 9781072664451

Cover Illustration by RAK

All Rights reserved. No part of this book may
Be reproduced or transmitted
in any form or by any electronic or mechanical
means, including photocopying, recording,
or by any information storage and retrieval system,
without written permission of the author.

DEDICATION

To Rebecca for her strength and resilience to life's challenges.

Other Novels by William Kerr

Dragon Path
(Path of the Golden Dragon)

The Red Hand

The Collector

Death's Bright Angel

Judgment Call

Mark of the Devil

Night of the Angels

Deadly Logic

Night Scream

Tears of the Gods

MURDER BY DECEPTION

Chapter 1

Jefferson County, Colorado

Present Time

Sonny Weaver stretched his arms high in the air, fists doubled as he yawned. The mid-October sun had already dropped behind the foothills leading west, up into the high country. A scattering of cumulus clouds had turned a soft pink against what had become a darkening purple sky. Creek-side cottonwood yellows, spruce blues and pine tree greens were beginning to merge into early evening shadows.

The two-mile round trip along South Valley Park's major hiking trails, Swallow Tail and Coyote Song, had been anything but tiring, even with the backpack of iced-downed beer carried over his shoulders. In fact, midway through the hike, they'd found a fairly secluded place off the trail under a shaded overhang of one of the erratically formed, red sandstone formations. It afforded enough privacy from other hikers where he and lovely, auburn-haired Emily Jo had stopped for a good hour.

There had been a little kissing as well as a fair amount of mutual, hands-on exploration, exciting enough to raise the body temperature on each, yet not to the point of forgetting there were others on the trail nearby. It must, however, have been the 6-pack of Sam Adams Boston Lager they'd consumed – him four cans, she two – that brought on the fullness and sudden desire to sleep.

Those moments were now only the fleeting memory of an enjoyable afternoon as Sonny turned toward the restroom which was nothing more than a single-door, unisex portable toilet.
Standing off to the side of the parking lot, it sat inside a walnut-stained, wood-framed enclosure to give the impression of privacy.

It was one of those toilets that by the end of the weekend at every county and state park, you needed an oxygen mask just to open the door. God forbid if you had to do anything other than take a leak. Made him proud he was a man and only had to find the nearest tree.

"C'mon, Emily Jo, it's gettin' dark. That road up the mountain to your mama's place on the weekend, it's a sonofabitch. You know that." Speaking as much to himself as to Emily Joe, he continued, "Dork-heads comin' down from up there, all beered-up, ninety miles an hour, lights blindin'. Just as soon run you off the mountain as look at you."

The door to the toilet snapped open as Emily Joe stepped out, zipping up her jeans with one hand. "For Christ's sake, quit your hollerin', Sonny." Taking the handkerchief from her nose with her free hand and nodding back toward the toilet, she added, "I sure as hell wasn't planning on spending the night in that thing." With eyes momentarily scrunched tight, nose and face wrinkled in disgust, she muttered, "My God, that was bad. Let's go."

Having already shed the backpack from his shoulders, Sonny swung it up onto the bed of the new, silver-colored Ford F-150. The clanging of empty beer cans echoed across the parking lot, all but two other vehicles having already departed.

Ignition, headlights, shift of the gears and the truck pulled up to the lot's exit as darkness began to descend. With a quick look to the left and right and seeing no traffic either way, Sonny shouted, "Shazam, baby, and we're off!" With gravel and red sand spraying out behind the truck's rear tires, Sonny whipped the steering wheel to the right and fishtailed onto the two-lane Deer Creek Canyon Road.

"Damn it, Sonny," Emily Jo cursed. "You're drunk. You need to stick to that three-point-two stuff they used to have in the grocery stores if you can't hold your beer."

"Fuck you, smartass." He considered a moment. A narrow smile spread across his face before saying, "And that's not a bad idea."

Emily Jo backhanded Sonny's right shoulder. "Not in your dreams until you're sober."

"C'mon, Emily Jo, I'm sober as a priest."

She laughed. "Not Father Jonathon. Not my priest. He can out drink you any day of the week and never show it."

Just after they passed the small, tree-shrouded bridge that crossed over swift-running Deer Creek and a sign that pointed the way to Grizzly Drive and a development of oversized homes, Sonny jammed on the brakes. Tires squealed against the asphalt, bringing the truck to a jarring halt. "Holy shit, you see that?" He flicked on the high beams.

"See what?" was all Emily Jo could get out before her mouth opened in an ear-shattering scream. One hand squeezed Sonny's arm. With the other hand white-knuckled on the passenger door armrest, she demanded, "Is it a man or what?"

The thing, six feet of more in height, stood on two feet, most of its body covered in hair, face narrowed, almost human, but not. It glared at them, its eyes showing reddish green in the glare of the headlights. They couldn't hear it, but they could see the mouth, pulled back into a snarl, fang-like teeth bared in the sharp glow of the high beams. A moment later the thing dropped to all fours and started toward the truck, at first a slow lope before picking up speed.

Sonny still couldn't believe what had materialized in the middle of the road. Answering Emily Jo, he blurted, "I don't know and I don't fucking wanna know," as he jammed the gears into reverse and stomped on the gas pedal. The truck jerked backward, but the creature kept coming, faster, its face contorted with an animal viciousness that spoke only one thing – kill.

"Faster, Sonny," Emily Jo begged. "It's catching up with us."

Twisting his upper body and head around to look through the rear window, Sonny lost control. He mistakenly turned the wheel to the left rather than the right. The truck's rear end swung across the east-bound lane and off the road, through an aging barbed wire fence, through weeds, across a small opening between two trees and down into the creek. "Shit, Shit, Shit!"

His curses were drowned out by Emily Jo's shrieks and the full weight of the creature as it crashed down on the hood of the truck. Its front feet, covered in hair like those of a great dog, clawed at the windshield, then the top of the cab. Metallic screeching tore at their ears as the claws raked across the roof and ripped through paint in its attempt to tear its way into the cab.

Yelling and cursing, Sonny jerked the gears into low and stomped the gas pedal. With four-wheel drive, the front wheels seemed to catch, but the rear tires only spun deeper into the rock and sand of the creek's bottom.

With tears streaming from her eyes, Emily Jo kept begging, "Please, I don't want to die, I don't want to die."

Its full weight now on the roof of the cab, the enormous creature started jumping up and down until the roof began to give, crushing inward. The side windows suddenly exploded outward, leaving only shards of glass at the bottom of the window frames. The windshield splintered into a spider's web of cracks before bursting out across the hood.

Lightning fast, one of the creature's hand-like paws dropped down through the side window. Its claws tightened and sank into the flesh of Emily Jo's shoulder.

The last words Sonny heard or thought he heard through Emily Jo's terrifying screams were, "Sonny, help me."

Sonny grabbed her left arm and tried to pull her to him, away from the creature's grasp, but it was no use. Shouting, "Emily Jo!" he felt her yanked away, her body dragged through the narrowing slit of the open window, her clothes torn from her body as she was pulled across jagged glass.

Emily Jo's screams were submerged by a growl that turned quickly into a long, triumphant howl that made even the trees seem to shudder with fear of the unknown.

Chapter 2

Northeast Florida

While life doesn't always meet our expectations, it was one of those times a couple of years back when things couldn't have been better. The old farm house overlooking the Atlantic Intracoastal Waterway between Jacksonville and St. Augustine grabbed me the first time I saw it. Several weeks later following a cash sale, the house was picked up, lowered onto a barge and towed north up the Intracoastal to a little place called Palm Valley, Florida.

Once offloaded and firmly on a new foundation, I poured a fair amount of savings into fixing up the house. In addition to new plumbing and wiring, a paint job in and out, I had a new kitchen installed as well as tile flooring throughout the lower level, new carpeting on the stairs and upper floor.

Since my mother had passed away, I also brought down much of her antique furniture before selling the family's home in Charleston, South Carolina. My pride and joy, however, has been a wide, screened-in back porch looking over a new floating pier jutting out into the Waterway. The house had become what I called my final duty station.

You may ask who the hell am I? Matthew W. (as in William) Berkeley. What few friends I have call me Matt. Former Navy Special Warfare officer, past head of security for the congressionally funded North American Archeological Research and Preservation Agency (NAARPA) and now retired.

Between scuba diving down in the Keys and kayaking on the Intracoastal Waterway, I've been able to hold down my weight and stay relatively healthy despite entering what many consider *the later years*.

Some say I'm merely faking retirement because of the trouble that has followed me from the earlier phases of my life.

Others who know me say I wouldn't be happy if I couldn't find a dead body or two strewn along the way. Actually, I'm just trying to find a little peace as I grow older.

I suppose in the minds of the young, gray hair and early sixties meets the definition of *later years*, but to me, it's all in the mind. As long as I'm mentally and physically capable of carrying the load and faced with a challenge to solve now and then, I'm good to go. So far as challenges go, unknown to me that morning, one was waiting just around the corner as I'll later explain.

There've been a number of interesting, exciting and yes, scary moments with the Navy – Viet Nam and various special ops thereafter – but the bureaucracy of duty in Washington and driving a desk instead of a ship pretty much deadened the thrill.

Lured by a former university professor with the promise of something different, I took what one might call early retirement at the rank of Commander and entered civilian life to provide security for NAARPA's archaeological exploits, both here in the States and in a number of other countries. Surprising how many bad guys inhabit the world of artifacts, the dead and their remains.

There've also been a few love interests over the years. In that regard, however, the past months have definitely been a disappointment. My current love interest is, or I should say *was*, Lieutenant Polly Bartelow of the Jacksonville, Florida Sheriff's Department. Beautiful, highly intelligent yet fearless when the occasion required, we've shared a number of law enforcement adventures as well as each other's bed.

It was good until she was promoted to Captain and temporarily assigned to the Florida Department of Law Enforcement's headquarters (FDLE) in Tallahassee for advanced training. An eight-week course, no less.

All went well the first couple of weeks. Together on weekends, but then time began to lag between visits. Work load, field trips to various law enforcement facilities throughout the state and studying the various aspects of the organization's support of local law enforcement was the excuse. From a couple of my contacts in the FDLE, it appeared, however, that a lot of that work and learning process was being shared with a guy from the Tampa Police Department. A guy she'd known in the past and who was undergoing the same familiarization process. Unfortunately for me, it appeared they were getting a lot more familiar with each other than was necessary.

Hope springs eternal, or so I wanted to believe. Just because she was thirty-or-so years younger than me, I still considered myself able to carry my own, in bed or otherwise. So, what the hell was this younger guy all about? Dr Phil, where were you and your "life strategies" when I needed you?

I guess the only thing I could say was, "It is what it is." Something like the old Doris Day song, "Que Sera, Sera" which, if I remember correctly, meant whatever shall be shall be.

With the sky a deep Atlantic blue and the sun inching its way westward, warming the October day, it was with thoughts of "Pretty Polly" that, paddle in hand, I was on my way down to the pier for a bit of kayaking on the Intracoastal. As I reached the pier and tossed the paddle into my faded green, badly scared L.L. Bean kayak, the cell phone in my jacket pocket clamored for attention.

I thumbed open the flip top on the antiquated mobile device and punched the TALK button. With eternal hope still in my heart, I answered, "Polly?"

"Who the hell is Polly? It's me, John Nabhe in Denver. I need help. Your kind of help."

Disappointment knows no bounds, but I'd be damned if I was going to share my dashed hopes with a guy who once saved my life. "Not many want my kind of help anymore. What's happening?

"Coupla things you might find interesting. Anybody with you?"

"I was just getting into my two-seater kayak to do a little paddling on the Intracoastal. To my chagrin, the second seat specifically designed for female occupancy is empty."

He gave a half laugh. "You're slipping, Berkeley. Unless

you're on the hunt for trouble, and even then, you've usually got a lady companion somewhere close by."

"Not today. Hold on. Power boat passing."

I held my hand over the phone as a speed boat shaped like one of those stretch-bodied, low-slung cigar boats used by drug smugglers on TV – think *Miami Vice* – roared down the waterway. Bow up at least ten to twelve degrees, two big, black 150 horsepower Merc's hanging off the boat's transom, it cut a distinct "V" through the mud-brown water.

A guy and two well shaped blonds in mini-bikinis and suntanned to the max were balanced in the cockpit. Each woman held up a beer bottle in one hand and waved in my direction with the other as the boat whipped past. Its bow wake spread like storm-driven surf in search of something to overturn. When the waves hit my floating pier, one after another, it felt as though I was bouncing up and down on the end of a bungee cord.

Once the near-deafening sound of the boat's monster-sized outboards passed, I half shouted, "Still there, John?"

"Yeah. Sounded like an F-16 just went through your backyard."

"Boat with a hot rod driver shooting through a no-wake zone. But what the hell, glad you called. What's this about *my kind of help*?"

"Remember the dig in Arizona? The Anasazi? They're calling them the Ancestral Puebloans now. The killings we had that nobody wanted to believe who or what did them?"

"I've tried to forget, but yes, I remember."

"We've got something like that out here. And yeah, after what we went through together, you're the only one I could think of who might be able to help."

"In Denver?"

"Close by, before this thing gets somebody else."

Chapter 3

Denver, Colorado

I've been to the Mile High City a couple of times, but flying into Denver's International Airport has always been a thrill. It's the one with the white fiberglass roof designed with 34 tepee-like structures representing snow-covered mountain peaks. Of course, now, it's got the weirdly shaped hotel sitting next to it that, for me, totally screws up the image.

Beyond that, to see the Rockies off to the west as the plane lines up on its final approach is also something special. I should have known, being October, the first snow fall had already blanketed the high country, the definition of 'high country' considered to be from eight thousand feet elevation, reaching to over fourteen thousand.

And yes, I checked the Weather Channel before the flight. When you're a dedicated Floridian from a beach town, a rare change to autumn colors is great, but snow is the last thing you want. I must admit, however, the crest of snow-covered Long's Peak, Rocky Mountain National Park's crowning glory, is still a majestic sight, whether you like snow or not.

As the wheels of Southwest flight 2796 touched down with a heavy, jarring crunch and a whirlwind of reversed engines erupting against my ears, my thoughts were more on John Nabhe, a son of the Navajo Nation and currently a member of the Denver American Indian Commission. John is actually an adopted name. His Navajo name is Niyol Naabahii, translated, Wind Warrior.

A number of years ago, in the days when we worked providing security on a NAARPA dig in Arizona, Utah, New Mexico and southwestern Colorado – better known as the Four Corners – that's exactly what he was: my wind warrior in every sense of the word.

Back then, findings of the Anasazi, the Ancient Ones – sorry about that, Ancestral Puebloans as John mentioned on the phone – was just getting to be a catchword in the world of archaeology. Unfortunately, their artifacts were beginning to find their way into the black market, aided by unscrupulous collectors and, sad to say, some of John's own people in the northeastern corner of Arizona.

Both embarrassed and infuriated over what was happening, he helped me bring in the FBI. Although there were some close calls, we stopped a lot of the thieves, including one of his cousins. As the old saying goes, he's got more cousins than Bayer's got aspirin. I have a number of scars as souvenirs from that assignment.

As in the past, I'd dealt with such thievery a number of times, but on that dig, it was some of the other unnerving events I've tried to forget. Other-worldly events, you might say. Native American legends of shape-shifters and trickster spirits, events we could never factually prove. These beliefs became linked to the unsolved deaths of several of our team members which locals attributed to such creatures. Even some of the tribal police wanted no part in the investigations. Whether the deaths were to drive us away from lands said to be sacred to the Navajo people or as a distraction to the multi-million-dollar sale of stolen artifacts, we never knew. Either way, their murders were terrifyingly real regardless of the motive.

John's call three days ago talked about certain recent things that had taken place in the foothills just west of Denver. Things that couldn't be explained, he said. Things similar to that which we'd run into during the Arizona portion of the dig. He'd given no further explanation. I still wasn't one-hundred percent sure what the hell he was talking about, but thinking about those times in the desert – the medicine man, his chants echoing in the night, the brutal killings found the following mornings – they were already leaving a churning motion in the pit of my stomach. I couldn't put the Four Corners out of my mind.

But here I was, freed of all entanglements. Though there had been no "Dear Matt" letter, Polly had finally called and knew that I knew about her new playmate from the Tampa Police Department. I told her I was taking off for the mountain west and not waiting around for her to finish her little fling. That pretty much cut whatever bond was left between us. Like it was *my* fault she'd found somebody else. Guess I should have patiently waited until she got her fill of the other guy, pun definitely intended.

It was another twenty to thirty minutes of offloading before I could make my way through the C terminal to the train, a quick rumbling ride past B and A terminals to the Epson Terminal, the end of the line. As I passed through the doors into the terminal, there was John standing behind the rope separating arrivals from the rest of the world. He was not much changed over the twenty or so years I'd known him.

Since the Four Corners dig, we'd exchanged Christmas cards and at least one or two telephone calls each year. He'd gotten a law degree and was currently practicing in Denver. He had a grown son and daughter working with the Bureau of Land Management in Montana and Wyoming, respectively, but unfortunately lost his wife of thirty-five years to heart trouble.

Now in his middle fifties, five-ten or eleven, about my height, he had burnished bronze skin, as smooth as that of an apple, and a broad face with an eye-catching smile. Favored with a full head of black hair, it was swept back into a braided ponytail that reached several inches below his shoulders.

Actually, he was still a well-muscled, good-looking man in cowboy boots, weathered jeans, an open-collared shirt of typical western-cut and a suede jacket with leather fringe along the bottom of the sleeves. As always, a pair of Serengeti sun glasses rested just above his forehead. He made a lot of heads turn, especially those of the opposite sex. He could have climbed atop the larger-than-life cowboy statue in the middle of the terminal and not have drawn as many stares from admiring women as was happening at that moment.

Once past our initial greeting and small talk, we headed down through the mass of humanity to baggage claim and snatched my one piece of luggage from the conveyer belt. Not much was said until we were in his pickup truck, easing our way into the continuous flow of departing traffic. As we passed Denver's famous, rather overwhelming statue of the blue stallion with the fiery-red eyes, standing 32-feet high on its hind legs – the demon horse many call it – I finally said, "Time's up, John. Nice to see you again, but I just spent X amount of dollars and three hours on a plane coming out here at your request. I've done that without any real explanation about your problem. It's time you enlighten me."

The smile was no longer on his face. Keeping his eyes on the road and the swirl of traffic heading out from DIA along Pena Boulevard toward Denver and God knows where else in Colorado, all he said was, "Wait. You're in a Hampton Inn in Littleton, one of Denver's southwestern suburbs. We'll check you in, have dinner and then a meeting with members of the Indian Commission at the Museum of Nature and Science."

"Why the Indian Commission and why at the museum? If I remember from long ago visits, that's damn near on the other side of Denver from Littleton."

"First, the Commission has an interest in what's been happening, and second, they have a dedicated meeting room at the museum. This is their scheduled monthly meeting. Only reason you're staying in Littleton, its closer to the action. Tomorrow morning, you'll meet a young man who'll do a show-and-tell about what happened to him and his lady friend."

This was too much. I swiveled around enough to stare at him and barked, "What the hell kind of action and experience that you can't tell me about?" My irritation level was starting to move into the red zone.

Still maintaining his stone-like expression, eyes on the highway as we merged onto I-70 headed west, he said, "You'll learn more tonight at the meeting. After that and tomorrow's get together with the kid, you'll know everything we know. I promise, what you're going to hear will get your attention as well as your imagination."

Chapter 4

Dinner was at a steak house near the hotel. Probably three quarters full, the surrounding conversation had muted our own talk about past archeological excavations in the greater Denver area: Lamb's Spring, Black Foot Cave, and the Magic Mountains' site near Golden. We had just finished the main course, each savoring a cup of coffee and trying to decide if our waistlines could tolerate dessert when two large, powerful looking men entered the restaurant. Not sure why they caught my eye and made such an impression. Perhaps it was the mysterious nature of John's so far limited information concerning why he asked me to come to Denver. Maybe it was because I was already spooked by my memories of the Four Corners dig and didn't realize it.

Both were dressed against the chill of the autumn evening. One was white, a little over six feet tall, bald on top with a scraggly goatee that faded back on both sides into a heavy five-o'clock shadow. He wore scuffed and battered cowboy boots, faded work jeans and a heavy plaid flannel shirt with what appeared to be a pack of cigarettes in the breast pocket.

The other, obviously Latino, probably Mexican, was neater in appearance than the white guy. Several inches shorter but built like a battering ram, he sported a handlebar mustache, otherwise cleanly shaven, pressed khaki slacks and shirt under a dark windbreaker.

The young lady behind the lectern greeted them, picked up two menus and said something, nodding toward an empty booth. Both of the men shook their heads, apparently about the booth and pointed in our direction as though we were waiting for them. They immediately made their way forward in near lock step, the young receptionist following with the menus.

Keeping my eyes on the two as they headed our way, I asked John, "Friends of yours?"

John swiveled his head around. A deep frown crossed his face as he said, "Not hardly, but I'd swear they're the two I saw at the airport. They were hanging around that big cowboy statue in the Epson terminal while I waited for you." He lowered his voice as they drew nearer. "And again, down in the baggage claim area. The Mexican guy was standing just up from you. Grabbed a bag off the carousel and quick put it back like he'd made a mistake." John grunted and added, "Gotta admit, them showing up here gets to be a little too much."

They passed our table, each looking us over as though trying to memorize our facial features. Or to make sure they'd identified the right men. One thing I noticed on the white man, the collar of his shirt and a tattoo, the top part of a vine with a mottle-colored snake head bent forward, mouth open, fangs and forked tongue visible. The rest of the image retreated down beneath his shirt.

Almost as soon as they took their seats, menus spread out before them, the same waiter who had served our table approached them with two glasses of water. He asked, "Anything to drink?"

Without looking up from the menu, the white man said, "Whiskey, neat. Stranahan's Original.".

The Latino ordered, "Tequila Avión."

"I'm not sure we have the Avión. We do have – "

The man's teeth clinched in a low growl. "You have it. Get it."

"Yes sir."

Almost afraid he might say something to further provoke the Hispanic, the waiter hurried to our table. With a wary look out the corner of one eye at the other table, he stuttered, "Can I... can I get you anything else? Dessert?"

John threw a glance over my shoulder toward the two men, gave a slight shake of his head, and said to the waiter, "No, just the check."

As soon as the waiter left, John took a final sip of his coffee, patted the residue off his lips with the napkin and said in a low voice, "The way those two guys looked at us, I got like a sharp blade running up and down my spine and it activated the run or fight button. In this case, run seems to be the best option."

"Gotcha."

The waiter returned with two drinks on a tray, delivered them to the men, then brought our check. Before the waiter could leave, John opened the leather-bound cover holding the check and took a look at the bottom line. He slapped a hand full of twenties on top of the check and said, "Keep the change."

With the waiter's thanks echoing in our ears, we headed toward the exit. Before we went through the doorway, I looked back at the men. Both chugalugged their drinks. The Latino threw some money on the table and they were up, the white man turning over his chair as he rose. Ignoring the chair, they hurried, almost ran toward the exit and us.

Without waiting for the door to close behind me, I shouted, "Haul ass, John. They're coming and they don't look like they want to make nice."

Out of the restaurant, I nearly yanked the handle off the passenger-side door of John's pickup truck as bullets clanged off the side of the bed and walked their way toward the door. I literally dove headfirst into the cab, slammed the door behind me and yelled, "Go, go, go!"

We were already moving when the rear window splintered into a giant spider web. Particles of glass sprayed across the cab as two bullets streaked between the two of us and smacked into the windshield with resounding thuds. I'd swear I felt the heat of the rounds as they burned their way past my face. Even though after the fact, I automatically ducked.

"Damn, that was close!" I didn't know at the moment, but I caught some splinters of glass in the back of my neck. Lack of pain is a wonderful thing until it catches up with you.

"Sonofabitch," John shouted. "I knew damn well something was wrong with those guys. And they shot up my truck, goddamn it, my brand-new truck."

Working the accelerator and the brakes at the same time, John whipped the steering wheel around as we shot past the exit from the parking lot, tires screaming against the asphalt, car horns cursing at us for cutting them off.

"Following?" he shouted.

I turned and looked back as best I could through the splintered rear window with the two round holes spaced no more than an inch apart. "No lights turning out of the parking lot, but keep going wherever you're going."

"Police station a couple of miles up the road."

Chapter 5

Moonlight drew irregular patterns among the gnarled thicket of Gambel oaks. Hiding the opening to the long ago abandoned mine from view of nearby hiking trails, their covering of leaves had begun to fade and wither in the chill of late autumn.

Below, several hundred feet and to the north, occasional cars and pickup trucks created cones of light as each hurried along Deer Creek Canyon Road. Their beams on high gave early warning, or so they thought, against the creature they now feared inhabited the darkness. The creature so luridly described in newspaper, radio and TV accounts following Sonny Weaver's encounter. The lights themselves appeared checkered on and off by the rows of cottonwood trees stretching along the banks of Deer Creek.

As viewed from the abandoned mine entrance, looking east, a narrow bridge spanned the creek. It served as the entrance to Grizzly Drive and the fifty or more homes nestled among the lower hills. For the most part, the homes stood dark, their owners having deserted the community during the past month and a half. Even those still showing an inadvertently left-on, outside flood light gave no evidence of human life.

The murdered and ravaged, dismembered bodies of three residents, all women hiking alone during late afternoon or early morning among the hillsides and shallow ravines, two male hikers from the Denver suburbs farther up in adjacent Deer Creek Canyon Park's Golden Eagle Trail and the disappearance of two local children, a boy and girl, ages five and six respectively, brought about the initial departure of residents from the community. Whether the perpetrator was a rogue bear, mountain lion or depraved human, hunting parties led by law enforcement and

Colorado's Parks and Wildlife Department failed to produce any leads.

The final straw for those few remaining residents was the attack on the young couple along Deer Creek Canyon Road: the crushed top of their pickup truck's cab, the unexplained claw marks on the hood and roof and the vicious killing of the woman, dragged through the vehicle's smashed window. Shreds of clothing, flesh and blood on the broken glass and snagged on brush leading up the creek were all that was found. Ultimately, all trace of the woman vanished at the water's edge.

Even the few bears and what mountain lions that roamed the higher and more densely wooded areas of nearby Red Mesa and Plymouth Mountain had ceased their nocturnal visits around the old mine. It was as though they sensed something stronger and deadlier had come to inhabit their world.

His eyes pierced the darkness in search of movement among the deserted homes, possibly someone returning to claim something they'd forgotten; a car stopping along the road for its driver to relieve himself among the trees or into the creek; someone on one of the hiking trails, unaware of his presence and needs. He enjoyed the killing of humans more than initially thought, even the taste of their flesh, especially the females. He remembered the first, long ago, the hatred that had boiled up within him at her unfaithfulness, yet the sweetness of her flesh.

Once those hunting him got too close, however, he would move deeper into the mountains where humans would be less wary. And there would always be protection if he needed it. He thought of his protector, old, weak, but as cunning as ever. The grunt that rose in his throat could have been interpreted as either a growl or a chuckle. Despite the odor, sharp, irritating to his nostrils and lungs, he moved back into the mine, patiently waiting to fulfill his cravings for the taste of new-found prey. They'd come. He sensed it. This was the night.

* * *

Our visit to the Littleton Police Department, the nearest to where we were at the time, wasn't the worst experience I've ever had, but then again, it wasn't the most pleasant since we were already late for meeting with the Indian Commission. Their lab technician still on duty, Lilly Mendoza, bifocals resting halfway down the bridge of her nose, black hair tied back in a bun, was in faded jeans, gray blouse and red-on-white athletic shoes. Though a little hefty and wearing a tired look on her face, she was definitely not a bad looking woman. Following a quick visual examination of the pickup truck, she took photos of the bullet damage, passenger side, tail gate, rear window and windshield before prying out six flattened and battered rounds.

Her findings simply verified what we said during a relatively quick interrogation by Detective Max Roland of their Investigations Division. I could tell he definitely wanted to get back to the Thursday night NFL game between Denver and Kansas City which he placed on mute.

We explained what happened. As for what prompted the action, John told him it might possibly have had something to do with things happening around Deer Creek Canyon. He couldn't think of any other reason why somebody would be shooting at him or me. That's all he said, but the detective seemed to understand, which of course continued to leave me in the dark. I got the idea everyone at the station knew about John and Deer Creek Canyon long before our impromptu visit to the station that night.

In addition to sending her two assistants to search the restaurant's parking lot for empty shell casings, Lilly the lab tech wanted to keep the truck overnight for more forensic snooping. Primarily so their ballistics guy could hopefully determine from the recovered rounds the type weapon or weapons and the possibility they had been used in other crimes.

Of those found useful for examination, I later learned that four of the rounds were identified as 40 caliber S&W and the other two were nine millimeters, indicating as John and I knew there were two shooters.

John, using a combination of smile and charm, convinced her he'd have the truck back early next morning. The frown on her face broadcast that she didn't like what she was hearing, but since it was John, she'd go along. I've worked with forensics people before, but never heard of anything like that. If there was the possibility of retrievable evidence, they'd keep it. It seemed all John had to do was smile and the world followed his lead.

"Seven o'clock tomorrow morning and not a minute later. I've got a long day ahead."

It was evident she was a hard nut to crack. To hopefully mollify her, I volunteered, "I'll rent something to get us around over the rest of my stay." I said that not really knowing how long that stay would be.

After a medical tech picked glass slivers out of my neck, cleaned the various nicks with alcohol that burned like hell, applied Polysporin, gauze and tape and said I would live, we were finally cleared to go. An hour late, we were at last headed across town to the Denver Museum of Nature and Science and the Indian Commission meeting.

Chapter 6

The Denver Museum of Nature and Science was and is considered one of the nation's foremost educational institutions in archeological and paleontological research. My people – NAARPA, that is – have worked with their paleontologists on various excavations in Colorado, Wyoming and Utah. The museum sits off Colorado Boulevard as part of a massive, city-owned complex known as City Park which also includes the nationally renowned Denver Zoo, lakes, boat houses and a golf course.

The side of the building facing the boulevard is surrounded by a phalanx of trees which, without a strategically placed line of security floodlights, would cast a shadowy pall on the building. Once parked, John led me to an entrance where a night security guard was waiting. Again, like the police station, John was immediately recognized, and we were allowed entry without question. I hadn't realized he had become such a celebrity in the Mile High City.

The entry hall was cavernous with numerous ticket outlets for non-member visitors, for an IMAX theater, a planetarium as well as for special exhibits requiring additional fees. Since the escalators were not operating at that time of night, we headed for an elevator located between the deserted food court and the museum's gift shop. Looking through the windows as we passed, like most such shops, it appeared to be little more than a semi-educational come-on and room full of colorful gimmicks to entice kids and make additional money for the museum. I can't argue with that. Museums need as much funding as they can get to survive and do the work they do.

With exception of the fading *clop, clop* of the security

guard's leather heels against the tile floor as he moved deeper into the building, it felt like even the faintest whisper would echo throughout the chilling stillness of the hall. It actually felt good to get into the elevator and hear the hum of a motor and the sound of cables running through well-oiled blocks as we moved upward.

When the door opened, we found ourselves on the third level and a carpeted walkway that, over a waist-high safety wall, looked down on the first floor. By that time, only relatively dim security lights illuminated the way. It was enough to see, but a little eerie as museums go when closed to the public for the night. It reminded me of the several movies about a night in the museum when exhibits came to life, especially as we passed the Egyptian Room.

The entrance was open to a large sarcophagus standing well over six feet tall. Its various, somewhat faded, hand-painted colors were highlighted by a single spot light angled down from the ceiling. It gave the oversized coffin a macabre look. Beneath an elaborate headdress rested what we Americans would call a typical, ancient Egyptian face with eyes that appeared to follow us as we walked past.

Naturally, having been in the business of archaeology, I remembered the word *sarcophagus*, broken down into its two main syllables, meant *to eat flesh*. Great! That's all I needed. First, two bozos shooting at us earlier that night and now a sarcophagus, casting a set of eyes on us, wanting to eat my body. I felt those eyes boring into my back until we turned and crossed a bridge spanning the open distance to another section of the building, making our way through the Explore Colorado, African and South American exhibits.

We stepped out onto a balcony overlooking a glassed-in atrium, and what a view. A solid wall of glass, three stories high. In the distance, lights danced off a lake that made up a large part of Denver's City Park with the full splendor of the city's skyline aglow in the background. Past that, I could only imagine the Rocky Mountains reaching up into the night sky.

"There they are," John said, pointing to our right.

I have to admit I did a double take. He was right. Though on our level, the meeting was being held in a ribbed, glass-enclosed room shaped like a Quonset hut. It was suspended from the museum's uppermost ceiling and attached to the building's exterior framework. It literally hung out over the atrium some forty feet below. Again, the city's lights were clearly visible through the room's far glass wall. And yes, there sat the members of the Indian Commission in plain view with paper work, glasses and pitchers of what appeared to be water on the table.

To one side stood a large, portable white board with notes appended to its face and a small table holding a commercial coffee maker surrounded by cups, sweetener, stirrers and a platter of cookies. The door, glass as well, contained an integrated, frosted glass sign which read, *Harry T. Lewis, Jr. Community Room.*

The quiet murmur of conversation suddenly went silent as we entered. The eyes of the nine people, six women and three men, seated around what was little more than a long, Formica-surfaced work table, turned in our direction. Each person had a nameplate directly in front of him or her, facing inward as though others around the table couldn't remember everyone's name. There were two empty chairs on one side, one with the nameplate before it reading *John Wind Warrior*, my John. In my usual astute manner, I deduced this was where we were supposed to sit.

There were at least four others in chairs along a side wall. More than likely visitors interested in the proceedings. One of the older ones, a man, wizened and wrinkled, with long white hair, work boots, faded jeans and a red and black plaid jacket, seemed vaguely familiar. Why, I didn't know. John was the only person I knew in Denver or, to my knowledge, all of Colorado.

Not one to enjoy heights, I was definitely a bit uncomfortable, knowing the room was hanging some forty feet above the atrium floor below. My discomfort quickly disappeared when I focused on an absolutely stunning woman at the far end of the table as she said, "Come in, John. Thank you for calling to let us know you'd be late. Please take a chair and introduce your visitor."

"Sorry about the inconvenience." he said. "Appreciate all of you waiting." As he sat, he motioned for me to take the vacant chair next to him. Quickly looking around the table, he added, "Someone either didn't like the way we looked or didn't want us to get to the meeting. They decided to take target practice with us as the targets. Whether coincidence or tied to tonight's subject matter, I don't know."

It was hard to take my eyes away from the woman whose nameplate read, *Roberta Pine Woman, Co-Chair*. I wondered what *Pine Woman* would have been in her native language, but that was the least of my thoughts. She looked to be in her early to mid-forties, maybe even younger. Though sitting, I judged her to be fairly tall, a trim five-eight to five-ten. Narrow face, long, below-the-shoulder-length raven-colored hair, dark eyes and skin light brown with a slight reddish tone.

While it's said you can identify Native Americans by their high cheek bones, her cheeks, highlighted by the double row of ceiling lights, were the most beautiful I'd ever seen. Lips, the lower lip slightly thicker than the upper, unimaginably kissable. Just the look of her was replacing all memories of Pretty Polly back in Florida. It wasn't love at first sight, but it was definitely fascination on my part.

"Is there something wrong?" Roberta Pine Woman asked, looking in my direction.

I stuttered a moment before answering, "I'm sorry. I was staring. Bad habit. Forgive me. I didn't mean to cause you any discomfort."

Thankfully, she nodded, a slight smile on her face. "Forgiven."

She knew damn well why I couldn't take my eyes off of her. She was the best-looking woman in ten states and probably with the intelligence to go with the beauty, a fact of which I would later learn, as well as for another lady I was yet to meet.

The rest of the commission members were all in business dress as though having come to the meeting direct from various downtown offices. All but one whose nameplate read *Vincent Brave Wolf, Co-Chair*. He was a youngish, full-faced, rather overweight gentleman whose clothing looked as though he might be a hands-on building contractor or some kind of construction engineer.

They all nodded in my direction and murmured their hellos as John said, "This is Matt Berkeley who I told you about. As I said, we worked together a number of years ago providing security for an archeological dig down in the Four Corners, but mostly in Arizona, southern Colorado's Canyon of the Ancients and a fair amount of time in Utah's Hovenweep area. He was with the North American Archeological Research and Preservation Agency. Better known as NAARPA. Head of security."

"Have you explained to Mr. Berkeley why we invited him to join us this evening?" Roberta Pine Woman asked.

"Not in detail."

"Little or no detail," I added. "Only that recent events in the Denver area were similar to a situation we experienced during the Four Corners dig."

"And you came here based on so little information?" asked one of the other women, Bonita Morning Star as noted on her nameplate.

"Yes ma'am. I've known John for many years. In fact, I once had several opportunities to trust him with my life."

"And vice versa," John provided as an addendum.

"Very well," Roberta Pine Woman said. "Since John seems to have been so reticent to detail our problem, Vincent Brave Wolf, my fellow co-chair, will hopefully enlighten you about the situation. Vincent."

Roberta Pine Woman, her diction, mannerisms and ability to give directions gave me the impression she was a professional at whatever she did.

The engineer or contractor or whatever he was started with,

"I don't know how familiar you are with the greater Denver area, Mr. Berkeley. If –"

"Very little, so guide me."

"There have been at least eight murders over the past two months, initially thought caused by some kind of animal, perhaps a mountain lion come down from the high country, or a human serial killer. The possibility of it being a human was strongly considered after the third killing. All occurred in Jefferson County in a small community of homes adjacent to Deer Creek Canyon Park. The area is west of Denver and the suburban city of Littleton. In the case of Deer Creek Canyon Park, it's under the jurisdiction of the Jefferson County Sheriff's Office."

Brave Wolf was interrupted by the *bing-bong-bing* ringing of a mobile phone. One of the commission members, Dr. Ernest Long Bow on his nameplate, answered and said "Yes?" This was followed by cupping the phone and, as he left the room, saying to everyone present, "Excuse me, I'll be right back," his words trailing him out the door.

One of the women, Inez Young Girl, got up from the table and walked over to the coffee maker. As she filled her cup, she looked back at me and asked, "Coffee, Mr. Berkeley?"

I shook my head. "No, but thanks anyway."

A man named Robert Yellow Horse spoke up. "While the doctor is on the phone, *The Mountain Gazette*, a local newspaper reported on the murders in an uncalled-for way. Trying to stick a name to the killings, like the Green Valley Killer or Night Phantom Killings, jokingly called the killings Colorow's Revenge."

"Colorow?" I asked.

"A Ute chief who used to prowl in the area with his band of Indians." He glanced quickly around the table, a guilty smile on his face and said, "Sorry about that." Looking at me, he added, "I'm supposed to say Native Americans."

There was soft laughter around the table with someone saying, "You're forgiven."

"Anyway, Colorow is said to have been a huge man, over

six and a half feet tall, over two hundred seventy pounds. He disliked and harassed white people: Settlers, miners, trappers. Eventually hunted down by government men, wounded in a gun battle. He escaped north, but subsequently died of pneumonia. Blamed white men for his troubles. Therefore, the name Colorow's Revenge. Interesting story, but that's not what's troubling the Commission. It's what Vincent is about to tell you."

There were murmured discussions around the table as well as a loud, indiscernible muttering from behind me. Loud enough for me to take my eyes away from Roberta Pine Woman and swivel around in my chair to see who was making the noise. It was the old man I noticed when we first came in. "You look familiar. Have we met?" I asked. "Sometime in the past?"

He stared at me, continued his muttering, his upper lip curled as though in a snarl. He suddenly jabbed his right arm in my direction, leaned forward and shook a gnarled index finger in my face. I expected him to say something, but no. No words; only his eyes. They were like fire, ablaze with what I could only describe as *sheer hatred*, but why?

"Mr. Hataali, is there something wrong?" Roberta Pine Woman asked the old man, her voice cutting across his mutterings.

The man sat back in his chair, eyes closed as though in a trance. The noise stopped, but his lips continued to move almost as though saying some kind of incantation to himself.

One of the other women turned to me. "Don't worry about him, Mr. Berkeley. This is not the first time he's done something like this."

I nodded in her direction as the Doctor returned to the room and took his place at the table. I knew, however, the old guy, in whatever garbled language he was using, was talking to me. More than talk; more a threat.

"Vincent," Roberta Pine Woman said, "If you would continue."

The co-chair picked up with, "As I said, human, a serial killer or so most thought. Understand, however, since the most recent killing, what I'm about to tell you are solely the Commission's thoughts. Thoughts of something human, yet not quite human. Certainly, for all we know, not thoughts under consideration by the Jefferson County Sheriff's people. We haven't discussed it with them since the last killing."

He reached across the table for a glass and poured some water from a half-filled pitcher. I held a glass out which he also filled while I asked, "What happened at the last killing that made you think otherwise? Human... but not quite human."

Vincent Brave Wolf pulled from beneath a sheath of papers a section from a weekly newspaper, the masthead reading *The Mountain Gazette*. He looked at it for a moment before pushing it in my direction. The lead article on the cover page was entitled, WOLF MONSTER KILLS LOCAL WOMAN. Below the title was an exaggerated black and white caricature of a wolf, half animal, half-human, covered with hair with an elongated snout, oversized fangs and claws. The eyes were red, the only color in the entire picture. The creature was in a crouch as though about to attack.

I scanned the first three or four paragraphs before demanding, "What the hell is this? Somebody's idea of a Halloween joke? I know it's October, but this is –"

"No, no, Mr. Berkeley," Ms. Pine Woman said, her head shaking. "It's based on what the boy described, or young man I should say. You'll need to read the whole story. It's what he told the Sheriff's people. They've been very close about it, but unfortunately, he was allowed to be interviewed by the media."

"So far, all I've heard is there's a young man or boy I'm meeting tomorrow. What boy, Madam Chairman? John?"

John answered before Roberta Pine Woman could speak. "Young man, boy, whatever. He's the person I said we're going to meet tomorrow, the person interviewed by the media."

"But you still haven't told me..." I stopped in midsentence. Enough said. I figured to hell with it. I wasn't going to ask again. Giving him a quick sideways glance, hopefully showing my irritation with how little he had told me, I flipped through the newspaper in search of the continued article.

After a quick scan of the remainder of the article, I continued. "Based on what little I've read I finally know who the boy is. The article and some of the other sketches take up full pages. I'll read it again, but you've got to tell me what it is that's *your* problem." Pointing at the newspaper article, I asked, "What's the Indian Commission's particular interest in this stuff? I can't help you if I don't know. Otherwise, it's the county sheriff's problem in which I am not going to get involved."

I was pissed and it was beginning to show. I wasn't being told everything. Why couldn't John and the others come right out and give me all the details? I needed a minute or so to cool down.

Pushing back my chair, I got up, almost stepping on the crazy old man's feet behind me, and walked to the far end of the glassed-in room. With the city lights spread out before me and after several deep breaths, I turned back to the Commission members.

While returning to my chair, I said, "I came out here to help based on John's request and our past friendship. Just tell me the problem, and I'll tell you if there's anything I can do."

"With my name, you think I like it?" Brave Wolf said, his face lined with obvious anger. "This rag even tried to interview me after they published the article. My name. I know it's because of my name, but I refused."

"Explain."

It was the woman who offered me coffee, Inez Young Girl, who spoke. "The boy in the article and his girlfriend were attacked, supposedly by some half-man, half-wolf creature. The thing stood on two feet, but ran on all fours. The article is using such terminology as shape shifter, skin walker, wendigo, the whole lycanthropy thing and associating them with the Navajo people.

"Vincent is Diné Navajo and with a name like his? Brave Wolf? The paper went straight to him. Of course, I'm sure you know, wendigo had or has nothing to do with the Navajo. It was the Algonquian-speaking people along the Great Lakes region and Canada; their monster who lurked in the forests, but I suppose it still makes good press.

"Since skin walkers were part of Navajo mythology, some of us have already had phone calls asking if the Navajos had anything to do with the murders. Even threats directed at the Commission. That's why, based on what John told us happened at your... I believe both of you called it your Four Corners dig, we're asking for your help."

John touched my arm. "It's what the media were told by the young man who survived the attack."

The old man behind me began to moan. I felt a sudden movement, and then his hands were on my throat, squeezing, people shouting, screaming, and trying to pull him away. He refused to lessen his grasp until I reached back and grabbed both of his arms. I dug my fingernails into the underside muscles and ligaments of his wrists controlling the movements of his hands. He howled in pain, but refused to let go until John and Vincent Brave Wolf, as big and heavy as he was, literally dived across the table, to drag him away from me. Almost knocking me over, they threw him to the floor and held him down until he gradually quieted.

"Let's get him out of here," Brave Wolf said.

They picked him up by the arm pits and drug him across the carpet, through the door out onto the balcony overlooking the atrium and left him there. He squatted against the wall just outside the glassed-in meeting room, his breath heavy, eyes ablaze, staring at me.

When John and Brave Wolf came back in and everyone was again seated, Roberta Pine Woman apologized and asked if I knew why he attacked me.

"If it's what I think it is, it's a long story. I thought he looked familiar, and I think I know who, and yes, what he was and perhaps still is. It was the Four Corners area, Arizona, where I knew him, or more correctly, knew of him.

Our dig team called him Grandfather Medicine Man, and

yes, several other names I won't mention. He hated us. Thought we were destroying the history of the Anasazi people, his people or so he claimed. After some of the actions John and I had to take, he felt I destroyed his image as a medicine man."

While I went more into detail about the Four Corners episode, what I did not know at that moment was what was happening slightly less than twenty miles to the southwest of the museum. That's as the proverbial crow flies. It was what the old man had created was about to do.

Chapter 7

From farther up the hill and off to the right, a set of eyes followed the automobile's headlights as they crossed the bridge over the shallow waters of Deer Creek. Unaware of being watched, Richard Lamb increased the pressure on the accelerator as the car climbed the upgrade on Grizzly Drive. He turned onto Bear Cub Circle and pulled into the driveway of a two-story, cream-colored stucco home that was still illuminated by floodlights mounted just below the roof line. They'd been left on to hopefully discourage burglars and vandals from taking advantage of a completely deserted community. Besides it would help the Sheriff's hourly roving patrol see anything unusual. At least, that had been his thinking.

He hit the remote-control button and waited for the garage door to go up. An overhead light went on revealing a space stuffed with boxes, a hanging rack full of hiking clothes, fishing and hunting gear, a menagerie of children's toys, two mountain bikes, lawn equipment and a small green, John Deer tractor. There was barely enough room for the single car.

Once the door was fully up, Richard pulled into the garage and turned off the ignition. He sat for a moment, staring into the rearview mirror affixed to the top of the windshield. Through the rear window, he could see only a lighted part of the front yard and driveway; past the stretch of light, darkness.

A slight shiver ran along his body. He envisioned the graphic in the newspaper of the wolf-like creature said to be hunting the foothills and doing all the killing. He patted the stock of the Remington 1100 American Classic, a 12-guage, auto-loading shotgun. The magazine held four, Hypersonic Steel shells advertised to "take lethality to new heights." The butt rested on the floor beside the center console, the end of the 26-inch barrel leaning against the passenger-side door. "Can't believe she asked me to come out here," he muttered to himself. "In the middle of the fucking night no less with some half-crazed…"

Richard forced the thought aside as he stepped out of the car and punched the wall-mounted button for the garage door to go down. After unlocking the back door, he entered the house and switched on lights as he went. "Now where the hell would she have put the damn things?" With a shake of his head, he continued talking to keep himself company in the silence of the empty house.

"A hotel room, two kids sleeping six feet away and we're gonna have sex? No chance." In his wife's high-pitched voice, he mimicked, "'I forgot my birth control pills and I have to keep the schedule, sex or no sex.'"

"Bullshit!" He shook his head, ran his fingers across his forehead in surrender and trudged his tired, increasingly overweight body up the stairs to his wife's bathroom. First the medicine cabinet and each of several vanity drawers; not there. Next the bedroom. He rummaged through her dresser and bureau drawers; again, not there. Back down to the kitchen and an upper cabinet where both of them kept most of their daily prescription meds out of reach of the kids. Success! At the back of the cabinet partially hidden by a bottle of Aleve and a large container of calcium tablets was the 28-day pack of Microgestin.

Jesus, he thought. *If I can see the damn pills, why couldn't she?* Out loud, he added, "Hope they find and kill the damn thing so we can all come home."

Richard slipped the pack of Microgestin pills into his oversized jacket pocket, made sure all the house lights were out and exited into the garage. He thought a moment about turning off the outside floodlights, but decided, *What the hell!* Since they were on a timer which he'd have to reset, he muttered, "Screw it."

Rather than pressing the garage door opener by the side of the kitchen door, he decided to play it safe. He waited until he got into the car, started the engine, locked the doors and pushed the remote control clipped onto the sun visor mounted above the steering wheel. Once the door moved fully into the up position, he backed the car out onto the driveway, stopped and punched the control, waiting for the door to descend.

He was about to attach his seat belt and shoulder strap when, without warning, something slammed against the driver-side window, a crash of metal against glass only inches away. Once, twice, a third time. He saw it for only a split second, in the glare of floodlights, his vision distorted by the first cracks in the glass. Some kind of creature, standing, its body covered with hair, elongated lower face, claw-like hands swinging something at the car. In that instant, the entire width of the window exploded against his shoulder and the left side of his face. His screams filled the car, not so much from pain but from the mind-numbing fear.

Richard's brain finally responded. Frantically, he grabbed for the shotgun and pulled it upward. The front sight just above the muzzle snagged on the passenger door's arm rest, then the door handle before springing free, his index finger wrapped around the trigger.

At the same time, he felt a stabbing, almost paralyzing pain in his left shoulder as claws sank through the jacket's cloth, deep into the muscle. For a moment, his own cries drowned out the snarling and growling that tormented his ear.

The thing yanked him closer to the now open window, pinning his left arm against the door. Its face pressed next to his, breath hot, odor of decayed flesh. Almost immediately, there was a piercing pain at the back of his neck; claws squeezed against flesh. He felt himself being pulled even tighter against the door.

He tried to swing the shotgun up and around with his right hand. With the uncontrollable awkwardness of the movement, his finger tightened against the trigger and the weapon exploded. The blast pressure within the relatively contained interior of the car ruptured his right eardrum; the hot wetness of fluid filled his ear.

As the recoil jammed the butt of the gun into his ribcage, the car's headliner disappeared and steel shot opened a hole in the roof. While fighting to break loose and still crying, screaming, shouting for help that would never come, the shotgun roared again. The shot took out much of the dashboard, the windshield and the passenger-side window.

He felt his body jerked up by the shoulder and neck and drawn partway out of the window. Broken glass ripped and tore his arm and upper torso. On fire with pain, he lost his grip on the shotgun.

Richard's cry of "No-o-o-o!" became only a croak as something closed over his throat, tighter and tighter. It cut off his airway. He could feel his face on fire. His eyes bulged from the pressure. His ability to struggle grew weaker. With one final, futile gasp for air, a white-hot fireball erupted somewhere behind his eyes. The light instantly turned to darkness as the rest of his body was heaved up and out through the window.

For only a moment, the night was silent, the quiet quickly broken by the tearing of cloth and flesh and snapping of bone. Growls, low and guttural, with what one might mistake for a garbled word spoken here and there, turned into a long, triumphant howl.

The creature lifted its head toward the night sky and sprinkling of stars for all to hear. The howl echoed around the deserted homes, the sound spreading among the surrounding foot hills and along the trails leading up into the high country.

A small gang of elk grazing in one of the pastures in the park above the community raised their heads as one and looked down toward the vast area of homes. With a wheezing snort from the only bull in the gang, they turned and quickly trotted farther up into the trees in the direction of Plymouth Mountain and safety.

Chapter 8

He was surprised they'd found his work so quickly, but he knew they would come. They'd been there before. His appetite satisfied for the moment, despite the sickening odor created by tiny winged creatures that had largely ignored his presence, he hid the remains of his trophies in the deep coolness of the old mine to await his return.

It was shortly before first light when he heard the dogs, barking, yipping, running close together, then apart, one with nose close to the ground, a second with nose held high, sniffing the air. They'd been used before. His ears twitched at the sounds, each bark now identifiable with its particular owner.

He had so far eluded them by going higher into the mountains. Sometimes there were large rocks from which to jump, one to another, leaping great distances without touching the ground, always moving higher. Other times he'd used small creeks, their waters rushing down the foothills to join the South Platt River, absorbing his spoor, but now was different. He had known better. Sooner or later the dogs would corner him, and the men would kill him. They might even allow the dogs to attack him, tear the flesh from his bones. Last night's opportunity, however, had been too tempting to ignore.

His protector had also known, had sensed his growing taste and hunger for human flesh following each kill. With the dawn still hiding beneath the Hog Back, or so the jagged hills just east of the park were called, lights on the bridge blinked their signal. From the mine, he immediately cut across the high ground on all fours, staying low behind the scrub while descending to the first trail past the entrance to the park, then left.

His powerful hands and feet, functioning like paws, barely

touched the ground; long, unbelievable strides. He first smelled and then saw the creek, its waters chilled by the night air and light snow that fell higher up in the forest, quickly melting into runoff. Once there he splashed his way toward the bridge.

With one mighty leap, both hand-like paws hit the top of the bridge railing some ten feet above the water and pushed off. The toes and balls of his feet added punch to his upward motion, lifting him even higher. Had there been someone observing from the deep shadows that covered the creek banks, they would have been awed, spellbound, amazed at the acrobatic agility and strength of the creature.

He landed on two feet on a pad of thick neoprene in the bed of an aging pickup truck. His arrival was as soft and fully balanced as would be for a world class gymnast descending from a set of horizontal or parallel bars. The slight jarring of the truck from his sudden weight barely created a cry from the vehicle's ancient springs.

The truck quickly reversed. As it turned sharply onto Deer Creek Road, the left front fender scraped the end post of the railing on the opposite side of the bridge, sending an angry metallic screech echoing along the creek. Straightening, the truck headed west in the direction of the higher mountains and safety from hunters still to come.

The acrid smell of the mine still in his nostrils, the creature smothered a hacking cough with his arm and looked back. His trail had ended at the water's edge. Nothing remained of his scent or track for them to follow. As the truck bumped along the asphalt road, he stretched full length beneath a sheet of tarpaulin on the neoprene pad in an attempt to relax his muscles.

His exertion, exacerbated by the stench created by the winged creatures at the back of the mine where he'd taken what little remained of that night's kill, brought a deep, mucous-driven cough from the depths of his lungs.

There was, however, something else that drew his attention. For the first time, he felt a stinging pain at the ankle joint of his left leg. He pulled back the tarpaulin. In the dim light of that time just before dawn, he saw hair was missing, revealing a lengthy gash. Beads of blood were already drying.

He pulled the leg to him, wiped the wound with paw-like fingers and licked the blood away. Small price to pay, he thought, for such an unexpected yet delicious prize, the man who had so foolishly returned to his hunting grounds. As the cough subsided and he settled onto the pad, he pulled the piece of tarpaulin back over his body. Had he been a cat, he would have purred, thinking contentedly of a faraway place and a love he once had… until he ate her.

* * *

Jefferson County's Pyramid Peak at 7,487 feet is no match for Colorado's other peak of the same name. Located some ninety miles to the west as the eagle flies, the latter peak rises to its majestic height of 14,025 feet not far from the world-famous ski resorts of Aspen and Snow Mass, Colorado. Even at that height, it's one of the lowest of the State's fifty-seven "fourteeners," so called for their elevation, 14,000 feet or more. Its lowly cousin sitting in what's considered to be little more than the foothills of Jefferson County, however, happened to be in the right place at the right time.

Shortly before dawn, a damp mist hung over the canyon when the old man heard the far-off sound of dogs, the splash of his grandson in the creek followed by the impact of his body in the bed of the truck. Not turning the truck's lights on, he immediately backed the black, rust-marred pickup truck off the bridge, not noticing the sound of the left front fender scraping against the bridge's end post before turning west on Deer Creek Canyon Road. Unless they were also driving without lights, no one followed. The old man had driven the route many times to become familiar with every twist and turn of the road, and there were many.

It was a little over four miles to the three-way intersection where Deer Creek Canyon Road continued west toward the high mountains while its shorter namesake, Deer Creek Road, bore left in a more southerly direction toward the lower Pyramid Peak. Immediately to the right was a graveled parking area that once led to the mines and smelting operations of Phillipsburg.

Gold, bismuth, copper and tin, but the small deposits were soon depleted. Result? Mines and Phillipsburg were abandoned. It was the story of those and other mines in the area and their nearness to the project as he called it that had provided a solution for his plans. That morning, however, a sign at the entrance to the lot read RTD PHILIPSBURG PARK & RIDE.

Two buildings sat to the side of the parking lot, one a dilapidated, two-story hulk, gray ghost of a structure that was literally rotting away. The decrepit framework seemed to lean against the sheer side of a cliff as if to maintain its balance. Wood siding was missing in places, leaving gaps for the weather to enter. The roof was warped, shingles missing and falling apart. The old man chuckled to himself. A hand-painted sign, black on white, stuck out from the side of the building. It read, PRESERVATION PROPERTY. KEEP OUT,

The other building, a two-story, yellow clapboard-siding affair, appeared vacant, was rundown but might be habitable with a little work. There were several lines of cars and pickup trucks parked on the graveled area, empty, their drivers having already taken early morning
RTD buses into Denver.

He maneuvered the truck around until it was in the second line back from the lot's entrance between two cars and a pickup, facing toward the exit. He turned off the motor, hunched low in the seat and waited. From his vantage point, he could see the intersection. As expected, two patrol cars soon entered the intersection, one continuing west up toward the small hamlet of Homewood Park, the other turning south.

He checked a badly scared pocket watch every few minutes. Thirty minutes, forty-five, daylight fast approaching.

Birds were already on the wing, chirping, cawing, screeching. An hour went by until both patrol cars returned, one from the south, one from the west. They entered the parking lot, one to loop around the other and stop side-by-side in order for the deputies to talk. The old man ducked down even farther, praying to all the gods he knew to keep his grandson from moving or making a sound beneath the tarpaulin in the back.

It seemed an eternity. Through a small opening in his driver-side window, he could hear their motors running, the drone of the deputies' conversation, but there was no opening of car doors, no footsteps approaching on the gravel. More conversation until finally, two motors revved, gravel crunched and they were gone, both moving east back in the direction of Grizzly Road and Deer Creek Canyon Park.

Waiting another ten minutes to make certain no more patrol cars came around the curve, he started the engine, pulled forward through an open space to the intersection and headed south toward the foot of Pyramid Peak and an old logging road. Another mile or so past widely scattered, medium-sized mountain homes, a closed volunteer fire department station with a huge wire cage to the side filled with aluminum cans and he was there.

The old man brought the pickup to a slow roll before pulling off Deer Creek Road onto a narrow dirt and gravel pathway which appeared to have seen little use over the past years. He'd found it quite by accident several months earlier. Undergrowth and weeds crowded in on the passage from years of obvious neglect. Within a few yards, he had to gun the engine to get the truck up the road which angled sharply upward through the thick cover of pines and cedar. He stopped once he reached a wire fence with a gate secured with a chain and large padlock, a fence and gate he'd built.

A quick glance into the rearview mirror and he could see his grandson in the bed of the truck, the tarpaulin wrapped around his body. He wasn't certain how to treat this man, but he knew the future held little promise of survival for the creature. In his mind that was what his ward had become. A man creature, more animal than man in his cravings and bodily needs. The process had started in Europe and progressed since his return. The old man felt shame for using his own blood-kin, his daughter's son, as he had, but at least it had given his grandson purpose.

The tarpaulin shook with the man's cough, an effort to expel the fluid that had collected in his lungs, the fluid that had originated at some point during the intermittent periods spent in the old mine. He felt sorry for his grandson, but the man's actions, largely choreographed by himself, had served their purpose. These had been the lands of those who came first. First Nation people as they were called: Ute, Arapaho, Cheyenne as well as Navajo on their journey south, not the white man. Their tribes, their nations had been robbed and run off the land.

If he could use the unsuspecting white man who provided him with safety to keep the land from further destruction and disrespect for those who came before, he would take whatever measures were necessary. For him, the arrival of his grandson had been a message sent by the gods.

The old man sat for a moment, thinking, planning. Had he been seen? If so, had they identified and were tracking the old pickup? He felt reasonably safe, but he couldn't be sure. He knew sooner or later, as they widened the search area, they would come. There was one way, however, to prove if the pickup was under suspicion. Return to the scene of the crime.

Once he'd mulled over what happened that morning and felt certain of what he had to do, he got out and unlocked the gate, drove the pickup through, relocked the gate and pointed the nose of the truck up the logging road which had become little more than a derelict firebreak through the densely populated forest of Pyramid Peak. The truck shimmied its way around the numerous twists and turns filled with weeds, rocks and tire-busting ruts, until it emerged into a small, unkempt clearing.

The track ended at a single structure. It backed up against the trees at the rear of the clearing, the word *clearing* being more a misnomer than anything else due to knee-high weeds and wild shrubbery which had grown over the years. A shack, well over thirty, maybe forty years old he imagined, was held together by lines of warped clapboard siding and a planked roof spotted with patches of dark green moss and mold. A small wood-floored porch, covered by the same roof, clung precariously to the front of the building.

Two windows, one on each side of the solid wooden door, were covered with layers of newly installed, opaque plastic sheets to shield the one-room shack from both weather and prying eyes. A few feet to the left side of the house was a three- by four-foot-deep hole in the ground which the old man had dug for disposal of waste. Off to the right of the structure sat the remains of an abandoned well.

An online review of Google maps showing a ten-square-mile area with no other structures nearby had alerted him to the place. In fact, except for the few occupied homes down along Deer Creek Road, there were none on this side of the mountain.

Once parked and out of the truck, he tapped his ward on the shoulder and spoke, his graveled voice in the difficult Athabaskan language of the Diné, the Navajo people. "Hok'ee," he called his grandson by his native name, "we're here. A place where you must hide." He received only a grunt in response. "Come inside. You are sick, need rest."

Despite a deep grinding cough, the creature rose, pulled the tarpaulin about his body as one would a blanket for warmth and, with one free hand grasping the side of the truck bed, catapulted his way to the ground. His exertion caused a spasm of coughing, but he walked to the door and opened it.

Inside the shack was a small stone fireplace. Its flame, lit earlier by the old man, provided heat against the morning chill. Two bunks sat flush against the left wall, separated by a small, use-worn, black chest of drawers. Though unlit, a portable propane heater and attached fuel canister sat atop the chest, its heat element elevated to point that its heat would flow several feet above the bunks. An old, permanently food-stained walnut wood table with a kerosene lamp sitting on its surface and two closely-matching chairs, one on each side of the table, occupied the center of the room.

The old man hurriedly lit the lamp, using a small box of matches lying on the table. As additional light filtered across the room, Hok'ee saw that the furniture looked as if it came from a Goodwill or Salvation Army store, not what he'd become use to during his years away, a time and place now seeming as distant as his long-ago youth.

At the back of the room, a line of plank shelves four deep bracketed to the wall held bottled water, canned goods and coffee, paper plates, cloth and paper towels, bottles of liquid dishwashing soap, plastic utensils and several rolls of toilet paper.

Beneath the shelves sat a large ice chest. Hok'ee, his native name meaning *High Backed Wolf* for the excessive amount of dark hair on his body, especially for his race, moved to the chest, raised the lid, sniffed, and grunted his approval.

At the end of one of the bunks sat the only new looking object in the room: a shiny black portable toilet seat with a bucket centered beneath the opening. The bucket was lined with a plastic disposal bag. Near the back door was a bag of lime and a small shovel for covering waste matter in the hole outside.

The old man led Hok'ee to one of the bunks. Still in his native tongue, he said, "After last night, Hok'ee, you cannot be hungry. I saw in my dream what you were doing, but you need rest, sleep. I have business at another place. Stay here. You must not be seen."

Hok'ee pushed the long mat of hair away from his face. Using the Navajo names for *Grandfather* and *medicine man*, he spoke. "Sicheii, I have done as you asked, but I am sick. You are the Hatathli. You must help me."

"I will do as promised, but for now, rest." Taking a small bottle from his coat pocket, he handed it to Hok'ee. "Drink. It will clear your cough and help you sleep. We will talk when I return."

The old man knew his promises were like seeds of the cottonwood tree, wisps of fluff caught on the wind, most never to fulfill nature's plan.

Chapter 9

It was 6:30 next morning following the Indian Commission meeting when the phone rang and a computerized voice announced the day, time and year. As it turned out, I probably should have asked for an earlier wake-up-call, but the day before had been long and tiresome. I needed the sleep, regardless of what the lady lab technician said.

After a shave, shower and dressed as if heading out for a hike in the mountains, I went down to breakfast. Joined halfway through by friend John and a final cup of coffee while we discussed the coming day, we were off.

A longer-than-I-thought-necessary time at the local Enterprise Rental office awarded me with a burgundy-colored Hyundai Santa Fe SUV. It really wasn't the Enterprise guy's fault for the excessive time.

At my request, he and John labored over a Denver metropolitan map, highlighting in bright yellow the way from the office to the Littleton Police station. A safety measure in case I lost John and his bullet-riddled pickup truck in the morning traffic. It was a good thing. As luck would have it, he went through a green light that suddenly turned red, forcing me to stop as the pickup disappeared in the distance behind a wave of morning traffic.

With the map lying flat on the passenger seat, folded several times and showing only the Littleton area, it was a little after 8:30 when I arrived at the station. John must have slowed, waiting for me to catch up since he was just getting out of his truck.

Lilly Mendoza, our now favorite lab tech, stood at the entrance of the building, arms akimbo, lips drawn tight to one side in a where-the- hell-have-you-been grimace. In other words, *If I was here at seven, why in the hell weren't you?*

"You're an hour and a half late," she said. "I was about to put out a BOLO for your arrest. Both of you."

"Sorry about that," I said, both hands out as though plea bargaining. "My fault. Late sleeper, big breakfast, and…" nodding toward the Hyundai Santa Fe in the parking lot, "time it took to lease the car."

"Bull shit! John, get your truck around to the garage," she ordered. Motioning with her right arm and index finger, she added, "Around that side of the building. And you," her eyes lifted over the top rim of her glasses, boring in on me, "there's a waiting room inside. Wait there. I'll send him out when the paperwork's done."

Twenty minutes later, we were on our way to pick up a young man by the name of Sonny Weaver. He was waiting in the parking lot of a McDonald's on Santa Fe Drive in Littleton, several miles from where he and his girlfriend had been attacked. He told John when they earlier spoke there was no way he'd go back alone to the place where the attack had happened. After what John finally explained about the specifics of that night, I couldn't blame the guy.

Following John's directions through the last portion of the morning rush hour, it was probably a twenty- or twenty-five-minute drive before we turned off on Deer Creek Canyon Road. It was as though somebody had thrown a switch when suddenly the city was left behind and we were winding our way up into the foot hills.

Two law enforcement vehicles marked JEFFERSON COUNTY SHERIFF passed going in our direction, but I didn't pay any attention at the time other than to note they were both exceeding the speed limit. No flashing lights or sirens, but that's what cops do, don't they? We passed a sign stating SOUTH PARKING LOT, SOUTH VALLEY PARK.

"That's where we'd been hiking, South Valley Park, before…" Sonny took a deep breath. "… before it happened. We've still got another mile or two up to the bridge."

He was right. Another mile, the upgrade slight but

noticeable, until we reached the bridge he was talking about, the bridge leading to Grizzly Drive. There was enough room on the shoulder just past the bridge to pull over and park next to a rust-on-black pickup truck. A lengthy strip of yellow crime-scene tape hung loose from a nearby tree, a macabre memento to the death of a young woman.

A lone man, who apparently didn't give a damn if there'd been a murder near that very spot only a week or so ago, was in ankle-deep water on the edge of the creek, panning for gold I assumed. He had on old clothes and rubber boots up to just below his knees. His face was covered by a wide brimmed hat pulled down over his forehead.

I pointed at the man and asked, "Gold?"

Sonny answered, "Yeah. Lots of people do it up and down the creek. Small grains of gold sometime wash down from the mountains." With anger in his voice, he added, "S.O.B. probably doesn't give a shit if part of Emily Jo's body comes floating down the creek. Just keep on panning."

"Sorry to ask, but I understand they've never recovered her body. No part?"

Sonny shook his head and sighed. "Nothing. Not a thing we could even bury and say it was her. Her mom, single, divorced, a basket case. It really hurt her. Visited her last Sunday. Lives about five, six miles farther up the mountain, but I went around the other way. Not on this road, not alone."

We walked along the creek bank, past the man panning for gold. He never looked up. Maybe ten, fifteen yards farther, I pointed to a pair of deep tire tracks on the bank that cut through the weeds where they went down into the water. Parts of an old barbed wire fence and several small bushes had been crushed along the way.

"That where you backed into the creek?" I asked Sonny, at the same time, giving John a scouring look for having kept me in the dark for so long. "Last night, Mr. Nabhe finally, and I say *finally* with some emphasis, told me what he knew about the attack. Mostly from an interview you had with one of the local newspapers."

"Tire tracks? Yeah, that's them," Sonny answered, slowly nodding toward the tracks. "That's where he... the thing caught up with us." Though an adult, he seemed momentarily like a little boy having trouble finding the words. Shaking his head, he closed his eyes, tight. I knew he was trying to shut out the memory, but couldn't.

Finally, he went on with, "Never seen anything like it. Hopped right up on top of the truck like it was nothin', jumpin' up and down. Crushed in the top. Windows popped out. The thing reached down and drug Emily Jo right outta the window. I tried to..." He broke down, tears edging their way down his cheeks as his right hand reached out, fingers working as if grabbing, grabbing, grabbing for the tragically disappearing vision of his Emily Jo. He turned away from us. "I'm sorry I..."

John put his arm around the young man's shoulders. "Nothing to be sorry about, Sonny. I'm sure you've been stronger than I could ever be, carrying such a memory."

Knowing John, I knew that wasn't so, but then wasn't the time to say anything other than, "It's okay, Sonny. I've seen all I need to see. I would, however, like to drive up on Grizzly Drive to see Deer Creek Canyon Park. Take a look at some of the trails where others have been attacked."

To John I asked, "You said there were also two children missing?"

"Yeah. Unlike what was left of three women and two men up there, nothing found."

I could hear dogs barking in the distance. It sounded like at least two, maybe more. "They allow dogs in the park?" I asked.

"Don't know," Sonny said. "Been up there hiking, but don't remember whether or not I saw anybody with dogs. Some of the county parks allow dogs on leashes, some don't."

It was a slow walk back to the SUV, purposely to give Sonny a chance to wipe away the tears and compose himself.

When we passed by the man panning for gold, it was the first time I noticed he was somewhat bent, not from the panning, but from age. As before, he turned away from us, his hat pulled down such that I couldn't really see his face. Again, I wondered why he would choose this place where such violence had occurred, and so soon after the event. Most people would avoid it like the plague.

As I passed the dirty black pickup truck, an old Chevy Silverado from back in the early 2000's or late 1990's, I saw the left front fender had been badly scraped, a line of shiny bare metal at least eight to ten inches long. *Recent*, I thought, but it didn't really hold any relevance at the time.

Back in the SUV, I circled around the truck and turned onto the bridge, noticing a deep gouge and streak of black on an end post on the opposite side of the bridge. I immediately remembered the scrape on the old Silverado pickup truck. Coincidence or...?

Since I wasn't into paint analysis, we drove onto Grizzly Drive past a conservatively designed sign displaying the words *CANYON CREEK ESTATES... PRIVATE... NO SOLICITORS.* When Sonny told me the entrance to the park was farther up the road, I forgot the gouge on the end post and the scrape on the truck because we never got to the park.

Two metal barricades that looked like oversized sawhorses blocked Grizzly Drive just before the intersection with a street called Bear Cub Circle. Immediately behind were two sheriff's department black-and-whites parked sideways as an additional barrier, one a Ford Explorer, the other an F-150 pickup truck with a mean looking, heavy duty brush guard wrapped around the front grill. I pulled the SUV as close as I could up to the blockade.

As one of two uniformed deputies walked forward, I pushed the tab for the window to go down and asked the deputy, "Trouble at the park?"

He was a young, blond haired, clean-cut looking guy, sharply pressed uniform, the name *R. Innes* engraved on a brass-plated name tag over his right breast pocket. As he moved closer to the SUV, he said, "Everything's closed. You need to turn around and –"

"Ralph, it's me, John Nabhe." John shifted in my direction, leaned forward, his chin just above my right arm. "What's happening?"

The deputy leaned down so he could see inside the vehicle. I pulled back as far and as straight as I could. He rested his hands on the door and said, "Hi, John. Man, you don't wanna know. Bad stuff." He tilted his head slightly to look toward the back seat. "Sonny Weaver, didn't expect to see you out this way so soon."

"Came to show Mr. Nahbe and Mr. Berkeley where it happened."

"What bad stuff," John asked. "Like before?"

"Yeah, real bad. One of our patrols found the victim around midnight last night."

"Who's here? Sheriff Ferguson? Chief Kay?"

Ralph, as John had called him, slapped at a deer fly that had landed on the side of his face before answering. "Damn flies. Sheriff and Undersheriff are gone, but yeah, Chief Kay's here, along with Captain Lundgren, Felicia Gonzales and her people, and as you would know, Doctor Wong doin' his thing."

With a level of sarcasm in his voice, he added, "His majesty the coroner, Prince Collum, doesn't like the sight of blood. No sign of Bishop, the DA. Guess he's sleeping late."

"Is it at the park?"

"No, on Bear Cub Circle." He nodded over his shoulder to the street off to his left. Still don't know what he was doing here, alone at night. From ID in his wallet, looks like he's the owner of the house he was at. They're trying to find and notify next of kin. Tough job since all these folks out here've scattered to the four winds after all the killings."

John said, "Since I've been involved, unofficially from the beginning, because of all the rumors and such about the wolf creature, how about calling Chief Kay and ask if I can come up. Tell her John Nabhe's got the man from Florida I told her about.

We might be able to help."

Innes chuckled, all the time shaking his head. "You sure you wanna do that? Just talking about it makes me wanna puke. I've seen enough of that kind of stuff in Afghanistan."

"Like I said, we might be able to help."

Ralph stood back from the window, hit the button on a small, shoulder-mounted radio transceiver and turned his head toward that shoulder. "Chief Kay, Deputy Innes. Got some people here who wanna see you."

While the deputy was talking, John whispered, "Ralph there's a former Army Ranger, two tours in Afghanistan. Doesn't talk much about it. Good man."

There was a moment or two of silence before a female voice replied, "Not a good time, Deputy. Who is it?"

"John Nabhe, the Weaver guy, both you know and..." The Deputy looked at me, one eyebrow raised in a silent question.

I gave him my name. "He says Matt Berkeley."

"That the man from Florida John told me about? John, can you hear me?"

John leaned as far as he could across me and said, "Yes, ma'am."

"Not pretty."

"Understood."

"Okay, you and Berkeley. Park your car down there and walk. Leave Mr. Weaver with the car. He can keep the deputy company. He doesn't need to see this."

I looked back at Sonny, sitting in the far-right corner of the backseat, eyes closed, vigorously shaking his head. "She's right, no way."

I put the rest of the windows down to give Sonny some fresh air. It was one of those Colorado fall days John told me about – snow one day, summer-warm the next. This was one of those warm days, low seventies.

As John and I got out of the SUV, me pulling my light windbreaker off and throwing it back through the driver-side window, I heard Deputy Ralph Innes say, "They're on their way, Chief."

Bear Cub Circle was lined with Sheriff's Department patrol cars, a couple of unmarked black sedans and a white van with JEFFERSON COUNTY REGIONAL CRIME LAB stenciled across the sides and rear doors. There was also a Coroner's truck, engine idling, supposedly to take the body away when the Crime Scene people were finished taking photos and locating any visible evidence.

It was the third house down from the intersection where it looked like all the action was taking place. It was strange not seeing neighbors standing outside their homes, gossiping about what was going on, but then I remembered what John said. No neighbors, all gone because of the supposedly half-man, half-wolf creature lurking in the hills.

As we walked, John explained, "Chief Kay is Kay Pierson-Sanders, Chief of the Criminal Investigation Division. Smart lady. Degree in criminal justice and public safety, did time at the Senior Management Institute of Policing at Boston U., and a graduate of the FBI National Academy. Not sure why she's here instead of one of her section leaders. Big case, I guess."

"Impressive. Doctor Wong, the Medical Examiner?"

"We don't have Medical Examiners in Colorado. We have elected coroners. Wong's full name is Wong Yan Lung, but everyone calls him Dr. Wong, the Chief Deputy Coroner. He's a forensic pathologist. The Coroner is Wes Collum, but for whatever reason he's seldom at the scene."

"The Deputy mentioned a Felicia Gonzales. Who's she?"

"One of the supervisors at the Regional Crime Lab. She'd be here for the photos, blood, bones, flesh, God knows what else."

"Who was the other person he mentioned?"

"Captain James Lundgren, heads the Special Investigation Section. Works for Chief Kay. Guess he's involved because they think it could be some kind of domestic terrorism. Never really cared for him. Unless they run us away, you'll meet 'em all."

Chapter 10

The last of the vehicles blocking the view of what had to be the front of the victim's home was the Coroner's truck. Rounding the front of the truck, I stopped to take in the scene: an off-red Lexus RX four-door sedan in the driveway of a two-story house, cream-colored stucco over concrete block, clay tile roof with two flood lights mounted below the roof line. The place spoke of big-time money along with the other homes on the circle. The car's driver-side window was broken out.

What to me looked like a small picnic tent, green top, open on four sides, had been erected on the lawn. Several people were standing around underneath, talking. The only one I immediately identified was the Chief Deputy Coroner, Dr. Wong, as John had called him. He was the only Chinese person in the group. Call me a quick study, but what the hell.

Motioning toward Wong, I asked John, "The woman next to Dr. Wong? Chief Kay?"

"Uh-uh. Felicia Gonzales, the lab lady."

I could see between their legs a large something in black lying on the ground. Since murder victims don't usually stand around talking to law enforcement personnel, my mental processes quickly told me it had to be the victim in a body bag.

"Chief Kay," John called to a woman whose back was to us.

Chief Kay turned around, separating herself from the group. In civilian clothes – dark slacks, matching blazer over a white blouse – she appeared to be in her late thirties or early forties, skin a smooth milk-chocolate in color. A pleasant looking woman, her hair was swept back away from her face, ending in a tight little bun at the back of her head. The most surprising thing about her was the fact that she was pregnant. The "baby bump" told me she was about eight months along, give or take a week or two.

"John," she said, a verbal footnote adding, "Mr. Berkeley." Approaching, hand out to shake John's hand, she said, "Actually, John, I was going to call you to see if you could add some thoughts to what we've got here in light or our past conversations. In this case, I'd prefer showing you photographs, but looks like you can see the real thing if you think you're up to it."

As she extended her hand to me, she gave a half smile, half grunt and said, "You also, Mr. Berkeley, if –"

John cut in. "I promise you, Chief, he's seen his share."

After the preliminaries of introducing me around, John asked, "Vic got a name?"

Chief Kay answered, "Richard Lamb per the ID's in his wallet. Found the wallet on the ground, apparently ripped from of his trousers during a struggle. We're trying to locate his wife, but no luck as yet. As you know, after all the murders, the homeowners around here moved out. They're scattered from here to kingdom come."

"Know her name?"

"As a matter of fact, we do," said Dr. Wong, a short, firmly built man, distinctly Chinese, wearing a black windbreaker over a set of green scrubs. "From his wallet and from a bottle of Microgestin in a zipped-up pocket of what's left of his jacket. Birth control pills for Pauline Lamb. We think that's more than likely why he came back to the house, to get the pills. Looks like she won't be needing them for a while unless she has a lover on the side."

Felicia Gonzales gave a soft chuckle. The sour frown on Chief Kay's face, however, made it evident she didn't appreciate Wong's last words which I suppose were a normal bit of autopsy room humor.

I'd known a medical examiner back in Florida who thrived on the same kind of flippancy in her work. I suppose that's how they tolerate some of the things they have to see and do.

Without saying anything, the Chief nodded toward one of the crime scene personnel standing near the body bag. He immediately knelt and unzipped the bag a little more than halfway down the length of the corpse. Since I was standing back several feet but relatively close to what was obviously the victim's car, I wanted to take a look inside the car and said to no one in particular, "Go ahead. I'll be with you in a minute."

After only a few steps across a heavy-duty, opaque plastic sheet covering the ground next to the car, supposedly to keep shoes from stepping on blood-soaked grass and soil, I leaned down and looked through the remains of the shattered window. Dried blood and scraps of clothing clung to jagged pieces of glass across the bottom of the opening.

"Whoa!" was all I could say when I saw what looked like a war zone inside the car; a singed, ragged headliner framing a hole blown in the roof, a destroyed dashboard in front of the passenger's seat with half the windshield, forward door pillar and side window demolished. "Shotgun?" I asked as much as stated to a deputy standing nearby.

"Yes sir. Shotgun's already bagged and in the crime lab's van. So's a two-foot-long piece of steel rebar they think was used to break the side window, probably from one of the houses under construction down the way."

My immediate thought was, I had never seen a wolf or any other animal use a metal rod to break a window, but it passed as I thought of the shotgun. "To have had a weapon that powerful with him, he must've known something might be out here, something from which he might need protection."

"With all the recent killings, that's what we figure. He's behind the steering wheel, grabs the gun, tries to pull it around, but couldn't."

For a moment I studied the front seat of the car, the steering wheel and then the window. I could see the scene unfolding in my mind. "Window busted inward, but very little blood on the seat or the steering wheel. Like you say, he made a try for the gun, but whoever or whatever had him, yanked him back. His finger automatically pulled the trigger, once, twice. Boom, boom, out he went, leaving skin and blood on the broken glass, big time blood smears on the outside of the door, half his clothes and shotgun still inside."

The deputy looked hard at me. "You law enforcement?"

I shook my head. "No, but I've worked with a number of them."

"Who? What?"

"Well, uh, FBI, DEA, Interpol, Special Branch of the London Metropolitan Police, more commonly known as New Scotland Yard, Charleston, South Carolina Police Department and the Jacksonville, Florida Sheriff's Office. Quite truthfully, none of them particularly cared for me. Especially CIA, one of their agents, egotistical sonofabitch. Saved his life, and he still tried to kill me."

The deputy gave a disbelieving chuckle. "Who the hell're you kidding?"

I also had to laugh, since I'm pretty sure no one else would believe me either. "No, I don't much kid."

John walked up and tapped me on the shoulder, at the same time addressing the deputy. "I promise, Deputy, this guy's for real." Then to me, he nodded back toward the tent and said, "C'mon over. You need to see this, and like the Chief said, you're not gonna like what you see."

The group parted as we walked beneath the tent. Dr. Wong said, "John wouldn't tell us what he was thinking. Wanted you to see the victim. Get your opinion." The body bag was still unzipped, but had been partially closed, still revealing the face and upper chest. Dr. Wong pulled the bag open to thigh level, revealing what was left of the body as I knelt down for a closer look.

I at first closed my eyes. "Shit!" I didn't want it to be happing again. It couldn't be. God only knows how I had tried to bury the memory of what I'd seen down in the Four Corners.

Realizing what I said, I looked back over my shoulder and apologized to Felicia Gonzales, the Crime Lab lady, and Chief Kay. "Sorry about the language"

Felicia Gonzales, a rather thin, dark-haired, not unattractive Latino as the name would suggest, shrugged her shoulders. The movement was accompanied by something that sounded like, "Nyeaay," followed by a simultaneous *no-problem* palms-up

Chief Kay answered with, "I've heard worse. What are you seeing?" As best she could in her condition, she placed a hand on my shoulder and eased herself down on one knee beside me.

It took me a moment to fully digest what had happened to the poor bastard. First the skin and flesh at the end of each shoulder was torn and ripped as though gnawed down to the grayish-white of the bone. Where the rounded heads of the humeri – the large bones at the upper extremity of each arm – should've been, they had been twisted away from the Glenoid cavities or sockets of their respective scapula, the back part of the shoulder. Meaning simply where the arms were supposed to be connected to the shoulders, they weren't. You might say, they were gone, missing in action.

As I explained to those around me, having been part of the world of archeology for a couple of decades, I did learn a thing or two about bones, their function and their names.

Mid torso, the upper abdomen appeared to have been sliced or more likely clawed open. Hard to tell which. From what little I know of the body's various organs, the killer had taken virtually all the liver on the right side of the abdominal cavity as well as part of the gall bladder. Maybe even part of the right kidney. Hard to tell on the latter two since everything was such a mess.

Since the breast bone had been yanked upward and ribs and muscle pulled back with what had to be brute force, it was obvious the heart sac had been torn open and the heart ripped away from the aorta and the artery to the lungs. The stomach, for the most part, appeared to be intact except for a small tear where the edge of the liver would have been. Farther down, past the midsection, the penis, scrotum and testicles were missing.

"What do I see? It's what John and I saw years ago on a couple of archeological digs down in the Four Corners. Some said it was caused by humans, some said it was animal, while some said it was a mixture. Man who walks on four feet. A shape shifter like the newspaper article inferred."

I stood, reached down and gave a hand to Chief Kay as she maneuvered her way into a standing position. I heard the barking of dogs from higher up in the hills, their barks growing in volume, coming closer.

A man in civilian clothes walked over from the house and said to Chief Kay, "They're bringing in the dogs. That means nothing found, or they would have called."

Chief Kay touched my arm. "This is Captain Lundgren, head of our Special Investigation Section."

We shook hands. I said, "John mentioned you and your position. Something about domestic and international terrorism?"

He was tall, over six feet, several inches taller than me, not overly big, just tall. A handsome man with graying hair like mine. I always say, guys with gray hair have to be good guys. That however is an assumption that might not always prove to be true.

"Yes. Just in case, since we haven't been able to get any closer than we were with the first murder. Actually, tagging along on this one to see if I can add something to the investigation." He glanced sideways at Chief Kay. His jaws tightened just short of a scowl, he said, "My idea since the Chief hasn't seen any reason to include me and my experience."

"I think John will agree with me," I said. "This doesn't seem to have anything to do with the kind of terrorism I should think you'd normally deal with."

John entered the conversation with, "I concur. Whatever it is, it's similar to what we had in the Four Corners. It *was* terrorism of a sort, meant to scare us off a couple of archeological sites. To be honest, I don't think it's the kind of action you would normally work with, Captain. If not coincidental and they are like the Four Corners' killings, it's much more insidious. Killings for a purpose, something none of us know about. Not yet, anyway."

He narrowed his attention to Chief Kay. "If you're going to catch this killer, you're going to have to determine, what's the purpose? Only then will you find the man… or thing behind the killings."

Chapter 11

John and I were about to leave when two handlers and their dogs rounded the crime scene van and cut across the lawn, both dogs on leather leashes. I first thought they were German shepherds, but as they came closer, I realized there were certain differences. The larger one was a shepherd, brownish-tan with the usual black "saddle" coloring along its upper back, but the other?

I was interrupted in my dog identification thoughts by Chief Kay speaking to one of the two men. "Okay, Andy, let me guess. You got nothing."

The man with the shepherd, a tall, slender white guy with what looked like I thought to be a scoped Remington 30-06 hunting rifle hanging by a leather strap from his left shoulder, answered, "Except something I've got for Felicia and her lab, not anything specific. Butch…" He nodded toward the shepherd, "…he caught the scent of what he picked up here at the scene. Ran my ass off trying to catch up with him 'til he stopped outside a bunch of Gamble oaks, about seventy or eighty feet off the trail. Set back and some distance above the lower trails. I tried to look, but couldn't see anything.

"I put Butch on a long leash. Back under the trees he went. I could see his movement against the lower leaves and limbs 'til suddenly he disappeared. Like gone into a cave or maybe an old mine. There's some of them scattered around. Pulling on the leash stopped. He must've gotten in maybe five to ten feet, but he wouldn't go any farther.

"When he came out, I could smell it on him. Some kind of odor. Pretty sure it's not somethin' dead. Wasn't strong, but acidic, hurt the nose. Like maybe ammonia. You get close, you can still smell it on him. We picked up the track again, but it stopped at the creek. We crossed over to the other side. Gone."

Dr. Wong moved closer to the dog, ruffled the hair on its back, sniffed his hand, then returned to his position next to the deceased.

Andy, as Chief Kay called him, reached in his jacket pocket and pulled out a small plastic bag. "One thing we found before we crossed the creek is this." He held up the bag which contained a broken twig with a couple of leaves, something brownish black and some blood.

"Looks like a clump of long hair and blood. Must've been runnin' fast and caught a leg or hind quarters on the bush when the thing, whatever it is, was headin' that way. Could be from a dog, coyote, bear, but you can run this through your system." He handed the bag to Felicia Gonzales for lab analysis.

"Thanks. We'll do a check." She looked toward Chief Kay. "Should have something by tomorrow."

"And you, Will? No body parts, no blood, fluids, bones?" Chief Kay asked the second handler who carried a bolt action .375 H&H Magnum. I recognized the rifle since a friend of mine back in Florida used to hunt big game in Africa with one exactly like it.

Will, obviously American Indian, short, but built like an NFL halfback, big legs, big arms, said, "Nothing, at least nothing like a body or that man's arms. Kinda like Butch there at the cave, whatever it is. Like Foxworthy said, like a tunnel under the trees. I couldn't crawl through there without gettin' all scratched up. Ginger went back in there. Coupla sniffs and came on back." He nodded toward the body bag. "Thought sure we would at least get some blood, but like all these murders over the past month or so, nothing, zilch, or in my language, *ádin*. Frigging amazing."

"Think, for whatever reason, the dog has lost its sense of smell?" Chief Kay asked.

"No ma'am," the man said, shaking his head. "I was also thinking there was a problem, but we went back to the training grounds last week. Tested her with blood, bones, even buried a cadaver part back in some trees, one of the parts we'd gotten from the medical school they couldn't use. Bingo. Got it, no sweat."

"Who trains your dogs?" I asked.

"We're both trainers and handlers out in the field," Andy, the white man, answered. "And you are? Don't remember seeing you before." Tossing a thumb in John's direction, he asked, "You with John here?"

There it was again. Every breathing soul in and around Denver, probably the entire state of Colorado knew John Nabhe.

Chief Kay answered, "Yes, he is." She explained who I was and why I was there.

The man, first wiping a curl of dark hair away from his forehead with one of the largest, boniest hands I'd ever seen, extended that hand in my direction. "Andy Foxworthy, and no kin to the comedian with the same last name. I'm what they call a Director at Large for the Colorado Chapter of the Search and Rescue Dogs of the U.S. SARDUS for short. I live here in the Denver area, but the chapter's address is over in Otis, Colorado."

He must have seen the blank look on my face and added, "That's a spot on the map just east of Fort Morgan and just west of the Nebraska line. Will and I, we both train the dogs and go out into the field with them."

He nodded at Butch, the German shepherd sitting quietly at his feet, head cocked and looking at me as though wondering if I was friend or foe. "Butch is part of our urban and wilderness trailing team. One of the best at what he does."

I asked the second man, Will, "Your dog. I thought it was a German shepherd. It isn't, is it?"

We shook hands. "Will Long Arrow. Up from Cortez, down near the Four Corners."

"I'm familiar with Cortez," I said. "Used it as a base of operations a couple of times."

Long Arrow continued. "Unlike John, he's Navajo, I'm Southern Ute. Anyway, no, her name's Ginger. She's a Belgian Malinois. Trained for human remains detection. She does remind you of a German shepherd, but she's smaller with a slightly different body shape. More squared off, but talk about energy. At times, she's like on a sugar high.

"Today's the second time she's been up near that cave, or whatever it is back in there, the same one Andy's talking about. Same odor. Like Andy, I had her on a leash. She went in maybe four, five feet, but it stopped her cold. Reckon ammonia is as good a description as any. Even I could smell it back where I was. Like regular air, then you could smell it, then clean air, then like ammonia, on and off. When she came out, she was swinging her paw at her nose, like trying to clear something out of it. Like the odor, I guess. Had kind of a hacking cough. Took her a few minutes to get over it. Never heard her cough like that before."

"I'm sure Mr. Berkeley isn't all that interested," Captain Lundgren said. "We've got –"

I cut him off. "As a matter of fact, I really am interested." Talking to Foxworthy and Long Arrow with quick glances toward Chief Kay to make her a part of the conversation, I said, "Any idea what might be causing that odor inside the cave or possibly an old mine shaft? I've been told there use to be some gold mines around here. Particles of gold still washing down the creek back there." I pointed over my shoulder toward Deer Creek. "Saw a man panning for gold this morning."

"Yeah, could be, but no," Foxworthy replied. "After smelln' that smell and the dogs' reaction to it, ain't no way we're goin' in there to find out. You got any ideas, you're welcome to share 'em."

"Couple of ideas, but not in the use of your dogs. Just interested in the way dogs can be trained to detect certain distinct odors and be of so much help in cases like this."

"You a dog handler?" Lundgren butted in, sarcasm coating the edge of his words.

"No, but I happen to know a man and wife team with a dog that's unique in the world of detection, an area totally different from finding human remains or following human scent. They work with the University of Washington's Center for Conservation

Biology. Normally, conservation of wildlife is their main interest, but their dog, a Labrador retriever, has been used in police and animal control cases. Dogs in the program are called CK9 dogs. Their handlers told me about this one after it was used in a case in Montana."

"What's this dog so good at?" Lundgren asked, once again his question tinged with a sarcastic what-the-hell-do-you-know attitude.

"Scat."

"What?" The question came from Lundgren and Chief Kay at the same time.

Dr. Wong was standing with the last of the EMT people near the now completely
bagged corpse. He laughed. "From the word *scatology*, the study of feces or fossil excrement. Animal droppings, dung, poop otherwise known as shit. I think I know, but tell us, Mr. Berkeley, what good would something like that do for this case?"

"Only if you two…" I nodded toward the two dog handlers, "… have noticed fairly large animal droppings around or near the cave."

"No," Foxworthy said. "You, Will?"

"Nope. Seen rabbit poop, fox, deer, but I know what those look like. Seen no bear up here. From what the papers are describing and the size of the thing, nothing that big, like a mountain lion, that eats meat, for sure."

"As are all the dogs in the program – Rex is his name – he's trained to find scat and recognize the animal species that left the scat. He can recognize wolf and mountain lion. The latter called panther in Florida where I come from. He ignores all other species, including human. In the case of the odor in the cave, I'm thinking droppings, guano, from a rather large colony of bats. I'd have to check, but there's a possibility he could ignore that odor, also."

Dr. Wong shook his head. "I'm not so sure, Mr. Berkeley. If it's bats and the smell of ammonia, it's more than likely Mexican

Free Tail bats. Amazing and beautiful creatures, they're common in Colorado. Known also as Brazilian Free Tail bats. *Tadarida Brasiliensis*."

"As well as a pathologist, you're also some sort of uh...Bat Man, huh Doctor?" Looking at Wong out of the corner of one eye, Lundgren issued a soft chuckle beneath his words as though attempting to make a joke at the Doctor's expense.

What a jerk, I thought to myself.

"You'd be surprised, Captain Lundgren. I have numerous interests." Not missing a beat, Wong went on, "To continue, their droppings contain several chemicals: nitrogen, phosphorous and potassium, excellent fertilizer. It can, however, cause histoplasmosis in humans by inhaling spores of the fungus that grows in the dropping, but that's not what you smell if you're smelling ammonia."

"If you know so much about bats, Doctor," Lundgren asked with what was becoming, to me, an unusual degree of sarcasm, "just what is it? What would cause ammonia if that's what it really is?"

Wong looked at Lundgren with a cocked eyebrow before answering. "Droppings from a large colony, more than likely a bachelor colony of Free Tails – perhaps several hundred or several thousand – make an excellent home as well as food for dermestid beetles. Their numbers can become astronomical. The beetles' waste product produces ammonia hydroxide. Concentrations so great, it can become lethal to humans."

He looked at the two dog handlers. "To dogs, also. I'm glad they didn't enter any farther than they did. Humans definitely should not go in there without some kind of breathing apparatus. Ammonia, if strong enough, would blanket most other odors including, for example, decomposing body parts. Your dog, Mr. Long Arrow, regardless of how sensitive his olfactory nerves might be, would never have caught the scent of decomposing flesh or bones in such conditions."

"Not to change the subject from bat shit, ammonia or no

ammonia, but we're tracking a killer, not a wolf or mountain lion, Mr. Berkeley." It was Andy Foxworthy, still not understanding where I was going. From the way he was fiddling with the leash on the German shepherd, I could tell he was not having any of it and was ready to go.

"The graphic in the local newspaper, supposedly based on a nighttime, scared-as-hell description given by Sonny Weaver, who by his own admission had been drinking beer, depicts a menacing, half-crazed man-wolf creature. Then local media's attempt to interview members of the Denver American Indian Counsel, in particular the group's co-chair. What's his name, John?"

"Vincent Brave Wolf. Navajo like me, and everybody knows Navajo's believe in bad medicine men who deal in shape shifting. Men turning into wolves or the other way around. Especially sensitive for a man named Brave Wolf. Old wives' tales as far as I'm concerned, but, as one of our Commission members said, it makes good copy."

"As for the term *creature*," Chief Kay said, "since we don't know what the hell it is, from now on, it's *the killer*. We don't need to sensationalize this thing any more than it already is."

"Yes ma'am, understood, but as you say, since nobody seems to know whether or not the killings are by a human or animal or..." I was about to say *a combination of both*, but I caught myself and said, "The killer has a stomach and a colon that can hold only so much before he or she has to evacuate what's left after the digestive process. Rex might be able to at least identify its scat if it really is a wolf or mountain lion. Other than man, they are the most dangerous, meat-eating predators you've got in the Rocky Mountain region. Right?"

"Semi-correct," John said. "Lion and bear, the latter sometimes, but wolf? Doubt it. The nearest wolf packs in the U.S., gray wolves mostly, are pretty much across the northern states, Michigan to Oregon and in Yellow Stone National Park in Wyoming. There are some Mexican wolves in Arizona and New

Mexico, but to my knowledge, they're damn near extinct. Not gonna bet the farm, but to my knowledge, none seen in Colorado other than in State-sanctioned animal sanctuaries."

Foxworthy pushed in with, "Right, John, and I doubt it's a mountain lion. Not the way they handle their prey. After makin' a kill, a mountain lion usually drags the kill to a protected area and feeds on the shoulder and upper abdomen areas first. He doesn't leave it lying around like this."

He pointed toward the body bag and its contents. "And they don't tear off the arms like we got here, or like with the two women and hikers up in the park. The two kids, I don't know.

"After feeding, mountain lions separate the internal organs from the main carcass and hide 'em at a distance before covering 'em with soil, leaves and such. A mountain lion'll return to the kill again and again until the meat's all gone or until the meat's spoiled. I can tell you, like John says, I'll bet the farm it's not a mountain lion doing this kind of killin'."

I nodded. "If that's the case, by process of elimination, if there's no identifiable wolf or lion scat out here where the murders have occurred, that leaves man as the likely killer. That should at least put a stop to all the shape-shifting crap tossed around by the media."

Chief Kay turned away, one finger resting on the side of closed lips. When she pivoted back in my direction, she said, "If we do find evidence of…" She hesitated for a moment, a wry smile moving across her face, '… evidence of large mounds of scat, you can contact your friends, Mr. Berkeley. We'll see what they can do."

Lundgren's mouth dropped open before asking, "You can't be serious, Kay."

"You're damned right I'm serious, Jim. I'm gonna try any goddamn way I can to solve this case and stop the killings. If Mr. Berkeley's friends and their scat-hunting dog will help,
you're damn right I'm gonna try. At least narrow things down a bit."

To me, her words, a putdown of Lundgren or not, said she had a job to do, and by damn, she would do whatever it took. I knew she meant it. I also knew at that moment, if she would allow it, John and I were going to love working with the lady, baby in the oven and all.

Lundgren scoffed at my *dog* suggestion. "What you're suggesting, Berkeley, shit sniffing dogs, is a stretch of the imagination. Like your bat droppings, all BS and nothing more."

He turned to Chief Kay. "So far as I'm concerned, there's nothing here to do with terrorism, foreign or homegrown, that needs me or my people. Unless you've got something else, Chief, I'm outta here. You didn't ask or want me here in the first place. And as far as I'm concerned, you're making a mistake listening to this Berkeley character."

As he stomped his way across the lawn toward one of the unmarked cars lined up along the street, I wanted to say, *Up yours, so'bitch*, but I didn't. He might be annoying, but he might also be vindictive, something John and I didn't need if Chief Kay actually wanted our help.

Chapter 12

Once we set a time to meet with Chief Kay and Dr. Wong the next day, at their request I might add, we walked back to the rented SUV, woke Sonny Weaver and advised Deputy Ralph Innes we had permission from Chief Kay to enter Deer Creek Canyon Park. Of course, with her obvious passion for details, she had already spoken with the Deputy before we arrived.

As soon as he removed one of the metal barricades, backed the pickup truck out of the way and gave us a "Be careful" warning, we drove up the hill to the empty asphalt parking lot. A relatively sunny morning had turned overcast. Low hanging clouds pushed along by an increasingly cool wind folded their way across the sun. It was almost like an omen of things to come, things I was definitely not going to like.

There wasn't a helluva lot to see at the entrance to the park except a large, glassed-in message board containing a map of the park, a rack of brochures showing trail routes and a brief history of the area. A brick building with restrooms, which by this time all three of us desperately needed, and a couple of covered picnic tables stood off to the left.

Nearby, both to the left and the right of the message board were different trail heads leading to the park's higher elevations. With directions from the two dog handlers in mind, we decided to hike up to the cave, mine or whatever it was that created so much interest.

After thankfully relieving our swollen bladders, we took the trail marked Meadowlark as the wind begin to pick up. A light mist of rain hit my face causing me to shiver, making me wish I'd worn something heavier than the light jacket I'd grabbed before leaving the SUV. On a separate sign, already shiny wet from the rain were the words, "PLEASE STAY ON THE TRAIL" With no intention of doing otherwise until we found what we were looking for, we immediately started upward with Sonny Weaver bringing up the rear. No way, he said, was he going to wait at the entrance by himself.

Though John and Sonny had no trouble with the increasingly steep terrain, it wasn't long before I started sucking air. For a guy who'd been living at sea level for the past ten or so years, climbing a trail that starts at six thousand feet and quickly increases in altitude can do a number on one's oxygen intake. After several switchbacks, a quick glance at the gradient lines on the trail map showed we were at six thousand, four hundred feet, the point near where Andy Foxworthy said the cave or abandoned mine was located. It was, so he described, largely hidden by a thick copse of Gamble oaks.

As the trail curved to the left, just off to the right, maybe seventy or eighty feet, was a growth of the short, rather stunted-looking, tightly packed oak trees backed up to a particularly sheer outcropping of rock. If hikers obeyed the stay-on-the-trail sign, whatever was behind the trees, if in fact there was anything, would be difficult if not impossible to see. The trees were fully grown but no taller than ten to twelve feet, perhaps a few up to fifteen feet. Similar leaves, but height-wise, they were nothing like the forty, fifty or sixty-foot tall live oaks I was used to back East.

But where was the cave? Although it was now pushing toward the end of October and some of the leaves had already turned brown and fallen away, the trees were so bunched together and limbs so thoroughly intertwined, I still couldn't make out a cave or mine entrance from the trail.

Arms and fists braced against my side and catching my breath in spite of snickers from both John and Sonny about my inadequate lung capacity, I looked out over the countryside. To the south, higher ground, occasionally interrupted by narrow ravines and populated by pines, spruce, various other evergreens and a single patch of Aspen gold.

To the north, Deer Creek, the road that paralleled the creek where Sonny and his girlfriend were attacked and the bridge leading to Grizzly Drive. Farther on through the mist, I saw rolling hills and one of at least two imposing facilities where Lockheed-Martin did much of its research and fabrication of equipment for use by NASA and the military.

It was though the clouds had dropped even lower, gradually obscuring my distant vision, but to the east, I could still make out rolling hills and valleys dotted with what appeared to be anywhere from fifty, possibly sixty or more up-scale homes. There were also several partially completed structures and a couple of raw foundations on hillsides. I remembered seeing the sign just before being stopped by the crime scene tape and the deputy that read Canyon Creek Estates. All in all, from the looks of the mostly oversized homes, it was a rather posh community as the British would say.

Other than Chief Kay's people wrapping up at the recently deceased's two-story home, there was no sign of life except for a small cluster of mule deer grazing on a hillside – no cars on the roads, no people, kids, dogs or other pets walking or running around the neighborhoods. Even though most of the view was gradually disappearing in the fog-like mist, all in all, it was a perfect spot for observing the comings and goings of human prey.

"Think that's it?" John asked, pointing toward the Gamble oaks.

"Only one way to find out."

"You sure you wanna do this" Sonny asked, head tilted, one eye half closed, the opposite eye brow raised in a look of high skepticism. "I mean, like going in there if that… that thing might be in there?"

Funny how everybody I'd met seemed to give me the same *are you sure you want to do this* kind of question. I suppose fear might be the operative word.

"I'd rather not," I said to both men, "but since we're here, and since I've finally caught my breath, we need to check. If there's something bad in there, you'll have to catch up with me on my way downhill."

Followed by John and Sonny, I cut across knee-high grass and weeds and slowly circled the growth of Gamble oaks. I was careful to maintain my footing on the mixed gravel and weeds, slippery with the falling mist, while my two brothers-in-arms looked on. There was still no sign of a cave or anything else. I reached the side of the trees facing downward toward the bridge and road.

Only by getting on all fours could I see a way between the trees and the large outcropping of rock. It was like the dog handler had described where the dogs had entered. A kind of path had been made through the leaves that had fallen.

"Think I might have something," I yelled to John and Sonny. "How about getting over here for a little backup." I heard Sonny mumble, "I should've stayed with the deputy."

Once my intrepid crew of two were standing behind me, I said, "If it's the cave or mine or nothing more than a hole in the ground, I'm going to the entrance or maybe a couple of feet inside. Without a light, that's it, no farther. If you hear me scream, grab my legs and pull like hell."

Already on hands and knees, my shoulders hunched up against my neck to make myself as narrow as possible, I dug my elbows into the soft earth and pulled myself forward onto the approximately one-and-a-half-foot-wide path that followed around the slight outward curve of the rock face. From my vantage point at the entrance to the path, the curvature made it difficult to see whether there was any kind of opening or not. It was made even harder by the darkness that had taken hold, a combination of closely thatched overhead branches and cloud cover.

As I moved forward, stiff lower tree limbs scratched and clung at my clothing on the left side of my body and back like tiny claws. There was a claustrophobic feeling created by the densely packed oak tree limbs looming just above my head and to my left and the slab of rock on my right. Everything felt wet to my hands and to my knees through my trouser legs. From the way fallen leaves had been crushed into the damp earth, it was again evident something or someone had been using the path on a continuing basis. I hoped like hell I wasn't about to meet something bigger and nastier than me. There was no standing up to fight *or* to run. Not good.

I could understand why Will Long Arrow, the Navajo guy, didn't come in here. He was built like a tank, too wide. The Foxworthy guy, tall and skinny, could've fit even better than me. Unless, truth-be-known, he was afraid he'd meet something with big teeth and claws. I pretty much felt the same way, but like in horror movies, there always some idiot willing to go down into the pitch-black cellar when everyone in the audience is saying, "You'll be sorry."

Crawling my way around the curve of the rock and keeping my head down from some of the lower hanging limbs, suddenly there it was, an opening no more than ten to twelve feet in from where I'd started. The cave! Or more correctly, the entrance to what had once been a mine.

What kind of mine, I didn't know, but there was no mistaking that much of it, at least the entrance, had collapsed many years ago. On each side of the irregularly shaped, triangular opening was broken, near rotten timbers that once held up the entrance. There was a third timber that lay at an approximately fifty-degree angle between the two entrance supports, from the top of one to the bottom of the other. My guess, it must have once served as the lintel, the horizontal piece over the entrance that carried the weight of the rock and earth above.

There was also a splintered board hanging loose from the lintel piece, once white, now badly deteriorated with black, hand-painted lettering, a couple of the letters completely obliterated. As best I could make out, it read S something MPS something N, a space followed by an MI. Probably Simpson or Sampson Mine. The rest of the last word was missing where the board had split in two. The other part of the board must've been somewhere in board heaven.

The entrance was now no more than five to six feet wide at the bottom, angling up beneath the fallen lintel to about four feet high, ending in a slanted triangular-shaped opening at the top. Certainly not tall enough to be seen above the thicket of Gamble oaks. If I could get to my feet, bend my knees and stoop as much as possible without falling on my face or butt, I could enter. Otherwise, it was stay like I was, on all fours, and inch my way forward. That wasn't going to happen. I needed some kind of body leverage if there was something bad waiting for me in the mine.

Getting on my feet, still bent almost in half, I tilted my head back over my shoulder and shouted, "It's a mine, entrance partially blocked by a cave-in, but accessible. I'm going to take a quick look inside."

"You're sure?" John called back. "I know you don't like bats. I'm coming in."

"No, too little space. I'll only take a minute. If there's bats in here like Dr. Wong says, I'm pretty sure they don't come out this way with all the trees blocking the entrance. There has to be another way in and out. In fact, I can feel a slight movement of air."

Without waiting for a reply, I duck-waddled my way past the opening out of the rain which was beginning to make bigger, harder drops. I stopped and listened. No sound and no physical sign of life, animal or human. I moved forward until my body was mostly blocking, not only the entrance, but much of the light that was filtering through the oak trees.

Moving in one or two more feet and that's when it hit me: the smell of ammonia. Faint, as though caught on a momentary draft. Above my head and along the side of the mine were the remains of more timbers holding up the roof. From what I could tell in the near darkness, the mine seemed to open up the deeper it went. But again, ammonia. I sneezed. Whether my imagination or not, the sharpness of the odor and the sneeze was telling my nose this was not a good place to be. I remembered how Long Arrow had described the Malinois swiping a paw at her nose when she came out of the mine.

I wondered how far into the mine and for what length of time could a man or a wild animal go before the nose, windpipe and lungs would be damaged? And if there were bats, what about their droppings, the fungus spores, the beetle things Dr. Wong spoke about and the histoplasmosis stuff that could kill? Questions I couldn't answer.

As I started backing out, my right hand touched something pushed up against the rocks. Cloth, a rag, a piece of torn once-white cloth, filthy, crusted with dirt and... I knew immediately, dark brown, almost black coagulated blood. The dead guy, Lamb – what was left of his shirt was white. Was this his? The rag was wrapped around something. With the momentary fading aroma of ammonia, my nose automatically wrinkled at the rag's foul odor. Why hadn't the cadaver dog smelled it? Ammonia too strong for its olfactory nerves? Again, more questions.

I took the cloth in one hand, unfolded it and stared at the contents for a moment. "Damn it!" It was a bone, a humorous, the large, upper-most bone of a human arm. Oily to the touch, there were gnaw marks with thin strings of dark meat clinging to one end. Tiny critters crawled in and out of the meaty areas.

I pictured Richard Lamb's body, arms missing. Was it his? The only thing of which I was certain was that real live wolves don't use rags to wrap up bones. Regardless, it was not easy to forget the Four Corners and the unsolved case of the Navajo creature known as the man who walked on four legs or feet or whatever it was called.

A cold shiver ran up my spine and took a spin around my brain. I closed my eyes for a moment, wishing it all to go away, but I knew it wouldn't. Not until we found and killed the creature, or now in my mind, more likely the man who did this. Everyone knows werewolves don't exist, don't they? Or did ancient ones know something we don't?

Chapter 13

It was mid-afternoon before we left the Park. There had been a short break in the rain, but more clouds were already rolling in from the northwest for a late day shower along the Front Range. I was quick to learn that the term, Front Range, represents the urban corridor that runs north to south along the eastern face of the Rocky Mountains. In a way, it serves as a demarcation line between the mountains and Colorado's vast open plains to the east.

Along the route, some of the foothills bare such descriptive names as Hog Back, a line of jagged hills resembling a hog's back, and Flat Irons, five slanted rock formations that look like the faces of old-fashioned clothes irons. I could look at those hills from dawn to sunset, but for the life of me, could see neither hog backs nor flat irons. Perhaps that's because one's imagination doesn't really soar when living around Florida swamp land for a fair part of your life.

John drove. Despite the on-and-off rain, I held the wrapped bone in my hands halfway out the open, passenger-side window as far away as I could to keep the noxious, tell-tale odor of death out of the SUV. We dropped the arm bone off with Felicia Gonzales at the Regional Crime Lab for her examination with a promise she'd get it over to the Coroner's office and Dr. Wong ASAP.

After the bone delivery, I did a good scrub-down on my hands and left a message for Chief Kay with her Admin Assistant advising what we'd found, who had it and set the time for tomorrow's meeting with the Chief and Dr. Wong.

With hands thoroughly sanitized and back behind the wheel, we dropped Sonny Weaver off at his place of work and made a quick stop at my hotel for me to shed my dirt-stained clothes and get into something more presentable. Finally, we were on our way to downtown Denver. Our intended destinations were the Denver Public Library's main location at Thirteenth and Broadway across from the Denver Art Museum and then to the nearby History Colorado Center. Our plan was to do some research on the Deer Creek area. Primarily, the old mine. It was then that John received a call.

He pulled out his phone which was totally unlike the flip-top dinosaur I'd been using for the past twenty years. The front of the damn thing was all glass, multiple icons but nothing that resembled a key board. He caught me glancing at it. "An iPhone, best I've ever had."

So, what if the guy had gone modern on me. Call and receive calls, that's all I needed.

Touching a small *green phone* icon on the glass face, he swiped his index finger across the bottom of the thing to the word *Accept*. At first all he said was, "Afternoon, Roberta."

The conversation on John's end consisted of several yes's, no's and finally, after looking at his watch, he said, "We're on C-470 in Highlands Ranch headed over to I-25, then downtown. Quickest way this time of day."

There was a break before he said, "Not on our schedule, but no problem." He checked his watch once more. "Thirty minutes if you're free."

Silence again before, "Okay. Thirty if we can find a parking place, either in the Stout Street parking garage or, the gods be willing, along the street. Forty-five if we have to look." He hit OFF on his mobile and said, "Change of plans. Maybe the library and History Colorado tomorrow."

I couldn't help the smile on my face. Before he could say anything else, I said, "That was Roberta Pine Woman, right?"

In the middle of a short laugh and a sideways glance, he said, "I saw the way you looked at her at the meeting last night."

Keeping my eyes on the road and the overpass that curved over and down onto the I-25 North entrance ramp, I answered with all the seriousness I could muster, "Well yeah, she is definitely one good looking woman, I have to admit." I said that knowing she was one of the most beautiful women I'd ever met, and in all modesty, I've met a few.

Mustering my best business-like tone, I continued, "Since she's co-chair of the Indian Commission and at least indirectly involved in this, I've been wondering if and when we were going to keep her up-to-date."

I shrugged my shoulders as if to emphasize my interest was only in coordinating our efforts. Partially true, I guess. As we merged onto the Interstate and the rush of traffic, I admitted, "And besides, I saw the wedding ring on her finger."

John nodded up and down, a smug, Cheshire cat look on his face. "Huh-huh, and when did that ever stop you?"

I pushed down on the accelerator to keep from getting run over by an eighteen-wheeler before answering, "I learned a long time ago, think about making it with a married woman, there's always the husband who owns a big gun and an equally big jealous streak."

That at least got a laugh out of John and an admission on his part. "I've gotta be honest. She's not married."

"What?" In my surprise, I must have unconsciously made the car do a bit of a swerve. The driver in the lane next to us pounded an angry blast on his horn and waved a middle finger in my direction before speeding ahead. I would have returned the gesture, but I've always thought 'flipping the bird' was, to say the least, crude and boorish. More importantly, it displays a lack of common sense, especially on a busy Interstate, a place where road rage can get you killed.

"She *was* married. Burt Wilson, a white guy, major in the Army, stationed down at Fort Carson in Colorado Springs. His unit got called to Afghanistan. Been there a month. He and several senior officers were in a meeting with some Afghan politicians, army and police reps about additional security for Kabul, the capitol city.

"In the middle of the meeting, one of the Afghans got pissed about something and opened up with a .45 or similar. Killed Wilson, one of our colonels and a pro-U.S. Afghan politician before one of ours, a Lieutenant Colonel I understand, shot him.

Shooter turned out to be a Taliban sympathizer from what Roberta was later told."

"That's tough. How long ago?"

"About two years."

"Why the ring? To keep guys from hitting on her?"

"That's my guess."

Except for a, "Thanks for letting me know," I kept quiet for the rest of the drive on the Interstate until John said, "Take a right at the Auraria Parkway exit. I'll guide you. It becomes Market Street. Stay on Market to Seventeenth Street. Hang a right. It's a fair piece down to her building. If we don't see a parking space on the street, we'll try the garage."

It was another fifteen minutes fighting mid-afternoon Interstate and business district traffic before I finally turned onto one-way Seventeenth Street. The street's surface shone with a thin veil of mist that foreshadowed a heavier rain that was to follow. And naturally, no parking spaces along the street.

Stopped at a red light, my eyes followed John's index finger as he pointed toward an eight or nine-story building, saying, "That's hers. There on the corner with Stout Street, the Equitable Building. One of Denver's oldest. Once housed the governor's office until it was moved to the State Capitol Building in the late eighteen-hundreds. It's called the Queen of the City's office buildings."

And it looked it. The first two stories were of pink-hued granite, the upper floors gray brick, giving them a layered-cake affect. It was a look that immediately stood out from all the surrounding buildings. There was even a window and balcony approximately midway up decorated with nude cherubs, adding a kind of Italianesque touch to the building.

"Take a left on Stout. Parking garage on your left in the first block."

He was correct. Thankfully there were a number of empty slots on the second level.

Though only October, the much-thickened cloud cover

made it feel like the beginnings of winter had bypassed autumn. Once parked, it was a short walk to the Equitable Building through the chill of a quickening breeze that accompanied the lightly falling shower. A search of the building's occupants' directory located in the rather opulent, almost cathedral-like lobby and we headed for a bank of elevators.

A very nice, middle age lady kept the door open for us. "What floor?" she asked.

"Six," John replied.

"My floor, also."

And up we went.

After giving the lady a "Have a nice day" farewell as we got off the elevator, the two of us turned left, the lady to the right. We walked past three offices sporting different names until John said, "This is it."

The name etched onto a fairly large brass plate by the side of the door was, *Cochoran, Gresham, Kennedy and Wilson, LLC. Land Use, Zoning & Environmental Law.*

I asked, "Wilson? That Roberta using her husband's name?"

"Yeah, she's a partner."

Not too shabby, I thought, partner as young as she was.

We pushed through the door into a spacious, well-appointed reception area with dark, beautifully grained redwood paneling, expensive leather-upholstered chairs and several coffee tables with neatly stacked magazines. There were a number of professionally framed photographs-on-canvas of various Colorado mountain and high-plains scenes by, as I was to learn, famous nature photographers like John Fielder, Sara Marino, Eric Stensland and others. Two well-dressed men sat together, deep in conversation.

At the far end of the room was a silver-haired woman, her hair styled in a bob with bangs swept back slightly to one side giving her a relaxed, casual look. More than likely in her late fifties or maybe early sixties, close to my age, her skin tone never the less gave the appearance of a much younger woman. A pair of tortoise shell glasses, bifocals from what I could tell, did nothing to detract from her looks.

Truthfully, she could have won any number of beauty contests in her early years. Like Roberta Pine Woman aka Wilson, she was a definite WOW! More a senior WOW, I must admit, but WOW none the less. A name plate on her desk read **Gladys Knight**. Beneath the name in much smaller letters were the words in parentheses, *(Not **THE** Gladys Knight)*.

With a smile that could melt a mountain glacier and lips that were a delicious shade of light pink, totally in sync with the silver color of her hair, she said, "Good afternoon, John. Without a doubt, you're here to see Roberta."

There it was again. As I've indicated before, there couldn't be anybody left west of the Kansas state line who didn't know John Nabhe.

"Yes, ma'am. She called about thirty, forty minutes ago." Nodding toward me, he added, "And Gladys, this is Matt Berkeley. I used to work with Matt down in the Four Corners area providing security for various archeological digs."

Though not standing, she reached out across the desk and offered her hand. "Glad to meet you, Mr. Berkeley. Are you from the Denver area?"

I leaned forward, took her hand and felt the soft warmth of her skin. "Glad to meet you, Ms. Knight. To answer your question, no, just came up from Florida. And please, call me Matt."

John chuckled. "Besides archeology, he's also an old navy Commander who used to drive ships and riverine craft in Viet Nam."

Adding a caveat, I inserted, "But that was a long time ago."

"Changing the subject," John said, "what are you doing out here? You're usually in back with Roberta."

"Regular receptionist out sick and no temp available. The biggest of the four bosses said, 'You got it, Gladys.'"

John turned to me. "Gladys is a paralegal. She's Roberta's

right-hand, left hand, ace researcher and anything else Roberta needs. She could damn well handle court proceedings if she had to."

Meanwhile, Gladys punched a number on an office intercom and softly announced, "Roberta, they're here." There was a momentary pause before Roberta's voice responded, "Send them back."

Gladys turned back to us. "She's waiting for you. Since you were last here, John, she's moved to a newly renovated office. Fourth door on the left."

To be kept in the conversation and demonstrate my courteous demeanor, I smiled, nodded and added, "Thank you, Ms. Knight."

She returned the nod and offered that smile again, but did *not* say, "Call me Gladys." So much for my charm, clean-cut good looks, Florida tan, gray hair and highly cultivated manners.

The name on the door read ROBERTA WILSON, Esq. John tapped on the door and immediately opened it. Roberta was on the phone, but motioned us to enter. Two rain-speckled windows behind Roberta, their blinds partially open, looked down on Seventeenth Street, lights already beginning to throw a wet glare up from the asphalt. The lack of traffic noise told me the windows were the heavy thermal type, not something installed back in the nineteenth century when the building was built. On the wall between the windows were a number of framed diplomas and award certificates.

Roberta, as beautiful as when I first saw her, sat at a large executive desk between the two windows. The desk, as well as a credenza-like desk immediately at her back beneath the diplomas, was covered with legal-size blue folders. Some were open revealing various papers, others closed, stacked as though waiting for her attention.

Besides a desk-top computer, the only non-work-related item on the desk was a framed photograph of an Army officer, young, handsome, in his Dress Blue formal uniform displaying his major's rank and a number of miniature metals. Overseas service bars on his right sleeve sat just above the blue and gold braid. That told me he'd been overseas before his Afghanistan tour, probably Iraq, Syria or some other God-forsaken place. Two, rather uncomfortable looking chairs stood in front of the desk.

I did a quick glance around the room. One wall was intersected by a door opened to a separate office. Shelves on either side of the door held displays of Native American pottery, carvings, photographs and a magnificent collection of hand-carved and meticulously decorated wooden Kachina dolls representing spirits found in various First Nation cultures. A third wall with the door through which we entered provided space for shelves on either side of the door lined with law and case books, everything neat and orderly.

A fourth wall off to the right of Roberta's desk, like in the reception area, held a number of photographs on canvas of mountains and wilderness land. Speaking softly, John explained, pointing to one then the other, "Local guys, but known throughout the west. Stephen Weaver and Stan Rose, respectively."

Beneath the framed photographs sat a leather sofa, a broad-surfaced coffee table and, on the opposite side of the table, three straight-back chairs, leather upholstered with arms. The floor was a somber, richly hued wood. A finely woven space rug with patterns one would normally identify with Native American designs lay beneath the coffee table.

Roberta finished her phone conversation, stood and walked around the desk. She extended her hand to John and then to me, saying in order, "John, Mr. Berkeley. Thank you for coming. Coffee, soft drink, water?"

John said, "Whiskey, but since that wasn't part of the offer, coffee."

When she looked at me, I said, "Water. Good for the soul. Whiskey later."

Smiling, she asked, "Anything wrong with whiskey?"

"Absolutely not. If anything, it's a higher level of

goodness."

With a slight chuckle and a smile, Roberta called Gladys Knight and told her she wanted her in our meeting, to find one of the clerks to take over reception duty and to bring in water and coffee for all of us. When Gladys started to tell why she was at the reception desk, Roberta said, "Don't worry. I'll take care of him." That again told me Roberta wasn't afraid to carry her own weight among the heavies.

Afterwards she motioned toward the sofa. "Let's sit over there, less formal. To be honest, I never liked formality. While we're waiting for Gladys who normally works in the adjoining office," she pointed to the open door between the pottery and Kachina doll shelves before saying, "tell me what you learned this morning. Chief Kay called a little over an hour ago, wanting to keep me in the loop. Said you were at the crime scene and you'd fill me in. Already the Denver Post has put out a special edition on last night's murder as well as the local TV stations' noon news. No media-created half man, half wolf sightings as yet, but that will surely come."

With John and myself taking the sofa, Roberta in one of the chairs, before we could start, Gladys came in with a small laptop computer snugged between one arm and side and in her hands a large tray containing three cups of coffee, cream, sweetener and a glass of water. Now that I could see the woman from head to toe, I was even more impressed: the way she dressed, a smart open-front burgundy colored shirt over a white turtleneck sweater with white slacks; the way she walked, confidence in her movement; the slimness of her body, still well shaped – athletic, in fact – for what I assumed to be her age, and more significantly, no wedding ring on her finger. I couldn't help but think, with her looks, there were plenty of old guys like me who were more than willing to keep her company.

As soon as everyone had their beverages and Gladys was seated with the laptop for taking notes, John took the lead, telling what we heard and saw, me filling in some of the blank spots until

I described the abandoned cave. The ammonia odor, what I found and what I felt significant about it.

I also described my acquaintances with the people who owned the scat-sniffing dog. I had to admit, however, considering the rebar used to break Richard Lamb's car window, the wrapped bone and pending examination of hair and blood the SARDUS guy found, I was no longer sure the dog would be needed. That could wait until I knew what Dr. Wong and the lab people determined. The whole thing was starting to look more like a human, possibly deranged, but whose actions could be for any number of reasons.

There was silence for a moment until Roberta said, "While I was in court this morning, Gladys received a phone call from Burt Addelson with the Jefferson County Planning and Zoning Division. We often deal with the P and Z people in several of the surrounding counties concerning zoning and environmental impact. Tell them about the call, Gladys."

Up until now, Gladys had been taking voluminous notes on what John and I'd been saying, fingers flying across the keyboard, key clicks like staccato notes on a rag-time piano. With a quick exhalation of breath and a momentary arm and hand stretch accompanied by a wriggling motion with her fingers, she said, "Burt told me that a foreign corporation based in London, offices also in New York and Hong Kong, had submitted the various applications necessary for permitting and establishing a theme park in Jefferson County. It's for over a thousand acres adjacent to Canyon Creek Estates and the County's Deer Creek Canyon Park where all the murders have taken place. The company is currently opening an office here in Denver which would later transfer to Golden in Jefferson County in a building they're planning to build.

"The initial applications for Building and Rezoning Permits, Notice of Interest for Land Disturbance, Grading and related permits were submitted a month before all the Deer Creek area murders started. At that point, the P and Z office merely considered it another development to be reviewed, approved or disapproved, the latter because of its potential closeness to a residential community.

"According to Burt, however, an addendum to the applications was submitted when a large number of people started advertising their homes for sale in the Canyon Creek Estates community. That was after the two children went missing and body parts of the first five adults were found. Burt said owners are so frightened they're actually willing to take a loss just to get out. In many cases, they'd already abandoned their homes since they can't even get a realtor to place their property on the market. It's gotten worse after that woman was pulled out of the pickup truck.

"Here's the interesting part. In addition to the land first noted in the original submission, the addendum includes the entire Canyon Creek Estates where the homeowners are desperate to sell. Burt understands the company is offering fair market value for each of the homes."

"Unbelievable!" I said. "Fair market value when these people can't find a realtor or sell on their own? What's the name of this company? I'm familiar with a number of major development companies with headquarters in London, doing construction work throughout the U.K. They keep finding artifacts from centuries back when they start excavating to put in building foundations."

"Ralston World Wide Entertainment, LLC. It's an investment company from what Burt says. Wealthy investors, philanthropist who specialize in purchasing land for the purpose of conservation. They're currently funding similar projects in other western states, the U.K., Europe, Asia and the Middle East. Their objective is to offer entertainment, yet, at the same time, protect the land and its history."

I shook my head. "The name means nothing to me. Sorry."

John's face took on a puzzled look. Prefaced with a *humph*, he finally said, "I understand the first applications, but the addendum and in view of the timing, the murders and all the accompanying publicity. The whole thing seems... well awkward for lack of a better word. Even so, what kind of theme park would they put out there that's gonna protect the land and its history? Ferris wheels and roller coasters won't do the job."

"Burt says their applications are for the establishment of a museum that celebrates the history of Native Americans in Colorado." She looked down at her notes from her conversation with Addelson. "Ute, Cheyenne, Navajo, Apache, Arapaho, Shoshone, Comanche, Pawnee and Kiowa. They would also have, and I quote, 'an authentic Indian village.' Native American actors in authentic costumes would perform daily activities and explain the history of their respective tribes. There would be stables, riding horses and instruction with access to the trails up through Deer Creek Canyon Park.

"In addition, following the submission of the addendum, they approached the County this past week about assuming responsibility and upkeep for the park, a ninety-nine-year lease from the County at so much a year. He didn't know the dollar figure. Once the theme park is operational, other than voluntary donations from visitors, everything free to the public."

Roberta shook her head and raised her hands, expressing her exasperation with the whole thing. "I simply don't understand. These people have never approached the Indian Commission. We're the organization that has the greatest interest and knowledge of Colorado's indigenous people as well as that of surrounding states."

"Celebrating the State's native people sounds good," John said, "but I still think the whole thing, the addendum especially, is weird as hell." He shrugged his shoulders.

"On the other hand, if this company has already been looking for land out in that vicinity, I guess it makes good business sense to the company and sure as hell a God-send for the families out there, but fair market value? Like Matt says, unbelievable." He shook his head as though he was missing something

Taking a quick sip of water, I added, "Under the circumstances, I can understand the homeowners' point of view. With all the unsolved murders, some kind of monster sucking at their life's blood so to speak and law enforcement clueless in finding the killer, I know what they're thinking. Grab the offer, go somewhere else and live another day.

"On the other hand, from what little I've seen, the land below Deer Creek Park where the homes are located doesn't really look suitable for this kind of operation. I may be wrong. You can shape the land a lot of ways with bulldozers, backhoes and dynamite. But still, if they're so big on philanthropy and land conservation and if the people want to sell, why not buy what they want and give it to Jefferson County for an addition to the already established park?"

With a frown cutting across her face, Roberta said, "I honestly can't see any kind of entertainment venue where so much death has happened. What else did he tell you, Gladys?"

"With the initial submissions and the addendum, the land they want covers the entire Deer Creek area, both the park and Canyon Creek Estates. Since market values out there have literally plunged to zero…" She nodded in my direction in agreement with my earlier thoughts, "… some of the company's personnel have been negotiating with a large number of homeowners. Some closings are already scheduled. It's really very simple. Nobody wants to buy with all the horror stories in the media. I wouldn't."

Roberta shook her head. "People are now calling it *Death Creek Estates*. Burt Addelson told Gladys, property owners are already lining up at the Jefferson County Zoning office asking them to change the zoning to what's called 'Conservation Zone District, Colorado' in favor of the company's project. It's the zoning change the company will need."

"What the hell is Conservation Zone District, Colorado?" John asked.

Roberta answered, "It's for conservation of open spaces and development of parks and recreation facilities to meet the recreation needs of the county. It covers agriculture if no dwellings are within the area, but more importantly in this case, it includes public parks and/or recreation areas open to the public, things this company wants to do with their theme park.

"There are also special purposes under the recreation portion such as a riding academy and stables, golf driving ranges and other similar open-nature type uses. Even camp grounds and what they would encompass, everything for public use. We get involved where there may be questions concerning the environment and whether or not the organization or corporate entity is in compliance with the General Provisions and Regulations Section of the County's Zoning Resolution."

Gladys observed, "Lots of big fancy homes means the company must have deep pockets, let alone having to destroy the homes and clear the land to meet the requirements of a host of bureaucracies. Not only the county building and zoning restrictions and County Commission requirements, but those of the Colorado Department of Parks and Wildlife and potentially the U.S. Fish and Wildlife Service. That's a tough assignment. I'm sorry but there's something about this that..." Stopping in midsentence, her upper teeth gnawed on her lower lip.

The overall look on her face told me she also had reservations about the whole thing. I was beginning to really like this woman. She had a suspicious nature like me, and besides, she talked like me. "I'm with you, Ms. Knight. With the possibility of bad times hanging over their heads," I said, putting voice to my thoughts, "pretty damn convenient, this company showing up from London, New York and Hong Kong just in time to save the day with a bag full of money. You're right. From what I saw when we were out there this morning, big, expensive homes."

"Exactly what Roberta and I thought," said Gladys as she laid the lap top aside and went to Roberta's desk, rummaged through some files, finally retrieving a legal-size, thicker-than-usual sheet of paper. She returned to her chair. Holding up the paper, she said, "A topographical map of Jefferson County, Colorado. Burt faxed this over at my request. According to Burt, this highlighted area is the entire spread of land they're talking about." She outlined the area with an index finger.

Continuing, she said, "As you can see, the highlighted portion not only includes the initial land they wanted but also the park and the residential community. The boundary, including the park, goes west, well up into the mountains. Its northern boundary follows along Deer Creek Canyon Road to what was once known as Phillipsburg, an abandoned mining town back in the late eighteen-hundreds. Then south along what's called Deer Creek Road for another five miles on a line just below a number of homes along the highway."

"You think…" John hesitated for a moment, lips pursed, narrowed in thought. He took a sip of coffee, giving each of us an opportunity to follow suit, the rest with their coffee, me with my water. He started to say something, but shook his head. "No, Roberta, Gladys, you tell me what you're thinking before I waste everybody's time."

Roberta nodded to Gladys who answered, "A theme park, no matter how great it sounds, is not the company's true objective. Not this particular theme park anyway. To paraphrase an old saying, if it's too good to be true, it's most likely not. Get the property and then…? What's the word? Subterfuge, meaning any plan or action used to hide one's true objective."

Roberta took a sip of coffee before agreeing. "That's what we both think."

John smiled. "I couldn't have put it any better."

"But why?" I asked. "Any evidence to back up what you're saying?"

Gladys answered, "They come into the greater Denver area cold. No coordination with the Indian Commission or the History Colorado Center, one of the finest depositories of First Nation People history in the State, nor contact with any of the State's universities or tribal organizations. That's what I've been checking most of the afternoon."

There was silence, each of us looking from one to the other, waiting for someone to speak. I broke the silence. "Ms. Knight, you mentioned a place called Phillipsburg. You called it a mining town, now deserted, abandoned. What kind of mining?"

"Glad you asked," Gladys said. "I just happened to look it up." She turned the map over and read from a line or two of handwritten words. "'Numerous mining and smelting operations producing gold, bismuth, copper and tin, but the deposits quickly depleted and the town was abandoned.' This from the history of Deer Creek Canyon Park and surrounding area. There was also gold mined on nearby Sampson Mountain, named for the man who discovered the gold."

I stood, stretched to get the kink out of my lower back and shoulders and walked to one of the windows behind Roberta's desk, overlooking a rain-swept Seventeenth Street. Various colored umbrellas – black being the predominant color – sheltered people as they exited the many office buildings along the street.

They were accompanied by the sluggish movement of heavy vehicular traffic, headlights bright on the left, red tail lights to the right reflecting off the sheen of water on the one-way street, windshield wipers swishing back and forth in rhythm.

I checked my watch. Four thirty, getting off time and the beginning of rush hour, people heading off to shop, have a drink, or go home to their own private world. I turned. "Getting late," I said as I walked back to the sofa and the dwindling level of water in my glass. "Let's talk about the killer."

"Go for it," John said. "That's why I asked you to come out here. Thought your experience might give us something we've overlooked."

Looking at Gladys and Roberta, I said, "Following your lines of thought, if the killer is a man, not a genius, nevertheless intelligent, someone who gives some consideration to each of his killings, why all in the same general location?

"If he's killing for killings sake, or for cannibalistic reasons in view of what it appears he's done to the bodies, why not kill in other locations. One in Denver, others in the various suburban communities around Denver. One or two farther up in the mountains in Jefferson County if that's where he's hiding. Create as much confusion as possible for all the law enforcement agencies throughout the greater metropolitan area.

"Either that or he's got a specific reason for killing locally and in some cases, leaving leftover body parts for people to find and create fear. In other cases, hiding leftover body parts for later use, parts that... pardon my frankness, ladies... that fit his appetite. Possibly somewhere deep in that abandoned mine. He didn't mean to leave that wrapped arm bone at the mine entrance. That was a mistake. As I said, everything else has been for people to find, to build an entire community's fear of who might be next."

"What're you saying, Matt?" Roberta asked.

Almost as an echo, Gladys asked, "Yes, what are you getting at, Matt?"

It was like a lightning shock of acceptance. They'd both finally called me *Matt*. John had a big wide grin on his face. He realized the same thing. His boy was now part of the tribe, so to speak. It took me a moment to refocus.

"Based on everything we've discussed today, in my opinion, like John told Chief Kay this morning, there's a reason killing's have been so localized, but what's the reason? What's the killer trying to tell us? I think there's something he wants, but what? Answer? The land."

I nodded in Gladys Knight's direction. "Your word, subterfuge, says it all. It's a game of deception. Murder by deception, if you will."

I pointed to the map now lying on the coffee table, circling the highlighted area with my fingers. "If I'm correct, it's not some hairy monster we're dealing with. The killer enjoys killing, to be sure, probably somewhat wacko in the head, but he's nothing but the means to an end.

"Somebody's pulling his chain, and it's not for a theme park. Everything carefully planned, carefully orchestrated. The land is what that somebody wants, more than likely something they think or know is under the surface and worth killing for.

"Gladys, what was it you said they mined up in that

abandoned mining town you mentioned? Do you mind if I call you Gladys?" *Gladys,* surprisingly, had suddenly become one of the loveliest and most important words in my vocabulary. That surprised even me.

"Please do," she answered with a smile that, for the first time, appeared to be on the edge of an invitation, but that was probably only my wanting it to be so. "It was Philipsburg. Gold, bismuth, copper and tin as well as gold on Sampson Mountain."

That smile caused me to take a moment to get back on track. Drinking the rest of the water in my glass gave me a moment to steady my thoughts before saying, "It doesn't have to be gold or anything like that. Probably something we'd never think of. Something really off the wall, but extremely useful and valuable. Like you said earlier, there are locations in other western states Ralston Entertainment's trying to buy, maybe other places in Colorado."

"I can certainly do some snooping with some of the other Colorado counties and with Utah and Wyoming at least," Gladys said. "We've worked with them before, but what exactly am I looking for?"

John and Roberta started to speak at the same time, but John nodded in Roberta's direction who answered, "Mineral deposits, known or suspected, but not currently being mined. And Gladys, find out if they're looking for mineral rights. Matt, anything else?"

"That's it. More specifically, if there's anything around the Deer Creek Canyon area. If there is, I'm pretty sure we'll find the *why* for all the killings and hopefully who is really running the show."

Chapter 14

Except for the yellowish glow from the kerosene lamp on the center of the table, the room was wreathed with shadows, otherwise dark. Images of the two chairs, their backs twice normal size, were superimposed as shadows against opposite walls. Even though the fire in the fireplace had dwindled to little more than hot, glowing ashes, the mass of hair covering his body was still sheltering an overabundance of internal heat.

He felt wet all over, almost claustrophobic because of the closeness of the tiny, one-room shack. He'd grown used to sleeping near the mouth of the abandoned mine and the cool night air. At least here, he could hear, and yes, smell the falling rain. Its patter on the roof and against the opaque, vinyl-covered windows created a sleepy, mesmerizing sound.

Groggy, his head weighed like his brain had thickened to the hardness of wet clay, thoughts difficult to grasp, to sequence, to find meaning. He forced back the blanket covering his body, attempted to push up on one elbow and fell back. He tried to breathe as deeply as he could, his breath in short gasps. With each breath and exhalation, there was a watery bubbling sound within the chest. Groans became harsh, prolonged bouts of coughing, forcing up globs of blood-flaked mucous as he tried to think.

Besides the warmth, besides the dampness, he felt a low throb of pain shoot up the length of his left leg. Why? He slowly remembered the taste of his own blood from the cut just above the ankle. What else could he remember?

What was it his grandfather had given him to drink? Bitter, yet a warming sensation as it flowed down his throat. Something to make him sleep, but for how long? He eased his head to one side, searching for the first, then the second of the two windows, the second blocked from his view by the chest of drawers. The first, however, indicated darkness had fallen over the mountain side. He'd slept too long, hungry. He lay there as thoughts crowded his mind, at first from long ago, snapshots from his past.

* * *

Loneliness. It had followed him most of his life. It was there now. A constant ache from day to night, from night to day. Before he was born, his father, a roustabout working on an oil rig in Texas, died in a blowout when the pressure control equipment failed. To find acceptance in the outside world, his mother named him Keith; Keith Nalzheehii, the hunter, Hunter substituting for his Navajo surname as he became older and ventured from the Reservation into the white man's world.

From the beginning, it was the hair, black with a brownish tint, silky, long. Even while small, the boys teased him, called him Hok'ee, High Backed Wolf, because of the unusual amount of body and facial hair and his ability to run faster and jump higher than anyone. "Hok'ee" Nalzheehii, the fastest boy on the Reservation. Even though his mother trimmed the hair on his face and the back of his hands at least once a week and later, as he grew older, taught him to shave, it did little good.

It was not only the hair that made his peers wary, but Hok'ee grew taller and stronger than any of the other boys on the Reservation, his voice maturing and deepening earlier than the others. A few of the boys took pity on him, but many of the older ones bullied him, made him walk on all fours, jabbing him with sticks from all sides, forcing him to run, each step faster and faster.

They taunted him with despicable words about his mother having mated with a wolf. "Wolf, cry like wolf," they shouted, daring him to outrun the coyotes, rabbits and deer when they went hunting. Catch the creatures, kill them and skin them.

Once while butchering a rabbit, a fly flew against his face. As he swatted at it, some of the blood from the knife in his hand splattered across his face and lips. He remembered the taste, still slightly warm. It had a strange wildness to it. Some of the boys saw him. From then on, he became High Backed Wolf with Blood on Face. He liked, not only the taste of the blood, but because they feared not only his looks, size and strength, but his swiftness, ability to kill and eat his prey without fire to cook.

It finally came to an end. Supposedly to protect the girls, they would often throw small pebbles at him, the pebbles becoming rocks over time. One night, in the flood lights outside the Reservation's youth club, in spite of the barrage of rocks, the accompanying laughter and the goading by both the boys and girls, he ran at them. At first on two feet before dropping to all-fours and howling like a wolf.

They continued their laughter, pointing in ridicule until they saw the hate on his face, or what part of the face they could see. His eyes took on a reddish green color in the glare of the flood lights. They scattered, some running into the youth center, others to the nearby road toward their homes.

He caught two of the slower ones, an overweight boy and his younger sister, nipping at them, clawing, especially the boy who stumbled and fell. Hok'ee stood over him snarling, his teeth white, menacing as the boy begged not to hurt him. Satisfied, Hok'ee turned and walked away, leaving the boy whimpering with fright. After that night, the bullying stopped, but he found himself more alone than ever, always alone.

The girls ignored him, even when he proved himself at track meets. He was faster than all the boys from high schools within the Navajo territory: Chinle, his own school, Kayenta, Tuba City, Ganado, Window Rock. Even so in competition outside the territory with white, Mexican and the few black boys from Holbrook and Gallup.

Following high school, he outwardly adopted the name Keith Hunter in favor of the white man's name his mother had given. He again proved himself athletically superior during his two years at Diné College, sometimes competing against the State's two major universities, the University of Arizona in Tucson and Arizona State University in Tempe.

Basketball found him excelling until the NCAA, without medical proof, declared him ineligible since they said his super human movements and overwhelming strength had to be due to steroids. And surely, he must frighten members of the other teams with the wolf-like hair on his body. Hair which he refused to shave off his arms and legs and was evident beneath his uniform.

By then, he had grown exceptionally tall, well over six feet, slim yet muscular, his face, once shaved, narrow and handsome. At the college, he excelled, not only at basketball and track, but in long jump, gymnastics such as pommel horse, still rings, vault, parallel bars and horizontal bars, the latter areas unusual for a person his height.

After two years at Diné College, he qualified for the 2008 Beijing Olympics wining three gold medals and one silver, spread across the 1,500 meter and Long Distance 10,000-meter races, the 4X400 meter Relay Race and the Long Jump. Shortly afterwards, however, he was disqualified for the same unproven reason – use of hormonal drugs, especially for his unusual hair growth. Again, disappointment, a characteristic that seemed to follow him throughout life.

Alone, his mother now dead, he relied on his grandfather for a place to live. His grandfather, the only one who by then showed understanding and compassion for his externally imposed failures, the one who served as medicine man for their small community.

Keith saw an advertisement poster in the window of the general store: **STETSON BROTHERS CIRCUS, APPEARING IN FLAGSTAFF, FRIDAY, JUNE 16TH. COME ONE, COME ALL.** On the poster were animated pictures of elephants, caged lions and tigers, trapeze artists, clowns, a tattooed man, a bearded lady and more, but it was the bearded lady who caught his attention. If she could be part of the circus, why couldn't he? He spoke with his grandfather who gave him enough money for the round-trip bus fare to Flagstaff and a ticket to the circus. After seeing the show, he felt that, with all his soul, this was something he could do with his life.

Once he found the two Stetson brothers, revealed his hair-covered body, and demonstrated his ability to run, both on two feet and on all fours, to jump great distances, horizontally and vertically, he was offered a job. To play the part, he reverted to the once hated name the boys had called him: Hok'ee – High Back Wolf, along with his surname, Nalzheehii, the Hunter.

They built a set with fake trees, large rocks of steel frame-enforced papier-mâché, and used him as a wolf, howling, snarling, children clinging in fright to their mothers and fathers. He was hunted by two ruggedly costumed cowboys, one being the show's animal trainer. Of course, they always made their kill to the shouts and applause of the audience.

Two years, traveling throughout the western United States, twice into Canada greatly enlarged his world. It was there in Canada, a town called Edmonton, the capital of Alberta Province, that he had his first sexual encounter with Lydia, the bearded lady. He learned from Lydia that the beard on her face, in addition to a modest amount of hair on her chest, was called Hirsutism. In her case, it was caused by some kind of ovary syndrome. She didn't know, however, if it was the same as the hair that covered his entire body. Nor did he, except he knew he didn't have ovaries, or didn't think he did.

It all came to an end when, during one of the shows, the animal trainer, unknown to Hok'ee, decided to use his whip instead of a rifle loaded with blanks. The whip, an eight-foot-long, braided bullwhip of kangaroo hide so the trainer bragged, was once used by Gunther Gebel-Williams of Ringling Brothers and Barnum and Bailey fame. It had a thin, twelve-inch leather fall at the end.

With the other man as backup, the trainer took his whip to Hok'ee, popping him several times with the leather fall, again and again to the delight of the audience. In pain, enraged at what was being done to him, taunted by shouts of encouragement for the trainer from the stands, and cornered in a crevice between two of the giant boulders, Hok'ee grabbed the whip, yanked the trainer to him and, howling into the man's face, bit off part of the trainer's nose and upper lip. Though it was considered self-defense by the Stetson brothers as well as the Canadian Royal Mounted Police, he was fired.

One of the policemen, a Frenchman, originally from French-speaking Montreal where he had joined the RCMP, told him about circuses in France. So beloved by the French people, he should go to Paris where any one of the circuses would surely welcome him.

Once back in the States, after obtaining a passport which had not been required in Canada while traveling with Stetson Brothers, and with what little money he had saved plus some from his grandfather, he went to France. There were circuses by the dozens: *Cirque Fenando, Cirque Medrano, Cirque Plumé*, they ranged from the Mediterranean south of the country to the north, east and to west.

It was *Cirque de Montmartre* that caught his eye, and he caught theirs as well. This time, however, he became the aggressor, two unwary lovers his prey. In the arena, the center stage was designed to resemble a park, much like the *Bois de Vincennes*, the largest park in Paris. Props for the scene consisted of a closely packed group of plastic trees and flowering shrubs that could be wheeled on and off the central performing area. A mockup of a line of Roman columns overlooked a silvery, moonlit pond.

Two lovers, whispering, kissing, unaware of the danger, strolled along a path as the hair-covered werewolf lurked behind the trees, silently following. Within months, he became famous, known as *le Loup-garou de Paris*, the Werewolf of Paris. Thousands came to see his act, his picture on every kiosk throughout the city, each *Arrondissement* or section of the city, on each street corner of the greater metropolitan area.

But the most exciting thing in his life was Arielle, a trapeze artist, who with wig and make-up, posed as one of the two lovers, wooing and swooning along the path, soon to be ravished. With the sound of background music creating more and more suspense, the werewolf stalked the loving pair, finally pouncing on the man, tearing and ripping cloth, fake blood spouting from the man's chest and throat before giving up the fight and dying.

Once the frantic, screaming Arielle was in his clutches, he would look into her eyes, see her beauty, relent and let her live, showing the softer side of his wolfishness. The crowds loved it, much like the bloodthirsty citizens of ancient Rome, enjoying the killings or a show of well-deserved mercy in the Coliseum.

The city and as far away in the north as Calais and along the Mediterranean coast, Marseille and Toulon, fell in love with the stories and film shorts of *le Loup-garou de Paris*. Hok'ee became the toast of the country.

Within months, Hok'ee and Arielle became lovers. She called him *Ma chaude couverture d'amour poilue,* my warm hairy love blanket, and his life for the first time finally found a sense of meaning, of fulfillment, of happiness. It was in his second year with the circus. His fame had grown, not only in Paris and throughout France, but people came to see him from several of the surrounding countries: Belgium, Luxembourg, Germany, Spain and Italy. Arielle took leave to go home to be with her invalid mother in Lyon in the southeast of France, absent from her trapeze as well as their performances together. More important to Hok'ee, absent from their nights of erotic lovemaking.

Days became weeks until, lonely and missing her, one evening after the show, Hok'ee ventured by Arielle,s apartment in an attempt to make himself taste the familiarity of her presence, to remember their closeness, his feeling of being wanted. As always, it took him a moment to differentiate Arielle from the neighborhood in which she lived – *le Quartier des Prostituées*, the Neighborhood of the Prostitutes. Her excuse was that she sent much of her earnings to her mother and could not afford better lodgings.

As he walked along Rue Saint-Denis and past the open-air market, prostitutes were displaying their come-hither wares in front of the poorly lit doorways that led up into the rundown, two- and three-story buildings. When they would see him, they would huddle together seeking safety in numbers. After a nervous moment or two, someone would timidly ask, *"Le Loup-garou de Paris de le Cirque de Montmartre?"*

He would answer in words he had practiced many times. With what little they could see of his facial expression and hear in the tone of his voice asking for their understanding, he would say, *"Oui, c'est moi, mais n'ayez pas peur. Je veux pas de mal."* His words meaning, yes, that was him, but not to be afraid. He meant no harm. He would hear a sigh of relief, the women slowly dispersing as he walked farther along.

Though the blinds were drawn, he saw the glow of lights in two of the windows. Her apartment, he knew, third floor, last two windows at the side of the building. His mouth dropped, at first shaking his head in disbelief. Two silhouettes, dancing, close, kissing.

As he watched, denial followed by, "No." The words grew louder. "No-o-o. Arielle!" Her name suddenly burned his tongue, his mouth, his ability to reason. With a lifetime of rejection as a boy, as a man, rage took control, rising like a white-hot flame throughout his body, his mind.

Without thinking he rushed through the building's open, poorly lighted doorway and up the two flights of stairs to Arielle's apartment. The strong odor of sweat and urine, of over-cooked cabbage and burnt meat enraged his senses even more. He stopped for a moment, listened to the music, to the lilt of her laughter, her voice in a husky whisper, saying, as best he could understand, *"Au lit, mon chéri."*

With the words *lit,* bed, and *mon chéri,* my dear, and a howl that echoed through the dingy hallway and down the stairs, Hok'ee kicked open the door. He threw himself against Arielle and her new lover, clawing, biting. With Arielle screaming, begging him to stop, the man tried to fight back.

Ignoring Arielle's pleas, Hok'ee swiped his claw-like fingernails across the man's face, picked him up and, with the strength of a crazed animal, heaved him through the window onto the street below. Having lost all control, he turned on the woman he loved, the woman who in his mind had rejected him for another.

She ran into her bedroom, tried to shut the door, but he forced his way through. Grabbing her by her shoulders, he lifted her off the floor, threw her on the bed and sank his teeth into the side of her throat.

It was if he was again on the hunt of his youth, the rabbits, the coyotes, the young deer, the kill and the blood. With one hand over her mouth to smother her cries, his teeth sank deeper. Powerful jaws crushed the brittle horseshoe-shaped bone suspended in muscle and ligaments at the top of her throat. He tasted her flesh, the heat of her blood. Finally, her struggles ceased, her eyes, earlier filled with fear and pain, began to take on the glazed stare of the dead.

Hok'ee, lungs still heaving from his exertion, knew her life had ended, but realized he could not stop. Not until he tasted more of her flesh and the fluids of her body. It was as if she had given herself to him. He took her, accepted the gift of her soul, of everything that had once been Arielle, the woman he loved. He also knew his life would never again be the same. That his days as the famous *le Loup-garou de Paris* were over.

Chapter 15

A sound! Hok'ee's ears took on a new alertness, his eyes narrowed. Suddenly he was awake, his senses alive. Thoughts of Paris, of Arielle, lost in the past. "Sicheii?" he whispered for his grandfather. "You return?" No answer.

The sound again: The cast iron latch to the door, its thumb-press slowly pushed downward, the slightest creak of rusted metal against metal. He quickly rolled the blanket to appear as if someone was beneath its cover. As the door pushed open, with the silence and swiftness of a wolf, he sought the safety of a darkened corner, partially hidden in the space between the end of the rear wall shelving and sink. The brownish-black body hair added to his near invisibility.

Two men appeared in the opened doorway, their features caught in the glow of the kerosene lamp, each with a rifle. The shorter of the two, a thickly built, dark-skinned man wearing a western-style hat was in front, water drops falling from a handlebar mustache. The much taller man behind him pulled back a rain hood from his head, revealing a totally bald scalp that shone in the light from the kerosene lamp.

Hok'ee knew immediately: Latino in front, white man behind.

The shorter man stepped forward, quietly, trying to avoid any squeaks from the wooden floor boards. He raised the rifle, pointed at the first bunk; an empty mattress. Then the second bunk behind the chest of drawers and muttered, "*Si. Es él.*"

Hok'ee winced at the explosion of bullets, one after the other. He heard and felt the *thunk, thunk, thunk* of the rounds as they hit the cot and its rolled blanket. When the firing stopped, the Latino moved closer to the cot, rifle at the ready, pointed toward what he thought was the thing he'd come to kill. He stopped as the white man spoke from the doorway.

"You sure you got him?"

"*Si.* Got him, or it, or whatever it is."

Before anything else could be said, Hok'ee sprang forward out of the darkness, crushing the man against the bunk. The rifle, flung against the wall, was fired toward the ceiling by a suddenly broken finger. Before the man could react, Hok'ee's teeth sank into the thickness of his throat, cutting off the scream.

The man in the doorway, shaking, raised his rifle, wildly shouting, "Carlos, get the fuck outta the way so I can shoot him." When the only reply he could hear was a wave of deep-throated growls, he said, "Fuck this shit!" and fired. Shot after shot, wild. One glanced off the top of the propane canister fueling the portable heater, sending the heater tumbling from the top of the chest of drawers. A loud, high-pitched hissing sound of propane gas escaping from the canister suddenly overshadowed the growls.

Another tore into Hok'ee's back, splintered the left shoulder blade and exited just above the lung's upper lobe. For a moment, there was only surprise at something hitting his body until the nervous system went full speed ahead. His growl grew into a high-pitched squeal-like cry of pain. Like a streak of fire, the pain shot down into his back, searing along nerve endings of the nearby spinal column, filling his chest with a burning sensation he'd never known before.

Releasing his grip on the man whose wind pipe had been crushed and letting the body fall back to the bed, Hok'ee howled as he spun toward the door. The white man, momentarily frozen at the sight of the thing before him, quickly recovered and raised the rifle once more.

As Hok'ee, with a singular burst of energy, leaped high over the table in the middle of the room to avoid further bullets, the man fired. Two rounds, three, trying to follow Hok'ee's movement, each bullet passing beneath Hok'ee as he jumped. One hit the kerosene lamp. It exploded in a burst of yellow-orange flame, sending burning kerosene splattering across the room, igniting everything in its path, including the residue of gas seeping from the cracked propane canister.

Seeing Hok'ee hit the floor and pivot in his direction, the man turned, moved sideways through the open doorway, rifle in one hand, butt against his shoulder. Two more shots and the firing pin clicked empty. He threw the rifle back at the creature as he ran out into the night toward the old logging road.

Hair singed from the fire and disregarding his wound and the possible amount of blood he might be losing, Hok'ee charged forward onto the porch and into the rain. Knowing he could run faster than the man, he dropped to all fours, immediately stumbled and fell against a partially rotten tree stump. The pounding pain in his left shoulder, arm and back screamed at him, making the arm almost useless.

Pushing against the stump with his right hand to regain his footage, he ran on two feet, seeing himself in the races of his youth. With each breath came sharp guttural growls through clinched teeth, not only from pain, but from hate. This time, his quarry, human, not rabbit, not fox, not deer.

The man was no match for the creature whose howl was getting closer and closer. Already he could hear the splashing of rapid footsteps following behind along the muddy trail; imagined the creature's touch, claws raking at his back. No use.

Out of breath, he stopped, turned and pulled a hunting knife from a scabbard on his belt. Lungs heaving and wiping the rain from his eyes with the sleeve of his jacket, he shouted, "Come on, you fucking nightmare, you goddamned animal. Just you and me. Come on."

Suddenly, the creature was gone. Wind coursing through the trees and rain pelting against his jacket were the only sounds. The woods around him were dark, the darkness folding like a shroud around him. Then he heard it.

A snarl from somewhere behind, then off to the side, to his right or was it to his left? The crack of a broken limb or twig from nearby. He turned in jerks, almost slipping in the mud, regaining his balance, slashing out with the knife in every direction. "Where the fuck are you?" he yelled. "You –"

His words were cut off by a wolf's howl and the rock-hard impact of Hok'ee's good shoulder into his chest. Thrown backwards, he felt the creature's weight press down on his body. He couldn't tell whether it was the continuing growl and snarl of the thing or his own helpless cries he heard. Fighting for his life, he jabbed the knife once, twice, three times into the side and back of the monster, grunting with each strike. He felt the blade hit something hard. Bone!

Suddenly the only sound he heard was internal, his own screams as teeth ground deep into his face, covering his mouth and nose, shaking his head from side to side like a wet rag. He tried to cry out, but the sound was muffled by his own blood that poured into his mouth, clogged his nostrils. As quickly as the weight had hit him, it lifted and settled on his midsection, the knife torn from his hand.

Ignoring the pain in his shoulder and using both hands, Hok'ee plunged the pointed end of the knife's blade deep into the man's throat, that space between the top of the breast bone and the base of the Adams apple. It cut through both trachea and esophagus. Despite the man's body twisting one way, then another, arms and legs thrashing about, Hokee continued forcing pressure downward on the handle of the knife, the width of the blade blocking the man's airway.

Lungs crying for air, heart deprived of oxygen, but no longer able to inhale through the severed, blood-drenched trachea, the last thing the man heard was the deep-throated growl of a creature that had become his worst and final nightmare.

Hok'ee rolled away from the man's body and lay for a moment, quiet, the mud and crushed weeds like a cushion against the pain in his shoulder and chest, now more intense following his struggle with the white man. Slowly, he rose to his feet and looked back up the trail. Scraggly pines and tree limbs of mountain

Aspens, now leafless from autumn's rain and wind, formed a grotesque tableau, crooked and misshapen against a backdrop of fire.

The cabin! Lightning darts of flame and accompanying smoke leapt high above the tree tops into the rain-soaked night. He listened to the crackling of the fire when suddenly gunshots, like a short string of firecrackers, filled the night. He winced at the sound before remembering the Latino, his rifle, its bullets exploding in the fire. His anger mounted even more at the memory.

With eyes closed, head reared back, mouth open wide, his lungs and throat erupted with a long, agonizing howl of hatred at the two men who had caused this, a howl that echoed around the mountain side. The cry gradually became a near-silent whimper of frustration, turning into a wet, phlegm-coated cough as the reality of the moment stroke home. His grandfather had abandoned him, left him to die at the hands of strangers. There could be no other answer. Tears slipped from the corners of his eyes. He felt the familiar cloak of loneliness, the loneliness that had haunted him throughout his life. He thought of Arielle, their mutual needs, but for only a moment.

With a final look at the fire, Hok'ee knew it would bring men who would want him dead. Only one place remained that offered safety. The place dogs and men had feared to enter. Reaching down and pulling the knife from the man's throat, he turned and, holding his left shoulder, limped down the trail toward the highway, weakened, blood oozing from his various wounds. If he had to die, he wanted it to be on his own terms.

Chapter 16

Yesterday's rain had stopped sometime during the night, leaving the morning air clear, clean and on the borderline of cold. Following John's directions, from C-470, part of an unfinished beltway around much of the Denver metropolitan area, I merged onto Johnson Road in Golden, once a center of coal mining, now a bustling city in the foothills a few miles northwest of Denver. An immediate left onto Jefferson County Parkway in Golden and we entered a campus of buildings serving the Jefferson County government. Dead ahead was a roundabout and farther on a massive, strikingly conceived building constructed of either off-white sandstone or granite.

A rounded section of glass and stone topped by a glass dome, perhaps eight to ten stories high, stood at the building's center. Two wings, each five stories high, presumably containing the main office spaces, stretched out in opposite directions from the center building. It must have taken up at least five acres of land. The reflection of early morning sunlight on the building's glass dome was almost blinding.

"That's the county's Admin and Courts Facility," John said, "known locally as the Taj Mahal for its obvious extravagance. Quite a building, but that's not where we're going. Take a right off the roundabout and keep going, then right on Welmer Street. There." As we turned onto Welmer, he pointed to a rather ominous, dark stone building, the sign in front reading, SHERIFFS COMPLEX DETENTION CENTER.

"That's the jail. Keep on around, down the hill and turn into the next parking lot. Entrance to the Sheriff's offices is in the lower part of the building."

Once parked and into the building, we encountered a sign-in process, the unloading of all pockets and metallic objects followed by a quick pass-through the telephone booth-like metal and explosive detector. It was similar to TSA's Advance Imaging Technology, otherwise known as AIT, used for airport security. We were then escorted to Chief Kay's office in the Criminal Investigation Division.

Our escort knocked on the door at precisely nine o'clock, the arranged time for our meeting. "Chief Kay," he announced, "John Nabhe and a Mr. Berkeley for their appointment." He immediately closed the door behind us.

I was surprised as we walked in. After seeing the county's Taj Mahal and the scope of this building, a quick glance around told me this wasn't what I expected. I found her Office somewhat drab. Government desk, chairs, vinyl gray flooring and a ten to twelve-foot conference table, the only piece of furniture in the room that appeared worthy of a Division Chief. I'm sure if they knew, the county's property tax payers would be pleased with such austerity.

Scatted about the walls were some framed lithographs, some hand signed, some plate signed, all African art and an antique engraved foil map of the Colorado Territory pictured long before statehood. There were also framed pictures of Chief Kay with various people presenting what appeared to be diplomas or awards, one with whom I assumed was Sheriff Donny Ferguson who I had yet to meet. Another was on the steps of the state capitol with the Colorado Governor who I recognized from a ten o'clock TV newscast the evening before.

"Come in, John, and you, Mr. Berkeley," Chief Kay said, rising from behind the desk. "Doctor Wong should be here shortly. Let's sit at the conference table. Coffee?"

John answered for both of us. "Yes, ma'am. It'll definitely help while we go over everything from yesterday."

Although still relatively early in the morning, Chief Kay looked tired. Unlike at the crime scene, a stray hair here and there, bags under her eyes, a slight slump of her shoulders as she moved.

Even the clothes she was wearing – a light-colored blazer, blouse and slacks – looked as tired as she did. Possibly my imagination, maybe the fit of the clothes, but she looked even more pregnant than she did yesterday. Like the baby could make his or her entrance into the world at any minute. Maybe it was the increasing size that was the cause of the slump.

She nodded toward to a small table off to the side with a black, twelve-cup coffee maker and carafe still three-quarters full, a line of clean coffee cups, creamer, yellow packets of sweetener and stirrers.

While John proceeded to the coffee maker, I said, "You look tired, Chief. Already a full day?"

She sighed. "Last night, domestic disturbance. Neighborhood just outside Golden. Our jurisdiction. Husband threatened to kill his wife. Their teenage son called nine-one-one. One of our uniformed deputies shot in the shoulder; husband shot, dead. Our people had been out there several times before."

She motioned toward the coffee machine. "Pour one for me, John. Black, no creamer. Creamer makes me a little queasy now days." She patted her abdomen. "And yes, Mr. Berkeley, yesterday rolled right into today."

A knock at the door and an equally tired looking Doctor Wong entered with a small leather briefcase. "Kay, gentlemen," he said as he came to the conference table. "A busy night for both the Chief and me. Any coffee left?"

"One or two cups," John answered. "I'll get it. You look as beat as Chief Kay."

Once we were seated, Chief Kay said, "The good doctor spent part of his evening and this morning with me. Him with the dead husband, me concerned with our wounded deputy until the EMT's took him away.

"My lieutenant who heads up the Crimes Against Persons Section is away on special training and my CI Section Leader, Captain Gelespi, sick with the flu. Otherwise I wouldn't have been there. Not with this." She glanced down and nodded to her greatly expanded waistline before gesturing to John, "You first."

"Matt," John said. "Take it."

To make a long story short, I covered everything: discovery of the old mine hidden behind the clutch of Gamble oaks, the ammonia odor which had been described by the dog handlers and the arm bone wrapped in what I believed to be cloth from Richard Lamb's shirt. Whether or not the Chief or Doctor Wong had received any information concerning the bone from Felicia Gonzales at the Crime Lab, I didn't know.

Chief Kay inserted, "She called, and yes, you did right. She supervises our forensic chemistry services, latent fingerprint processing, DNA and serology analysis. Her people will be doing DNA tests from blood on the cloth and marrow from the bone, but that'll take at least a week," adding, "better than the month or so it used to take." Glancing at Wong who had taken a seat at her side, she said, "Tell us about the hair and the blood Andy Foxworthy found yesterday morning."

Following a sip of coffee, Wong explained, "The blood, human, not animal. The hair, again, human, not animal. If both came from the killer, he or she is human and not some kind of half wolf, half man. Like with the bone, once DNA is established, we'll check to see if there's a match with any DNA found on the cloth and bone. My bets on Mr. Lamb from the other nights killing. We'll naturally be checking to see if there's a match with any other we have on record."

Wong looked at John and then me to determine if we had any questions.

As much a statement as a question, I said, "What you're telling us is that, at this moment, you consider our…" I held up two fingers of each hand and wiggled them representing quotation marks, "… our *unknown creature* to be human, whether man or woman. If so, there's no longer any need for my friends' scat sniffing dog. At least to hold off until a DNA match with Mr. Lamb is either confirmed or not."

"I had forgotten about the dog, but yes, I think that's the

prudent thing to do for the time being."

I thought for a moment before saying, "I do, however, have a question about the hair. If I remember correctly, it looked like a thick hank of black or dark brown hair, anywhere from three to five inches long with hours-old blood on the roots and skin particles. With that length, you'd think it would have come from someone's head, right?"

"Yes," came from both Chief Kay and Doctor Wong. "But…" Wong started to say.

I kept going. "The dog handler said he found it caught on a bush on the trail of what he was tracking. If so and the hair is human, he or she was either moving on all fours for the hair to be from the head or on two feet for it to be from a lower part of the body. If the latter, who's got hair that length on a leg, arm or anywhere else on their body?"

John said, "Or on all fours and from *anywhere* on the body."

Chief Kay said, "Doctor, you're the medical man. Got any ideas?"

Doctor Wong pushed back into the curvature of the chair, exhaled a rush of air and pursed his lips in momentary thought before leaning forward and saying, "I did some research once we determined both the blood and hair were human. Ever heard of bearded ladies of the circus?" With a sly smile on his face and a mischievous twinkle in his eyes, he surveyed the three of us who each nodded. Chief Kay also threw in a, "Who hasn't?"

Quickly following another sip of coffee, he explained, "What one normally associates with the bearded lady is nothing more than excessive facial hair. Its formal name is hirsutism. Normally on the face, that being the cheeks continuing down from the hairline, upper lip and chin. Hence, the bearded lady. Also, often on the chest and abdomen which I should think one would not normally see in a circus atmosphere."

"Unless doing a strip performance," John inserted.

Dr. Wong chuckled. "Well yes, I suppose so." Continuing

with a more clinical description, he went on, "Can be genetic, but usually caused by an underlying endocrine imbalance sometime after puberty. In other words, hormonal disorders which can originate in different organs of the body. Hirsutism affects between five and fifteen percent of all women, regardless of ethnic background. And yes, men can also suffer from hirsutism, but it's much more acceptable to society – beards, mustaches, etc. Perhaps not even recognized as such."

He unzipped the briefcase on his lap and pulled out several sheets of paper stapled together. Before displaying the contents of the pages, he went on. "There is also a condition known as hypertrichosis, also called Ambras syndrome, an abnormal amount of hair normally over the entire body. And yes, informally called werewolf syndrome, because the thick dark hair looks much like that on the mythical werewolf."

I thought of the Four Corners dig and the killings we had experienced, but kept my mouth shut, waiting to see where this would lead.

"There are two distinct types. Generalized hypertrichosis, which occurs, as I said, over the entire body, and localized hypertrichosis, which is restricted to certain areas. Based on what young Sonny Weaver describes when he and his girlfriend were attacked, I would think what he saw was the generalized type. All man, all hair, but acting as a vicious animal with apparent cannibalistic tendencies, the cannibalistic description based on what we've found."

Doctor Wong then opened the papers, slowly turning one page after another, showing black and white photographs of several adult males, one adult female and a man, seated, holding a four or five-year-old boy in his lap. In each case, their bodies, except for the palms of their hands, were covered with thick dark hair.

There were also color pictures of circus posters dating back to the eighteen- and nineteen-hundreds. I based the time on the type of commercial art, coloring and lettering, of both women with massive facial growth and men whose bodies were completely covered.

Doctor Wong started to place the papers back into his briefcase when it hit me. "Wait a minute, Doctor. One of the circus posters looked much more recent that the others. The writing was in French. Could I see that one again?"

"Certainly." He handed the papers to me.

I thumbed through them until I came to the one that caught my eye. At the top, the words in large bold print, **LE CIRQUE DE MONTMARTRE PRÉSENTE LE CÉLÉBRE LOUP-GAROU DE PARIS POUR VOTRE PLAISIR ET EXCITATION**.

Immediately below was the picture of a human figure, its body thickly covered in dark brown hair, a wolf-like face with an extended snout, blood dripping from its teeth and lips. The creature's feet straddled a woman, her hands raised to ward off his attack. In the background, a line of Roman columns overlooking a silvery, moonlit pond. "Chief Kay, do you have a magnifying glass?"

"Yes." She rose from her chair, her weariness evident in her movements. She went to her desk and produced a large magnifying glass from one of the drawers, returned to the table and handed it to me.

"Thanks." In the lower right-hand corner of the poster, too small to read in the photograph's reduced size, were tiny words, but there was only one thing in which I was interested. With the glass increasing the size of the words and numbers, I read aloud, "Two thousand sixteen and what I think is the printing company's name." Nodding, I said, "I thought the art work and lettering was a lot more recent than all the others."

"What do the words say, up at the top?" John asked. "I can make out it's about a circus, but the rest?"

Chief Kay responded, "The circus Montmartre presents the werewolf of Paris for your pleasure and excitement."

"I didn't know you spoke French, Kay," Wong said, a

quizzical smile on his face.

"Five years with the New Orleans Police Department. A little Cajun, also. Speak better than read, the opposite of what most people tell me."

"You're onto something, aren't you?" John said, nodding in my direction.

"Yeah. I once worked with Interpol when I was in Paris looking for a stolen religious piece of art, a triptych presented to Churchill by Stalin at the Yalta Conference back in Nineteen forty-five." Looking at Chief Kay, I continued, "What I'm getting at, I strongly recommend you check with the Paris Police Prefecture, a unit of the French National Police.

"They've got to know something about this guy playing werewolf with the Montmartre circus. Is he still with the circus? If not, where did he go and under what circumstances? As wild as you might think, if he came to the States, he could be our killer."

"In addition to Interpol," she said, "did you work with the Paris police on this stolen piece of art?"

"No, ma'am. You might say, I kind of uh…" With more of a double grunt than a chuckle and a shake of my head at the memory, I admitted, "… I kind of made myself scarce from the French police following several killings near the Eiffel Tower. My departure was surprisingly made with help from the CIA and New Scotland Yard."

Chief Kay, head cocked to one side, raised an eyebrow and asked, "Would you like to tell me more of the story or should we leave your Paris adventures for another time?"

John laughed and answered for me. "Probably best to say, Matt's led a very interesting, sometimes charmed life over the years and leave it at that."

With a sideways glance at me and what appeared to be a reluctant smile on her face, the Chief said, "I'll do that. I'll also discuss contacting the Paris police with Sheriff Ferguson at the status meeting later today. Now that that's settled, I believe the two of you had more to share with us."

John and I looked at each other, nodding, both remembering our discussions with Roberta Pine Woman, aka, Wilson, and Gladys Knight. John was the first to speak. "Either we have some kind of deranged human, probably a man, maybe even by way of Paris, who simply enjoys killing and eating human prey, or we have some kind of deranged human who is being used for a given purpose."

"And what would that be?" Wong asked.

I explained our discussion with Roberta and Gladys, the end-result being there was something someone wanted, either above or beneath the surface of the earth in the Deer Creek area. From that meeting, it was our joint opinion that the killings were merely a deception coupled with mass fear within the community, a means to an end which we have yet to identify.

"Come on, Mr. Berkeley," Chief Kay said, "that's a stretch if I ever heard one. Explain."

I went on to describe the company, Ralston World Wide Entertainment, LLC out of London, trying to buy all the property in the Canyon Creek Estates adjacent to Jefferson County's Deer Creek Canyon Park, ostensibly for a theme park. I recommended, "In addition to Roberta Pine Woman's law firm trying to get as much information as possible about the Ralston Company, you might want to get your county lawyers doing the same. Whether you think it's a stretch, as unimaginable as it might be, this company could well be pulling the strings of our killer just to gain access to the land. Why? Find the killer and we might learn the secret, or vice versa."

There was a loud, hurried knock at the door, followed immediately by man in a sergeant's uniform. "Chief, we just got a call from the volunteer fire department out on Deer Creek Road. Fire last night, shack midway up on Pyramid Peak. Deserted or so they thought."

"So why contact us?"

"When they got there, they found two bodies, one in the fire and one just on the old logging road leading to the shack. The one on the road, they didn't see him in the dark. Found him later. They had run over him, but they don't think he got there by himself. From the looks of both, they also don't think at least one of them was killed by the fire.

"They're recommending you and your folks get up there and take over what they say is way outside their mission statement."

"Tell'em to stand by the scene 'til we get there. We're on our way."

"I'll call Felicia to get her crime scene people out there," Doctor Wong said. "I'll be there shortly."

He headed toward the door, stopped abruptly, turned and said, "First, Chief, I agree with Mr. Berkeley about contacting the Paris police. Can't hurt, and John, you and Mr. Berkeley might like to come along. Pyramid Peak is right next door, geographically speaking, to where all the murders have occurred." He looked at Chief Kay who was already on the phone. "Okay, Chief?"

Clamping a hand over the mouthpiece, she shook her head and, with an I-give-up look of near exhaustion on her face, said, "Why the hell not. The more, the merrier."

Chapter 17

With an All-in-One computer and keyboard sitting off to the side of her desk, she could look visitors straight in the eye, an action which gave the vastly overweight Joni Wickett a sense of authority and power over the needs of others – those she deemed inferior to her position. In this case, however, she didn't really know what to do with the old man, Indian by the cut of his face and complexion. Or was it Native American or First Nation's People or Person? She never knew what was considered politically correct anymore.

Whatever, he stood before her desk, bronze-colored face wrinkled with age, snow-white hair, faded jeans, equally faded red plaid flannel shirt and, she had noticed as he entered the office, scarred, heavy-duty work boots caked with mud. The definite look of a farmer right out the pig lot. *Yes, indeed*, she thought, *inferior*, but there was something about his eyes that scared her.

Though his voice was low, each word presented a warning that brought a strange prickling to the skin on the back of her oversized neck. A feeling that spoke of something completely unfamiliar in her experience. Still, Joni considered herself a professional at her job. Just as important in her mind was her responsibility for protecting her boss, *my man* as she spoke of him to fellow workers. He hated unwanted interruptions to his normal routine. For whatever reason, she knew this was a time to stand her ground.

Making herself as official looking as she could in her secretarial chair and placing both elbows firmly on the top of her desk, the overabundance of skin and flesh surrounding the elbows folding down along the desk's surface, she said, "I'd be more than happy to help you, Mr. ahh…"

"Samuel Hataali."

Although knowing there was no entry on the appointment list for someone with that name, Joni nevertheless turned to the computer. After clicking on the icon for that day's business calendar, she quickly glanced at the monitor, gave a low *hummmm* before looking back at Samuel Hataali. With a feigned shadow of disappointment clouding her face, she said. "I'm so sorry, but there's nothing showing you have an appointment. He's currently preparing for an important meeting this afternoon. If you'd like, I can schedule something for you, perhaps tomorrow or – "

The old man interrupted with, "He...will...see me." His words were spoken softly, yet with emphasis to show his determination. He tilted his head slightly downward, eyes boring in on Joni's face as though seeking a connection, a means to force his will.

Joni Wickett knew she could not, would not tolerate such arrogance, such insolence. Standing, all five-foot-two of her one hundred-and-sixty-five-pound torso, she stretched to make herself as tall as the tips of her toes could bear. With arms crossed, resting on her size forty-eight, full-breasted womanhood, battle-ready, eyes narrowed, a nobody-fucks-with-me look on her face, she said, "Either leave this minute, or I'll call a deputy to take you out."

Her toes finally giving way under her overwhelming weight, she dropped flatfooted and immediately reached for the phone on her desk. Halfway to the instrument, her hand froze in midair.

Samuel Hataali's eyes took on a particular glow. Their dark brown gaze trapped her and seemed to pull her into their depth. She tried to turn her head, to blink away his stare, but she couldn't. She lost all control of her hand. The weight of her body pulled her back into the chair as though every ounce of motor power, every shred of will power had been drained away.

She tried to speak, but there were no words to call out, no power to scream. Her vocal cords were paralyzed. The only movement visible on her face was a small welling of tears on the bottom rim of each of eye. From her nostrils ran a minute flow of clear mucous, hovering just above her upper lip.

The old man moved closer, leaned across the desk, his eyes speaking the strength of his power. "Rest, fat one. I *will* see the man."

With that, he moved toward the door marked CAPTAIN JAMES LUNDGREN, CHIEF, SPECIAL INVESTIGATIONS SECTION.

* * *

James Lundgren, seated, his back to the door of his office, was engrossed in a spread of rising crime graphs displayed on a computer monitor that rested on top of a dark, cherry-stained credenza situated behind a matching executive desk. He failed to hear the door open and close. A sudden chill in the otherwise heated room created a momentary shiver across his shoulders.

"Nice day, Mr. Captain Lundgren."

The voice made him spin his lean, six-foot-two frame around in the leather, high-back swivel chair. In the process, he rammed his left elbow against the corner of the desk and its shiny glass top. At the same time, his left knee slammed into the edge of one of the drawer's metal pull handles.

"Goddamn!" he cursed, grabbing his knee, his face distorted not only with pain but at the sight of the old man standing on the other side of the desk. He jumped to his feet, favoring the now bruised, quickly swelling knee and demanded between clinched teeth, "What the hell are you doing here? I told you never to come to my office. Only to call on my personal mobile phone."

"Today is special day. Like spirit, no one saw me. Only the large woman outside your office who will not remember." The old man slowly turned his head in one direction, then another. "Nice office. Wood panels, dark like desk. Best one in building, I think. Dark like your thoughts. Of course, only the best for big man like you." The last sentence dripped with unmistakable sarcasm.

"Get to the point, Hataali. Like I said, you're not supposed to be here. That was our agreement, and what's so damned special about today?"

"Time is special. Time for you to honor our agreement. My grandson and I have finished our work. People in houses go, try to sell to your people. I want agreement signed so our sacred ground will remain empty, no longer desecrated by white man and others. Your promise, remember?"

Lundgren reached down, rubbed his knee, took a deep breath, sighed and said the first thing that came to his mind. "Tomorrow. I'll get the agreement signed today, notarized and recorded with the County to make it official. In the morning."

He thought for a moment, mentally searching for a discrete location where he wouldn't be known. "The RTD Park and Ride lot at the old Phillipsburg ruins. You know where it is. Five a.m. Come alone. Just you and me." He pulled open a drawer, fumbled around for a moment and pulled out an envelope. "Money for you to –" When he looked up, the door to the office was open and the old man gone.

Immediately reaching into his coat pocket, he pulled out an iPhone 7, tapped the telephone icon, punched one of the numbers for automatic dial and waited. When he heard the word, *Yes*, he said, "The old man was here, but I'll have him taken care of tomorrow. My people have already taken care of the other one."

The words, "You idiot," came over the mobile's tiny speaker like a dagger's point to his inner ear. "You mean you don't know? Don't they tell you anything over there?"

"Know what, for God's sake?"

"Your people are dead and the... the thing they were after is gone. So, what the hell are you going to do about it?" The line went dead.

Captain James Lundgren sank back into his chair, mouth open, eyes searching the ceiling for answers where there were none. "Damn it! Just goddamn it to hell." Sitting up, he shouted, "Joni." No answer. "Miss Wicket, goddamn it." Still no response.

Groaning at the fire in his knee, Lundgren got up from behind his desk and hobbled to the open door. He poked his head around the door frame and saw her sitting at her desk, staring straight ahead.

He moved past the doorway, pounded on the top of her desk with his fist and again shouted, "Damn it, Joni, what the hell is wrong with you? Wake up!"

Joni Wicket jerked forward, her breasts acting like bumpers against the edge of the desk. They kept her from falling face down onto her computer's keyboard. Immediately pushing back, she turned toward Lundgren and stuttered, "I... I must have... I must have fallen asleep." Shaking her head, bewildered at what was happening, she added, "I... I'm so sorry. I don't know what –"

"The old man," Lundgren demanded, "Did you send in him to see me?"

"I uhh... I don't know. What... what old man?"

"The old Indian, damn it. He was just here."

With her face turning red with embarrassment, Joni's body began to shake in an attempt to hold back the sobs as she said, "I didn't... I didn't see any old man and... and please believe me, I didn't send anybody in to see you."

Remembering Hataali's words, *"Like spirit, no one saw me. Only large woman outside your office who will not remember,"* Lundgren looked toward the door leading out into the hallway. Eyes narrowed, he muttered to himself, promising, "You're a dead man, you old bastard. Fucking spirit or no spirit, dead, even if I have to kill you myself."

Chapter 18

It was almost noon when we arrived at the turnoff giving access to Pyramid Mountain. Not hard to find. Some distance in from the road, yellow crime scene tape was looped along the wire fence and across what looked to be a homemade gate opening on an old logging road. Or was it just a weed-covered fire brake leading up the side of the mountain?

And yes, there was our faithful Deputy Ralph Innes, uniform, side arm, department-issued Taser stun gun and all. I pulled in to the sparsely graveled area leading up to the gate behind a Sheriff's Department black and white pickup truck and lowered my window.

"Don't bother turning off the engine," Innes said. "There's a graveled turnaround area about a hundred yards farther up the highway. Couple of deputies' cruisers up there already. They want as few cars at the scene as possible. Walk back, and Chief Kay said it's okay for you to come up. About three quarters of a mile up." He pointed over his shoulder at the beginning of a thick line of lodge pole pine and spruce trees shading the road, fire brake or whatever it was meant to be, leading up the mountain.

"I'm heading up there. The Chief wants me to question some civilians I met when I went door-to-door along the road here. Only two crime scene people still up there looking for evidence. Most of 'em already gone by the time I found these people. Another deputy will be here. He'll let you through."

Sounded like Chief Kay had a lot of trust in Innes, allowing him to question witnesses in place of trained crime scene techs, or herself for that matter.

Minus the SUV, it was a good fifteen minutes later when the new deputy who John also knew swung open the gate for us.

John and I started our way up the road. At least I decided to call it that. Once into the trees and following a multitude of tire tracks cut deep into the weeds and mud, we found a late model pickup truck parked halfway off the road. It had been pushed off to the side. Yellow crime scene tape encircled it, tied to trees at the front and rear of the truck. "Must belong to the bad guys," I said.

John chuckled. "According to the deputy who came into the Chief's office to tell her what happened, past tense, *belonged to,* is probably more accurate."

Perhaps another four to five minutes of walking – quite honestly, to a flatlander like me, already breathing hard and trying to keep pace with John, it was more like climbing – and we found another area on the road cordoned off with the same familiar yellow tape. The weeds and mud in the roughly rectangular area had been beat to hell and back. "Looks like something bad happened here," John said.

Two crime scene techs were taking photos of the area. To one side were more tire tracks and the remains of two saplings recently cut to make a way through for vehicles. Bark on some of the nearby trees appeared freshly scraped as some of the vehicles attempted to pass.

"Hi, John," one of the techs said, his face hidden behind a camera. "Chief Kay said you'd be coming." Lowering the camera, he pointed to what was obviously a crime scene. "Must've been one helluva fight. Vic number one had apparently been run over by a fire truck. It was dark when the fire department people came up here. He's already been moved up to the cabin or what's left of it." He motioned toward the tire tracks going around the taped off area. "Follow those tracks on up. Primary crime scene's up ahead; a burned-out cabin. About another half mile."

Once again, there it was. Damned if everybody in the State of Colorado didn't know John. Laughing to myself, I shook my head and kept trudging upward. Although the air was clear, I could smell the remains of burnt wood and thought I could hear voices up ahead.

When we finally reached the clearing, there was the now familiar crime scene tent, most likely the same one that had been in front of Richard Lamb's home in Canyon Creek Estates. The difference was, this time there were two body bags instead of one. The nearest was stretched out the full length of an adult body; the one beside it a lump, something doubled over into an oversized fetal position.

Call me weird, but what immediately surfaced in my mind was the old Wrigley's Doublemint chewing gum ad that had something about double your pleasure, double your fun. My only excuse for that little ditty is that, as you get older, thoughts like that seem to pop out of nowhere at the strangest times. Like I said, weird.

A fire investigative team was working the ruins of what had once been a cabin. What little was left of the collapsed roof had been ripped up and largely removed. I suppose such action was done to determine if there were any more human remains underneath. There was also a man and a woman talking with Deputy Ennis back near the tree line. They were obviously the civilians he had mentioned, each wearing jeans, work shirts and scuffed-up western boots.

A small table was set up next to the cabin's charred remains with two crime scene techs brushing soot and whatever else from what appeared to be two weapons, both rifles. Looked like AR-15's from the design of them, their nylon polymer stocks and hand grips melted into almost unrecognizable shapes, the built-in rubber butt pads burned away.

Under the tent was Chief Kay, Doctor Wong, one of Wong's people and Felicia Gonzales. Chief Kay called out, "You two, come on over here." She looked like she was about to drop, no sleep since last night, completely exhausted, even more so than in her office several hours ago.

As we made our way through the weeds and dirt-turned-to-mud from last night's rain, she pointed to one of the body bags. It was the one with fetal-shaped lump inside. "That one's pretty well burned to a crisp. Tough to identify except from dental records if we can find any or maybe DNA from blood in bone marrow if it hasn't been boiled away. Another *if*, if we can find a match on record.

"The other man," she nodded to the second bag, "looks like maybe our psycho killer might be the one who took him out. Appreciate if you two would take a look and tell me what you think, if at least one of them might be who shot at you several nights back."

When they're fresh dead, they aren't really a problem for my nasal passages, but burnt? I've only seen one body that had been burned to death. Bad scene, bad smell. To me it was almost like thoroughly burnt liver combined with a sulfurous charcoal odor. Let's just say, burned human flesh is definitely not like beef on the barbie.

I knew, however, there was no way around it when Dr. Wong's tech unzipped the bag containing the lump. "Damn!" The smell and the knowledge that it was once a living, breathing person can make you gag, if not audibly, certainly mentally. I immediately grabbed my handkerchief from a back pocket and put it over my nose.

Trying to keep at least a foot or two away, I leaned over the lump of charred flesh and asked Dr. Wong, "Do you think he or she died from the fire, or died from some other means before the fire?"

"All I can say is that the individual, most likely a male, was relatively short in statue and probably heavyset. A lot of flesh burned away, but still a fair amount left. As to cause of death other than fire, I can only tell you that after the autopsy.... if at all."

Meanwhile, Wong's assistant had unzipped the second bag down past the chest to the dead man's waist. John stood there, studying the face which was the only visible portion of the body. That part above the abdominal area was covered by a partially open water-resistant North Face jacket and a plaid flannel shirt, open at the throat, the collar button like it had been ripped away.

"I don't know. With that much damage to the face, almost impossible," he muttered, loud enough for me to hear. He looked at Chief Kay and said, "Not sure." To me, he said, "Matt, take a look."

I stood, moved around and away from the burned lump, thankful when I heard the sound of the zipper on the body bag being closed. Stooping over the second body I saw a white man, as tall as me if not taller, facial skin and flesh ravaged around the cheeks, mouth and nose. The torn-up face looked a lot like what a gator or a shark would do to prey caught in its mouth, violently shaking and ripping at something live trying to escape. Like John said, pretty hard to make a facial identification from what remained.

"From the blood on the lower throat just above the breast bone," I said, "looks like a stab wound, possibly with a serrated-edged knife. As wide as it is, maybe all the way up to the hilt, then yanked out. Not smooth." Pointing, I added, "Ripped the skin on this side of the wound pretty badly. You might even find the missing collar button down in there."

While the rain had washed much of the blood from his face and throat, the clothing, mostly around the chest and abdominal areas – shirt, unzipped jacket and upper part of the trousers – were totally discolored and stained with what appeared to be blood. "Is there damage to the chest and abdominal areas?" I asked Dr. Wong.

"With all the blood on the body, strangely enough, no bite marks, no skin punctures, nothing. Only the face and throat. Like you, I wondered where all the blood that far down the body came from, unless..."

Leaning over, John looked at the man's throat, quickly continuing Wong's thought pattern with, "Unless our guy here did some stabbing himself, like wounding his attacker during the struggle. Wounding him pretty badly for that much blood to have accumulated before he had maybe a...uh...a knife taken away from him, like the one that ended up in his throat."

"I agree," I said.

Chief Kay said, "We've got people scouring the woods, trying to see how the killer escaped, but no blood's been found. Nothing to show which way he might have gone. Of course, the rain could have washed it away. No knife, either. If there was one, he must've taken it with him."

There was something just above the man's collar, dark green, just enough to show. I asked, "Doctor, can you unbutton the shirt again so we can see what's under the collar?"

Without a word, Dr. Wong knelt next to the body, unbuttoned the top three buttons just below the collar and spread the material. "As you can see, it's a tattoo of a vine with a snake entwined around it. Goes down under the left arm and apparently onto the back."

I let out with a, "Sonofabitch! That's him, the man in the restaurant with the snake tattoo. He's one of the two who shot at us. Gotta be! And the other one? Could well be the Latino who was with him."

Chief Kay backed away from the bodies, deep in thought, an index finger pulling her chin down as she looked back at the burnt-out remains of the cabin. "If these are the two who shot at you, why are they here? What happened to the burnt one and who killed that one?" She pointed toward the white man with the punctured throat.

It was Felicia Gonzales who spoke, the first words she'd said since we arrived. "Why are they here? To kill the killer. What other reason? Our killer, monster, wolf man or whatever it or he is, had to go somewhere to hide. Disappeared to where, we didn't know, but somebody did. Had to have been the cabin. Like John said back at the other crime scene, somebody's behind all of this. Somebody's been helping our killer, but decided it or he was no longer needed, no longer an asset."

Why it dawned on me, I don't know, but I said, "The other crime scene."

"What about it?" Chief Kay asked.

"Not exactly the crime scene itself, but the bridge. I was thinking coincidence at the time. There was a deep gouge streaked with black paint on a post at the end of the bridge going up to Grizzly Road and the other crime scene. The post at the end of the bridge next to Deer Creek Canyon Road.

"A rusty old Chevy Silverado was parked in a pull-off beside the creek where a man was panning for gold. The truck was black and its left front fender was badly scratched, a line of bare shiny metal maybe eight, ten inches long. The scratch looked like it had recently happened.

"It didn't dawn on me then, but the truck and the man could definitely be how the killer escaped from the dogs. Never saw his face. Had a wide-brimmed hat pulled down over his forehead. He was stooped, so I'd say he could be fairly old. Damned if we weren't standing more than twenty feet from the guy."

"Didn't see the license plates, did you," Felicia asked.

"No. Didn't have a reason to check at the time."

It was at that moment, out of the side of my eye, I noticed Ennis had finished with the two civilians who were starting down the road leading from the cabin ruins. "Witnesses?" I asked Chief Kay, nodding over my shoulder toward the couple.

"Yes, in a manner of speaking. Why do you ask?"

"Mind if I speak with them?"

"By now they should've given Ennis everything they know, but if you want to."

I jogged my way across the weeds to the road and called to the couple. "Could you wait just a minute? I've got a couple of questions."

They stopped, turned around and the woman said, "We've already told everything we know to the deputy. Other than seeing the fire from our house, none of it makes much sense."

When I caught up with them, they both accepted my hand shake, first the woman, then the man. "I might be able to make some sense out of it for you. I'm Matt Berkeley. I'm not police. I'm here as more of a consultant, an advisor to the Sheriff's Office concerning the killings around the state park. I had experience with a similar situation down in Arizona several years back."

The woman shook her head. "If it was as bad as we've had around here, it must be terrible to have to come back to something like this. What questions you got?"

"How far do you live from here?"

"Mile, mile and a half, down on Deer Creek Road. Other side of the road just to the north. Why?"

"Since the sheriff's people spoke of you as witnesses, did you see the fire?"

It was the woman who answered. "We did. I saw it first. Must've been around nine o'clock. I came out on the porch to see if it was still raining. It was, but what I saw was more of a glow against the clouds. Not really flames. I called Caleb out to see if he saw the same thing I was seeing."

"She did," Caleb said. "I remembered the old mining cabin in that direction up on the mountain. Since I'd seen somebody putting a wire gate on the fence down on the road a couple of months back, thought maybe they'd bought the land and had been stayin' up there in the cabin. And yeah, that glow Emma talked about looked like that cabin might be on fire."

"Then what did you do?"

The woman answered. "Caleb started to go inside to the telephone to call the fire people when we heard the most god-awful sound from up on the mountain. Sounded like a wolf howling. I'm telling you, it sent shivers up and down my spine."

"Mine, too," Caleb added.

"Gun shots? Did you hear any?"

"Way off. Sounded like a string of firecrackers goin' off, but with the rain comin' down on the tin roof over the porch, we weren't really sure."

"What did you do after that?"

"I waited a minute to see if there was more firecracker sounds or another howl, but there weren't. Neither of 'em. That's when I went inside and called Jim Flannigan, head man of our volunteer fire department up the road."

"You got any idea what that howling was?" Emma asked. "Don't think it was anything like those artist drawings in the local newspapers, do you?" She paused a moment, more than likely thinking about the pictures in the papers. "About what that boy saw, the thing that pulled his girlfriend outta the truck?"

She momentarily closed her eyes and wrapped her arms about her body in a tight self-hug as though trying to make herself the smallest possible target against the unknown. "We saw those body bags up there, you know."

"To be honest, I think it may have been, but not the half wolf, half man thing pictured in the newspapers. Whatever happened at the cabin was caused by a human being."

"Think you gonna catch him?" It was Caleb, at the same time scanning the surrounding trees as if the killer was hiding behind one of the huge spruce trees.

I nodded my head in answer. "We've learned more about this man this morning than we have in the past several weeks. Yes, I think we'll catch him and I think it'll be sooner than later. I won't hold you up any longer." I once again shook hands with both of them, added my thanks for their cooperation, turned and hurried back to the cabin area.

While at that moment I would have preferred to join the search for our killer, wondering if it could be the man once called the werewolf of Paris, my watch showed almost one o'clock. I had to drop John off at his law office in Littleton followed by a meeting with Roberta Pine Woman at two. We were to meet with Chief of the Minerals Resources department at the Colorado Geological Survey office in Golden. My area map showed it as part of the Colorado School of Mines campus, a mile or so from Chief Kay's office.

Before I learned from John of Roberta's marriage, the death of her husband in Afghanistan and her apparent disinterest in any kind of relationship, the meeting would have been something to which I would have eagerly anticipated. From what

I now knew, I considered the meeting little more than a business session with an acquaintance.

Regardless, if we could obtain the kind of information I wanted, in fact expected, it might help us determine the *why* – in legal parlance, the motive – behind everything that had and *was* happening. If successful, that could hopefully open up all other avenues toward solving the murders and who was actually behind them, not just some hairy, mentally disturbed individual who liked the taste of human flesh.

CHAPTER 19

I pulled into the parking lot of the Moly Building that housed the Colorado Geological Survey offices, an unassuming, flat-roofed, red brick building located in what was called Mine Park on the west side of Golden. Several feet in front of the entrance door rested a large rock with the organization's logo painted in black.

I knew the type of information we needed, if it existed at all. The primary question was, is there the possibility of underground wealth behind the killings and could we link it to the sudden appearance of the Ralston World Wide Entertainment people attempting to buy the land?

Other than a receptionist situated behind a four-foot-high, granite-topped counter, there appeared to be no substantive security arrangement other than a couple of cameras strategically positioned at corner walls just below the ceiling. No doubt much less security than the United States Geological Survey offices would have only a few blocks away.

As soon as I announced who I was and why I was there to the receptionist, a pleasant looking woman of somewhere within the middle-age grouping, I heard my name called from one of the several doorways to my left.

"Mr. Berkeley." A conservatively dressed black man, tall, slender, close-cropped hair, a slight mustache which wrapped around the ends of his mouth to a stubble-bearded chin stepped forward. Damned if he didn't remind me of Hollywood's Denzel Washington. He wore khaki slacks, cordovan loafers, a brown, open-collared shirt, sleeves rolled up to mid-forearm. The latter indicated to me this man was here to work.

At the same time, he approached, hand extended, and

introduced himself. "Simon Grant, Mineral Resources. Everyone calls me Simon. Welcome to Colorado Geo Survey. Ms. Knight is already in my office, pouring over some of our derivative maps." We shook hands with him adding, "Come on back."

I'm sure he recognized my surprise when he explained, "Mrs. Wilson was called to substitute for one of their other people in court. Ms. Knight is taking her place, but has been one of our primary contacts over the past several years, in particular concerning zoning laws in various parts of the state. One of the other partners in the firm assists with environmental issues." He laughed. "We do so since budgetary cutbacks have forced us to lose our own in-house legal team."

It took me a moment to remember Wilson was Roberta Pine Woman's married name, the one she used in her professional life. "Yes," I nodded. "I've already met Ms. Knight and was impressed." I didn't say, however, not only with her intelligence, but everything else about her. "And please call me Matt."

He led the way along a lengthy hallway to a large windowless room with wall-size, computer-generated projections covering three walls. Two of them appeared to be little more than informational tables. One titled *Resource Category Description/Notes*, the second titled *Numeric Rating System Description and General Criteria*, the latter with color-coded information showing the State's areas with the highest potential for minerals in red, down to the least potential in light gray which covered most of the State's eastern plains.

The third wall projection, centered between the two informational tables and taking up the greater part of the wall, floor to ceiling, appeared to be the most interesting. Entitled *Colorado Mineral Commodities Mapped Regions*, it was a map of the state broken into four major regions: West-Central, Central Mountain, South-South West and Front Range.

It was the latter with which I was concerned. You might say it was our target area. Each region was sectioned into red and blue squares or quadrangles depicting where mineral deposits are located or areas currently being mapped. For simplicity sake, I called it *the minerals map*.

A lengthy waist-high, standup worktable accommodating four workstations stood before the minerals map. Each workstation was equipped with a desktop computer/monitor, wireless key board and mouse. Various papers and reference materials lay next to two of the stations. Shelves beneath the workstations held a veritable library of note books and what I assumed to be more reference material.

A fair distance behind this four-position worktable stood a raised platform with a twelve-to-fifteen-foot conference table and chairs placed so that the occupants could readily view each of the three individual wall projections, in particular the dominating minerals map.

Casually dressed and as lovely as I remembered, Gladys Knight stood behind the worktable, at the moment sideways to me. She had a computer tablet with some kind of special pen in her hand, taking notes. I was able to make out *Samsung* on the back of the tablet, but that was all. Ushered through the door by Simon Grant, I said, "Ms. Knight, a pleasant surprise. I thought Roberta was going to be here."

She turned, a smile on her face, took off her glasses and said, "Did you forget so soon? It's Gladys."

I returned the name reminder, an index finger pointed in her direction. I'm sure an overly pleased grin was on my face at the now firmly established first-name basis. "No, I didn't forget and I'm Matt, remember?"

She laughed. "I do remember." She put her glasses back on, adding, "I see you've met Simon. He's Colorado's rock and mineral man."

Simon motioned for us to move to the conference table on the platform. "Up there, you'll have a view of all three projections at once. I can manipulate them to show whatever areas and minerals in which you have an interest. As you can see, I've taken the liberty of placing coffee and water, glasses and cups on the table. If there's anything else you want, let me know."

"Thank you, Simon," Gladys said, stepping onto the platform and selecting a chair. "Coffee for me. Matt?" Whether my imagination or not, it was as though she placed a slight emphasis on my name, a smile added as an extra punctuation mark.

"I'll take water," I answered, filling a glass from a carafe in front of me.

Simon poured two cups of coffee from a thermos-type and passed one to Gladys.

"Thanks, Simon," she said. She took a single pink packet from a bowl, tore off one end and added sweetener to the coffee, stirring as her eyes and smile continued in my direction.

Normally, I would have been flattered, but it seemed as if she was sizing me up. I could sense the mental gears turning. Looks, size, intelligence, empathy towards others, maybe even for small animals for all I knew. In other words, is he good enough for me to waste my time or forget it?

Simon started the conversation. "I have some idea why you're here based on what Mrs. Wilson told me, but why don't you give me a short brief."

Since it was Roberta who had set up the meeting, I nodded to Gladys for her to take the lead.

Keeping to a bare minimum, Gladys told about the murders in the Canyon Creek Estates community and in and around Jefferson County's Deer Creek Canyon Park. As a result of the fear brought about by the killings, she explained the departure of the community's residents and their urgent desire to sell their homes. She finished with Ralston World Wide Entertainment's attempt to buy and rezone the land for a theme park, primarily dedicated to the history of Colorado's indigenous people.

"In terms of the Ralston people," she said, "it seems that everything is so convenient. The killings, the abandoning of the homes, Ralston's sudden emergence as the homeowners' financial savior, everything seemingly part of a well-developed plan on the company's part. The question is, could the company have a reason to want the land for other than a theme park? Something not visible, something beneath the surface of the land, something so valuable they would kill to get it?"

Simon's eyebrows peaked upward with sudden interest, followed by, "That's quite an assumption without actual evidence, but perhaps not far off." He took a sip from his cup before saying, "I work closely with my counterparts over at U.S. Geological Survey. I was aware of what was happening at the park and found it interesting that, like Colorado, something similar has been happening largely to privately owned land in five other states: California, Wyoming, Montana, Idaho and Alaska. Companies simultaneously attempting to buy the land. If government owned – local, state or federal – obtain ninety-nine-year leases on the land.

"Understand, my U.S. Geo contacts tell me there have been a few murders within these areas, but not an anomaly when one considers we're talking about five states. Certainly not as you describe here in Jefferson County. There have, however, appeared to be an unusual number of threatening and intimidating acts by each of the companies, especially for privately owned land. Each offer is for a different use that normally requires rezoning. Why this is happening, we're not certain, but we've centered on one possibility which in a way mirrors your concerns."

I swept both hands around the room at the three projections and asked, "If they're not asking for mining and mineral rights, why is this happening?"

Gladys inserted, "I agree. In our case, I called Burt Addelson over at Jefferson County P&Z about the Ralston people and mineral rights. He says they've received nothing as of yet."

"A question we asked ourselves. Their reasons make little sense until one looks at the mining potential of the lands. To date, nothing so far as our U.S. cousins can find in the way of mineral rights being sought. They're checking into the background of each of the companies, including your Ralston Entertainment people."

Gladys raised a hand. "If not mineral rights, what do you

and your contacts over there think it might be? That one possibility you mentioned?"

"We, like you, think there's something there, but unlike you, not something they want brought to the surface. We think it's to keep the land free from the extraction of certain minerals. To preserve the various lands in each of the states from any kind of further exploration and/or development, be it for oil, coal, natural gas or other specific mining operations."

I shook my head, admittedly somewhat confused at something he'd said. "I uh... I don't understand. You said different companies in different states. Are they working in tandem? Could each of these companies be part of an umbrella organization trying to maintain its anonymity?"

Simon took a final sip of his coffee and stepped down from the platform, taking his cup with him. While picking up a laser pointer from one of the workstations, he moved toward the minerals map straight ahead of us. Turning, he said, "Let me tell you a story, but before I do, a question. Rare Earth Elements or minerals. We call them RE's. Are you familiar with these particular minerals?"

"I know they exist and are used in a lot of things," I replied.

Gladys gave a slight tilt of her head, a short wave of outstretched hands showing, "Somewhat. Our firm has represented two or three environmental organizations in the past in relation to RE's as you call them as well as coal mining and drilling. The hydraulic fracturing or 'fracking' process for oil and natural gas, but I'm certainly not familiar with their names or properties, RE's that is, or the methods for obtaining them."

"There are seventeen of them listed on the Periodic Table," Simon explained, "but you don't just go out and dig them up like diamonds, gold or a lump of coal. They have to be extracted from other minerals, the most abundant, a fluorocarbonate known as Bastnäsite."

He typed an order on one of the computers on the worktable, causing a color map of the world to replace the Colorado minerals map. With a few more typed orders, both China and the United States stood out, giving them an almost three-dimensional affect and distinguishing them from other countries.

With the red laser pointer, he highlighted China and then the U.S., each country immediately showing areas outlined in red backslashes, others with blue backslashes. Several of the blue slashes appeared to be crisscrossing different areas in Colorado and other western states, a single red in California and a smudge of red in southwestern Colorado.

"Red are the known Bastnäsite deposits and blue are suspected or potential deposits. As you see, there are more red areas in China. They constitute the largest percentage of the world's resources. The phosphate mineral Monazite is the next largest source of RE's, but in no way can it compare with Bastnäsite."

I asked, "Can you enlarge Colorado so we can get a better idea where those deposits and potential deposits might be?"

"Certainly." With a hand wave over the computer, the smallish outline of Colorado grew to at least ten times its size, showing recognizable county outlines. "Big enough?"

"Like magic."

There were three small red backslash areas in southern Colorado and two blue slash areas in what I thought to be Jefferson and Boulder Counties, west and northwest of Denver, respectively. Pointing to the most westerly of the two blues, I said, "There. Is that the Deer Creek area?

Simon enlarged the county outline.

"That's it, Matt," Gladys said with sudden assurance. "Possible Bastnäsite. Tell us, Simon, why is Bastnäsite and rare earth elements so important that, in our case, they would be cause enough to kill for? Or to keep others from getting. In other states, apparently scare or threaten people into selling their land, or if threats don't work, kill in the few instances you mention?"

With more typing on the key board, Simon brought us back to the world map followed by more typing which superimposed a list called RARE EARTH ELEMENTS and names of the 17 RE's: Lanthanum, Cerium, Neodymium, Samarium and on and on. After each element was a bewildering list of uses.

"As you can see, following extraction of the RE's from the different forms of Bastnäsite, there are many, many uses for each of the elements." Without even looking at the listings of uses, Simon rattled off, "Camera and telescopic lens, photographic filters.

"So far as the driving public is concerned, permanent magnets used in ABS braking systems, cruise controls, car stereos, speedometers and gauges, even the tiny electric motors controlling door locks, power windows, heater and air conditioner fans, electric mirrors, windshield wipers.

"Other everyday things such as cell phones, the red phosphors in color TVs, fiber optic cables, even stadium lighting for nighttime sports and to strengthen metal compounds such as aluminum baseball bats, bicycle frames and lacrosse sticks." He took a deep breath before adding, "You name it, virtually every item we use in this modern world of ours relies on RE's, not the least, implications for the military."

"As I get older," I said, "I seem to have more questions than answers. If we – the U.S. – along with China have so much of the stuff, what's the problem?"

Simon stepped back from the worktable and computer, turned, nodded and gave a short chuckle. "You're not alone. You're much like anyone else learning about RE's for the first time. A quick bit of history and all will be revealed."

As he spoke, Simon typed another order, making the list of RE's disappear. He then began walking back and forth, sometimes using the laser pointer for emphasis, swinging the beam toward the world map, China and the U.S. still highlighted, or directing it up and down to emphasize a statement.

"In the Nineteen-ninety's the U.S. and other nations went to the World Trade Organization arguing that China was severely restricting production and export of RE's, thus making the price of

RE's out of reach for many manufacturing countries. At the time, the mining of Bastnäsite and extraction of RE's was actually booming in the U.S., namely through a Denver based company named Richmond RE, Incorporated. They had mines in California and three in southern Colorado – Gunnison, Freemont and Custer counties. Why the U.S. became involved in the petition is beyond me."

"Likewise," Gladys said. "If they were producing and making money, I would have thought Richmond RE would have lobbied against our participation."

"They did, many millions of dollars-worth, but to no avail. As a result, the WTO found that China had broken free trade agreements by restricting production and export of rare earths. In 2014 China agreed with the findings and in January 2015, lifted all restrictive export quotas, thus causing an increase in supply of rare earths and a vast reduction in price.

"Richmond RE found itself losing millions since the cost of production far exceeded the rapidly decreasing market price. As a result, the company suspended operations in California, mothballed all their equipment and closed down the Colorado mines, selling much of the equipment to guess who? China! The monetary losses made their lobbying costs look like pocket change.

"Richmond, the only major producer in the U.S., subsequently went into bankruptcy, Chapter Eleven from which, after several years, they've finally received court approval to exit. That was some months ago. Can they reorganize to the point of resuming production of rare earths and compete on the world market with China? As I see it, it can happen only with the current Administration's help and determination."

"What do you mean?" I asked, probably more indignantly than I should have. "That seems like a no brainer."

"Past presidential administrations have let mining for Bastnäsite languish for a number of reasons, one of which has been the impact on the environment and court actions by environmental groups. Not only the cost factor, but environmental concerns. Extracting, refining and recycling RE's produces radioactive slurry and toxic acids.

"Mining in Colorado and other western states also demands adherence to laws requiring restoration of mined lands and protection of water resources. That in itself is an extremely expensive proposition. China, whose leadership speaks a good game, now a major player in the Paris Accords on climate change, in reality has no such environmental restrictions when it comes to RE's.

"What has suddenly caught the attention of this Administration?" Gladys asked.

"National defense, the military and its requirements."

"Namely?

He went back to the keyboard he'd been working with and typed in another command, instantly bringing up a list of rare earth related military equipment. "For example, tuners and filters for guidance and radar control in the PATRIOT air defense missile system, ceramic coatings for jet engines, precision-guided munitions, stealth technology, the Navy's AEGIS radar and missile array system, the most advanced shipboard system in the world for antiaircraft and antimissile defense, lasers, nuclear shielding technologies for our forces. My God, as you see from the list, I could go on forever."

Shaking her head, Gladys asked, "Why have we allowed ourselves to get into such a situation?"

Simon laughed. "Why? Not paying attention to our country's priorities. Not helping develop better and environmentally safer ways to process RE's."

I was beginning to feel like I was being preached to, but on the other hand, I could see where he was coming from, having spent a large part of my life in the military. Certainly, with the early years of the AEGIS radar and missile array system.

Simon continued. "While I have different feelings about the current Administration, they have been the first to realize we cannot depend on China or anyone else for an adequate, cost-effective source of RE's. Only those produced by and in the United States or perhaps in a friendly nation such as Canada will serve our national interest, in particular if we are to maintain our military readiness without dependence on a potential enemy.

"The President has recently ordered several federal agencies to increase exploration, mining and the process of critical minerals, including Bastnäsite for the extraction of RE's, and streamlining permits for private mining companies. This of course flies in the face of environmentalists, but it all comes down to national security. It's really up to the Administration to assist in the economic and regulatory hurdles, largely environmental in terms of putting money into developing cleaner methods of processing RE's and other minerals and to get the necessary level of production.

"As a side note, why do you think the administration decided to increase the number of troops in Afghanistan? It wasn't just military necessity."

"What do you mean?" Gladys asked.

"Afghanistan is said to have over a trillion dollars-worth of unearthed minerals. An envoy made up of government and highly placed private industry people have already been to Afghanistan to meet with their mining officials to discuss extracting rare earth metals. As for the increase in troops, let's just say, most of the sources for rare earths are located in Taliban-held territories. Get the picture?

"Regardless, the immediate problem, once all others are worked out, it takes a mining company several years from the point of acquisition of the property to even start production. Hopefully, Richmond RE can get their California and Colorado mines back in operation with a minimum of time and expense."

Trying to get back to the reason why Gladys and I were there, I said, "While definitely important, you've been talking about rare earth elements and their uses on both an international and national level which is way above our pay grades. We're here for one reason and one reason, only. The murders in Jefferson County and the sudden availability of a buyer who wants to buy up all the land. That includes the leasing of Deer Creek Canyon Park for a purpose which quite honestly hasn't made much sense until now. Like you and your friends over at U.S. Geological Survey, Gladys and I both believe there's something more, something we can't see, something in the ground."

Gladys cut in with, "To get to the point, are there deposits of Bastnäsite, the mother of all RE's, in Jefferson County and if so, could this be the reason why Ralston World Wide Entertainment is trying to buy all this land? For the same reason, do you believe that's why the other companies are trying to control the land in the other states?"

To answer our questions, Simon returned to the front of our table and replied, "Yes, we are aware of significant potential deposits in nearby Boulder County and south in the San Juan Mountains as well as here in Jefferson County, just south and east of Pyramid Mountain. Specifically, around the Deer Creek Canyon area.

"Since the President's executive order, we, both Colorado and U.S. Geological Survey, believe they are attempting to buy or lease the land, not to mine for the mineral, but to stop, repeat stop, mining for Bastnäsite and to keep the monopoly of RE's with China. We definitely believe somewhere in the background lurks China with the money and wherewithal to carry this through.

"The U.S. Geo people have notified our suspicions to their boss, the Department of Interior, who is in the process of informing the Departments of Homeland Security, Justice, Energy, Defense and the President."

I took a final sip of water, stood and said, "We appreciate you sharing your knowledge and suspicions, Simon. The way we figure it, whether it's China or anyone else, so far as the killings here in Jefferson County are concerned, somebody local is pulling the strings. That's why I was asked to come here, to help stop the killings and find out who's responsible. Find the killer and we'll find the high rollers, be it China or anyone else."

As Gladys started to stand, I pulled her chair back for her and said, "We need to talk, and I could use a drink. Have you got the time?"

She stood, turned and took my hand as she stepped away from the table. "I'll make the time."

Chapter 20

It was later that afternoon that Deputy Ralph Innes was quick to notice Joni Wickett's eyes. They seemed glazed over as he entered the office, but when he told her Captain Lundgren had sent for him, it was her single word, "Go," that stunned him. It was usually like an interrogation about what business he had with the Captain, since he was not part of Lundgren's Special Investigations Section.

Wondering why the Captain had called him, he stood before Lundgren's desk at ramrod attention. His muted green, long-sleeve tactical class-A shirt, black tie tucked between the second and third buttons below the collar, and spotless khaki trousers had been pressed to the point that he looked like he'd just stepped out of the U.S. Army's Manual of Uniform Regulations. Added to that, his seven-point gold Jefferson County Sheriff's badge over his left shirt pocket, the patch on his left shoulder, the holstered weapon, double magazine holders and other equipment arranged for easy access on his leather duty belt gave the impression he was ready for command inspection. He'd only been given an hour before the meeting, but he'd learned to keep a clean meeting-ready uniform always available in his locker for such impromptu occasions. In this case, special occasions that padded his take-home pay.

"Relax, Deputy. What I want to know is why the hell you didn't call me? Let me know what was happening?"

Innes allowed his body to take on a more *at ease* stance, his hands initially outstretched in a sorry-about-that gesture, and said, "First thing, Chief Kay had us doing a door-to-door search for anybody down along Dear Creek Road who might have seen or heard anything. I found one couple who the Chief had me interview. She kept me busy the rest of the morning doing this, doing that. Never was a time when I could call until I did."

"Damn it, Deputy, regardless of anything else you were doing, you should have known the minute that Indian guy showed up — what the hell's his name? The one with the Indian Commission bunch."

"John Nabhe, Sir."

"Yeah, John Nabhe, and that Berkeley person. You should have known when they showed up it had to do with the case. You and I, we get paid to keep our eyes, nose and anything else on this thing."

"Yes, Sir, you're right. It's just the timing wasn't right."

James Lundgren pushed away from his desk, stood, turned and looked out the window overlooking the building's parking lot, his hands coupled behind his back. "Just don't let that kind of slipup happen again." He turned and walked around the desk, firmly planting himself on the edge of the desk, an act which caused Innes to take several steps back.

"Like I said, Ralph," Lundgren continued, "we've got an extremely sensitive job to do."

"Sir?" The deputy knew whenever Lundgren called him or any of the other junior ranks by their first name, he wanted something and whatever he wanted was not going to be easy.

Lundgren thought for a moment before saying, "I've got a problem, which means *we* – you and me..." He pointed a finger at Innes and back at himself "... we have a problem. The men who I would normally have handle the situation for me are no longer available. Know what I mean?"

"I think so, Sir." Innes had a feeling the shit was about to hit the proverbial fan.

"There's a man who, if he has the opportunity, could and will upset all of our plans."

Innes caught the *"our plans"* bit. Not Lundgren's plans, *our plans*. He wasn't part of anybody's plan. He just provided information for a little extra money. He wasn't supposed to, but what the hell? A man has to look after himself, doesn't he? "I don't understand, Sir."

"If this man, an old man, an Indian, does what I think he can and will do, we'll all suffer. You, me and a lot of other people, *big* important people, can go down. You get my drift?"

Innes's face dropped. He spun around, walked to the door and just as quickly turned back toward Lundgren. Nodding, he said, "Yes, Sir, I think I'm getting your drift and if I'm right, this is way over my head. If you want this person out of the way, I mean permanently, you're talking to the wrong man.

"I've been sneaking info to you because, you and I know, Chief Kay doesn't like you and didn't want you involved in this particular case. That's all. The only way I would take out anybody permanently would be in the line of duty."

Lundgren literally burst off the side of the desk, took three rapid steps, grabbed the deputy by the arm and pulled him back into the middle of the room. While Lundgren was taller than Innes, he was certainly no match strength-wise for the younger man. It was respect for rank, something engrained in him from his Army days that kept Innes from slamming his elbow into Lundgren's midsection.

When Innes jerked his arm free, Lundgren ordered through clinched teeth, "Sit down and don't move until I say you can move." Pointing to one of two, leather-covered arm chairs, he pushed Innes down onto the chair and added, "You listen to me, damn it. I go down, you go down with me."

"I still don't know what for sure you're talking about," Innes said, his face red with anger.

"I'll tell you what I'm talking about. That fucking Indian. I want him gone, and I know damn well you know how to take care of him, Mr. ex-Army Ranger."

Innes tried to stand, his head shaking in rhythm with, "No, no, no. Not happening."

Lundgren pushed him back into the chair and leaned down in the man's face. "Oh yes, it'll happen, and you'll be the one doing it. You've got a mother and younger sister in Colorado Springs, right? You want to keep them safe, right? All up to you."

Innes's eyes narrowed, his hands automatically turned into fists, tight, knuckles going vivid white under the pressure. "You son of a bitch."

"Thought so. That out of the way, I've read your record. Bronze star, sniper in Afghanistan. How many kills? Ten, fifty, a hundred or more?" He straightened up and stepped back. "Best shot in your Law Enforcement Academy class, weren't you? Why's that? Experience, that's why."

"You're fucking crazy, Lundgren."

Lundgren ignored the charge. "One man, one time, *pow*!" He slapped the palms of his hands together, the explosive clap in Innes's face caused Innes to jerk back. "That's all I need," Lundgren went on. "No more after that. Got it?"

"How can I be sure? If I do this, you know damn well I'm hooked. There's always my mom and my sister, isn't there? I'm your shooter anytime something or somebody gets in your way, your so-called important people's way. Like I said, you're one crazy son of a bitch."

The Captain walked around the desk, opened one of the drawers and took out a key ring with a key and remote entry transmitter hanging from it. Tossing the key into Innes's lap, he said, "Parking lot, Twenty-seventeen black Ford Explorer in my personal parking space. Cargo section. Lift the floor board. Spare tire's been removed. There's a red bag inside. Don't open it. Take it, toss the key inside and close the lift gate.

"On the driver-side door, there's a key pad, five keys, two number each. Hit the five-six and seven-eight keys at the same time. That locks the car. Go home. Only then, open the bag. When you do, you'll find an old friend waiting inside. Got all that?"

With his head tilted down toward his lap in apparent surrender, Innes nodded and took a deep breath, "Yeah, I got it."

"Smart. Tomorrow morning, RTD bus stop. Be set up no later than 4:30 on the cliff above the ruins of the old dance hall building, Phillipsburg. You know where it is. You patrolled up there after the Lamb killing. I'll be there with the Indian in the parking lot at five. Just like Afghanistan, when I leave or before if he causes trouble, take him out."

"For Christ's sake, Lundgren. Take him out just like that? That's murder. I'm a cop, for God's sake. Protect, not murder."

With a low, grunt-like chuckle, Lundgren gave Innes a quick, stinging slap across the left cheek. "Yeah. Just keep thinking, mama and sissy down in Colorado Springs, all safe and warm, and you'll take him out just like..." Lundgren made a loud *snap* with his fingers. "... that."

Minutes later Innes approached the Ford Explorer, pointed the key transmitter in its direction and punched the OPEN icon button. He heard only the click of the lock in the driver-side door. A second punch and door locks from around the vehicle sounded the open click. He searched for and found the button and raised the rear lift gate to the cargo compartment.

Pitching a small ice cooler, a kid's baseball bat, ball, first baseman's glove and a soccer ball over into the rear seat, he lifted the floor board. The first thing he saw in place of the spare tire was a red, heavy duty, zip-up carrying bag with a large AAA printed on one side.

Ignoring Lundgren's warning, Innes stepped back for moment and scanned the parking lot. Satisfied there was no one nearby, at least close enough to see what he was doing, he unzipped the bag and pulled out a light brown metal case weighing what he thought to be anywhere from twenty to twenty-five pounds. Stamped into the metal was the seal of the Department of the Army. Right below were the words, FOR OFFICIAL GOVERNMENT USE, ONLY.

Turning his head from side to side to once more check for anyone close by, he popped the four snaps securing the case and lifted the lid. "Aw shit!" He immediately slammed the lid down, snapped the case shut and replaced it in the red AAA bag.

Lundgren was right. It was like seeing an old friend or one

like he'd used in a war he'd wanted to forget. Inside rested a camouflage-tan Knight's Armament M110, a 7.62mm NATO caliber, semiautomatic sniper rifle. He knew each function, each component part, each piece of accessory equipment, and most of all, he knew the weapon's killing power.

From his window overlooking the parking lot, Lundgren watched as Innes entered the Ford Explorer, opened the cover over the spare tire and pulled the red Triple-A bag to him. "Damn you, Innes," was all he could say when the deputy lifted the metal case out of the bag and opened it. "Jesus Christ, Innes! Thought they taught you how to follow orders in the Army."

Once Innes closed up the car and walked away with the red bag, Lundgren muttered to himself, "That's it. I've had enough."

He was about to head for the door and tell Joni Wickett he was leaving when the mobile in a locked desk drawer burped several low notes. "Damn it!" He unlocked and opened the drawer, withdrew the devise, hit the phone icon and said, "Was just about to leave."

"Your earlier visitor we discussed, the one you said was going to be a problem. Can you assure me the problem is being taken care of?"

"Yes. By the beginning of the work day tomorrow, the problem will be solved."

"Good. Don't fail me like your two idiots did up on the mountain. Too many things are beginning to happen. Chief Kay, Wong, that Berkeley man and his Indian friend. Happening too fast, and I want them shut down. Understand?"

"It takes people, time and money. I can't just –" Lundgren realized the voice at the other end of the conversation was no longer there. "Damn!"

While putting the mobile back into the drawer, he cursed, "Bastard! Thinks I'm his fucking slave."

He nodded, angrily knowing the threat the man behind the voice was holding over his head would always be there until he, James Lundgren, did something about it. "Someday, you blackmailing son of a bitch, just you fucking wait."

While across town...

* * *

According to Gladys, Golden, Colorado's origins go back to the discovery of gold in the swift running Clear Creek which cuts through the center of the city. Attracting the area's earliest settlers in the mid-19th century, Golden quickly became a major supply stop for gold miners seeking their fortunes in the adjacent mountains. I suppose history was the reason she selected the Buffalo Rose Saloon on Washington Street for a drink and talk about what we'd learned from Simon Grant at the Geological Survey office. She was unaware the saloon had recently been remodeled inside and out.

As we drove along the street, she eyed the *new* Buffalo Rose. "Not bad, I guess."

"What do you mean, you guess?" I asked as I followed a sign that pointed right to a parking garage about a block off Washington Street.

"The building, they've changed it."

The exterior did look new, but for me never having been there before, it really didn't turn me on or off. For those who had visited the place before, it was really a matter of one's personal likes and dislikes. "You want to go someplace else?" I asked.

She shook her head. "It's getting late and this is as good as anyplace else for a drink."

After we were parked and once inside, a little dark when entering out of the late afternoon sunlight, the saloon's interior was definitely welcoming after a chilly walk from the backstreet parking garage. The beer, a Coors Light – selected since Golden is the home of the famous Coors Brewery – was cold like I like it, just this side of freezing.

Seated at the bar, Gladys asked the bartender, not overly busy for that time of the afternoon just before the getting-off-work crowd arrived, why the remodeling since she'd liked it the way it was.

After explaining the reason for the renovations, he went on to elaborate on the building's history which the owners were determined to preserve. Dating back to the mid eighteen hundred's, the saloon had hosted such famous guests as Civil War Generals Grant, Sherman and Sheridan. There were also numerous shootouts inside the bar between the local Sheriff and some of the more notorious bad men of the time. What I liked, however, were the ghost stories, especially that of the "ghostly girl."

After stacking some clean glassware for ready use, leaning closer across the counter and speaking in a soft, mysterious tone, he shared, "Sometime when I'm here at closing time and cleaning up, I can hear her going up and down the stairs. There was an old swimming pool down in the basement, covered over now. Used back in the eighteen-seventies when this was both a hotel and restaurant called the Overland House. It's believed the little girl drowned in the pool, leaving her spirit behind."

Once we'd heard a full history of the of building, from grocery store, public hall for church services and dances to territorial council meetings when Golden was capital of the Colorado Territory, hotel and finally the Buffalo Rose Saloon, Gladys and I settled down to discussing what we'd learned at the Colorado Geological Survey office.

We were about to order a second round of beer and something from the bar menu when my dinosaur of a cell phone began to ring. I flipped it open, saw it was an unfamiliar number but with the name *Pierson-Sanders*. The name rang a bell. Even though I wasn't sure, I answered anyway. "Berkeley."

"It's Chief Kay. John with you?"

John must have given her my number. "No. I dropped him off at his office. He had some work to catch up on. Guess he still has to make a living."

"We need to meet," she responded. "Tomorrow morning,

eight a.m. Bring John. Response from the Paris police and where we think our killer has gone to ground. Too late to go out there tonight, but thought you might be good to go, if you know what I mean."

Wow, guess I'd become a real part of the team. At the same time, a red warning light blinked on and off in my brain, remembering the CIA when they made me a less-than-eager part of their team in London and later disowned me. Even tried to kill me when I defied them and went my own way. I was determined that wouldn't happen this time, primarily because of my respect for Chief Kay, and of course, John Nabhe, my old friend.

"We'll be there, but I'd like to bring someone else with me. Gladys Knight from Roberta Pine Woman's law office."

I held the phone to the side and looked at Gladys. "Eight o'clock tomorrow morning. Okay?" Giving me what I considered an excited look on her face, she quickly nodded in agreement. The more she smiled, the more I wanted to be with her. If only she would reciprocate the feeling, but that might be a little too much to ask.

I explained to the Chief, "Roberta set up a meeting with the Colorado Geological Survey office, but had to be in court. Gladys subbed for Roberta. Lots of info about the land as well as the *who* and the *why* we discussed this morning. This thing might be bigger than just Jefferson County, Colorado.

"Since you've been keeping Roberta filled in because of the Indian connection in the local papers, Gladys is also up to speed where everything stands concerning the killings."

I could visualize Chief Kay shaking her head, a look of exasperation on her face. There was a moment of silence before she answered, her tone definitely mirroring the look I imagined. "I guess. We keep adding one here, one there, I'm going to have to get the Sheriff to deputize half of Jefferson County and part of Denver."

I laughed as the line went dead. Looking at Gladys, I asked, "With that turn of events, ,how about dinner? Give us a chance to get our stories straight."

There was that smile again. "Love to. I'll let Roberta know about tomorrow."

Chapter 21

That night Innes called his mother five, six times to warn her and ask where she could go for the next several days until he could work things out, but there'd been no answer. Nor had she returned his calls. Had they already found her? Kidnapped her and his sister? Killed them? All because he'd allowed himself to be a sneak for Lundgren on the wolf man case for a couple of extra bucks a month. As a result, he was now supposed to kill a man, an Indian.

For Christ's sake, he didn't even know the man's name. Worry along with anger at himself clouded his mind. The one thing he knew for sure, if anything happened to his mom and sister, he'd make Lundgren pay and anyone else he could find who was involved.

Between calls, he stripped and cleaned the rifle, the M-110, the SASS he called it, an acronym for Semi-Automatic Sniper System. The more he worked, preparing the weapon for Lundgren's ordered mission, the angrier he became. He'd killed before, many times, but in the service of his country. In fact, in the five years he'd been a Jefferson County deputy, he had yet to kill in self-defense or otherwise.

The thought of him, a law enforcement officer, committing murder gnawed at him, tightened the sinews of his conscience to the point that killing Lundgren would be the lesser of two evils. But could he? And what would happen to his mother and sister if he did? He sat there, wishing his mother would call, praying to God or whatever power he could think of for an answer, but there was no response.

It was a little after 0400 hours the next morning, still dark, when Innes, his mind now operating in military time and efficiency, pulled off Deer Creek Canyon Road onto a dirt road he'd found after leaving Lundgren's office the afternoon before. The rutted, single-lane road meandered upward toward the top of the cliff that towered over the old Philipsburg dancehall ruins and the RDT Park and Ride bus stop. Farther on was a vacant dilapidated farm house and barn where he hid his late model Dodge Ram Pickup.

As a precaution, he wore an old pair of ACU's – Army Combat Uniform – with the operational camouflage pattern he'd worn in Afghanistan, minus the tactical vest. Covering his head was a lightweight balaclava colored to match his ACU, his eyes the only facial feature showing through the single narrow slit.

He removed the gun case from the rear seat floorboard and, using his department-issued tactical flashlight, made his way over a strip of meadow filled with high grass and through a stand of pine trees to the top of the cliff.

Innes had slept fitfully that night, but he knew now that the time had come. He had to put thoughts of his mother and sister aside and concentrate on what had to be done. He checked his watch – 0437.

Last night's late news had shown sunrise a little before 0700. Based on that, he figured first light no earlier than 0600. For his purpose, however, the four strategically placed dust-to-dawn LED streetlamps in the car park and their silvery-white spread provided sufficient light regardless of when daylight arrived.

He switched off the tactical flashlight once, one by one, cars and pickup trucks began to pull into the lot. He wasn't surprised when their drivers remained in the vehicles, safe from the chill morning air until the first bus of the day arrived.

Kneeling some feet back from the cliff's edge and remaining hidden by shrubbery and weeds, he placed the metal carrying case on the ground before him. Slowly, silently he released the four snaps, raised the lid and removed the rifle before pushing the case aside. Though working in the dark, every movement and every accessory component, its mount or insertion, was automatic. Steps the sniper in him could still accomplish with eyes closed.

First the QD sound suppressor. With the magazine removed, no round in the chamber, the safety select lever set to SAFE, he slid the sound suppressor over the barrel and rotated counter-clockwise until the quick-detach locking latch was fully engaged.

Second, with the bolt locked, the rifle still on SAFE, he inserted the 20-round magazine into the magazine receiver well and slapped the bottom of the magazine with the palm of his hand to ensure the magazine catch was engaged. He then released the bolt, automatically loading the first round into the chamber.

Third, he lowered the legs on the bipod adaptor already attached beneath the barrel's hand rail system to provide increased stability and accuracy in target acquisition and aiming. Once that was done, he slid forward and placed the bipod legs firmly on a slight downward-sloped edge of the cliff. He knew the rifle's earth-toned brown barrel with its similar-colored sound suppressor would not be visible from the parking lot below.

Innes removed the covers from the eyepiece and objective ends of the 3.5-10X 40mm day scope secured above the rifle's flip-up/flip-down rear sight and adjusted the scope for elevation and range before zeroing it for the magazine's 7.62 caliber bullets. All the while his mind had been feverishly working on what he had to do, on what would be the lesser of several evils. Miss the intended target and risk his mother's and sister's lives, kill the Indian and be a puppet, dangling from another man's strings for the rest of his life or... kill Lundgren?

At exactly 0500 hours with the parking lot beginning to fill and the first RTD bus taking on passengers destined to the various Denver suburbs and into the city itself, Lundgren's Ford Explorer turned into the lot and proceeded midway to the rear, pulling almost even with the front of the old dance hall. Innes chuckled. *Couldn't be better*, he thought, perfect location for a dead-on shot.

As the bus pulled away and turned left onto Deer Creek Canyon Road headed east, an old model Chevy pickup, road-dust covered with a wide strip of bare metal on its left front fender, turned into the lot, followed by three or four other vehicles. The pickup stopped momentarily, allowing the driver time to survey the lot until Lundgren stepped out of the Explorer. The pickup slowly moved forward and maneuvered around a group of parked empty vehicles until it came to a halt several feet from Lundgren.

Innes watched the Indian exit the pickup truck and walk to within four or five feet of Lundgren's position. Using the scope's "hash mark" reticle or crosshairs, Innes made a slight adjustment to the distance before moving the crosshair from one man to the other. He lifted his head from the scope and watched the two conversing. Lundgren handed the Indian an envelope. The man opened the envelope, unfolded a single sheet of paper, read something and immediately ripped it apart. He threw the papers to the ground and crushed them into the gravel with his boot.

While he couldn't at first make out the words, Innes knew from the angry expression on the Indian's face and loudness of his voice that the Indian was threatening Lundgren. He saw the man spit at Lundgren who automatically stepped back. Just as quickly Lundgren looked up and rapidly nodded toward the top of the cliff; the signal to shoot.

Innes placed his right eye on the scope's eyepiece and centered the crosshairs on the Indian who was now calm but moving slowly, threateningly forward. Innes lifted his eyes away from the scope, surprised to see Lundgren backing toward his car, looking toward the top of the cliff, his head rapidly bobbing up and down, a desperate plea for Innes to fire.

His eye back on the scope, right index finger resting on the rifle's two-stage match trigger, the Indian was once again in the crosshairs. Innes squeezed only slightly until he felt resistance at the end of the trigger's first stage. Only a little more pressure – 4.5 pounds of force per the operating manual – would send the trigger through the lethal second stage, propelling the 7.62 caliber round over twenty-five hundred feet per second toward its target who would be dead before the sound reached his ears.

"Fuck you, Lundgren," Innes whispered. He shifted slightly so the scope's crosshairs sighted on Lundgren's chest, his finger ready to send the trigger into its second stage when he saw through the scope an arm and hand lash out toward Lundgren. The hand gripped a hunting knife. It whipped forward and sliced at Lundgren's throat, again and again as Lundgren stumbled backwards, trying to dodge the blade.

He heard Lundgren shouting, "Fire, goddamn it, fire."

Innes moved the rifle and scope as fast as he could to keep up with Lundgren and the Indian, but the bipod's legs, caught in the weeds, refused to move other than in a jerking motion. As the knife caught up with and sliced across Lundgren's throat, left to right, right to left, he saw Lundgren grab his throat. Blood spurted from between his fingers from an obviously severed carotid artery on the left side of the throat, a lesser flow of blood from the right.

Suddenly, he heard two shots and saw the Indian turn, open mouthed, bloody knife still in his hand. A startled look covered his face before he dropped to his knees and fell forward into the dirt and gravel.

Standing beside a pickup truck was a fully bearded man in work clothes, an AR-15 rifle in his hand, still pointed at the Indian. Finally, he lowered the rifle to a waist-high position and quickly moved forward while several disbelieving onlookers stood on the far side of the pickup, watching from the partial safety behind the truck's open bed.

Once the man reached the Indian's body, he kicked the knife aside with the toe of his work boot and used the same boot against the Indian's ribs to insure there was no reaction and no danger to himself. Satisfied, he pivoted toward the group and called, "For Christ's sake, one of you call nine-one-one. Need the law and medical people."

When no one moved, he raised the rifle, fired a shot into the air and shouted, "Don't just fucking stand there like idiots, do it, somebody."

Lundgren lay on his back, a tremor coursing through his entire body, the gush of blood from the left side of his throat beginning to subside, the tremor slowing to a stop. With everything happening so fast, Innes figured it had now been between one and two minutes since the knife's blade had made the cut. He had seen something similar in Afghanistan: shrapnel tear though a man's neck and blood erupt from a torn artery. He knew Lundgren had for the most part already bled out. The man was as good as dead.

Slowly so not to be seen from below, he worked his body, the M-110 and its bipod legs back from the edge of the cliff through weeds until he reached the bushes where he earlier left the gun case. Getting to his knees, he placed the rifle on SAFE, popped the magazine from the well and extracted the single round from the chamber. He then removed the sound suppressor, folded the bipod legs and placed the weapon into the case before snapping it shut.

Innes felt drained, stunned at what had happened, what he'd seen. He shook his head, muttering, "I can't believe it. The whole damn thing, like a frigging nightmare."

At least he had not killed in cold blood, but there was still his mother and sister and that goddamned group of higher-ups Lundgren mentioned. He had to do something, but what?

Chapter 22

I made an extra early start, having promised both John – still without his truck – and Gladys I'd pick them up for the eight o'clock meeting with Chief Kay. From the Hampton Inn in the western suburb of Littleton, I followed my map east to the Denver suburb of Greenwood Village for Gladys, north to the Chessman Park area of Denver for John, and back northwest to Golden and the Jefferson County's government campus.

For a guy having lived for a number of years in Palm Valley, Florida where ten cars make a traffic jam, the Denver area's morning rush hour can be a nightmare. Especially for one not familiar with traffic patterns and streets that suddenly change names or become one-way, usually the other way, after only six or seven blocks.

By the time we arrived at the Sheriff's complex of offices, I felt like I'd been driving for the past twenty-four hours, bleary-eyed, exhausted. The seemingly ever-present Doctor Wong was all smiles, chipper, already with a cup of coffee in his hands.

I forgot my own feelings when I saw Chief Kay. Not only tired, her face was full of worry. She looked like she should already be in a hospital's delivery room rather than investigating half a dozen or more murders.

It wasn't the most diplomatic thing to say, but I said it anyway. "I'm sorry, Chief, but you look worn out. You sure you shouldn't be home instead of here?"

Dr. Wong chimed in. "Same thing I said when I first came in."

"Damn it, you two," she shot back, an index finger waving at me, then Wong. "You're both echoing what my husband said this morning, and I'll be damned if I need three husbands. My lower back hurts and I feel like I need to pee every fifteen minutes, but for whatever reason, I'm breathing easier, taking deeper breaths than I have in the last month or so."

Wong gave me a strange look at her last words, a look like he knew something I didn't, but I wasn't going to push the matter any further.

Chief Kay glanced at the large clock on the wall before saying, "Instead of talking about my condition, time's a ticking and things to do." She immediately turned to Gladys and with a weary, somewhat forced smile, held out her hand. "You must be Ms. Knight. Welcome aboard. Everybody calls me Chief Kay and this is Doctor Wong Yan Lung. Doctor Wong is our Chief Deputy Coroner and forensic pathologist."

With introductions made, she nodded toward the conference table. "Long day ahead, but before we get started, anyone for coffee?"

Looking longingly at the table with the black, twelve-cup coffee maker and a full carafe, the line of clean coffee cups, yellow packets of sweetener and stirrers, I said, "Like a thirsty man in the desert. I'll pour and serve."

Before we sat, Wong said, "One thing before we get started. I completed the autopsy last evening on our two men from up on Pyramid Mountain. First, the one found on the trail, cause of death was cardiopulmonary collapse caused by the deep stab wound in his throat that severed and displaced the trachea or windpipe. In simple terms, the lungs collapsed from lack of air intake followed by the heart from lack of oxygen to pump the blood. Not to speak of the amount of blood the man loss, internally and externally.

"As for the other man, we couldn't identify a specific cause of death. We did determine, however, there was no soot in either his sinus cavities, trachea or in his lungs. It's reasonable to conclude he was dead before the fire started. Thought you'd like to know. We are, however, still trying to identify the two men. As of this morning, no success."

Once everyone had their coffee, Chief Kay and Doctor Wong took up residence on one side of the conference table, Gladys, John and me on the other. On the table in front of Chief Kay lay a poster board, facedown, and a red file folder.

The Chief started with, "I invited Captain Lundgren to attend since you told me on the phone yesterday afternoon..." she paused and looked at me, "... this might be bigger than just Jefferson County, elsewhere in Colorado and other states. With that in mind, my thought was perhaps some kind of national or international plot or conspiracy. Might be in the Captain's realm of interest, but I checked with his secretary this morning and he's not in yet. We can't wait. Let's hear what you and Ms. Knight learned at the Geological Survey Office."

Gladys and I took turns relaying what we'd learned from Simon Grant. It was a basic tutorial on rare earth elements and potential Bastnäsite deposits in the Deer Creek Canyon area as well as other locations in Colorado and five other states. Since the U.S. Geological Survey people had already determined there were enough similarities in each case – land with known or suspected Bastnäsite deposits – they had notified various other interested federal departments via their own superiors in the Interior Department."

With an index finger tap, tap, tapping on the surface of the table, Chief Kay seemed to be studying the framed antique engraved foil map on the wall behind me depicting the 1860's Colorado Territory. She seemed deep in thought until she finally said, "All very interesting, but I'll leave the big picture to the feds. I've still got a wacko serial killer to find. If he leads us to some kind of national or international conspiracy behind the killings, I'll bring Lundgren in and share what we find with the feds."

Chief Kay continued, "With the exception of you, Ms. Knight, the rest of us have seen this rather macabre advertisement." She picked up the poster and turned it over, showing the circus advertisement with the heading reading **LE CIRQUE DE MONTMARTRE PRÉSENTE LE CÉLÉBRE**

LOUP-GAROU DE PARIS POUR VOTRE PLAISIR ET EXCITATION. Below was the now familiar picture of the creature, its body thickly covered in dark brown hair, a wolf-like face with an extended snout, blood dripping from its teeth. The thing's feet straddled a woman, her hands raised to ward off his attack, mouth open in a terrified scream. If you thought about, you could almost hear her scream.

Gladys automatically drew back in surprise. With a rather sour laugh, she said, "You've got to admit, graphically, it certainly gets your attention. I'm sure to horror aficionados a werewolf attacking a young woman can be entertaining and definitely exciting, but what is the significance of a French circus poster?"

Doctor Wong quickly explained about the hair found snagged on a bush near Deer Creek and the determination that it was from a human, possibly suffering from excessive body hair disorder known as hypertrichosis. It was the poster, its 2016 date and Mr. Berkeley's recommendation that prompted Chief Kay's query to the Paris Police.

Gladys shifted slightly forward and looked around John at me, her eyes conveying either a question – why in the world did you do that? – or admiration for my intelligence. I chuckled inside, thinking probably the former.

Laying the poster aside, Chief Kay opened the red file folder lying in front of her and slid it across the table to John, seated in the middle of the three of us. To me, the papers and their somewhat less than perfectly printed letters looked like something received on a fax machine.

The top sheet displayed a logo, its colors blue, white and red, the French national colors, followed by a title and address: *Direction Régional de Police Judiciaire de Paris, 36 rue du Bastion*, *75017 Paris, France.* Written information following the letter head and throughout the following pages was in French.

"We received this late yesterday afternoon just before I spoke with you," she said, looking at me. "It's from the Regional Directorate of the Paris Judicial Police."

She paused a moment, again looking at me. "The people who Mr. Berkeley once successfully avoided." She chuckled. "I'm still waiting to hear about your great escape from the Paris *gendarmerie*."

Eyebrows knitted, Gladys again shifted forward to see past John. "Matt?"

I gave her what I call the old Marine salute, both hands up in the air and a *who me?* look on my face.

Chief Kay gave a rather pained laugh, one hand reaching around to her lower back. "Ms. Knight, it appears you and I need to interrogate Mr. Berkeley a bit more about his adventures in Paris, but another time."

John pulled the sheath of papers closer in front of him, scanned the first page and said, "Damn good thing you can read French, Chief."

"Remember," she answered, "South Louisiana French with a mixture of Cajun. Having gone through the document, unfortunately, there's a lot I didn't and still don't understand."

For the first time since introductions were made when we arrived, Gladys volunteered, "What you can't decipher, I'm pretty sure I can. Three years of French at UNC –"

Taken by surprise, I interrupted by repeating, "UNC?" My immediate thought was University of North Carolina, one of my two collegiate alma maters.

Gladys explained, "University of Northern Colorado. I also spent several years in Luxembourg when my late husband was posted with IBM. French with a bit of German thrown in, though French is the majority language in Luxembourg."

"John, damn it!" Chief Kay popped the top of the table with the flat of her hand. "Give that woman the papers so she can tell us what they say."

"All yours, Gladys," John said, pushing the papers in her direction. "Let's take a break so you can read through and give us a quick rundown."

While Gladys took bullet notes of what she read, the rest

of us finished our coffee, took restroom breaks – Chief Kay charging ahead – re-filled our cups and discussed the rare earth information until Gladys looked up, exhaled a sigh indicating she was finished with the task and said, "I think I now understand the significance of the Montmartre circus poster. I need a quick break and then I'm ready to give you a synopsis of what it says."

After I placed a cup of coffee with sweetener on the table for Gladys and she returned, she began with, "The Paris police, a department within the overall French National Police, has provided what amounts to an investigation which spanned two separate administrative districts within the city of Paris, the First and Eighteenth *Arrondissements.*

"To begin, the Circus Montmartre located in the north of Paris, the Eighteenth *Arrondissement,* hired this man with all the hair and started his act in January, 2015. Because of the type act, the police did a bit of research on him. Name on his employment papers was Keith Nalje, nickname Hok'ee, or something like that. Definitely not French. American Indian from a place called Chinle in Arizona. He was issued a Foreign Talents Visa by the French Ministry for Europe and Foreign Affairs based on information provided by one of their French Consulates in the U.S."

John and I immediately looked at one another, both saying at the same time, "Arizona, the Four Corners."

John added, "Chinle is in the Navajo Nation, just south of the Four Corners area. But the nickname, Hok'ee, if that's correct, literal translation, high backed wolf."

Gladys looked at both of us and said, "Like in one of the Navajo legends Roberta told me about. The one about shape shifting, man to wolf."

I responded, "Possibly. But go on."

Returning to her notes, she continued, "The police and their health department suspected he was afflicted with some kind of disease – the excessive hair. They didn't say what kind of disease." She looked at Doctor Wong. "That might be your hyper… uh hypertrichosis Matt told me about."

Looking back at her notes, she continued, "Before coming to Paris, he was part of a circus called Stetson Brothers Circus. Traveled mostly in the western parts of the U.S. and Canada. In Edmonton, Alberta Province in Canada, during one of the acts, apparently something similar to his act in Paris, he bit off part of the nose and upper lip belonging to another performer. Though considered self-defense by the Stetson brothers as well as the Canadian Royal Mounted Police, he was fired.

"Some months later, he arrived in Paris and joined the circus. The show as well as this Keith Nalje became famous, not only in Paris, but throughout the country. He became known as the *Loup-Garou* or werewolf of Paris. No problems experienced, no contagious medical disease and therefore no further investigation."

Gladys took a sip from her coffee, cleared her throat and asked, "Any questions?"

"Very good, Ms. Knight, but where does your First *Arrondissement* come in?" Wong asked.

"Seems he developed a relationship with one of the performers, a young female trapeze artist named Ariel Bisset. To make a long story short, she lived in the First *Arrondissement*. That would be what everyone calls the Right Bank of the River Seine, well south of the Eighteenth.

"The report explains the particular area where she lived as a red-light district. A frequent visitor and easily recognized by the ladies of the night, he was seen entering her apartment building one night. A short time later, a man was thrown from a window of her third-floor apartment. Screams from the apartment were heard. The Bisset woman was found dead shortly thereafter, her body partially eaten." Looking up from her notes, Gladys added, "Sounds like she was making a little money on the side and the Werewolf of Paris didn't like it."

Following another quick sip of coffee, Gladys said, "Somehow, our hairy friend escaped, apparently through a trapdoor to the roof and across several rooftops, never to be seen again. There are different theories on how he left the country with the assumption he ultimately returned to the United States, but nothing concrete.

"His record is still open with both the National Police, the European Union Agency for Law Enforcement Cooperation, better known as Europol and the well-known Interpol for the international side of things. End of story."

Everyone sat quietly for a moment, absorbing the information, in particular the murder and the part about the victim being partially cannibalized.

Chief Kay broke the silence by saying, "Thank you, Ms. Knight, for a thorough reading of the document." She shook her head. "I think, if nothing else, this gives us more than we've had in identifying our killer, but why, for God's sake, would he be doing this? Here, of all places?"

"Doing it because he's been told to do it," I said. "Told by someone he trusts, somebody close. John?"

John thought for a moment before bolting upright and snapping his finger. "I'll be damned," he muttered to himself, then louder, "I'll be dammed is right. Matt, the old man who sat behind you at the Indian Commission meeting, the one muttering to himself, who grabbed you and tried to choke you when you mentioned the Four Corners. For the last year or so, he's been talking about land in Jefferson County that belonged to a couple of the tribes. Ute, Cheyenne, Arapaho, Apache, even Navajo, old hunting grounds and how the white man has desecrated them."

I rubbed my throat at the memory. "Yeah, he almost pushed my Adams apple up through my mouth. You remember his name?"

"Samuel something, but Gladys, your boss knows. Call Roberta and ask her. The next question is, is this Keith Nalje guy from Paris, originally from Arizona, our man? A perfect match for the killer, but if it *is* him, where the hell has the man gone to ground?"

Chief Kay answered, "We've searched up and down that damn mountain and found nothing. Used the dogs, but the rain that night must have washed everything away.

"I even put together equipment for two of our men to go back into the old mine to see if that's where he's hiding, but when they got in there, even with flash lights, they claimed they got so claustrophobic from the head gear, HazMat suits and the dark, they had to come out." With a grunt of disdain, she added, "I think they just got scared of what they might find and –"

She was interrupted by a loud knock on the door which quickly swung open. A unformed deputy rushed in, almost out of breath, yelling, "Chief, you gotta come. Don't know why it's taken so long for us to get the word, but its Captain Lundgren. He's dead, supposedly murdered by some Indian guy."

While Doctor Wong immediately jumped up from his chair, Chief Kay closed her eyes. With face wrinkled into a tight, painful frown and one hand spread against her forehead as if pressing away a sudden headache, she slumped lower in her chair and whispered, "God in heaven, what more can happen?"

Chapter 23

Hok'ee lay in a fetal position just above a depression in the mine floor. Clinging to the roof of the mine were hundreds, if not thousands of dark brown bats, their colors lost in the gloom. Guano bats, he'd once heard them called, lived in the caves of northern Arizona. From where he lay, his ears were unable to distinguish other sounds above the barrage of high-pitched squeaks that echoed through the mine. Only short hours ago, they returned as a vast swarm from somewhere in the back of the mine, an opening, an air shaft. He didn't know nor did he care, but he did know it was a signal that daylight was returning to the outside world.

Peering over the rim of the depression, he could barely make out what appeared to be the tons of bat droppings with millions of tiny beetles that lived in the waste. Their movement caused the floor to be in a constant, seething motion. Or was it his eyes? It made him dizzy.

He blinked, rapidly at first, groaning at the deep burns which were, unknown to him, caused by the sharp, pervasive presence of ammonia. Created by the beetles, the heavy acrid odor permeated that part of the mine, sometimes pushed toward the mine's entrance by an intermittent flow of air. He blinked, rapidly at first, before forcefully shutting his eyes. When opening them, however, the beetles' squirming, wave-like rhythm continued.

It was the constant exposure of ammonia in the air that had increased the now ever-present burning sensations in his throat and lungs, shortness of breath, the constant wheezing and coughing. He could feel the blisters that had formed on the skin beneath the damp mat of hair, his arms, his legs, along his chest and abdomen, all agonizingly painful to touch.

It was, however, the bullet that had destroyed his left

shoulder blade before exiting just above his lung and the devastating infection boiling within the stab wounds, one in his back and two between ribs in his left side that would soon determine his ultimate fate. He was dying and he knew it.

If only he could live long enough to see his grandfather once more, ask his forgiveness for leaving the cabin where he'd been told to stay. Would the old man come in time? Surely, he knew this would be his grandson's only place of safety. Others had come, wearing strange things over their bodies and faces, but had backed away from the darkness before finding him.

Somehow Hok'ee made his way forward to see the early morning light, to feel the slight refreshing breeze that had always been present. If only for a moment, to witness the sun's first rays as they reached up over the eastern edge of the foothills and the valley where the white people had lived.

On his knees, his left shoulder and arm being useless, he used his toes to push against the soft earth, sometimes mud from dripping water, and rock debris, his right hand and fingers to claw his way toward the distant entrance of the old mine.

Almost there, the cleansing glow of sunlight beginning its reaching into the mine, he caught the faraway sound of sirens. So many, they drew near along Deer Creek Canyon Road, then moved away to the west. He stopped before he got to the entrance, fearful their westward movement was a trick to lure him out.

With his lungs and throat enraged by a deep, gurgling cough that rattled his entire body, tears filled his eyes as he turned and started back into the mine.

* * *

I had planned on taking John by the Littleton Police office to pick up his bullet-ridden pickup truck which had been released by Detective Max Roland and lab tech Lilly Mendoza. This was to be followed by dropping Gladys off at her downtown office, but with this unexpected Lundgren bombshell, no way was I going to miss the action. That is, if Chief Kay agreed. It was the words *supposedly murdered by some Indian guy* and John's mention of Samuel what's-his-name at the Indian Commission meeting that allowed John, Gladys and me to follow the Chief and Wong out to the murder scene.

Upon arrival, there was a uniformed deputy with two large sawhorse-type barricades blocking entry into the Park and Ride lot with yellow crime scene tape ringing half the cars and trucks in the lot. As Chief Kay's car pulled into the entrance, the deputy approached, listened to the Chief's words, nodded, then proceeded to swing one of the barricades aside. Once she was through, he waved for us to follow a rather circuitous route around many of the taped off vehicles until we reached a relatively clear area some distance from what appeared to be the actual crime scene.

I parked behind the Chief's car and watched her literally drag herself from the driver's seat, holding onto the door as though she might fall at any moment. Wong loped his way around the front of the unmarked Crown Vic, took her arm for support and shut the door. He looked back at me, shaking his head and rolling his eyes, an *I'm-not-believing-she's-here* look on his face.

John was the first to speak. "Let's get out but stay in the background unless we're called." Which we did, hanging out near the base of a cliff which overlooked the parking lot and two buildings, one dilapidated, the other old, vacant looking but still usable from the looks of it.

Gladys pointed to the older building with a sign nailed to its front saying, PRESERVATION PROPERTY – KEEP OUT. "The old Philipsburg dance hall I mentioned during our meeting at Roberta's office. What's left of the old mining town."

I nodded but was more interested in what was happening near one of the two body bags some distance away. To paraphrase the old saying, Chief Kay was madder than a wet hen. She was literally laying into a law enforcement officer, a man in full uniform and two gold stars on each collar. About my height, a little less than six feet, Latino in looks, clean cut in a dark blue or black uniform, well pressed shirt and trousers. I couldn't tell which color, blue or black, at that distance. He had a full head of black hair matched by a neatly trimmed mustache on his upper lip.

"That's Undersheriff Mike Vasquez," John said. "Chief Kay's immediate boss. Sharp guy. Bachelor's Degree in Criminal Justice and Public Safety, graduated from the FBI National Academy. Worked his way up from patrolman through every department. Also active in the community, volunteering as a youth football and baseball coach in Golden. Appointed Undersheriff two or three years back."

I couldn't help but laugh. "Well right now, Mr. Undersheriff's getting his ass reamed by Chief Kay. Let's see if we can get a little closer and hear what's happening."

Inching forward, using a ruby red Nissan Altima as cover, I heard Chief Kay say loud and clear, "God damn it, Mike, that Indian just now this morning became part of my case."

"I didn't know that," Vasquez tried to cut in to no avail.

"No excuse. From what you tell me, that man over there..." she pointed toward a large, bearded man in work clothes being interviewed by crime scene personnel. "That man says Lundgren met the Indian and gave him some papers. The Indian looked at them, tore them up, stomped them in the ground and killed Lundgren by cutting his throat, thank you very much.'

She again pointed toward the bearded man. "And based on what that same man says, who by the way just happened to kill the Indian, it took place between five and five-thirty. Still dark, for God's sake. Why would Lundgren be out here, a frigging parking lot in the middle of nowhere, meeting somebody, presumably this Indian man. If that's the case, it makes me think maybe both of them were somehow mixed up in all this killing shit."

Vasquez stepped back, trying to keep at least spitting distance from the Chief. "C'mon, Kay, I was just tryin' to help. You've been lookin' like you had one foot in the grave all this past week, carryin' that baby around, at the same time refusin' to take maternity leave and tryin' to catch that damn wolf man thing. I have no intention of taking over the case. Fact, you and the Sheriff haven't even cut me in on what's been happening over the last couple'a days. Now how about tellin' me just what *has* been happening?"

"Later, Mike." Looking down at the two body bags, she asked, "Which one's Lundgren?"

Standing beside a young, slightly overweight white man in scrubs boasting a goatee, mustache and, on top of his head, a knot of hair – a man bun I'm told – with a name tag reading 'Wallace Bookman', Dr. Wong said, "Wally says this one's Lundgren. How about unzipping the bag, Wally, so Chief Kay can take a look." As an aside, he added, "Wally's just started med school at CU. Wanted the experience."

"Like you, he likes dead people, huh?" Holding her bulging abdominal area, the Chief looked on as Bookman unzipped the bag far enough to reveal Lundgren's face and throat, the slit, from one side of the throat to the other, barely visible through the blood, now mostly dry, a reddish-brown, a sheath of which stretched down below the bag's opening.

"That's him, poor bastard. Never really liked him, but not a good way to go." She suddenly bent forward for just a moment and gave a short grunt and grimace as though experiencing a sharp pain. Quickly recovering, she said to Bookmen, "Zip him up and let's take a look at the other one."

Turning in our direction, she called, "John, you and Matt come over here. Ms. Knight, you might not want to see this unless you're used to seeing dead people."

Gladys hesitated for a moment before starting forward with John and me. "I'm game," she said.

As we dipped below a line of yellow crime scene tape, I noticed central to the attention of several CSU personnel was a black, late model Ford Explorer and an old rusted-out Chevy Silverado, its left front fender badly scraped, bare metal showing through the eight- to ten-inch wound. I knew immediately it was the pickup truck parked near the bridge over Deer Creek where we'd seen the man panning for gold. "I'll be damned."

"Be damned what?" John asked.

"That pickup truck." I pointed. "The same one we saw –"

Chief Kay cut me off. "John, you know Undersheriff Vasquez? Mike, John Nabhe. John's been helping out as a member of the Denver American Indian Commission after all that Indian shape shifting BS in the local media."

"John," Vasquez said, extending his hand. "Been awhile."

"Mike. Since you coached my nephew's junior football team. Sorry I couldn't have seen you under better circumstances."

I should have known the Undersheriff would already know John since everyone I've met has known him.

John introduced both Gladys and me, Gladys as assistant to Roberta Pine Woman, president of the Indian Commission, and me as having experience with similar type killings in the Four Corners area.

Chief Kay said, "John, take a look at this other one and tell me if he's the one we talked about this morning."

"Wally," Wong said, "Let Mr. Nahbe see the other one and hopefully identify him."

Bookman offered, "Not much to see. Two bullets in the back, apparently one snapped the spinal column, the other in the area of the liver."

After Bookman unzipped the second bag, displaying both chest and face, John moved closer and said, "That's him. Samuel whatever, at the Indian Commission meetings, always complaining about white people desecrating the land."

Without looking at what could be seen of the body, Gladys said, "I called Roberta on our way out here. His last name is Hataali. Samuel Hataali."

"Yeah," Bookman said. "That's the name on his Arizona driver's license."

John thought a moment before saying, "Makes sense. Hataali, Hatathli, somewhat different spellings and pronunciations, but all the same. In other words, shaman, medicine

183

man. Knowledge of the traditional religion, powerful in the curing diseases of both body and spirit, often with incantations. Because of the incantations, they're sometimes called singers. It never wrung a bell with me that... Matt, at the Commission meeting, you recognized him, didn't you?"

"Not at first, but after he tried to strangle me, I finally placed the face and the voice. Our Grand Father Medicine Man from the Four Corners, but I couldn't put a name with the face."

I turned to the others. "My government-funded organization was sponsoring several digs in the Four Corners area. He was determined to stop our investigation into the killings of our workers. He's older now, but yes, I recognized him." To Gladys I asked, "Where did the Paris report say the werewolf of Paris came from?"

"The what?" Undersheriff Vasquez ask, confusion written across his face. "What the hell'er you talkin' about? Werewolf of where?"

"Our unknown killer," I said. "I'll leave it up to Chief Kay to explain. Gladys?

"Chinle, Arizona."

John jumped in. "Chinle, Arizona, Navajo Nation, just south of the Four Corners. I see what you're getting at."

It was time for Chief Kay to interrupt our three-way conversation. "And, so do I. You're thinking Mr. Hataali here could well be the trusted agent, the middle man for our killer, and if so, what the hell did Captain Lundgren have to do with him?"

The last words I said to her were, "You got it, Chief, and that truck over there, the one your people are going through, that's the one –"

A pained expression came over her face as she bent part way and looked down, grabbed her lower abdomen and said, "Oh, my God. Something popped. I think it's... it's happening."

We all saw the spreading stain of moisture on her slacks between her legs. She began to pant, her breath in irregular gasps followed by a grunt, and another.

Dr. Wong grabbed her by the arm and, since I was the closest, ordered, "Help me, Matt. It's the amniotic sack. It's ruptured."

With the Undersheriff's nearby curse, "No shit! Of all the goddamn times," ringing in my ears, I took the Chief by the other arm and said, using the only terminology I knew, "In other words, her water's broken."

"Yes, damn it."

Wong placed his free hand on her abdomen. At the same time, she gave another grunt, followed by a low hum, in and out, softer, louder, softer, louder, interrupted periodically by another grunt as contractions came closer apart.

"Her contractions have started, and I bet my *fung shui* approved cabin in the mountains, she's been feeling them for the past several hours. Damn stubborn woman."

While she continued to moan, every few seconds muttering, "Damn it, damn it to hell," Wong reached behind her back to the pocket on the far side of her jacket, dug around for a moment, then pulled out her car keys. "John, get the Chief's car."

"Why not use the Coroner's van? It's got a gurney or whatever in it."

"Where we place dead bodies? No way. When you get her car over here, open both rear doors and the front passenger door, lower the front seat as level as you can with the back seat to give us more room to work. And Bookman, get us an EMT and call Littleton Adventist Hospital. Tell them we'll be there as soon as we can."

He turned back to one of the people gawking at what was happening. "Crime Scene, I need alcohol and three pair of latex gloves, your largest plastic evidence bags, paper if that's all you've got and something for suction afterwards."

To Bookman, his assistant, "Get me the emergency kit in the van and towels, sheets, anything clean and absorbent."

One of the crime scene people ran over with their large kit on wheels, pulled out a plastic bottle of alcohol and the gloves.

Another handed Gladys several large evidence bins, paper evidence bags and a tube with a bulb-like suction device at one end.

As John braked the Chief's car to a halt, jumped out and opened the two rear and front passenger doors, Wong called, "Ms. Knight, Mr. Berkeley, either of you ever witnessed a delivery?"

Gladys, already at my side, said, "No. I wasn't really into watching when they delivered my daughter. Just pushing and cursing every man I'd ever known."

I added, "I've seen a couple of episodes of *Call the Midwife* on PBS, but –"

"That'll have to do. Both of you, scrub down with this alcohol and get those gloves on. Let's get her in the car. We've got work to do."

Once she was in the car and on the back seat, we pulled off her shoes, slacks and panties, the latter soaking wet with a large blood spot on them. I whispered to Wong, "Problem?"

"No, from the opening of the cervix. Normal."

"Does it normally happen this fast?"

As he worked, bent over and trying to spread her legs and see up the birth canal as best he could, he said, "It happens when it happens. I don't know how long she's been feeling the milder contractions. Keeping it to herself, ignoring it to stay on the case." Straightening up, he breathed, "So far, so good, Kay."

Amidst Chief Kay's grunts and groans, I said, "Gladys, you help Doctor Wong at this end. I'm going around and hold her shoulders, hands or whatever she needs. Here's my jacket to wrap the baby in when it… you know."

Gladys took my hand for a moment and smiled. "Yes, I know."

Once on the other side of the car I leaned over and told Chief Kay, "Doctor Wong says you're doing great." I tucked one of the folded towels Bookman brought over under her head.

Between contractions and loud, agonizing groans, eyes shut against the pain, teeth clinched, she squeezed out, "Great, my ass, *oohhhh*. I told 'em I *grrrrrr* I didn't want a natural birth, damn it, and now see what's happening?"

Between groans, she did open her eyes, and I'll swear to this day, tilted her head back as I held her shoulders, looked me in the face and threatened, "You and Wong, you screw around with my kid like you did the Paris police, I'll kill you."

About the same time, I heard Wong instruct, "Push, Kay, push. It's time."

A handful of screams and the next thing I heard was, "Ahh, the head. Ms. Knight, suction, nose and mouth" Moments later, "The umbilical cord. Use that clamp. I'll do the rest."

To me and I'm sure to Chief Kay, it seemed forever before finally, a healthy looking, film-covered, dark chocolate baby boy emerged. With a firm pop between his shoulders, our new born took his first breath and let out a loud cry. I heard people clapping in the background.

Farther on, Bookman was preparing to load body bags containing Captain James Lundgren and Samuel Hataali into the Coroner's van. I looked down at Chief Kay and her baby boy wrapped in my jacket. It seemed ironic. Two lives savagely snatched away, one just arrived.

Welcome to Life 101, young man.

Chapter 24

As two EMT personnel were getting Chief Kay and her son, Julius Dwayne Sanders, into an emergency response vehicle, more commonly known as an ambulance, Dr. Wong, Gladys and I cleaned up using more of the Crime Scene Techs' alcohol and what remained of a roll of paper towels that mysteriously appeared from somebody's car. With Wong following in the Chief's car, we watched as the ambulance turned left onto Deer Creek Canyon Road headed toward the hospital as arranged by Wally Bookman per Wong's instructions.

By explanation, Chief Kay had earlier whispered her son's predetermined name to me while we waited for the ambulance to arrive: Julius for Julius Irving and Dwayne for Dwayne Wade, her husband's two, all-time favorite pro basketball players.

Satisfied we now had some idea it was the dead man, Samuel Hataali, who more than likely had been coordinating our killer's activities, I was about to usher Gladys and John back to the SUV when I heard a voice calling.

"John, Berkeley, hold up a minute." It was Undersheriff Mike Vasquez. "We need to talk. With Captain Gelespi who heads up our Criminal Investigation Section under Chief Kay still out with the flu, now classified as pneumonia, I'll be taking over for the Chief. Wong's gonna be busy cutting up Lundgren and the Hataali guy, so it's you two who know more than anybody else about the case. I need a quick update. Today, this afternoon, four o'clock my office. Can you make it?"

It was easy to notice that, with his *cutting up* comment, Vasquez didn't show a hell of a lot more remorse over Lundgren's untimely, rather rudely delivered passing than Chief Kay. I've got to admit, while it was a nasty way to go, I never thought very highly of the man. From the get-go, something about his cavalier attitude with Chief Kay, his boss, as well as his cutesy "bat man" comment toward Wong hit me the wrong way.

It was John who first answered the Undersheriff's invitation. "Sorry, Mike, I've got a client begging to meet with me for the last week. I've been putting him off because of all this stuff." John looked at me. "Matt?"

I nodded. "I'll be there. Have to take John to pick up his wheels at the Littleton Police Department before he meets with his client, then Gladys to her office, but I'm good for four o'clock. I'll give you everything I know since I got here from Florida."

I saw the quizzical look on the Undersheriff's face when I mentioned John's wheels and Littleton Police Department. "I'll explain the bit about John's pickup truck and the Littleton Police when we meet."

When he gave me a thumbs-up, the three of us headed for my rental SUV. I opened the front passenger door for Gladys while John piled into the back seat. As I started around the front of the vehicle, I heard my name called, this time from a different direction and barely audible, "Mr. Berkeley."

I turned. The voice had come from my right, but I couldn't see anyone. Again, as if not wanting to attract John's and Gladys's attention, the same voice softly called, "Mr. Berkeley, over here. The red Dodge Ram."

Damned if it wasn't Deputy Innes, but what was he doing here in an Army field uniform with a desert-like camouflage design? Looking back at Gladys and John in the SUV, I raised an index finger and yelled, "Back in one."

Innes was standing on the far side of the truck's cab, apparently not wanting to be seen. Coming around the rear of the truck, I said, "Deputy Innes? What do you want, and why are you in that garb?"

He motioned me forward. "Day off, getting in some hunting. Heading home when I heard the call on the police scanner I keep in my truck. Just didn't want the Undersheriff seeing me.

If he does, there goes my day off. Got a minute?"

"Yes, but did you know who was in one of the body bags?"

"Yes sir. Lundgren. Heard it on the scanner. They didn't know who the other man was at the time. Anyway, need a favor."

That caught me by surprise. Curious to hear what he wanted, I asked, "Why the hell would a Jefferson County Sheriff's deputy need a favor from me? What kind of favor?"

"We need to meet. Tonight, if you're free? Maybe get a beer, my dime. I know things I can't tell anybody else, at least not right now."

"What kind of things? You're losing me."

"About the murders. Things if I tell anybody on the force, I'm dead meat. In other words, either dropped from the force or worse. With your background, working with the CIA, FBI and others like you said back at the park, I just need to talk. Maybe get you to help."

"I didn't tell you anything about my background. Who'd you get that from?"

"From one of the deputies at the crime scene."

I can't say I wasn't interested, but the blaring sound of the SUV's horn added impetus to my decision. "Where and what time?"

"How about the Farm House Restaurant at the Breckenridge Brewery. It's in Littleton off Santa Fe Drive, not far from where you're staying. Eight o'clock. Give me your mobile number and I'll give you directions."

"No need. I'll find it. Eight o'clock. Almost my bedtime, so you better make it interesting."

With that, I rounded the bed of the truck and double timed it back to the SUV. Both Gladys and John chimed in with, "What was that all about?" with John adding, "Wasn't that Deputy Innes?"

Although I wasn't going to mention my late evening plans at the brewery, there was no sense lying about the rest of my conversation with Innes. "He's off today. Out hunting and heard about it on a police scanner in his truck. Knew about Lundgren from the scanner. Wanted to know who the other guy was."

"Why not ask Vasquez?" John asked.

"Scared Vasquez would cancel his day off if he saw him."

"That's BS, and you know it. My guess, he told his immediate boss he's sick."

I let it drop with, "You're probably right."

* * *

The meeting with Under Sheriff Mike Vasquez went well enough. In fact, I liked the guy. He was all business, asked the right questions, some I wasn't prepared to answer about my somewhat questionable dealings with other law enforcement agencies – local, national and international. There was one, however, had I ever killed another human being?

Apparently, somebody, probably Chief Kay, had done their homework on my background to which he'd gained access. Never the less, I considered the killing question off limits within the context of why I was there.

Since he was already versed on the earlier murders and disappearance of the two children, presumably dead, we first covered the news media and graphic wolf man drawings surrounding the horrific murder of Sonny Weaver's girlfriend, which, based on John's request, had drawn me to Colorado in the first place.

This was followed by Roberta Pine Woman's and the Denver American Indian Commission's interest in the case, the Richard Lamb crime scene, the abandoned mine, the burned-down cabin and the deaths of the two men on Pyramid Mountain. And yes, relative to the two men on the mountain, what happened at the restaurant and why John's pickup truck was with the Littleton Police, bullets along the body of the truck and through the rear window into the windshield, including the fight with his insurance company to get everything repaired.

We also covered Gladys's and my meeting with Simon Grant at the Colorado Geological Survey as related to rare earth elements and possible related incidents in other states. I could tell this somewhat satisfied his curiosity concerning Gladys's presence at the parking lot that morning.

Of greatest interest seemed to be John's and my experience during the digs in the Four Corners area, knowledge of Samuel Hataali, both past and present, including of course, the Werewolf of Paris, and how it all seemed to come together.

With exception of the rare earths, Hataali and the Werewolf of Paris, including Wong's hypothesis regarding the man's excessive body hair being a case of congenital hypertrichosis, I got the impression the man was no slouch when it came to knowledge of all the prior events. Certainly, those before I arrived. He'd stayed current on all of Chief Kay's and the crime lab's scene-of-crime reports except notes covering our meetings with Wong and the Chief. The big question which neither he nor I could answer was the Lundgren-Hataali relationship.

It was evident he was trying to sound me out to determine if he wanted to include me in any more of the investigation. This was confirmed when he asked, "Where do you think this wolf man character – think you said his name Keith Nalje from the Paris police report – where he's hiding and what do we need to do?"

"I'm thinking the same as Chief Kay. Pyramid Mountain has been searched from top to bottom and on all sides. So far, no signs of our so-called wolf man. Pretty sure he used the old abandoned mine shaft in Deer Creek Canyon Park back while stalking the homes below. The Chief rented some safety gear and sent two of her people into the mine. Supposedly because of claustrophobia from the hazmat gear and over-the-head breathing apparatus, they didn't get far enough to find anything or anybody. When we first found the mine, I tried to go in, but could only go less than ten feet because of the ammonia odor."

"Ammonia?" he asked, wrinkling his nose at the same time.

"Dr. Wong thinks it's a combination of bats, maybe thousands, farther back in the mine and beetles crawling around and eating bat dung. Beetle waste creating ammonium hydroxide which can be deadly. Also, something else from the bat droppings that can cause a kind of fungus, histo something or another. It causes severe respiratory problems in humans. Put the ammonia and the histo stuff together and they can do a number on the body and brain."

"Then how the hell do we get in there to find out if he's there?"

"Use the gear Chief Kay rented."

"It's not gonna be me, that's for damn sure. Talk about claustrophobic? I couldn't even go with my family into Carlsbad Caverns down in New Mexico as big as it is. If none of our people are willing or able to go, then who?

All the while I'm thinking to myself, *You're probably the biggest fish in the ocean, but you've gone this far, why not take the hook one more time?* "Me. Otherwise it may be too late and you may never know."

Vasquez laughed. "You've gotta be kidding."

I joined in the laughter, only my laugh was on me. "Sounds pretty stupid, doesn't it, but somebody's got to do it. I'm a scuba diver. I'm used to wearing similar gear like Chief Kay rented. I'm not claustrophobic. I also think there's another person who might go in with me."

"Who the hell would be that stu-" Vasquez caught himself before continuing with, "…uh willing to do that?"

I had to laugh again. "You're right. Stupid, but Dr. Wong would consider it scientific exploration. He's into bats big time, but if I go, I'm going armed."

Vasquez thought for a moment before saying, "You got it. Deputy Dog for a day. The Sheriff can swear you in and we'll issue you something from the armory for the time it takes to go in and out. Tomorrow, be here at eight a.m. and we'll go from here, but what about Wong?"

"I'll stop by the Coroner's office on my way out. I'm betting he'll jump at the offer. Understand it's one of the buildings farther up on Jefferson County Parkway. Have those two sets of hazmat and breathing equipment ready. And by the way, I prefer a Beretta M-9, ten-round magazine with nine-millimeter hollow points or something similar. And before I forget, what's happening to the guy who shot Hataali?"

"He's coming into the office tomorrow, but the best we can determine, he saw and heard the argument, saw Hataali attack and cut Lundgren and shot Hataali to keep him from doing any more damage. Too late, the damage had already been done, but he couldn't know that. We'll determine what action to take tomorrow once we've interviewed him and the other witnesses."

After stopping by to see Dr. Wong, who when asked, said, "Damn right, I'll go," I hit rush afternoon traffic on C-470 South, the main route to my hotel in Littleton.

With a quick stop to purchase a bottle of Jameson Irish Whiskey for its well-known therapeutic and mellowing affect after a long day, it was a little after five-thirty before I slid the room key card into and out of the slot beneath the door handle.

Pushing open the door I took only the first step before blurting out, "Gladys, how the hell did you get in here?"

She smiled, removed her tortoise shell glasses, started unbuttoning her blouse and said, "I need a shower. How about you?"

Chapter 25

I must admit, a beautiful woman has always taken priority over most other things in my life. With that in mind, I can't remember when I've had such a memorable shower. It sure as hell made me forget about Mr. Jameson and his delectable blend of Irish whiskey.

Later while snuggled beneath the covers of a king-size bed, tracing lightly the outlines of Gladys's face, her shoulders and down into the cleft between her breasts, I said, "Not that I have any reservations about your surprise visit, but how *did* you get in? Tell the front desk you're my wife or somehow jimmy the door's electronic lock system?"

She tilted her head slightly in my direction and smiled. "No to the wife thing. As to picking the lock, I've gained various talents during what I consider my first life other than simply being a paralegal. I suppose you could say my work with Roberta was and is my second career."

I couldn't help but chuckle. "You danced your way around that one. Explain."

Shifting to her side and leaning closer, the touch of her skin and the warmth of her body against mine almost made me forget wanting an explanation. In fact, all I could think about was how perfect we fit together.

My momentary mental lapse was interrupted when she answered, "If you recall, I said in the meeting with Chief Kay and Doctor Wong that I accompanied my husband when he was posted to Luxembourg with IBM several years ago. All true, except the IBM part. We were recently married CIA operatives assigned to our Embassy in the Duchy of Luxembourg's capital, the City of Luxembourg. That was in Nineteen eighty-eight.

"Our work encompassed several adjacent countries: France, Germany and Belgium with emphasis both on Berlin after the wall came down and Brussels as NATO Headquarters. Both cities were at that time flooded with Soviet GRU, their military intelligence operatives, and KGB, its foreign intelligence side, reorganized as the SVR in early nineties when the Soviet Union regurgitated itself into the Russian Federation.

"As you can guess, we were both quite young. Only Roberta knows my background. Why I'm telling you this, I'm not really sure." She paused momentarily, her expression betraying her uncertainty. "I suppose there's something about you and... and what we just shared."

Admittedly, her admission to having been a CIA agent was one hell of a twist.

Continuing, she said, "I was in Brussels when my husband, Walter, was on assignment in Germany, somewhere near the Polish border. This was not long after Poland had declared its independence as a satellite state of the Russian Federation. Things were terribly unsettled, Russia still smarting from the loss of Poland and East Germany.

"I knew there was some danger to this specific assignment, but I never knew exactly why he was there or what he was doing. That was par for the course for both of us. Neither knowing details about the other's assignment unless it entailed a husband and wife cover.

"In a nut shell, he disappeared. I never saw him again. I waited three months. During that time, I found out I was pregnant. With no word and no help from either our embassy or the German's in determining what happened, I returned to the States and took a leave of absence. It was then that I gave birth to my daughter, Beverly Ann, and my husband was declared dead by the Company, still with no explanation as to why or how he died."

I was at a loss for words and, yes, mesmerized by Gladys's revelations.

"Following this rather lengthy rejuvenation period, I

worked in the Operations Directorate in Langley, part of the Intelligence and Foreign Affairs office. Once Beverly Ann was old enough to stay with my mother who was still alive and lived in Denver, I served in several other overseas assignments in the Far East and South America, many visits back to see Beverly Ann, until the Company seemed to lose its original luster. That was a little over ten years ago when I came back home. I never remarried."

"Your daughter, Beverly Ann?"

"Married, teaches psychology at the College of William and Mary, Williamsburg, Virginia. Husband's a biomedical sciences professor. Two boys, twins, six years old. See them once or twice a year." She laughed softly. "As I look back on my life, I have to think their lives must be boring as hell."

"And you're happy with what you're doing, working with Roberta?"

"It's interesting, but I have to admit, not the same kind of excitement and sense of fulfillment of doing something for your country. As for you, through several of my old contacts, I've been able to patch together a few interesting tidbits about you, Mr. ex-Navy Commander Matthew William Berkeley. London with our agent, Royce Hawkins, otherwise known as The Hawk who didn't especially like your independent attitude."

"He was an ass."

"And of course, followed sometime later, the Island of St. Michael in the Caribbean where you killed him."

"He was trying to kill his daughter and me. Rather than him killing us, I simply returned the favor. I succeeded where he failed."

"England and Northern Ireland working with New Scotland Yard's Special Branch."

"People in Northern Ireland killed a friend of mine and kidnapped a British admiral and a woman I knew, threatening to kill her and the Admiral."

"Yes, so I was told." She shifted slightly, gave me an

I-know-everything look along with that luscious smile of hers. "An Admiral Sir William Douglas, First Sea Lord of the Admiralty. Your life is an open book, Matt Berkeley."

Shaking my head, all I could say was, "At the Prime Minister's request, I had no choice but to do what I did."

She went on with, "Then there's the German City of Koblenz and a secret document from World War Two."

"Lives were lost, and I fought back."

"And finally, from my friends, what happened and why you left Paris the way you did which I promise not to tell Chief Kay. I suppose it's these kinds of things that really stirred my interest, plus what I've seen since our first meeting. Otherwise, I'd still be the little old gray-haired, quiet mannered Miss Paralegal to you. Definitely not feeling the excitement of suddenly finding myself part of a murder investigation and in bed with the man I met only a few days ago, no matter how attracted I am to him."

My overall response was confirmed by a rather inane muttering of, "Wow!"

Pulling away and sitting up on her side of the bed, she stood and turned back to me. Her body was silhouetted by the glow of a small table lamp, its light caressing the silvery gleam of her hair and the creamy softness of her skin. All I could add was, "You're beautiful, Gladys. If tonight is the result, for the first time in my life, I'm glad someone, that someone being you, decided to look into my past."

Picking up her clothes from a chair where she'd dropped them earlier on our way to the shower, she headed toward the bathroom. Before closing the door, she looked back and said, "Once I'm dressed, you can tell me what that deputy said to you this morning and why he thinks you can help with whatever problem he has. You instead of his own people."

I couldn't help but chuckle and shake my head at the improbability of it all. "Good question. First met him at a crime scene up near the Deer Creek Canyon Park. Supposedly heard some gossip about me from one of the deputies at the scene or maybe from John. I don't know."

Before closing the door, she said, "My sixth sense tells me, if he's afraid to tell his superiors, it concerns the murders, but I think it's more than that. I think, somehow, he's been caught up in the mystery surrounding the Lundgren man. Things much bigger than him. For that reason, you need me and don't say no. Understand?"

As she closed the door, all I could do was nod.

* * *

Breckenridge Brewery's Farm House Restaurant, sitting directly across from the brewery, didn't look anything like the farm house where my grandmother used to live. Far from it, but it had a friendly atmosphere, and from the looks and sounds from the bar strategically placed not more than twenty feet from the entrance, pretty much a fun place.

The bar was a large rectangular shaped affair with a two-sided working and serving area in the middle. I could only see one working side of the bar, but a quick count showed me twenty or more beer taps in operation serving beer, ales, stouts, etc. A large dining area stood off to the left. While not blasting away at our eardrums, we could hear country western music in the background.

I saw Innes sitting alone near one end of the bar. He was dressed in civvies: jeans, an un-tucked blue and white checkered shirt, cowboy boots and a leather jacket hanging from the back of the bar stool. I wondered if the shirt was un-tucked to hide a sidearm and holster attached to his belt. Nevertheless, a good-looking kid, probably in his early to mid-thirties, about my height, dirty blond hair, clean shaven. Athletic build, but not as thick through the chest and shoulders as he appeared in uniform or in the camouflage ACU's he was wearing that morning. Hate it when these young guys make me feel sixtyish and above with the grim reaper drawing closer with each passing day.

He didn't see us until we walked up behind him and I said,

"Deputy Innes."

Holding a glass mug of beer, more of a large goblet than a mug, he turned on the bar stool, saw Gladys and almost dropped his beer. "You shouldn't've –"

"Wait a minute," I interrupted, holding a hand up to silence him. "Her name's Gladys Knight. She knows as much about what's been happening as I do and got more experience in this kind of stuff than you or me. *Big time.* You apparently have a problem with Lundgren and the investigation, and she's here to help. We're both hungry, so let's get a table in the dining room so we can talk."

Not sure that pacified the young deputy, but not my worry. As I said, he was the one with the problem or so he'd indicated that morning. We were there to listen.

A young lady took us to the rear of the restaurant and seated us near a large stone fireplace with a fire that was perfect for a chilly, late October night. Gladys and I sat on a cushioned sofa with our backs to the wall, facing Innes in a straight back wooden chair on the other side of the table. With a family of five at an adjacent table, there was only small talk about the weather and Innes's supposed unsuccessful hunting expedition earlier in the day until the waitress took our orders.

Innes ordered only another beer since he said he'd already eaten at the bar. For Gladys and me, however, amorous moments had definitely improved our appetites, leading to a butternut squash Alfredo for her and one of those "better-than-you're-momma-used-to-make" meatloaf dinners for me. Since the restaurant was part of the brewery, Gladys had an on-tap glass of Breckenridge Vanilla Porter, a dark, rather sweetish ale, and I settled for their Avalanche Amber Ale which quickly became one of my favorite brews.

For the most part, silence prevailed until Gladys and I were halfway through with dinner when the family sitting one table over finally departed. Taking a sip of ale, I asked Innes, "Why did you ask me for help? Why not John Nabhe? You know him, he knows you."

Innes thought a moment before saying, "He also knows Chief Kay, the Sheriff and the Undersheriff as well as half the force. Great guy, but for that reason, I couldn't trust him.

"You're an out-of-towner and seemed like you didn't give a shit. Uh, sorry Ma'am, I..." He looked down and gave a quick shake of his head as though attempting to hide his embarrassment before looking up and continuing. "I only hope I can trust you. Both of you, I mean."

Gladys chuckled. "I don't think you have to worry about Matt or your description of him. Talking with some past colleagues in my old job, the man shares very little until he's sure of what he's doing and what he's got. The words they used were, and I quote, 'Sometimes a rogue operator who ignores his superiors, but still gets the job done.'"

Innes gave Gladys a strange, questioning look. "What was your old job?"

She looked at me and smiled. "Since the cat's already out of the bag and we're asking Deputy Innes to trust us, let's just say, in my job, we called ourselves The Company."

"Oh."

I saw the proverbial light bulb go off in Innes's eyes.

"Yes, ma'am, I was an Army Ranger. I think I understand. I met some of your Company people in Afghanistan."

Looking around the dining room, I knew it was getting late since most of the tables had emptied and were being cleaned and reset by the wait staff in preparation for the next day. Finishing the rest of my meatloaf which was good, but not better than my momma used to make, I said in a much-lowered voice, "Now that that's out of the way, let's talk about your problem."

It took a pot of black coffee for all of us to ward off the effects of the ale as Innes told us what had been happening between Lundgren and him. Money on the side from some unknown source paid to him to keep Lundgren informed of what was going on in the Deer Creek murder case since Lundgren felt he was being cut out of the loop.

The final straw was Lundgren's demand to kill "The Indian," coupled with the man's threat against Innes's mother and sister if he didn't make the kill. And if Lundgren didn't take care of his mother and sister, some kind of mysterious higherup's would. Innes's story also included the fact that he had been a decorated sniper in Afghanistan, the M-110 sniper rifle and why he was wearing the camouflage fatigues that morning.

It was Gladys who broke the silence following Innes's explanation. "You're telling us you were there that morning to kill *'the Indian'*, but only reason you didn't kill *'the Indian'* was because *'the Indian'* killed Lundgren and some bystander killed *'the Indian'*. Right?"

"No, no." Innes shook his head. Taking a quick sip of his coffee, he explained, "With the threat against my mom and sister, whatever it cost me, I decided I was gonna kill Lundgren. Thank God, I didn't have to. I... I didn't want to kill anybody. Not like that, not in cold blood." Innes leaned over the table in our direction as if to emphasize what he was going to say. "Whether you believe me or not, it's true. I've done my share of killing in Afghanistan. I don't need a medal for one more."

Our waitress approached the table with a leather folder containing the check. Laying it on the table, she said, "I'm sorry, but we close at ten."

I took the folder, pulled out a credit card from my wallet and said, "We're through." When she left to do the credit card thing, I asked, "So what is it you want us to do?" *Us* being the operative word since I knew, if I agreed to help, Gladys was in this with me all the way.

"We need to get into Lundgren's home. His wife divorced him and took their two kids about two years ago so he lives, or I should say, *lived* alone. Look for something, anything that tells us who he was working for. The people he threatened would kill my mom and sister if I didn't kill the Indian. His place is in Golden, but I can't do it alone. I need more eyes and hands to do a proper search."

Gladys looked at me and I looked at her. I knew we were thinking the same thing. Someone, some organization higher up was pulling the strings for the killings and the land grab, land not meant for a theme park. It was someone big enough and financially powerful enough to go after lands, not only in Colorado, but in various other States, with known or expected reserves of rare earth elements. Things were starting to make more and more sense.

After the waitress returned with my check, I added a gratuity, signed and retrieved the credit card.

Gladys looked at me with a sly, rather mischievous grin and said, "I honestly had other plans, but breaking and entering will definitely add a bit of déjà vu to the evening."

Chapter 26

With the three of us in my leased SUV, not as colorful and easily recognized as Innes's red pickup truck, it took us slightly past eleven o'clock before we turned into a community located on the northwest side of Golden. The lighted, ornately designed sign at the entrance read TABLE ROCK RANCH. It was followed by what at one time must have served as a guard house for a gated community, now lighted but vacant.

For a lot of private communities, the cost of gated security has become too much for the few benefits it provided. If someone really wanted to get in to cause whatever mischief they planned, they'd get in regardless of some semi-retired, half asleep night watchman sitting in a gate house watching TV.

As we drove through the community, slow enough to look for the address, it was easy to see why there had once been a gate and guard house. Most of the homes, all large two- and even three-story affairs with more than likely finished basements, looked like they would be in the several million-dollar range or higher. If Lundgren could afford to live here on what I imagined his salary to be, either he or his ex-wife were independently wealthy. As Innes implied, there could well be under-the-table money coming from somewhere other than the Jefferson County Sheriff's Department. I seriously doubt, however, it's that kind of money, regardless of what he's been doing.

Having turned onto a street called Table Rock Circle, Innes said, "There, on the right." He stuck an arm from the back seat between Gladys and me and pointed toward a two-story home. The first-floor exterior was rough stone half way up, the rest darkly stained cedar shingles continuing through the second floor, the roof made of slate or some other non-composition material. A covered entrance porch swept the left side of the house, a low banister-like fence separating the edge of the porch from the lawn area. A couple of flower baskets hung from just below the roof line above the fence's railing indicating a woman's touch was still present. Or else Lundgren hadn't bothered to take them down following the divorce.

Sconce wall lights illuminated three garage doors to the right side of the porch. The smallest of the three was sized for a large riding mower or more than likely a golf cart. The golf cart made sense remembering, once inside the community, we passed the entrance to a club house and a par three golf course.

Like most of the homes we passed, at least a third of Lundgren's roof was covered by a large patch of solar panels, each reflecting light from the three-quarter moon. That bothered me. Moonlight wasn't exactly what we needed for our intended mission. The darker the better.

From what I could tell in the darkness, it was a lovely home with a well-manicured front lawn, several neatly kept flower beds, small shrubs and a single Aspen tree having already lost many of its leaves. Either Lundgren contracted a lawn maintenance service, or he did it himself. With what little I had learned about the man, I doubted the latter was the case. Again, how did Lundgren afford this kind of home?

"I'm going to park farther around the circle in case the neighbors have been watching TV and know Lundgren's dead." We continued until I found a spot shaded from the moonlight by a maple tree, its remaining autumn leaves still offering a brilliant red in the glow of a nearby street lamp.

Before we got out, Gladys rummaged through the small purse she had, found what she wanted and put whatever it was in her jacket pocket. My wild imagination envisioned my ex-CIA operative carrying a lady-sized semiautomatic, blazing away at the bad guys.

It was a leisurely walk past three other homes as though we were locals out for a late-evening stroll before we reached the shadows of Lundgren's covered front porch. Just to the right of the door was a bank of three windows covered on the inside by a single curtain. Between the windows and the door was a piece of clear plastic-covered paper taped to the wall with the words, ENTRANCE PROHIBITED BY ORDER OF THE JEFFERSON COUNTY SHERIFF'S DEPARTMENT. Since the home wasn't where Lundgren's murder had taken place, there was no crime scene tape, just the warning.

Speaking in a hushed tone, I asked Innes, "Looks like your brothers in blue have already been here. You don't' happen to have keys, do you?"

"No, but my coat can pad my elbow when I put it though one of these windows."

"Absolutely not," whispered Gladys. With that, she pulled out a set of pick locks from one of her jacket pockets. I could only suppose the set of picks and not a weapon was what she had earlier taken from her purse. As she positioned herself in front of the door, she said, "Never know when you might need these."

"You really did work for the Company, didn't you?" Innes said with renewed respect in his voice.

"For a while," she answered. With a couple of clicks, she turned the knob and added as we entered, "Better than broken glass all over the place."

Once inside and the door closed, I felt for the dead latch and relocked the door. As one would expect in such an affluent community, the low hum of a security alarm was barely audible from somewhere in the back of the house. We had only seconds before it would be sounding an alarm, notifying its parent security company and, for all we knew, the Golden police.

"Got it," Innes said, immediately disappearing into the darkness like he knew his way around. Moments later, the hum went silent.

As soon as he returned, Gladys remarked, "To have been able to shut off the alarm, we can only assume you've been here before."

In response he said, "Been here twice, the second time alone playing delivery boy. That's when he gave me the code to the security alarm."

"In that case, where do we start and what do we look for?"

Innes switched on a flash light, its reddish beam pointed to a large, rectangular door mat covering a stone floor. "Red filter over the lens. Less likely to be seen from outside." He directed it around the area. The light revealed that we were standing in a large entrance hall beneath a cathedral ceiling.

"Here." Innes handed me a similar lens-covered flash light from one of his coat pockets. "I only have two. Didn't know Ms. Knight would be with us. To answer the rest of your question," he directed to Gladys, "security alarm was straight back in the kitchen by the door going out to the garage. Easy enough.

"So far as my time here with Lundgren, we met in the living room over there." He ran the beam across the floor to a set of wide double doors opening on a large room with various pieces of heavy leather furniture and a large stone fireplace caught in the loom of the light.

"I did use a bathroom off what looked like a master bedroom down here, but never been upstairs, basement neither. He told me he had a family room down below, a finished basement with recreation area for the kids and a workout room, weights, treadmill, that kind of stuff."

"So where do you want us to look?" I asked.

"I'll take down here," he said. "The family room, a master bed room, kitchen, dining, and so forth. You take upstairs. If you don't find anything interesting, we'll meet in the basement. Knowing families, there has to be some kind of office, somewhere to keep personal things, bills, checks, house payments."

Following Innes's directions and guided by our single flashlight, Gladys and I headed up a set of carpeted stairs. Off a hallway that stretched from one side of the house to the other, there were two bedrooms facing the front of the house, each with its own oversized bathrooms. Of the two bedrooms, it was apparent they were for Lundgren's children.

One was definitely a boy's room with framed Colorado Rockies baseball, Denver Bronco football and Colorado Avalanche hockey logos. Various other sports paraphernalia hung on the walls including an autographed Bronco helmet, an autographed Rockies baseball bat and a set of crossed hockey sticks and a puck mounted just above the middle of the "X".

A small book case contained an entire collection of Harry Potter books along with several youth-related science fiction books and sports magazines. A walk-in closet contained clothes for a boy about twelve, maybe thirteen years old.

The second was a young girl's bedroom with all pink and white furniture, signed pictures of various female pop singers: Ariana Grande, Demi Levato, Katy Perry, Taylor Swift, Céline Dion with Dion's likeness superimposed over a poster for the movie *Titanic*.

The comforter on the bed resembled a show bill for the stage musical *Frozen*. Gladys informed me the show had made its pre-Broadway debut in Denver a couple of years back. Clothes in the closet and chest of drawers indicated the girl was more than likely nine or ten years old. Though divorced, it was apparent Lundgren still had visitation rights for his children.

"Thank God the kids aren't here," Gladys said as we crossed the hallway to a much larger room, the size of a master-bedroom if not larger but furnished as an office. Three large windows with open blinds looked down on a spacious backyard. Moonlight was bright enough to see the outer extremity of a stone patio that seemed to stretch the length of the house, pieces of outdoor furniture and a fire pit.

To the left was a playground with a swing set and sliding board, their metallic surfaces shining in the moonlight. Across the lawn on the other side stood a trampoline installed over a wide sandy area, I suppose for a landing as soft as possible should you take one bounce too many in the wrong direction.

Most interesting, however, was the fact there were no homes to the rear of the property, only open countryside with the darkened image of what Gladys called North Table Mountain in the distance.

Regardless of whether or not there were people living behind the house, we drew the blinds and switched on a table lamp. A dark cherry colored executive desk was placed so a person could enjoy the view of the mountain. In addition to the lamp, the desk was covered with a quarter inch piece of glass, individual pictures of the two children, a fountain pen set, an all-in-one, touch-enabled computer with wireless keyboard and a telephone/answer machine combo. Getting a hand towel from the office's adjoining bathroom to keep from leaving finger prints, Gladys activated the computer, but it was password protected.

Staring at the computer, she said, "If we only had the time, I might be able to..." She left it at that as she started opening the drawers on one side of the desk while I tried the other side.

The drawers might as well have been password protected in terms of content interest or lack thereof: extra pens, a ream or more of typing paper, unopened cartons of HP black and color ink for a printer sitting on a side table, a check book and several file folders containing various household bills, insurance, mortgage and homeowner association statements.

It was Gladys who, opening the swinging doors on a closet, discovered a two-drawer file cabinet. On top of the cabinet sat a medium-sized, combination-lock Sentry Safe. "Bingo!" she said.

I crossed the room and took a look at the safe. "Unfortunately, I'm not too swift with combination locks. You?"

She looked at me with a half-smile. "Once upon a time, long, long ago, in a galaxy far away named Camp Peary in Virginia, otherwise known as The Farm, there was a course. You know the rest. This towel's too thick. Got a handkerchief?"

I handed her a handkerchief. "It's clean."

Unfolding it to a single layer of cloth, she knelt before the safe and began manipulating the dial, slowly, listening for clicks that I never heard. Back and forth until Innes walked into the room.

"Nothing down below," he said. "Thought I'd see what's happening up here. Anything?"

Otherwise ignoring his entrance, her reply was, "Shhhhh." She tried the safe's handle twice without success, but following more turnings of the dial – right, left, right – the third time was the charm. The door opened to a safe filled with several files and two drawers in the lower half. Continuing to use the handkerchief, she opened both drawers, one at a time.

"Anything?" I asked.

"Money in each. Looks like stacks of fifty- and hundred-dollar bills. Could be several thousand dollars here. Wonder if he's been cheating on his alimony and child support payments?"

"Probably payments from the mysterious people he talked about," Innes said, looking over Gladys's shoulder. "Cash, tax free."

"Those file folders," I said. "If we're looking for anything incriminating, something that would link him to Samuel Hataali, those folders might be our best bet."

Gladys pulled one. "Closing papers for the house." A second one. "State and federal income tax filings." The third folder, however, caught her attention. She very quickly poured over several of the pages inside the file, thumbed through several more until she found a newspaper clipping and an envelope. "Interesting."

With a groan, as though her knees refused to work, she stood, forcing us to back our way to the desk and its lamp. "This might be what you're looking for, Deputy." Careful to use the hand towel once again, she shifted the computer to the side of the desk and spread the papers as well as the newspaper clipping out for us to see.

"A case down in Douglas County, the county seat, Castle Rock, to be exact. July, two thousand six. The top two pages are a letter signed by someone using only the letter 'B'."

As I read, Innes at my side, all I could say after reading the letter was, "You've got to be kidding." Sidestepping over to the newspaper clipping, there he was in all his glory, Patrolman James Lundgren, dark sunglasses, black helmet, black leather jacket standing with another patrolman next to their motorcycles, the words DOUGLAS COUNTY SHERIFF'S DEPARTMENT stenciled just below the motorcycle's wind screen.

From what I could tell based on the two-page letter and a quick read of the newspaper article, Lundgren stopped a car, found packs of methamphetamine and cocaine, cash and killed two Latinos, a man and woman. Investigation revealed the deceased male had a thirty-eight revolver in his possession. Killing was ruled justified because Lundgren feared for his life when the deceased reached for the weapon. The woman's death was called accidental. In other words, collateral damage.

The undated letter, however, told a different story. As Gladys said, it was signed by a person using only the letter "B". This person was in some capacity part of the staff for the Eighteenth Judicial District at the time of the event. Somehow B knew Lundgren planted the thirty-eight on the deceased male, took several thousands in cash and killed the man and his female companion to cover it up.

It didn't say how B knew, but this person was now blackmailing Lundgren to do whatever he had to do to secure certain land in Jefferson County. Who for? No indication. Otherwise, B would have the Douglas County case reopened with newly found evidence. The corker was that Lundgren was to contact a Navajo Indian named Hataali who had a way to significantly influence the outcome, regardless of the cost, human or otherwise.

An account had already been established in Lundgren's name in the Rocky Mountain Savings and Loan with funds from an offshore source as well as one in a California bank.

"That's why Lundgren was so interested in what was happening in the investigation," Innes said, backing away from the desk. "Chief Kay, who everybody knew didn't like Lundgren, kept him at arm's length.

"Of course, Lundgren felt like he'd been passed over when she made Chief, especially since she was a woman and a black woman to boot. Put all that together and I'm sure that's why Lundgren slipped me the money to keep him in the picture. Damn!"

Gladys nodded to the letter and newspaper article and asked, "Think all that's interesting? Look at these." She placed the contents of the accompanying envelope she'd taken from the folder on the desk and spread them out.

Innes and I shifted around for a better view of seven different color pictures, each showing Lundgren in different poses, none of which indicated he was aware he was being photographed.

"No shit!" was Innes's initial response. "Uh, sorry, ma'am, but talk about hot, these things are more than hot. Lundgren would've been under the jail if these things had gotten out."

I had to agree. Each photo had been taken using a thermographic or infrared camera at night, date and time noted in the bottom right of each photograph. The first picture showed Lundgren standing outside a car, weapon drawn, the car's driver-side window lowered. Lundgren's exposed face and hands as well as the car's hood and grill appeared bright yellow from heat, all the way down the to an orange tinted red showing somewhat lesser heat levels.

There were obviously two people in the car, their skin areas through the windshield a darker yellow than Lundgren's. Lundgren's clothes and the body of the car merged down into a deep purple in the coolness of the night air. Surrounding trees, grasses, the asphalt surface of the road were in various shades of light to dark purple dropping to total black in the darker areas.

The first four of the photographs were obviously taken from a point some distance off from the front of the stopped automobile using a zoom lens. Blurred images of dark purple-colored leaves in the top right-hand corner of each indicated the photographer was hidden.

The first and second photos showed Lundgren apparently exchanging words with the inhabitants of the car. A third showed Lundgren, handgun pointed into the open window and a bright yellow spurt of flame fired from the end of the weapon. Photo number four showed Lundgren, weapon apparently holstered, putting on gloves while a fifth had what appeared to be him reaching toward the open window with something in his hand.

"Possibly the planted thirty-eight revolver found on the deceased driver, maybe putting it in his lap" I said.

"You think?" Gladys asked.

"Gotta be," Innes said. "What else?"

Either some photographs were missing, or there was a lapse of time when the next photo was taken. It showed Lundgren standing behind the car, trunk lid open, leaning into the trunk with what looked like one of those cloth bags in his hands, the kind people use for grocery shopping. Everything was a deep purple color except for Lundgren's face and hands and two holes on either side of the man's legs – the still warm double exhaust pipes. His motorcycle was parked several yards to the rear, the engine beneath the gas tank still a bright yellow from the heat. The last photograph pictured Lundgren standing by his motorcycle, an obviously full bag of something being placed in a container mounted over the motorcycle's rear wheel.

We stood for a moment, staring down at the montage of thermal images until Gladys broke the silence. "Between the first and the last two photos, the photographer either had time enough to shift position to get the trunk lid shots, or there were two people snapping pictures."

"Agreed," I put in. "I'd also have to say, whoever snapped the photos must have known Lundgren was already a dirty cop and had some idea when and where the action was going to take place. Both that person with the camera and Lundgren may have been tipped off, and Lundgren had the location staked out, just waiting. It's apparent somebody else was waiting"

It was Innes's turn. "Whatever they knew or thought they knew, rather than turning the pictures over to the proper authority, they decided to keep it to themselves for this kind of use in the future. Blackmail in case they ever needed it."

Shaking her head, Gladys explained, "All very well, but we can't use them. Otherwise, they – your people – will want to know how Deputy Innes, as well as Matt and yours truly, suddenly came into possession of such damning information."

Innes looked like a corrected puppy with its tail between its legs, glancing from one side of the room to the other as though searching for an answer to Gladys's statement. "I don't know. I don't know what the hell I can do." Facing the two of us, he asked, "Any ideas?"

I was the first to answer. "We know this B character must still have some pull in legal circles, has had Lundgren on a leash, threatening to ruin the man's life if he didn't do as he was told."

"And we also know," Gladys said, "not only B but somebody or some mysterious organization, the likely source of the offshore money, its higher-ups whoever they may be, are involved, the ones Lundgren threatened you with, Deputy. Like Simon Grant over at Colorado Geo said, it's not just local. We're talking Colorado, Wyoming and the other states he mentioned with the potential for rare earth deposits –"

Innes broke in with, "What's that?"

"Like the letter said, land. Potentially extremely valuable land," I explained.

"We'll discuss it later," Gladys said while preparing to photograph the papers with her smart phone. "But who is B and how could he, thirteen years after the fact, be able to wield such power over Lundgren? I –"

The crash of glass being broken somewhere downstairs suddenly turned our completely illegal, night time visit upside down. "We've got visitors, folks," I whispered, "and I'll bet they're looking for the same thing we were."

Gladys placed the photos back in the envelope, swept all the papers into a neat pile, placed everything into the folder and rushed across the room to the closet. Once everything was back in the safe and the door closed, she spun the tumbler away from any of the correct numbers.

That done, I turned off the desk lamp, the initial darkness leaving us partially blind, and asked Innes, "You armed?"

"Yes sir. Smith and Wesson M&P, nine mil. Don't want to use it, but there's only one way we're gonna find out who's down there. Breaking their way in, you can bet your ass it's not the law. Let's go."

Turning off the table lamp and switching on his flash light with the red lens for night vision, he retrieved the relatively small, almost snub-nosed semiautomatic handgun from a holster beneath his shirt and motioned us to follow. As we made our way along the hallway and down the stairs, we could hear someone turning over the heavy leather furniture in the family room, ripping open cushions and the protective cloth covering beneath the furniture.

Simultaneously, someone else was snatching drawers from their cabinets in the adjacent dining area and letting their contents crash to the floor: eating utensils, plates, bowels, glass ware. Whoever it was didn't give a damn about hiding the fact they were here or had been here once they left.

Feeling a cool breeze filling the entrance way, in addition to a busted-out front window in the living room, I saw they had opened the front door, leaving it ajar apparently for a fast escape.

Almost to the bottom of the stairs, we heard what sounded like an order, one person to another, only in a foreign language. "Chinese," Gladys whispered.

At the same time, Innes eased his way down the last step and yelled, "Police, on the floor, hands behind your back."

More rapid Chinese followed by several shots in our direction. I grabbed Gladys who was two steps in front of me and pulled her back onto the stairs. With my usual agility, I tripped, fell backwards, and we both landed against the next four steps up, my back cushioning the fall, Gladys on top of me. Trying to quickly replace the air that had been forced out of my lungs by hitting the edges of the steps, I started to roll the two of us over and place myself on top of her.

More bullets! Halfway over, I saw Innes's flashlight fly out of his hand. Another volley of bullets followed the reddish light in its flight across the room. Rounds ricocheted off the stone floor, the sound in the confined area stabbing at my ears like a dozen jackhammers.

Two shadows raced by toward the open door. Innes, on his knees holding his right shoulder, was still able to follow the back of one of the shadows with a green laser integrated just below the pistol's barrel. He got off two rounds.

One of the men screamed and stumbled. The second man pulled him through the door with one hand, his weapon in the other hand, spraying bullets wildly into the walls and ceiling as they went. We were hunkered down like knots on a log trying to keep from being hit by stray bullets or shrapnel. Son of a bitch must have had a thirty-round magazine in that damn thing.

The slamming of car doors and the screech of tires on asphalt told us it was safe to stand, but how to get out of the house without people seeing us? Surely the whole world had heard the gunfire.

Innes was the first to react. "Quick," he said. "Back door to the patio. Open field out back. While all the neighbors are watching the front of the house and calling nine-one-one, we go over the back fence."

Picking up Innes's still glowing flashlight, I asked, "You okay? Looked like you –"

"Yeah, shoulder." He moved his arm up and down. With a slight grunt, he added, "Probably just a graze. I'm good. We gotta go. Double around behind some of the houses and back to the SUV."

And that's what we did. An ignominious retreat, I admit but, by all accounts the safest of any other option. Three houses over along the circle, we found a cinder-topped hiking trail leading down from nearby North Table Mountain. It ran between two homes into the community and out to the street.

The wail of sirens, growing louder by the second, was already cutting slices out of the night air. Taking up a nonchalant stride, we walked almost directly to the SUV, meeting several couples heading in the direction of Lundgren's house.

One of the men asked, "You know what's happening?"

Gladys answered. "Don't know. We were taking a late-night walk on the trail back there. Sounded like fireworks over that way." She pointed in the direction of Lundgren's house.

We moved on, got into the SUV and waited for the sirens to wind down once they reached what was now a crime scene. Only then did I start the engine and pull away minus headlights until we completed the circle. Slowing, I looked back to Innes in the back seat. "We've got to get that shoulder taken care of. Where's the nearest emergency room?"

"Negative. They're required to report gunshot wounds. It's just a scratch."

I watched in the rearview mirror as he again moved his right arm up and down to demonstrate. I thought I saw a frown on his face from a sharp pain, but I wasn't sure in the dark.

"There's an ex-Navy hospital corpsman over near where I live. With the Marines in Afghanistan same time I was. He'll take care of it."

By this time, I felt it safe enough to turn on the headlights. With a relieved swoosh of exhaled air from my lungs, we exited the fashionable Table Rock Ranch community, leaving what little paper evidence we found giving weight to Captain James Lundgren's relationship to Samuel Hataali and a man named B. Though we now knew there was the possibility of Chinese involvement, here again, as with the paper evidence and the mysterious B person, there was no one we could tell, and even if there was, no way to prove it.

Chapter 27

Dawn had yet to break through low hanging clouds over Golden, Colorado and the adjacent western foothills, promising a dreary, somewhat windy start for the day when the phone rang. He grumbled as he maneuvered his substantial weight onto one side of the bed in the direction of a bedside table and the incessant ringing. He quickly noticed the red LED digital numbers on the clock read ten after five.

"Jesus!" he muttered. He switched on the table lamp and reached for the phone, the speaker system permanently activated and turned up in volume because of his poor hearing.

"Yes?"

"Good morning, Mr. B." The voice was female, pitched somewhere between alto and baritone, a register lower than most women, but like smooth silk, a slight accent yet words precisely pronounced. "Much to be accomplished, Mr. B. Most important."

B pushed himself to one elbow and swung his feet over the side of the bed, raising himself into a sitting position. "I don't understand, and besides, I don't know you."

"You will. Town of Morrison, Flights Wine Cafe, parking lot, eleven-thirty. Do not be late. My driver will meet you. He does not speak English. He will give you a note with my initials and the organization's symbol. I repeat, most important."

Trying to get his feet into a pair of slippers that seemed determined to slide farther away with each attempt, he said, "But I'm scheduled to attend the Colorado Sheriffs Association's monthly business meeting here in Golden."

"Cancel. Morrison, eleven-thirty. Please, Mr. B, do not be late." The line went dead.

* * *

I had to admit, it had been a long night, what with our adventure at Lundgren's home and the drive back to the hotel via the Farm House Restaurant for Innes to pick up his truck. We agreed during the drive that, for the time being, we would keep that night's events between the three of us until we could dig up other evidence to substantiate our findings. I did get Gladys to tell me how she knew the intruders were speaking Chinese. After the death of her husband, her lengthy sabbatical during which the birth of her daughter occurred and several years at CIA headquarters, she had been posted to the U.S. Consulate General in Hong Kong and Macau for two years. She'd told me about the Far East, but not the specific locations.

What I did want more than anything was to make love with this beautiful woman who agreed to stay over, but as tired as we were after all that had happened, the best we could manage was to snuggle under the heavy comforter, hold each other close and fall asleep.

Gladys was gone when I woke up, home to shower and change before driving back to meet at the Jefferson County Sheriff's office at eight o'clock. She later told me she touched base with Roberta to get the day off. She also admitted that Undersheriff Mike Vasquez wasn't particularly happy when she showed up, despite my earlier explanations about her importance to the case.

After a quick "free" breakfast in the hotel's small dining area and enough cups of black coffee to awaken the spirits, I arrived for the meeting with Mike Vasquez a few minutes after eight. Gladys and John were already there. I saw Vasquez pass a five-dollar bill to John, at that same time saying, "John said you'd be late. I bet him a fiver, and yeah, just my luck, you're late. Doctor Wong is meeting us at the site with the Coroner's van.

"Couple of my deputies have taken all the gear you and Wong will need, including the Beretta you asked for. Surprisingly, we had one back in Evidence, picked up during a raid on an illegal pot grow. Like you asked, a crew is out there clearing the

Gamble oaks from the front of the mine. Parks Department doesn't like it worth a damn, but I told 'em we'd replant after we're finished. Sheriff wants to get the deputizing thing over with so let's go to his office. Paperwork's already there. Should only take a minute or two."

Speaking to John and Gladys, he added, "You two wait here."

After I was sworn in as Deputy Dog for the Day, or part thereof, Gladys and John with me, the Undersheriff in his car, we were on our way. Due to the still ongoing morning rush, two fender-benders blocking one lane and a light mist in the air making a gray day even grayer, it was a good forty-minute drive along C-470 and up into the foothills to Deer Creek Canyon Park.

When we arrived, besides a black-and-white patrol car and Dr. Wong's Coroner's van, the only other vehicle in the parking lot was a big Ford F-250 Crew Cab pickup truck. FRONT RANGE TREE MASTERS was stenciled on the truck's front doors with a relatively small wood chipper hitched up at the rear. Wong was walking out of the men's restroom just inside the park entrance.

As we made our way up the trail toward the mine, the Doc now in tow, four men were coming down the trail, each dressed in dungarees and green work jacket with the Tree Masters logo sewn on the front of each man's jacket. Farther on we could see the opening to the old mine and a massive stack of Gamble oaks, really nothing more than scrub oaks, their twisted and crooked trunks and limbs pushed off to one side. It proved to me that the Undersheriff was as a man of his word.

One of the men, apparently the crew's supervisor, said in passing, "Mornin', Mike. It's done. Didn't know how much we'd have. Back later this morning with a wood chipper big enough to do the job. You need any mulch for your yard?"

"Thanks, but no. I'll let the park people know you'll be back. And they'd probably like the mulch spread over the cut area until it's replanted. You know where to bill us."

Once we got closer to the mine opening, I appreciated

having a clean, unobstructed view of the entrance. It was much better than when I was on hands and knees during my crawl beneath the face-scratching, clothes-tearing limbs of Gamble oaks.

As with my first visit, near rotten timbers that once held up the entrance were on each side of the irregular-shaped, triangular opening. The third timber, a lintel piece I had assumed, lay at an approximately fifty-degree angle between the two entrance supports. The now familiar, badly splintered sign board with the peeling and faded black-on-white lettering still hung from the lintel. It was as I remembered except for one highly visible addition to the scene. A yellow crime scene tape was stretched across the entrance.

From the direct view that I now had, it was easier to see that the opening was no more than five to six feet wide at the bottom, angling up beneath the fallen lintel to about four feet above the ground, ending in a near point at the top of an off-centered right triangle. Though Wong and I would have to bend over to make our entrance, it would be better than crawling through wet leaves and mud like I did last time.

Again, true to his word, a couple of uniformed deputies had set up a portable table underneath a crime scene tent. Two zip-up-the-front white Hazmat coverall suits were laid out full length, from attached head-covering hoods at the top to booties at the bottom. The only non-white parts of the suits were the light green, tight-fitting gloves which appeared to be of some type of latex similar to surgical gloves and a small blue logo on the left side of each suit's chest with the imprinted word TYVEK.

With all of us crowded beneath the tent to avoid the mist which was slowly becoming a heavy sprinkle, I said, "Tyvek? Thought that was a building wrap for new construction."

Wong answered, "You're right, but it has many uses. It's a type of synthetic material of high-density polyethylene fibers. Extremely lightweight, almost like paper except much stronger.

"As for Hazmats, I wore similar suits several years ago while uncovering mass graves in South Texas, several miles in from the border. Authorities determined they were illegal immigrants who crossed from Mexico. It was obvious how they were killed, but authorities never identified why and who did it."

The Tyvek description was, if nothing else, educational, but the mass grave information brought a pall of silence over the scene until Wong asked, "Where are the respirators? We need them, not only because of the ammonia, but if I'm correct, some other very nasty things."

Unless my imagination had already begun working overtime, the very mention of ammonia and the memory of my last visit to the mine suddenly caused me to cover my nose with my hand. "There it is, ammonia." Looking toward the mine entrance, I asked, "Smell it?"

Everyone sniffed several times before shaking their heads and chorusing, "No."

There's an old saying that goes, 'Imagination is memory's twin.' In this case, for me it proved to be right.

"Respirators here, Doctor," one of the Deputies said. He reached beneath the table and pulled out two boxes, opened them and brought out a full-face respirator from each box. "The suits are new, unused, but we…" he nodded to the other deputy, "used the respirators when we tried to go into the mine the other day. We had them cleaned before we brought them out this morning."

I took one. The lower half of the mask was made of heavy-duty silicone which included the breathing apparatus, two activated charcoal filters and a HEPA filter. The upper portion provided a clear window of what looked and felt like Plexiglas. It appeared wide enough to allow both a direct and more than adequate peripheral view. In other words, both the Doc and I were going to look like a pair of extraterrestrials by the time we wrestled our way into the entire outfit.

Gladys helped me into my Hazmat suit, whispering what she remembered of the Paris Police letter and name and description of the supposed Werewolf of Paris, while John worked the other suit onto Wong. Covering the entire body, it felt a lot like a scuba diver's dry suit I once wore in Arctic waters, only much, much lighter. I could, however, understand why the two deputies felt claustrophobic once the hood and face-covering respirator were on. Unfortunately for the Doc, he was not the tallest person around. Since the suits were one-size-fits-all, the material around his wrists and ankles ballooned out, almost covering his green gloves and booties.

He was not the only one with a problem. The suits had no pockets which meant the Beretta M9 had no place to go. "The Beretta?" I asked. "Who's got it and where am I going to put it?" Pointing to the sides of the suit, I said, "No pockets. I need to keep my hands free as
possible."

"Problem solved," the second Deputy said. Nodding toward the other deputy, he went on, "Like I said, Denny here and me were the ones who tried to use the suits the other day and knew they didn't have any pockets." He pulled a duffel bag from under the table, sat it on the top or the table, unzipped it and lifted out a black police belt with a holster, the Beretta M9 and extra magazines in one of the belt's clip holders.

"A magazine already in the grip, one round in the chamber, safety engaged."

"Thanks. Don't know what we're going to find in there but feel better having a little added protection."

With the belt buckled around my waist, the Beretta on my right side and the respirator covering my head and face, its outer edges tight beneath the elastic seams of the Tyvek hood, the deputy called Denny handed Wong and me each a handheld flashlight, explaining, "They're good. Advertised to throw light out a little over several hundred yards. We used them when we tried to go in. Really lights up the place."

"That tells me, if you didn't see anything regardless of how far you went into the mine, our suspect, if he's in there, could be back two to three hundred yards or more from the entrance." I was surprised by the clarity of my voice, although it felt like I was talking through a wad of cotton.

"You got it," he said with a sly, glad-its-you-and-not-me smile on his face.

"Thanks a lot. That's about three football fields worth, maybe more. To be honest, I'm not really interested in going that far, especially if there's bats in there like the Doc thinks."

"I know what you're saying," John said. "When I saw all those bats in that cave we were in down in Arizona, I damn near ran over you getting outta there."

After a laugh and words of agreement as well as encouragement from everyone, the Undersheriff asked Wong and me, "You two ready?"

"As ever," Wong replied. Turning to me, he held up one of his green-gloved hands to show me a yellow, palm-sized device that resembled a miniature cell phone with a single control knob, several push buttons and a window showing a set of numbers. "A meter for measuring the amount of gas in the air if there is any, in our case, ammonia.

"Based on the two dog handlers and of course you, Mr. Berkeley, who've been near or just inside the mine, I feel certain there will be. It has an audible alarm when it detects the existence of the gas and a numerical value of the gas measurement in the monitor as it increases." He pointed to the small window. "With our respirators, it won't be any good for us, but if the man is in there, it will give us data on the amount of ammonia he's been inhaling, whether he's dead or alive.

"The only drawback, the meter does not measure airborne spores from fungus created by bat droppings, an altogether separate situation that causes the deadly histoplasmosis. If he's in there, it's unlikely we'll find him alive."

I gave a short, sour chuckle. "As long as we don't suck up any ammonia or fungus spores, I'm good."

Wong had one more surprise. He opened the cardboard box he brought from the Coroner's van and took out a shiny aluminum case. "A safety line," he explained. "Holds two hundred yards of red, thread-like nylon, very strong. Bright yellow markers every twenty-five yards. You can clip it onto your belt. Helps us from getting lost if the mine turns into a maze of different tunnels. The switch on the side allows automatic unrolling and take-up. Like a tape measure."

He tied the free end to one of the timbers at the mine entrance and clipped the case onto my belt.

Gladys squeezed my hand. "Be safe." In a softer voice near my right ear, she added, "We have things to talk about, and it's not about the werewolf."

Not easy to smile with your face largely covered by the respirator, I gave a wink and said, "At the top of my list."

"Mine, also." She smiled and again gave a slight squeeze on my hand as a promise of things to come.

With those last two words, I turned and ducked under the crime scene tape and lintel into the mine. Once able to straighten to my full height, I immediately switched on my flashlight, illuminating the tunnel. Wong did the same after he entered. Along the sides of the mine and above my head were vertical and cross timbers holding up the roof. All I could think was, *Keep holding, baby. Keep holding.*

Like I'd seen on my first visit, the mine opened out in width the deeper it went. With the light I could see the tunnel angling off to the left with a slight downward slope, so much so that the light beam went no more than a hundred feet before it hit solid rock at the bend. Even with flashlights blasting away for X numbers of yards, no wonder the deputies didn't see anything. They didn't go far enough. It really didn't make any difference. If we got to the end of the two hundred yards of safety line and hadn't found our quarry, the Werewolf of Paris could rot in there for all I cared.

I stopped for a moment. There was a slight movement of air flowing from somewhere back in the mine, much like the day I crawled just past the entrance. This was followed by a loud *ding* from Wong's gas meter. Ammonia!

Moving on, we tried to stay to the center of the tunnel and

not snag the extremely lightweight Hazmat coveralls on sharp edges of rock formations along the mine's walls or splinters sticking out from timbers. While the ground at the entrance appeared relatively dry and to have been cleared of any fallen rocks, as we moved deeper, rubble littered the floor, at times partially covering rusted rail lines where carts at one time had been used to carry ore and/or waste rock back to the surface.

"Fifty yards on the safety line," the Doc called out. "Ammonia level increasing." He flashed his light along the walls. "There, small veins of silver. Based on other mines in the area, Georgetown and Silver Plume, for example, several miles to the west, this mine was probably operated from the Eighteen-fifties through, at best, the Eighties when there was a drastic decline in silver prices. It would be interesting to know how much silver came out of this mine."

So much for Doc's mini history lesson. Rather than learning about silver mining, I was more interested in keeping my footing along the rails and around the larger rocks, loosened over a century ago by workers drilling or fallen from the natural shifting of the surrounding strata.

By this time, water was seeping from seams in the rock. It created a kind of mud from drilling dust and small rocks. In other places it formed puddles as much as an inch deep. The farther and deeper we went, the colder it became. Small, opaque colored stalactites extended down from the ceiling. I was thankful I'd worn a jacket beneath the full-body coveralls.

The more the mine opened out after another rather modest curve, the more the floor was covered by rock debris, causing us to do a kind of dance around some of the larger rocks to keep from stumbling and falling on our faces.

Thank God for the lights. Maneuvering my light back and forth, I discovered a room carved out of the rock off to the left just as Wong said, "One hundred yards. Though we can't smell it, ammonia level's getting higher." We stopped and surveyed the room's contents. It contained large pieces of machinery, rusted beyond use, several of what appeared to be pneumatic drills as well as one of the rail carts, everything corroded from the ever-present moisture.

Beyond the rail cart was an area that seemed to extend back into the darkness. To be sure our quarry was or wasn't hiding back in there, I walked up and shone my light along the sides and over the top of the cart. There was nothing more to see than a continuation of rusted equipment. As I stepped back, however, the light caught something in the cart, more than just something. A pile of grayish-white bones and two small skulls. "Aw, Christ!"

"Christ what?" Wong asked, stepping forward until he could see into the cart. He studied the bones for a moment. "It can only be the missing children, but there's nothing we can do for them now. We'll get them later."

Now that we'd found them, I hated to leave their remains in the cold and the dark, but I knew he was right. I followed him back into the main shaft.

It couldn't have been more than ten to fifteen yards farther along when the mine split in three different directions. "What's your guess, Doctor," I asked.

I waited for his response in the near silence which itself was unnerving to say the least. The earlier sounds of our footsteps and yes, the exaggerated sound of our breathing through respirator filters, had held the silence at bay, but this was different. Suddenly so quiet I could hear water drip, drip, dripping down along the walls and from the ceiling of the mine and the distant echoes of our voices when we spoke.

Most unnerving was the periodic groan of rocks grinding together somewhere from deep in the mine. In the back of my mind was the thought, *What if there's a cave-in and we're trapped with a flesh-eating, half man, half wolf and a blood thirsty cloud of bats swarming down on top of us?*

Wong saved me from my thoughts by answering my question. "Beats me. One way looks as promising as the other."

With that kind of non-answer, I moved first into the tunnel

to the right and pointed my light up, down, from one side to the other and saw the same old same old. Then to the tunnel that led straight ahead. Nothing different. Shaking my head, I stepped several feet into the tunnel on our left and stopped. "Damn it, I don't..." I felt the breeze, this time stronger. "There it is again, the movement of air."

Wong shone his light on the gas meter. "And the meter indicates an increase in ammonia. With the sudden increase, I'd say there are definitely bats in here"

"If there're bats," I said, "there has to be a way for them to get out and back in. That means an opening. If no one in the park or people living in Canyon Creek Estates has ever seen a swarm of bats come out of the mine, especially with that thick cluster of scrub oaks covering the opening, there's has to be another opening, an air shaft of some size. We're a little over a hundred yards into this damn thing. Let's check this passage out, at least until the end of the safety line. If we don't find our guy, we'll try the other two tunnels, again to the end of the safety line. If nothing by then, we're out of here. Agreed?"

"Agreed."

Moving forward, the flow of air became stronger, enough to rustle the loose material on my Hazmat coveralls. This seemed to make us move a little faster, a feat in itself because of the rocks and debris underfoot. So much so that Wong lost his footing and fell, dropping his flashlight. I bent and helped him to his feet. He checked his Hazmat suit to see if there any tears, but there were none. At the same time, I glanced at the distance marker on the safety line. "Hundred and fifty yards. We'd better find something soon or –"

"Shhhh. Hear that?"

"What?"

"Squeaks, high pitched and a *shhhhushing* sound in the background, like wings brushing against other wings. It's bats, Berkeley, bats. It shouldn't be far. I'm turning off my light. Keep your light on the ground in front of you so we don't disturb them."

As we made our way forward, slower than before, the squeaking and what the Doc called the brushing of wings against wings grew louder. It virtually masked the dripping of water and any other cave sounds, like the sounds of tiny little creatures scurrying out of the way as I walked. I stopped, took a step back before recognizing swarms of ..., "Cockroaches, damn it!"

Wong gave a weak laugh. "I should have suspected it. Cave dwelling cockroaches. Like the beetles I told you about, they also feed off of bat guano that drops on the floor."

Taking a deep breath and sweeping the little critters out the way with my feet when they refused to move, I continued along what remained of the railroad tracks peaking just above the rocks and muddy slush as the cave began a slight turn to the left. And then I saw it.

"Hold up, Doc. I think we found him," I whispered and held my hand up to stop Wong's forward motion.

On the floor of the cave, maybe twenty, twenty-five feet away lay a large bundle of hair with cockroaches moving freely around and on it. Whether man or animal, I couldn't tell. Above, hanging from the roof of the mine at the edge of my light's illumination glow, was a living mass of gray/black motion, clumped together, hundreds, maybe a thousand bodies and wings barely in motion, but enough to create a constant hum and to let us know they were alive.

Even though I'd volunteered to search the mine, damned if I wanted to move any closer to something that had the potential to kill me. At this point, however, I really had no choice.

With the flashlight in one hand and the M9 semiautomatic in the other, hoping the deputy was right about a round already in the chamber, safety off, I inched forward. I cleared my throat every few steps so as not to be a total surprise if the bunched-up thing on the floor was alive. The mound of hair, serving as host for any number of cockroaches, was curled in a fetal position.

Using the name provided in the French police report and John's pronunciation of the last name, I spoke as nonthreatening as possible. "Keith? Keith Nalje?"

At the same time, I saw a serrated knife lying several feet from the man or whatever he was. I kicked it well off to the side. I remembered the white man on the mountain, the stab wound in his throat made by what we thought was a serrated knife, but one that was never found at the crime scene.

At the sound of the knife clattering against rocks, there was a slight movement followed by either a groan or a snarl and what might have been a word I didn't understand.

"That you, Keith?" My M9 was pointed for what I hoped was a kill shot if he attacked.

Slowly, very slowly, the bundle of hair unwound itself and rolled onto one side, revealing what appeared to be a face, matted hair covering most of it, soured by a crust of vomit. Through a cough that seemed to rise from the bottom of his gut, cutting off what I was certain this time was a snarl, he pleaded, "Sicheii, why? I ... I killed for you." This was followed by more coughing that ended with, "Help me, Sicheii."

With those words I knew we'd found our killer, but who and what was Sicheii? Man, woman, thing? I watched as he tried to push himself up using his right arm and hand. The left arm hung limp as though useless. With the M9 still at the ready in case he charged, the beam of my flashlight picked out a mat of dried blood plastered against the hair of his left shoulder. Bullet wound or what, I couldn't tell.

Wong moved to my left side, allowing for the first time, the man to see both of us. I can only imagine that, in our body-covering white coveralls and hood, green gloves and respirator faces, we must have looked to the man like two nightmares from another world.

"We're here to help you, Keith," Wong said. "That your name? Keith?"

Followed by another spell of coughing which didn't seem to disturb the bats and their incessant squeaking, his words were little more than a whisper, but I distinctly heard him say, "Hok'ee.

Hok'ee... Hok'ee Nalzheehii." His breathing was slack, more of a wheeze, almost nonexistent as he attempted to sweep the hair away from his eyes and mouth, but he managed to continue. "Keith... white man's name my... my mother gave."

Somewhere behind the man we called Keith, I heard a continuous though uneven rhythm of plops. I took several steps closer, shone my light over Keith's head and stopped, not because of the man, but because of a depression in the mine floor that lay beyond. I could barely make out what appeared to be smoldering tons of bat droppings with millions of tiny beetles crawling in the waste. The plops were from falling bat excrement. The beetles' movement caused the floor to look like an undulating sea of motion.

Whether it was my imagination again at play or an actual, barely visible cloud of steam rising like a fog from the bat-waste covered floor in the otherwise chill of the mine, I didn't know, but my eyes began to water and I suddenly smelled the most sickening, putrid odor I'd ever experienced. That with the man obviously having lain in his own waste, the sewers of the world couldn't have been worse. Rationally, I knew, with the respirator, it couldn't be, but just the same, I gagged and almost threw up.

Stepping aside, I choked out, "He's all yours, Doc. Pretty sure he's too weak to cause trouble, but I'm ready if you need help." I held up the M9.

Wong moved past me, swept away the few cockroaches still clinging to the man, took him by the right arm and asked, "Can you stand?"

Without answering and with Wong's help, the man tried to push himself up, then dropped back to one knee. Exerting determination and what little strength he had left between bouts of coughing, he finally got to his feet, his upper body bent forward in obvious pain. There was what appeared to be a mixture of blood and yellow/green mucus seeping from both his mouth and nose.

When Wong placed a hand on the man's back to help steady him, the man's head snapped back. He let out a wolf-like howl that filled the tunnel, a cry straight out of the depths of hell, the sound echoing out into the distance and back.

I almost shot the poor bastard, but hesitated long enough to realize it was a cry of pain, of utter misery. For an instance, the squeaking and movement of the bats went silent.

Wong let go of the man's arm and shone his light on the creature's back. "My God!"

"What," I asked.

"His back and... and left side. Blood matted, and greenish pus seeping from the man's wounds. Knife wounds, I'm sure. Massive infection. Good God, all that and living back here, why he's still alive..."

I'd had enough. Quickly picking up the serrated knife from the floor of the cave and sticking into what I thought was a baton holder on the duty belt, Wong and I took turns holding the man up and pushing forward ever so slowly, often stumbling over and around the larger rocks and half buried rail tracks. From what I could tell, what had once been a big, powerful man was little more than hair, skin and bone, his body literally rotting away. I thanked God we had the respirators. Otherwise I was sure the stench from his body would have been overpowering, at least for me.

We were well passed the small room with the rusted equipment, now on our right, the remains of the children still on my mind, when the man forced us to stop, his words, "No... no." He dropped to one knee, then the other knee, the two of us still holding him up.

"What is it, Keith," Wong asked.

With his head bent forward, chin resting on his chest, a sudden froth of blood spewed from his mouth before he was able to say in a gargle-like groan, "Sicheii, forgive me."

There is was again, the word *Sicheii,* among his last words as he immediately became dead weight. Wong and I both tried to hold him up, but the weight of what little was left of his body was too much. We let go.

It was a good thirty minutes before Wong and I, each with

hands grasping the armpits beneath his shoulders, literally drug the body on its back to the entrance and out into what had become a chill mixture of clouds and sunlight.

With exception of John, everyone wrinkled their noses, took a step back and stared. "You found him," John said. No one else spoke.

The reaction was understandable when first seeing the mass of hair, blood and bile that covered it. And yes, the penetrating odor of sickness and death.

"Alive when we reached him, already dying. Dead before we could get him out." For the first time I wanted to keep the respirator on for I knew, from everyone's reaction, there was the stench of rot about him. In fact, I could see the look on everyone's faces as they automatically took several more steps back.

"Good Lord," Gladys breathed. "No wonder that young man, Sonny Weaver, described him the way he did. The face, what you can see of it and all that hair, covering his body. The man is huge. Look at his hands and his feet. Like claws."

Lying on his back, his full height was well over six feet. His hands revealed the skin on the palms clear of hair, but the fingernails, thick and long, curved like claws. The toe nails on each foot were shaped much the same.

"Undersheriff," Wong directed, "have one of your deputies go down to the Coroner's van and bring up a body bag, several pair of rubber gloves and some flexible dust masks. They're easy to recognize with a green exhale valve at the front. And yes, a stretcher. Once back, he can unzip and open the bag as wide as possible. With their help, Mr. Berkeley and I will keep on our Hazmat gear and place the deceased in the bag."

To the other deputy, he said, "Take as many pictures as you can of the deceased with your body camera, the mine opening and surrounding area. I'll call the crime scene people to come out with the proper safety equipment to cover the inside of the mine. As for our two missing children, I believe we found their remains, small bones, but there should be enough to make positive identifications."

"Oh, God, how awful," Gladys said, shaking her head. "Was he able to talk?"

"Some of it we understood," I answered, "but nothing about the children. Only what we think was his real name and another name he kept saying, but enough to know he's our killer."

John asked, "What kind of names? Can you remember?"

"Although he recognized the name Keith when we asked him, he finally said it was a white man's name his mother gave him. I'm pretty sure his first words were his own name. Hokee, like in the French police report. That was followed by something like *Nalje-e*. That make sense?"

John thought for a moment. "I think it does. Like I told you back in Chief Kay's office, Hok'ee is a Navajo name that means *High Backed Wolf*. If he's been covered with hair all his life, I can understand. As for the other, it's probably Nalzheehii meaning *Hunter*. Anything else?"

Wong answered, "The words, 'Help me,' followed by something like *Sichee*, and later, just before he died, he said 'No, no,' followed by 'Sichee, forgive me.' Nothing else."

John nodded. "Sicheii. Had to be. Navajo for Grandfather. He was calling on his grandfather to forgive him. Samuel Hataali, the man who killed Lundgren? It's a possibility."

Gladys said, "Sounds right. Sicheii, grandfather. The man who killed Lundgren, Samuel Hataali. You said so yourself, Hataali or Hatahli, Medicine Man." She looked at me. "And you remembered him. Said he was the man who gave you so much trouble on your digs down in the Four Corners. Called Grand Father Medicine Man."

Turning back to John, she continued, "You're Navajo, from the Navajo Nation in Arizona. You know the people and the history down there. If anybody can make the connection, you can." She stopped for a moment, exhaled a heavy sigh and asked the million-dollar question, "But we still don't know the relationship between Grand Father Medicine Man and Captain Lundgren, do we?"

Undersheriff Mike Vasquez started laughing. "Sorry I doubted you and your value to the investigation, Miss Knight. After that, if you get tired of all that legal stuff over in Denver, how'd you like a job with the Jefferson County Sheriff's Department? You've got my vote."

Chapter 28

B pulled the late model Buick LaCrosse into the Flights Wine Café's parking lot, the car's metallic silver dulled by highway back-splatter from cars earlier that morning while on his way to work. His one consolation was that the weather front bringing wind and rain to the area had moved out past Denver and onto the eastern plains. He noticed the building also housed a restaurant serving lunch and dinner which gave reason why the lot was nearly full.

He maneuvered the Buick to the lot's far corner along the retaining wall bordering Bear Creek and backed into an open space. By parking this way, it allowed him a view of the entire lot, vehicles already parked and those entering or leaving. His Seiko dive watch showed eleven twenty-five. Not that he was a diver, but the watch contained a bezel which he frequently used to time himself performing various functions like opening and closing arguments at a trial. This time, however, he shifted the bezel's zero-minute pointer to the eleven twenty-five mark and waited to see if the driver would arrive at the appointed time.

Lowering the window, he extracted a cigarette from a half-filled pack of Marlboro he'd opened only that morning, lit the cigarette with a gold lighter, inhaled and waited.

At exactly eleven-thirty, a black Mercedes Benz S-Class he hadn't noticed backed out of a parking space near the entrance. Instead of leaving, it backed rapidly in the direction of his car. Open mouthed, B watched as the Mercedes finally braked to a stop within inches of the Buick's front bumper, blocking him in.

"Damn!" was all he could say.

A heavily built, bull-necked man in black livery, Chinese, B was certain, stepped from the Mercedes' driver-side door, a folded piece of white paper in his hand. He approached the Buick, unfolded the paper and handed it to B through the already open window.

The top of the sheet contained the name 'Mr. B' and the gold-on-black theater curtain logo for the Ralston World Wide Entertainment, LLC. *Entertainment, my ass* was B's immediate thought. B took the paper and read its three short sentences. Once finished, he looked up and said, "Why and where am I going?"

The driver stood mute, arms at his side. B asked, "English?" before remembering his caller had said the driver did not speak English. "Oh, what the hell," he cursed.

He raised the window, grunted his five-foot-six-inch, two-hundred-pound mass – described indelicately by many as obese behind his back – from the car and flipped the still burning cigarette some distance away to the consternation of the Chinese driver.

He'd worn one of his business suits in order to cover the subcompact Glock 42 semiautomatic with six standard .380 rounds. The driver shook his head, pointed at B's left breast pocket and tapped it with his index finger. The same finger lifted the coat's lapel followed by the head nodding toward the inside of the coat. The driver shook his head more emphatically and pointed toward the Buick, muttering words that B knew from the way they were spoken meant put the pistol back inside the car. B also knew he'd have to lose some weight or buy a size larger suit coat if he was to successfully carry a concealed firearm without anyone recognizing the fact. Once the pistol was under the Buick's front seat and the car locked, B worked his way into the backseat of the Mercedes through a door held open by the driver.

Already irritated for allowing himself to take orders from a strange female voice on the phone, ruining the day's itinerary, his face had gone red with embarrassment for being so easily found out by some foreigner that he was carrying. He sat silently in the back seat, a clear glass partition separating him from the driver.

The Mercedes pulled out into traffic and, to his surprise,

turned left, heading west away from where he thought they would be going. "We're not going to Denver?" he shouted at the driver. There was no recognition he'd been heard. He beat on the glass partition and again shouted the question, but still no movement from the driver.

Exhaling a rush of air to express his frustration, B sat back, started to light a cigarette when he heard a loud, "*Bú xing!*" from a speaker just below the glass partition and saw the driver watching him in the rearview mirror. At the same time, the man shook his head and raised his right hand, firmly clinched into a fist.

When B didn't immediately react, again the driver shouted a sharp, "*Bú xing!*" followed by a one-handed slap against the steering wheel. Finally realizing what the man was demanding, B quickly placed the cigarette back into the pack and sat back as the word "*Hǎo,*" came from the speaker. It was accompanied by an affirmative nod from the driver. Embarrassed, B suddenly felt powerless, a feeling rare to him in his place in the universe.

He watched road signs and names of roads as they drove up the winding, two-lane road, higher into the foothills, Bear Creek off to the left, granite and sandstone cliffs on his immediate right. As they passed through small communities – Idledale and Kittredge – and the sign for Lair of the Bear Park, he nodded, knowing to some extent why and where they were going, at least the general location. The town of Evergreen, a mountain community with which he was intimately familiar after building a vacation home – his mountain retreat he called it – just southwest of the town some years earlier.

What did surprise him, however, was immediately after entering the town, the driver stopped, waited for two cars to pass in the opposite direction, and turned left. The Mercedes crossed the east-bound lane and entered a small parking lot for the Creekside Cellars Winery and Café. Only one space was open, adjacent to the entrance. It displayed a sign stating RESERVED. There was no hesitation on the part of the driver. He pulled into that space, turned off the engine, got out, opened the rear door for

B and pointed toward the winery's entrance.

Once inside B passed a number of customers waiting to be called to a table before turning left toward the large tasting bar only to hear above the normal lunch crowd conversation. On his way, he noticed all the tables and booths inside were full.

"Afternoon, Mr. B. She's waiting for you on the outdoor deck." It was a tall, middle-aged man who B had known beginning when he'd bought the land and built his retreat, back when he was still married. A two-story frame construction, outside of town just south of eight-thousand-foot Elephant Butte and west of the Three Sisters Mountains.

"Thank you, Evan, but a question. You might call it a blind date, sort of. What does she look like?"

"Oriental, Chinese or Japanese, long black hair. Maybe even Vietnamese. I can't tell the difference. I guess you can call her attractive, seen better, but let me tell you, all business. Paid me two thousand dollars to reserve the parking space and the deck outside for an hour and a half, just for you and her."

Evan nodded toward the winery's entrance and those waiting for an inside table, leaned closer over the bar and lowered his voice. "With the deck closed, hope they don't get so pissed it'll keep 'em from coming back." With a nod toward the outdoor deck, he added, "Be careful, Mr. B. She might be the domineering type."

"Thanks, Evan. I will." Remembering the voice on the telephone and imagining the power she held, at least over his life, he already knew in his dealing with these people how careful he had to be. He also knew, he had no choice but to stay in the race, no matter where it led, all the way to the finish line if he could live that long.

With a facial wall of annoyed looks from customers standing near the door to the outside deck accompanied by several overly loud whispers expressing their irritation, B looked straight ahead, trying to ignore their existence as he exited onto the deck.

One person, a woman, Chinese as B had expected, sat at a table next to the railing overlooking Bear Creek. The flow of the creek's waters offered a lazy, lapping-against-stones sound usual for late October, waiting for the coming spring that would bring torrents of snow melt down from the higher mountains to fill its banks. Several ducks swam below the deck, maintaining position as though waiting for bread and cracker crumb offerings from above.

Shadowed somewhat by an umbrella of cotton wood trees lining the creek, their limbs still carrying an abundance of autumn gold reaching out over the deck, there appeared to be a certain attractiveness to the woman's face. Or so it seemed at first glance. Though not unattractive, the closer he got, the face, a light bronze in color, took on a hardness that, to B, based on past experience was emblematic of power and, if need be, uncompromising ruthlessness when dealing with others.

Her hair, midnight black, was parted slightly left of midline and hung straight to well below her shoulders. One ear was hidden by the flow of hair, the other ear revealed only enough to show a single pearl earring.

Her face was relatively long. Shallow pockmarks along cheeks, chin and a rather prominent nose were partially hidden by makeup. Perfectly shaped eyebrows arched above eyes that seemed to look through B, their black pupils like lasers that could pierce into his inner most thoughts. Otherwise, she wore a black business suit, somewhat softened by a pink blouse with lapels that formed a V, stopping just above the cleft between her breasts.

On the table before her sat a plate of various cheeses and prosciutto, samplings enough for sharing with another. Two glasses were on the table, one partially filled in front of her, the other placed across the table before an empty chair. An open bottle of 2012 Petite Sirah sat in the middle of the table.

"Good afternoon, Mr. B. So gracious of you to accept my invitation."

B stood behind the empty chair. "You gave me no option, besides, I don't know you. Where is Mr. Chén? He's my usual –"

"Please be seated, Mr. B, so we can discuss what has

become a most disturbing situation."

Knowing he had no choice, B pulled back the chair and sat as the woman leaned across the small table and poured a liberal portion of wine into the empty glass before him.

"Due to unfortunate circumstances, Mr. Chén is no longer with us. My name is Sun Xiaolin. You may call me Doctor Sun as in your word *s-o-o-n*, the new Director of Rare Earth Minerals Advanced Research, China Rare Earth Group LTD, a corporation under direct supervision of the State-owned Assets Supervision and Administration Commission. Established by the President and the National People's Congress within the Ministry of Land and Resources.

"We are responsible for planning, administration, protection and national utilization of land and marine resources in the Peoples Republic of China. In case you are interested, I obtained my doctorate from Stanford University with one of the foremost earth-sciences programs in the United States.

"While Mr. Chén was perhaps not as forthcoming in explaining our mission, we have established various businesses within your country, Ralston World Wide Entertainment being but one example. By assuming Mr. Chén's mission, it is now my responsibility to ensure the continued monopoly of rare earth metals production and international sales remain with the People's Republic of China.

"Part of that responsibility is to take whatever action necessary to deny further production of rare earth metals in the United States. To do this, we are procuring lands known or suspected to hold fluorocarbonate minerals from which rare earths can be extracted. We have also bought by various means the cooperation of many of your most influential environmental organizations in this endeavor. I use the word *bought* since it applies to you as well. We appreciate your assistance in this effort."

B couldn't determine if the expression on her face was a smile accompanied with a nod in his direction or a smirk of satisfaction. Concentrating to keep his hands from shaking and displaying his nervousness, B pulled the pack of Marlboros from his coat pocket and started to three-finger a cigarette out of the pack.

"Please do not smoke in my presence, Mr. B," Dr. Sun said. "Bad for both our lungs."

Laying the pack aside, and with a sigh of capitulation to Dr. Sun's wishes, B took a larger than usual sip from his glass, foregoing the familiar twirling, sniffing and sampling of the wine. Swallowing with a noticeable gulp, he said, "When he first came to me, Chén discussed the need for rare earth minerals, inferring the possible mining of the minerals by a Chinese company, but he needed the land. He was afraid the knowledge might not be welcomed by my government. I wasn't aware of similar attempts being made elsewhere nor truly what you were doing."

"We have no desire to destroy your land. To keep others from doing so is our task. You, however, have made my work much more difficult because of your method for obtaining the land. A method, I admit, was a novel use of raw power, especially within your country. A method that has alerted not only local but national institutions when there could have been more acceptable means, both legally and ethically, of accomplishing the same results."

He couldn't keep himself from pleading. "I had no other choice. With what Chén knew of my past and my financial needs, he could have ruined me, ruined my life, sentenced my daughter to a slow and lingering death through his actions. No hope of a cure. I did what I had to do, damn it. That's the world I live in.

"These were the contacts I had, people I could control, people in the right place at the right time. People who could and would make it happen. Lives are lost every day. I see it all the time in my business. It hurts at first, but those left behind get over it."

Dr. Sun speared a piece of prosciutto and, with a small cube of cheese, put them in her mouth, delicately chewing while she took a cracker, crumbled it and dropped the crumbs into the creek for the ducks below. Never having taken her eyes off B during those very precise motions, she said, "An interesting philosophy, Mr. B. I would not enjoy a lasting relationship with you. Unfortunately, your actions now make it necessary to take steps I would otherwise not prefer."

B took a quick swallow of wine and asked, "What do you mean? I've done everything to make the land available. Made people pay the supreme sacrifice, all for you. Just pay me the rest of the money I was promised, and I'll forget you, Chén and everything to do with the land and those so-called rare earth things."

"I think not, Mr. B. To be honest, you now belong to me and our cause."

B jumped to his feet as rapidly as his weight would allow. "For God's sake, woman, what more do you want? I can't do anything else. If they find I'm involved in any way, they'll –"

Dr. Sun slapped the palm of her hand on the table as she demanded, "Sit down. You are making a scene for those viewing from inside and on the path across the creek. Your stepdaughter, Mr. B. a lovely young thing. I've been to see her."

"You what?"

"I said sit down," which he did. "So young, but strong with determination and belief in you, her father, the physicians and their research. If only the illness had not taken such a toll, but life is precious for those you love, is it not, Mr. B?

"A shame if her treatment were to abruptly cease because of a lack of funds, funds you do not have. No hope for a future cure. At best, something that would arrest the progress of the disease. Or because of your past misdeeds should they be made known. I include the murder of your wife for her adulterous ways. Most adroit how you managed the placement of guilt on her lover, but new evidence could arise that –."

"What evidence, goddamn it? There is none. All destroyed. You can't –"

"Not all. We can and will present that evidence unless you comply with our demands."

"God, I hate you people. Why I ever..." B's head drooped; a loose flab of flesh from his neck spread over his collar. Very slowly he lifted his head, his words hesitant, a sense of fear of the unknown in his eyes. He knew he was beaten. Shaking his head, he asked, "What... what is it you want me to do?"

"Save yourself, Mr. B. Save yourself. By doing that, you also lift eyes away from me, my organization and our endeavor." Dr. Sun shifted her plate and wine glass aside, reached beneath the table and withdrew a brown leather briefcase, placing it on the table in front of her.

"Taking a, what do you call it, a leaf from your wife's murder case, a leaf which I thought rather brilliant, let us once again save you and our efforts by diverting incriminating evidence to someone else. Someone quite well known and respected, but one who would also desire the land in question."

"How do we do that?"

"Actually, quite simple." Opening the briefcase, she withdrew a sheath of papers and a small plastic zip lock bag containing a red, made-in-China flash drive memory stick. She thumbed through the pages, speed reading as she went. Once through, she handed them across to B. "Follow the instructions for use of the material and information contained on the flash drive."

B took the papers and flash drive and read halfway down the first page. Stunned, he looked up and asked, "You want me to call a special grand jury and indict this woman? You can't be serious."

"Never more serious, Mr. B." With that Dr. Sun Xiaolin closed her briefcase, pushed back her chair, stood and said, "The deck is reserved for..." she checked her watch, "... for another thirty minutes. Why not finish the wine while you study the papers."

"I... I can't do it. You're asking the impossible."

"Your daughter, Mr. B. Remember your daughter."

"But this woman?"

"Yes, this woman, Roberta Wilson, lawyer, better known

as Roberta Pine Woman, Co-Chair of the Denver American Indian Commission. She and the now deceased fellow Native American, a so-called medicine man, Samuel Hataali whom you used, they will be your salvation. Most important, there are also three other names as you read further. I will be away for several days, but others will be watching your progress."

Dr. Sun lowered her head as though in a momentary bow. "As you Americans say, Mr. B, have a good afternoon." Reaching the door into the winery, she turned slightly before opening it and said over her shoulder, "There is also an American, a man named Berkeley. The man has an interesting history. Should he interfere further, we may see fit for him to be eliminated. Do as you are directed, and that will be determined based on your success."

Chapter 29

The week following our finding of Hok'ee Nalzheehii, aka Keith Nalje, aka Keith Hunter, the creature if you will, in the abandoned mine was, as it turned out, both good and bad. The best part was to substitute my hotel room for Gladys's condo in the Denver suburb of Greenwood Village and really getting to know this beautiful woman and her world.

I've had the good fortune to know several women, but none quite as intelligent, full of warmth and tenderness, and with a past as exciting, perhaps even more so, as mine. Nix the CIA part for me. My past dealings with their people have, for the most part, been erratic and at times finding myself on their hit list. Not a fun place to be.

Additionally, not as meaningful personally as my time with Gladys, was a meeting with the much slimmer around the waist line and recently returned to duty, Chief Kay, Dr. Wong and Undersheriff Mike Vasquez in the Undersheriff's office. The three of us, John, Gladys and I were invited as a courtesy for our part in finding Keith Nalje. As for Gladys, from what she later told me, her discussion with Vasquez shortly before the meeting centered around an invitation to work as a consultant with the Sheriff's Department on future such investigations. She didn't tell me at the time whether she had or would accept his offer.

Once we were assembled and following a *thank you* for our contribution from Sheriff Ferguson who had been pretty much a ghost during the investigation, Vasquez said to Chief Kay,

"Good to see you back, Chief. You sure you don't want more of your maternity leave?"

With a chuckle, Chief Kay answered, "And leave all the fun to you? No way. Where do you want to start?"

"Dr. Wong, the autopsy report."

Wong passed a copy of the report to Vasquez and the Chief. "The Sheriff received his copy this morning. I will, however, summarize its contents for the rest of you. First, Mr. Nalje, as we thought, was afflicted with congenital generalized hypertrichosis, also known as Ambras syndrome and, as I've described before, often called werewolf syndrome because of the amount of hair covering the body.

"Second, from his time in the mine and his continued inhalation of airborne spores from bat droppings, he did suffer from an acute case of histoplasmosis. His lungs and the linings of his mouth and trachea were practically destroyed.

"With the gunshot and numerous stab wounds that had become infected to the point of becoming gangrenous, the poison having spread throughout his body, those wounds and the combination of tissue deterioration and diminished functioning of his vital organs – heart, kidneys, liver, lungs – was determined to be the cause of death.

"Finally, thank the gods for our recently acquired DNA identification capability and its ability to give us relatively fast results. What you've all been waiting for, Mr. Nalje's DNA shows he was biologically related to Mr. Samuel Hataali which gives credence to our thinking there was someone of authority, in this case familial authority, directing or somehow influencing Mr. Nalje's actions.

"Mr. Nalje's DNA was found on Richard Lamb as well as the white man with the snake tattoo on his neck at the cabin on Pyramid Mountain. We were unable to determine any DNA on the second victim at the cabin. The body too badly burned. As for the knife you found in the mine, Mr. Berkeley, it had the DNA of both Mr. Nalje and that of the white man I just mentioned.

"I say the two were victims on the mountain although it is my opinion, they were there to assassinate Mr. Nalje and eliminate any link to others who might have been responsible for the various killings. An opinion, only." Looking at Chief Kay and the

Undersheriff, he added, "That is actually your decision to make.

"In addition to the DNA evidence, there are teeth marks on two of the three victims matching those of Mr. Nalje's teeth impressions. The third once again was too badly burned to retrieve any identifiable marks. The combination proves unequivocally that Mr. Nalje was responsible for the deaths of at least two of those victims.

"I'm relieved we were able, Mr. Berkeley and myself, to find the remains of the two children who were more than likely killed by Mr. Nalje. We're currently looking for the parents in order to establish their relationship through DNA. Concerning Mr. Weaver's young lady, perhaps someday. That's the best synopsis I can give of the report.

"As for Mr. Haatali's relationship to Captain Lundgren and, by extension, others, that's also for you, Undersheriff and Chief Kay, to determine. Any questions related to the autopsy?"

Regarding the Doctor's words when talking about the two men at the cabin on Pyramid Mountain, *eliminate any link to others who might have been responsible for the killings*, my immediate thoughts focused on Lundgren and the mysterious B person.

By not telling what we found at Lundgren's home as well as the surprise encounter with the two, gun-toting Chinese, we were in effect hindering further investigation. In other words, committing a crime. The best I could do at this point without consulting with Gladys and Deputy Innes was to lead the conversation toward Lundgren without any mention of the elusive B and any others.

"Undersheriff, the local rags had an article about weapons being fired at Lundgren's home the night following his murder. What was that all about?"

"Quite honestly, we're not sure. Our crime scene people found a large number of rounds embedded in the walls and stair well of the home's entrance hall as well as spent shells in a room off the hall from which the rounds were fired. More at the entrance and small porch area indicated whoever was doing the firing was exiting the house.

"In a hurry, I would say, firing at someone still inside while setting up a safety perimeter round themselves. From the shell casings and expended bullets, we were able to determine that, except for two of the shell casings and one round, they were 5.8 by 42-millimeter rounds normally associated with the Chinese made QBZ-95 semiautomatic rifle. These bullets are recognized to be made only by the Chinese."

"You said, 'except for two shell casings and one round,'" Gladys inserted. "What were they?"

Vasquez gave her a rather quizzical look. "Interesting you should ask."

Gladys shrugged her shoulders. "Curiosity, I suppose. It would indicate someone in the house might be shooting back at the QBZ-95 shooter."

Vasquez glanced at Chief Kay before answering. Receiving a brief nod of agreement from the Chief, he said, "Two shell casings but only one round found in the door frame leading to the outside. Nine-millimeter, from what we think was an M and P 9M2.0, Smith and Wesson. One thing seems certain, two nine-millimeter shells, one nine-millimeter round in the door frame and blood drips leading off the front porch and along the sidewalk to the street. That tells me someone was carrying the second round in their body as they left the house."

"M and P? What does that mean?" Gladys asked.

Chief Kay answered, "Military and Police. Why do you ask?"

"Just trying to keep things straight in my mind should I ever meet an M and P. You have no idea who the nine-millimeter shooter might be?"

Wanting to get away from something both the Undersheriff and Chief Kay seemed reluctant to discuss, I said, "While not looking for a lesson in firearms and ballistics, I'm sure your people did more than count shell casings while in the house. Did you find anything relating to Lundgren's involvement with Samuel Hataali or anyone else for that matter and why?" The letter from our unknown B individual, newspaper cutout and photographs kept weighing on my mind.

When Vazquez looked at his watch and stood, he said, "I've got another meeting, so we need to break this up." Looking at John, Gladys and me, he added, "Thanks for all the contributions you three have made. We wouldn't be where we are today if it wasn't for your help."

"One final question before we leave," Gladys said. "Based on what Matt and I learned from Simon Grant over at Colorado Geological Survey, various government departments and agencies are looking into land grabs in five other states as well as ours, efforts like that here in Jefferson County. Different named companies believed to be fronts for the Chinese government. Suddenly you have the use of Chinese weapons at Lundgren's house, something I wouldn't think common here in Colorado.

"At the same time, deposits of rare earth minerals, potential or actual, have been determined in each of these states. There seems to me to be the possibility of linkage with the Chinese. Are you going to follow up on that possibility?"

"Ms. Knight," Chief Kay said, "we've found our murderer. From that point, the case for the Jefferson County Sheriff's Department is closed. We will be looking at Lundgren's activities, but other than that, should there be an international conspiracy involving the Chinese or any other country, that's for the FBI and the Department of Homeland Security to take the lead. If we can help, we'll be more than ready and willing to assist. Other than that, we've accomplished what we started out to do and that was, find the killer."

Although she did add another sentence or two, in my mind, either the Undersheriff and his crime scene people found nothing in Lundgren's house exposing a 'dirty cop' history tying the man to the mysterious B character, or they were covering up for someone much higher than their pay grade. I hoped the latter wasn't so, but life is not always what you want.

Out in the parking lot, Gladys and I had just finished telling John we'd meet him for dinner at PappaDeaux Sea Food Kitchen for dinner not far from Gladys's condo when my cell phone gave its usual irritating *ding, dong, dong.* Flipping the thing's cover up and hitting the SEND button, I said, "Afternoon, David. Is this something good or bad?"

I held the phone away and explained to Gladys and John, "David Prosser, retired cop. Looks after my place when I'm gone. Wife, Jodie, keeps it tidy and sometimes cooks a meal for me."

I listened for a minute, then two going on three minutes before saying, "I'll get a flight out tomorrow morning. Frontier has a direct flight into Jacksonville. Puts me there a little after two in the afternoon." I'd already checked for I knew, once dream time with Gladys was over, I'd have to go home.

"Thanks for doing what you've done." Naturally he had to tell me Jodie would have dinner waiting in the fridge. "I'll catch a cab at the airport and see you and the contractor tomorrow afternoon at the house if you can set it up. After four if possible."

Gladys and John did a one-word duet by simultaneously asking, "What?"

"Late October Nor'easter. Limb on one of the big live oaks around my place broke off and fell on my back-porch roof. That porch is my favorite part of the house. Looks out over the Intracoastal Waterway. The limb also caused a leak in the roof over the kitchen. David's had the limb removed and a plastic cover put over the hole, but I need to talk dollars with the contractor before he'll do anything. For whatever reason, he won't talk by phone. Take a day or two before I can get back." I had to laugh. "I knew things were going too well."

Once John had gone and Gladys and I were in the SUV back to Denver, Gladys said, "We've got to talk with Deputy Innes as soon as you get back. We can't let this 'B' thing go any longer without telling Chief Kay and the Undersheriff. Agree?"

While I had avoided thinking about it, I knew sooner or later this was something that had to be done. I nodded. "Agree.

Wonder how much jail time we'll get for breaking and entering, burglary and shooting at the bad guys?"

Gladys laughed. "We can plead mental incompetency and ask for clemency."

* * *

Since the only clothes I had with me were those on my body, the rest left at Gladys's condo, and with plenty of things at home in the closet, I punched my way through the computerized boarding pass system in Denver International's main terminal, kissed Gladys good-by and headed for the TSA security check point. Once cleared I took the short train ride to Concourse A, stopping on my way to the boarding gate at a small book store for something to read.

That's when things literally hit the fan. At the entrance was a rack of the *Denver Post's* morning edition with Roberta Pine Wood's picture (aka Roberta Wilson, Esq.) in living color splashed across the upper half of the front page. Above the picture was the headline in bold caps, NATIVE AMERICANS LINKED TO KILLINGS. For a moment, all I could do was to stare at the picture and ask myself, "What the hell?"

I grabbed one, tossed a couple of bucks on the counter and headed for my assigned boarding gate, scanning the accompanying article as I went along the people mover. The only thing positive in the article was the statement that the *Post* had yet to confirm any of the allegations through its own sources. Of course, if that was the case, why print the picture and article? The only reason I could think of was to scoop other local media with the breaking news since they knew most of them would grab the information and run with it, regardless.

Once at the boarding gate, I called Gladys. When she answered, I asked, "Still on the road, or are you at the office?"

"On I-70, almost to the I-25 exit. Why?"

"Grab a copy of this morning's *Post* when you get there. If your boss wasn't famous before, she is now. Infamous might be the more accurate word. Picture on the front page and some kind of evidence suddenly found linking her, John, Vincent Brave Wolf, her co-chair on the Indian Commission, Dr. Ernest Long Bow and Samuel Hataali to the killings around Deer Creek Canyon Park."

Gladys was apparently speechless since all I heard was road noise over the phone and a nearby loudspeaker announcing, "Frontier Airlines Flight 858 to Jacksonville is ready to board. Boarding will proceed by row numbers."

"Gotta go, Hun. I'll call this evening and we'll talk. See you in two days… I hope."

Chapter 30

After landing in Jacksonville, grabbing a cab and the usual forty-five-minute drive out to Palm Valley that stretched into over an hour because of the early afternoon homeward-bound rush, I met with David and the contractor. Once we'd crawled around the roof, inspected the damage, discussed the work that needed to be done and agreed on a price, I wrote a check for David to give the contractor when the work was completed to David's satisfaction. With that done, David and the contractor long gone, and with half the porch still usable, I settled down with an ice-cold bottle of Newcastle Brown Ale from the refrigerator. The ale, an autumn amber thanks to David's wife Jodie, was just right for late October, whether in Florida or Colorado.

With the last few remnants of light slipping westward through the palms, cypress and live oaks on the far side of the Intracoastal Waterway and fishing boats headed for home, I finally had some quiet time to think about what happened in Colorado and what new evidence had suddenly surfaced. Evidence that placed Roberta, John, and the other Indian Commission members with Samuel Hataali and the various murders. Hataali I could see, guiding a mentally disturbed grandson to commit the killings, but the others? No way. Somebody was setting them up, and I had a good idea who it was. A man called B and whoever was yanking his chain.

If Chief Kay and the Jefferson County's Sheriff's Department were involved with this new finding, why hadn't she mentioned it? At the very least, said there was additional evidence which they were investigating. If this didn't come from Chief Kay and her people, again, who and why now?

In the final analysis, like so many times in my life when I

should have minded my own business, there was no way I was going to let John and his friends be roped into something they didn't do. Unless Chief Kay and her people would be willing to keep us in the loop once Gladys, Innes and I told them about what we'd uncovered in Lundgren's home, it would be up to Gladys and me to find the answers, or additional innocent lives were going to be ruined.

Once finishing a heated-up plate of Jodie's awesome downhome shrimp and grits with another Newcastle Brown, I made a couple of phone calls. First a thirty-minute call to Gladys that began with several mutual statements of how much we missed each other. It was a fact, but I wasn't yet ready to say *I love you* and apparently neither was Gladys.

With that out of the way, she told me the situation had taken off full bore, not only on local media, but had drawn national attention on the four major TV networks plus CNN, PBS's *BBC World News America* and internationally on the U.K.'s *Sky News*. I'd been so tired I hadn't even turned on the TV, let alone surfed the Internet for news.

"You wouldn't believe it," she said. "Roberta has taken a leave of absence from the firm, but speaking with Roberta, she says she, John and the others will definitely fight the charges. The whole thing is already beginning to look like a public lynching if you will. Believe it or not, people have dubbed the killings Colorow's Revenge among other racially tainted names."

I remembered during the Indian Commission meeting I attended with John, Robert Yellow Horse jokingly using the term based on Ute Chief Colorow's hatred of white people for encroachment on his land back in the late 1800's, the land that later became the park and the Canyon Creek Estates. Land that, along with the Ute, had also been part of the hunting range for the Cheyenne, Arapaho and, during their migration from the north, the Navajo.

"They're saying they wanted white people off the land so it could become a memorial for Native Americans and a museum celebrating the history and contributions of First Nation People." She went on to say, "The so-called evidence material points out that Roberta is Arapahoe, Long Bow, Ute, and John and Brave Wolf as well as Haatali, Navajo. They all plotted the killings together to get the land using the Navajo legend around shape shifting from man to wolf to kill and scare off all the people."

"All of that kind of information's really in this supposed evidence?" I asked.

"Yes, that and in the media, but no mention of the Ralston World Wide Entertainment and its theme park. That seems to have been forgotten, at least so far as the media is concerned."

"That's strange. Like you told us early on, the Jefferson County Planning and Zoning Department's got all the information about Ralston and what they're trying to do with the land. You'd think they would have tied the two together and said something to Sheriff Ferguson."

I thought a moment. "Whoever's behind this evidence appears to have forgotten about Ralston. That's either intentional or a slipup we might be able to go after."

By this time, I could hardly keep my eyes open and was trying to stifle yawn after yawn when I admitted, "Look, sweetheart, I'm dead on my feet. I've got another call to make. A guy named Tom Granger who used to be a U.S. Marshall here in the Jacksonville area. Once delivered a subpoena for me to appear before a Federal Grand Jury up in D.C. They were investigating a really bad government guy who tried to have the Canadian Prime Minister assassinated in addition to me and a friend, the latter two of us both here in the States *and* in Canada.

"Tom got his law degree and is now with the FBI in Washington. Fairly high level. Strangely enough, we became friends during a murder case in Jacksonville before he went big time. If I can reach him and set up a meeting, I'll catch a flight out of here tomorrow morning with a stopover in Washington. Afterwards, back to Denver."

"What can he do?" she asked.

"If he's as high up as he's told me, maybe fill me in on all this rare earth stuff Simon Grant told us about and what the feds are doing about it. At least in Colorado, whether it involves someone called B, the Chinese government or both, my gut tells me that's where everything started and where it's going to end."

* * *

Anticipating another several weeks in Denver and surrounding environs with November and colder weather a few days away, I was armed with a small carry-on suitcase packed tight with somewhat heavier clothing to hopefully protect from the first snowfall around the Mile High City. Thus prepared, an early flight on United put me in Washington's Dulles International at a few minutes before 10:00 the next morning with a connecting flight to Denver leaving that afternoon at 4:00.

That gave me barely enough time to put my luggage in a storage locker and a fast cab ride into the city for my appointment at 935 Pennsylvania Avenue, the J. Edgar Hoover FBI Building. Even though I'd spent several years at the Pentagon, the latter years with an additional closet-sized office in the Capital Building shared with seven other officers, I never really noticed the FBI building had two different floor levels: Eight stories on the Pennsylvania Avenue side; eleven on the E Street side. Nor was I aware that the building was constructed of precast concrete slabs, unlike many of the other older federal buildings of marble exteriors in Washington. Must admit, however, the FBI building was not my usual hangout in downtown D.C.

If influence and power was any indication by office location, the higher up in the building, the greater the influence and importance, Tom Granger had done well for himself in the years since we first met. After going through the usual security procedures and body pat down, the latter primarily because I had forgotten to take off my belt with the military style brass buckle, I was escorted to Granger's office overlooking Pennsylvania

Avenue within the Counterintelligence Directorate. After explaining my reasons for seeing him during our phone conversation last evening, this was where he said we would meet, one of two offices he had in the D.C. area.

Tom, in his late forties, was a good-looking guy, still wearing the usual dress uniform for government law enforcement personnel who rode a desk in Washington: dark suit, white shirt, power tie and immaculately polished shoes. His office had the same look, conservatively furnished, comfortable furniture but not extravagant.

After a quick updating of personal events in our lives over coffee – he'd divorced and remarried since we last shared a beer in Jacksonville; for me, the unraveling of my relationships, first with the brilliant and lovely Dr. Millicent (Millie) Bowman whose research in Boston took priority over my humble existence, and second, with pretty Polly on whom I earlier expounded.

That over and down to business, Tom said, "I know you carried all kinds of top secret clearances when you were on active duty in the Navy, but I'm guessing right now your clearance level is high enough to maybe read the editorial page in the *Washington Post*."

I laughed. "Sometimes I'm not even sure of that."

Continuing, he said, "Tell me exactly what it is you know about the Colorado situation. Based on that, I'll tell you as much as I can without getting into anything that's classified."

Thirty minutes later after running through events in the Denver area over the past several weeks coupled with information about Bastnäsite and rare earths Gladys and I received from Simon Grant at the Colorado Geological Survey, Tom said, "My directorate is very much involved, working with several other Departments: Homeland Security, State and Interior as well as receiving related foreign intelligence provided by CIA, DIA, etc. etc.

"Yes, there are locations other than Colorado in other states under investigation. Similar organizations, companies or corporations, if you will, fronting for what appears to be the Chinese. And yes, rare earth elements are the name of the game, buying up land without, to our knowledge, mineral rights thus far, through coercion or other means, such as the actions in Colorado."

I asked, "If not for mineral rights and mining operations, buying for what?" I already knew from Simon Grant what he and the U.S. Geological people thought, but I wanted Granger to verify Simon's information.

"Quite simply, to deny us the option of mining for minerals such as your Bastnäsite from which rare earth's can be extracted. Whether allied with this effort or not, several nationally prominent environmental organizations have been and continue to lobby against rare earth mining, using big bucks that appear above their normal cash flow.

"As you noted, the President is determined to exploit such mining in the United States and, as you also mentioned, even Afghanistan if we can finally clear out Taliban and Isis forces. It's the continuing and future monopoly of rare earths by China and their ability to reduce supply, especially for our military usage as well as that of our allies, that has taken on such urgency. To be honest, between you and me, our Commander in Chief is not necessarily on my favorite's list on many things, but on this, he's spot-on.

"Our job, my job to be exact, and that of the Counter-intelligence Directorate is protection of our nation's critical assets. That covers a wide area, including technology sectors, mining and extraction of rare earths for example. It also covers countering the activities of foreign operatives who mean to do harm to the United States. That's where we are right now relative to China and the rare earth situation.

"On a federal level, we were slow to realize what and why certain things have been happening. It wasn't until the U.S. Geological Survey and local agencies such as your Colorado people contacted the Interior Department that someone started to take notice. While evidence collected is thus far convincing, it's identifying the active players that have been the problem, especially our own citizens who are, knowingly or unknowingly, playing into Chinese hands and giving assistance. Those involved with what we think are front companies and those who may be working individually like this B person you mentioned."

Granger paused, giving me a moment to mentally review what he had told me before saying, "Without going further in the actual investigative process and where we stand, that's all I can say. I realize it's not much more than you've already determined from your own involvement in Colorado."

I decided to press the Chinese element a little further. "Let's say it's not the Chinese. The companies operating in various states are legitimate and buy the land. It would seem our imminent domain laws could intervene if we know there's Bastnäsite reserves U.S. companies could recover. Other than in the minds of certain environmental groups, that would certainly be in the public's interest, the nation's interest."

The look on Granger's face told me he didn't really want to go any further. Finally, he said, "Great idea in itself, but a bit tricky in this case. The feds would be working under the Fifth Amendment, locals under the Fourteenth. If we know there are actual rare earth deposits within the land or lands in question, yes. If we knew for certain, we wouldn't allow federally owned lands to be leased or private lands to be sold for other than actual mining of Bastnäsite or any other recognized, high-demand minerals."

"Certainly not knowingly to the Chinese," I interjected.

"Right, leased or sold if Bastnäsite was or is to be recovered by our own companies. It's my understanding in the vast majority of cases based on U.S. Geological Survey and some input from the Bureau of Land Management, we only *think* there are such deposits. The only four we're aware exist are three in southern Colorado and the one in California. All owned by Richmond RE, Inc., now closed with the company in bankruptcy.

"For other areas, potentials only, yet to be proven. One way or the other, environmentalists have kept us from making a final determination. Without actual plans to make some use of the property that would directly or indirectly benefit the public and to reimburse the owner, that would be the first problem. Even if we did, if the owner refused, then the government, federal or local, would have to go to court. That can drag on for years. We may not have years."

I pushed my luck a bit further. "On the flip side, say we definitely determine it is the Chinese for the purpose of keeping us from the land and its potential Bastnäsite deposits so they can maintain their monopoly of rare earths. There must be ways short of war we can stop them."

Granger gave a rather sardonic laugh. "You're asking for too much, my friend. Like I said, once we know for certain it *is* the Chinese, yes, there are ways. Unfortunately, because of the sensitivity of what's happening in other areas, both militarily and economically, I'm limited in what I can tell you. I'm sorry, but I can't say anymore."

After final words, handshakes and the arrival of an escort to usher me out of the building, once I started to leave the office, Granger handed me his card. "Has my office phone. If you call and you think it's something of a sensitive nature, just say, 'We need to talk about our problem.' I'll arrange for you to use a cryptographically covered phone at the Denver FBI office. Keep in touch, especially concerning information you learn about your B person. He could well lead us to the source of all this business."

I made it just in time to catch my afternoon flight out of Dulles and, with the time change and gaining of two hours on the clock, made it into DIA a little before six Mountain Time. Even though Gladys was supposed to meet me, I honestly didn't know how much I'd missed her until she was in my arms. Like homecoming, so natural, like the way it was supposed to be. Was I really the target of Cupid's arrow? Still to be determined, but damn, she felt good, and from what I could tell by the smile on her face and the kiss she planted on my lips, it was a WOW moment for both of us.

Chapter 31

The town of Greenwood Village just south of Denver is, for the most part, an affluent upper middle class, or higher, residential and business area, in particular the DTS district, short for Denver Technical Center. There you find both national and international headquarters for corporations involved in web and software design, electronic components, artificial intelligence, communications, aviation, aerospace including launch rockets, satellites and missiles, mining, investment and insurance. I could go on and on.

Gladys's condo, spacious and tastefully appointed with memories collected by a woman who had traveled much of the world, was just west of the Tech Center in Greenwood Village with a relatively easy commute to her work downtown.

Finally, home, at least I called it that if only on a temporary basis, a quick shower and a change of clothes, we had a take-out dinner from a local Greek restaurant consisting of gyro platters and calamari over a light-sauced pasta, washed down by glasses of ice-cold Ouzo. As tired as I was and with the dinner table cleared, I was ready for some very intimate time with Gladys followed by much needed sleep.

That, however, was not to be the case. Once the table was cleared, plates and the usual accessories packed into the dishwasher, except for two final glasses of chilled Ouzo, Gladys said, "Work time. Bring your glass and let's go into the den."

"You have got to be kidding."

With a laugh, she continued, "With Roberta taking a leave of absence, I was able to wrangle several days off, part vacation, part sick leave. While you've been flying around the country, I've been doing some research, but tell me what you learned since you left Denver."

Once settled into the warmth of the den before a gas log fireplace, I gave her a quick rundown on what had to be done with my house in Florida and a more in-depth description of the meeting with Tom Granger at FBI headquarters. The essence of the latter was, as we suspected after our visit with Simon Grant at Colorado Geological Survey, rare earth elements and evidence pointing to Chinese involvement through front companies in various western states. Thus far, however, they had nothing substantial enough to risk an international blowup.

"One of the problems the feds are having is identifying in virtually all cases local people who are inadvertently or purposely helping the Chinese. Case in point, our anonymous B person. Who is he, or maybe she, since the letter never really gave any indication as to which gender. Identifying Mr., Ms. or even a Mrs. B could be a major step in proving Chinese involvement. Granger's last words were, 'Keep in touch, especially any information you find about your B person.'"

Taking a final sip of Ouzo, Gladys went to her desk, unlocked one of the drawers and drew out several sheets of paper. "Part of what I've been doing is trying to get an idea who might fit the profile of our Mr., Ms., or you say, Mrs. B."

"You've got to admit, I'm an equal opportunity guy," I quipped, adding my wry sense of humor which, to my disappointment, brought only the mildest of smiles.

Continuing, she said, "Assuming the person is local, meaning the greater Denver metropolitan area – Denver, municipalities and metro districts in surrounding counties – I've made a list of people whose first and/or last names start with 'B' currently employed with governments in these areas. I started with one hundred and sixty-eight and, with a bit of snooping through Google and certain other systems to which I have access, I've whittled it down to ten names. Each with as much biographical data as I could find."

This lady had no end of surprises. Her words *certain other systems to which I have access* told me she was still able to use both present and past government contacts for information. "So, at this point, where does that put us?"

"Using the Internet's white pages, I was able to get Deputy Innes's phone number and spoke with him about meeting with Chief Kay and the Undersheriff."

I had a mental picture of the shock and frown on Innes's face when asked about the meeting. "With his job and future on the line, I bet he really went for that idea."

"Not much. After talking and explaining it was the only way to get them to keep the case open and go after the people behind all the killings and threats to his family, he was still pretty skittish about it, especially about the risk to his job. That's when I told him we thought it was the Chinese buying the land based on what Simon Grant told us. To deny the U.S. of certain strategic materials necessary for the country's defense. I can only assume it was his Army training and love of country that finally kicked in and he agreed."

"Have you set up the meeting?"

"No. Wanted to wait until you returned and showed you the list."

I shook my head and laughed. "After we admit to breaking and entering Lundgren's house, burgling his safe for incriminating evidence which we can't provide and, for all practical purposes, starting a shooting war with the Chinese, I just hope you get to show the list before they put us in a cell for safe keeping."

And yes, after she went over the list with me, I finally got my intimate time with that very lovely lady before slipping off into a sleep filled with people chasing and shooting at me in the dark. Whether it was the Chinese or Chief Kay and the Undersheriff, I couldn't remember.

* * *

With certain reservations which she didn't bother to

explain, Chief Kay reluctantly agreed to meet with Gladys, Innes and me the following afternoon. The fact that she appeared worn out and gave every appearance she'd much rather be home with her now several-weeks-old son, did not bode well for our meeting. There were also no courtesy questions such as *how are things going with you?* nor offerings of coffee.

The fact that Undersheriff Mike Vasquez's frown seemed plastered on his face also did nothing to promise a positive outcome. While we were not aware Dr. Wong was to be included, his was the only friendly, and yes, welcoming face around the table.

It was Chief Kay who first spoke first. "I'm not sure why we agreed to meet with you. As you were told, so far as the Department is concerned, the perpetrator has been identified and, with his mentor, is dead. End of story. The Sheriff personally made that announcement in all the local media along with the information about the Grand Jury and the people on the Indian Commission.

"People are moving back into their homes in Canyon Creek Estates. Others who may have closed on the sale of their property with that Ralston company have hired lawyers to cancel their contracts and return Ralston's money. The Deer Creek Canyon case is closed. How many times do we have to tell you?

"As you said on the phone asking for this meeting, Mr. Berkeley, you did not include John Nabhe in your requests for the meeting since he is the subject of a soon to be Grand Jury investigation along with the other three Native Americans. Unless you have something additional that bears on *that* case, something totally earth shattering, you three may well be wasting your time as well as ours."

I knew things weren't going well when Chief Kay resorted to *Mr. Berkeley* rather than the much friendlier *Matt* used when I was helping solve the murders. That being the case, since she agreed to the meeting, why not push a little further. "I assure you, Chief, we're not trying to waste your time. I do, however, find it curious from what you've said about considering the case closed, you waffled around Captain Lundgren's involvement. Surely, you're curious as to why he was meeting with Samuel Hataali, the killer's grandfather or whatever he was. And, based on witnesses, the so-called papers Lundgren passed to Hataali. Did they just blow away on the morning breeze?"

"How the hell did you know about the papers"? Vasquez demanded.

"Overheard the Chief when she was chewing you out." If Vasquez's eyes had been able to shoot nine-millimeter rounds, I would have been dead on the spot, but I wasn't through. "Nor have you shown any particular desire to determine Captain Lundgren's link to the Hataali man and his part in the whole affair."

There was a moment of silence in the room until Vasquez said, "That's an internal affair and none of your business."

Giving an evil eye in the direction of Innes, Vasquez said, "What I want to know is why you're here, Deputy? What have you got to do with this? And you, Ms. Knight, since you never got in touch about doing some work with us, work we talked about. The same question applies to you."

Gladys replied, "I think you'll understand once Deputy Innes explains his part in the investigation."

"His part?" boomed the Undersheriff. "What the hell part did he have to play other than directing traffic?"

I jumped in with, "Hear him out, damn it! Go ahead, Ralph."

The room became very quiet. Both Vasquez and Chief Kay locked eyes on me as though I dared talk back to law enforcement. Once they got over the shock of my impudence and apparently decided not to charge me with being a smartass, Chief Kay said, "Following that little outburst, I suppose as Mr. Berkeley says, go ahead, Deputy."

Setting the bezel on my watch, it was exactly fifteen minutes by the time Innes finished telling his story: spying for Lundgren during the murder case, people higher up pulling the strings, the order to kill Samuel Hataali with the secretly provided M-110 sniper rifle, the threat to his mother and sister now in California with a relative and witnessing the double killing at the RDT Park and Ride."

"Sniper rifle?" Chief Kay asked. "You were there the whole time? You were going to assassinate the Hataali man? You saw it all?"

"Yes, ma'am. The rifle's out in my car, unloaded. Don't know where Lundgren got it, but I need to turn it in."

"You're goddamn right you do," blurted Vasquez. "My big question is why didn't you use the damn thing? Shoot the Indian like Lundgren wanted you to. Lundgren might still be alive."

Innes studied the top of the table for what seemed like forever until Vasquez demanded, "Answer, damn it."

Looking up, first at Vasquez then at Chief Kay, "I didn't know the Indian. It wasn't a kill-or-be-killed situation like in Afghanistan. I couldn't just shoot him in cold blood. But Lundgren? Absolutely. He was gonna have my mother and sister killed if I didn't kill the Indian. Orders from somebody higher up, he said. I decided while I was out there, if I was gonna kill anybody, it would be Lundgren, but the Indian was too fast. Thank God I didn't have to."

Chief Kay and Vasquez both shook their heads. At the same time Vasquez said, "Shit!"

For the first time since we'd arrived, Dr. Wong entered the conversation and asked, "Is that all, Deputy?"

"No, sir." Innes looked at Gladys and me. "If one or both of you would tell what happened after that, I'd appreciate it."

Gladys and I took turns telling of the dinner with Innes, getting into Lundgren's house that night, what we found in the safe and our encounter with the two Chinese.

Dr. Wong was the first to break the silence. "From what the Crime Scene people tell me, with the number of shots fired, you're lucky to be alive. They found o ne nine-millimeter round and eighteen of the 5.8 by 42-millimeter rounds in the walls of the stairway and entryway. As the Undersheriff has already told you in our last meeting, the forty-two mils are of Chinese manufacture for their QBZ 95 assault rifle which goes to make Mr. Berkeley's idea of Chinese involvement more plausible."

At the word *stairway*, where we had hunkered down during the attack, Gladys and I looked at each other, both with facial expressions exhibiting how lucky we were before I said, "Yes, we were lucky, but since we were, there was really no alternative but to come here and give you the facts of what happened. And most of all, about Lundgren's past and blackmail by a man, or woman, called 'B.'"

Vasquez shook his head and asked Chief Kay, "What the hell are we going to do with these three? Charge them with burglary, destruction of private property, discharging a fire arm inside the City of Golden? Damn if this isn't a frigging mess if I ever saw one.

"And what the hell are we going to do about this B person? Reopen the case? Hell, there's already four other people under suspicion for the murders. What about them?"

"I'm tired, Mike," was her only reply, said with a sigh. "I'm not operating on all cylinders, that's for sure." She paused for a moment, apparently thinking about what she'd heard, before saying, "The Crime Scene boss said they opened Lundgren's safe and found nothing but house-closing papers, state and federal income tax returns, insurance papers, that kind of stuff. There was no mention of money, newspaper clipping and a blackmail letter from a person named B. If what Berkeley and Ms. Knight are telling us is true, somebody else got into that house and took whatever evidence that might have driven us to keep the case open."

Now we were getting somewhere. "Just a couple of more things," I said, "and then you can lock us up if that's what you want or need to do. As far as our B is concerned, I was in Washington as in D.C. yesterday. Visited an old acquaintance who heads up the FBI's Counterintelligence Directorate. We discussed what happened here, possible Chinese involvement as well as similar happenings in other states. Happenings involving the Chinese from what they can determine. If you recall, Chief, the rare earth minerals thing we learned about over at the Colorado Geological Survey. You remember, Undersheriff, I told you at our meeting following the Lundgren killing."

"Yeah, so?"

"That's what they think the Chinese are after. My acquaintance's last words before I left to fly back to Denver was, 'Keep in touch, especially any information you find about your B person. He could well lead us to the source of all this business.'" I paused for a moment, looking at Gladys. "Gladys may well have a lead."

Gladys passed around a sheet of paper to each person at the table." "While Matt was in Florida and Washington, I did some research. In my mind, whoever was blackmailing Lundgren and forcing him to cause everything that's happened is someone involved in or with law enforcement. Someone I would guess is fairly influential in political and/or law enforcement circles."

"Why so," questioned Vasquez.

"He was definitely aware of Lundgren's lurid past, had covered it up for future use and now was the future. Someone privy to law enforcement to have such knowledge. Someone still powerful enough to force Lundgren into being involved. Perhaps also involved in drugs, money under the table and who knows what else.

"As I told Matt, I researched everyone with the first and/or last name starting with 'B' currently working in law enforcement in the greater Denver area and surrounding counties. Lundgren's alleged killing of the two Latino drug couriers was in Douglas County, just south of Denver. I've reduced the names from one hundred sixty-eight to ten. I'd like to go over the ten names with you if I may."

"We're here when we could be heading home, so why the

hell not," said Vasquez, "but one question. I know damn well you're not just some lawyer's assistant, so what are you? What have you done before joining that law firm?"

I could see the wheels turning before Gladys finally said, "You're right. I was with the Central Intelligence Agency, twenty-three years. That's all you need to know."

Once again there was silence in the room, the kind that occurs in the deep of night at the bottom of a well. It was almost as though I was waiting to hear the haunting cry of an owl from somewhere off in the distance. Innes and I already knew, but the other three were open mouthed until Vasquez muttered, "By damn, I knew there was something about you. I knew it. That's why I offered you –"

Gladys interrupted him. "Ancient history. As I was saying, I'd like to go over the ten names on the sheet I passed around. Okay?"

"Do it," Chief Kay said.

"They're in alphabetical order with their current positions."

Gladys started at the top of the list with their current title.

Mr., Ms. or Mrs.. B. Suspects
Bassett, Johnathon, Esq.... Denver County...CPA, Director of Contracts & Accountability, also a lawyer
Bearman, Ruth Ann... Arapahoe County, Chief Deputy D.A., 18th Judicial District Office in Centennial
Bergan, Ralph W.... Aurora...City Attorney (legal counsel to the Mayor, City Counsel et al)
Bliss, Wallace M. ... Douglas County, County Attorney
Bishop, Christopher Warren... DA, 1st Judicial District (Jefferson County)
Boraz, Robert D... Golden...Golden City Counsel, lawyer
Branch, Millard R...Thornton...Municipal Judge, Thornton Municipal Court
Breen, Jean L ... Douglas County, Senior Asst. County Attorney (Human Services)

Buena Vista, Anna... Lone Tree, Sgt, Police Dept., Criminal Investigations, Investigation Services Division

Burnham, Barbara...Denver County, Magistrate, Denver County Juvenile Court.

Gladys went name by name, providing in depth information concerning each of the individuals, their ages, education, past employment including political positions, if any, marital status and current jobs. Once finished, she asked, "In your opinions, which name or names best fits the person who would be involved in Captain Lundgren's past, involved enough to know something with which to blackmail and pressure the Captain into overseeing the murder of innocent people?"

Chief Kay was first. "Lundgren was in Douglas County before he came here. Bliss was and is County Attorney for DougCo at the time Lundgren was with the Douglas County Sheriff's Department and now...? But I doubt from the other background info you gave that he's the one.

"Then there's Breen, Senior Assistant Douglas County Attorney now, but she was in Texas at the time you say Lundgren allegedly shot the two Latinos and took their money."

"That leaves Bishop, the D.A. for the First Judicial District, our district," Vasquez said before repeating much of Gladys's background information on the man. "Once a Municipal Judge in Illinois, left under a cloud. Then Town Attorney for Castle Rock down in Douglas County around that time, left over a dispute with the Sheriff's office.

"After that, Chief Deputy District Attorney for the Eighteenth Judicial District which includes Douglas County when Lundgren did his thing. Later ran for and elected to DA for our judicial district. Wife murdered under suspicious circumstances, but a male lover convicted. Understand he's in the State Pen down in Cañon City. You agree with our three picks?"

"I do," answered Gladys.

Dr. Wong asked, "Which do you think best fits the picture, Ms. Knight?"

Gladys answered without hesitation. "District Attorney Christopher Warren Bishop."

"What about you, Berkeley?"

"Same."

"Do you to know what you're suggesting?" asked Chief Kay. "This man is one of the most powerful men in Jefferson County, respected by law enforcement, has lunch with the Governor, golfs with the mayors of Denver and Golden. Thick with our Sheriff Ferguson. One of the highest conviction rates for murder-one and sexual assault cases in the State. Do you really think we can go after this man without bringing all the political shit down on Mike and me, let alone the Department?"

Dr. Wong, looked at his watch, pushed back from the table and stood. "I've got people standing by for an autopsy on what we think was a suicide, but I will say this. I've worked with several coroners' offices around the state, especially Denver and Douglas County. DougCo's coroner has been in her job for the past ten years. She has never had a kind word for Christopher Bishop since his days with the Eighteenth Judicial District. Unless proven otherwise, I go with Ms. Knight."

"What would you recommend," Chief Kay asked.

As Wong walked to the door, he turned and said, "Go quietly, go slowly, but by all means, follow up on Ms. Knight's lead. Determine motive and while doing so, should you find a connection between Lundgren, Bishop, Ralston World Wide Entertainment, and as Mr. Berkeley believes, the Chinese government, as well as what I believe to be bogus evidence concerning members of the American Indian Commission, arrest the man.

Chapter 32

Since we had not been bound by secrecy concerning the results of that afternoon's meeting and it was after six, well past normal office hours, I tried to call John at his home in Denver on his landline and on his mobile, but there was only the answer service in both cases stating his number and promise to return the call. After a third try, I gave up, knowing John had an active social life outside his law office, a life which had pretty much been stymied with his involvement in the case.

I joined Gladys on the condo unit's balcony for a chilled glass of German Riesling *Spätlese*, late harvest wine from the Rhine valley. Though it was still a few days to fallback from Daylight Savings to Mountain Time, the lights of the nearby Tech Center and surrounding businesses as well as part of downtown Denver to the north were beginning to push back against the coming darkness. Already the sounds of rush hour traffic were starting to fade to their nighttime level.

"You going to try to get hold of Roberta?" I asked.

"After we eat. Briefly talked to her before we went to the meeting with Chief Kay. Said she had an appointment with her lawyer concerning the allegations. Wouldn't be home until seven or seven-thirty. Warm-ups okay?"

"I'm good with anything you've got. Some of that spaghetti and meatballs I saw in the frig would be great."

After finishing dinner and the usual required cleanup, Gladys called Roberta. Wanting to give her some privacy, I settled in the den to go over the information she had assembled on Christopher Bishop. At this point, he was no more than a shot in the dark, but the best we had at identifying what appeared to be a *Mr.* B rather than a *Ms.* or *Mrs*.

The two primary questions in my mind were, one, if we were right, who was he working with or for and two, did the Jefferson County Sheriff's Department have guts enough to go after him? Would they take on the potential political fallout, allocate the resources necessary to check his movements, his associates, his finances? There was definitely big-time money involved in buying the land from homeowners as well as leasing park land from the county. Based on the D.A.'s salary or past city and county work before his present position and, from what we could determine, his current assets, it was a helluva lot more money than Bishop could raise.

Gladys came into the room. "She was home, just finished dinner. Told her about our meeting this afternoon plus what happened at Lundgren's house. Before I got to the list of suspects I'd prepared, our recommendation, and Chief Kay's and the Undersheriff's disappointing reaction, her doorbell rang. Thought it might be one of her people on the Indian Commission. Said she'd call back.

"She did say, the meeting I told you about with her lawyer included Vincent Brave Wolf and Dr. Long Bow. They developed a plan of action to fight the out-of-nowhere charges somebody concocted. For whatever reason, John wasn't there."

I couldn't imagine John missing such an important meeting. "Whatever they decided, it had better be good," I said. "The media and many of their readers and viewers from what I can tell have already anointed themselves as judge and jury and it doesn't look good."

* * *

Roberta looked through the peep hole in the door and saw, not a member of the Commission, but a familiar, yet unexpected, rather pudgy face. "What is he doing here?" she muttered to herself, eyes narrowing in a frown. Flipping the latch on the door's lock, she opened the door.

"Good evening, Mrs. Wilson. You don't mind me calling you by your business name, do you?"

"Uh, no, but you're the last person I would expect to see."

"I realize this is somewhat unusual, but there are things about the evidence concerning you and the other members of your Commission that simply do not add up. Before we go further in the investigation and expend the time and money involved in a Grand Jury, and I might add, further endanger your reputations, I felt there are certain things you might be able to clear up. May I come in?"

Roberta hesitated a moment before holding the door open. In terms of the law, not only unusual but unheard of, if not illegal. With the inward sweep of her hand she said, "Mr. District Attorney, uh Mr. Bishop, come in, please."

Once inside the small entrance way, he stood while she closed the door. "After you, Mrs. Wilson."

Roberta nodded and started into the apartment's main living area. Surprised at seeing the man, she failed to notice his hands, held close to his sides, were covered with skin-colored surgical gloves. A plastic, see-through, ten milliliter syringe and hypodermic needle was wrapped in the fold of the palm of his right hand.

As soon as she turned, his left arm shot out, caught her throat in the crook of the elbow, squeezed, shutting off any scream and pulled her back and down to his height. With the right hand, he immediately jabbed the needle into the sternomastoid muscle of Roberta's neck, just to the right of the spine's first cervical bone at the base of the skull. The thumb forced the plunger down through the shaft of the syringe, pumping three milliliters of liquid into the thick upper portion of the muscle. Pulling the needle free, he immediately relaxed his left arm and forcibly shoved Roberta across the room.

Off balance, her body stumbled over a coffee table and crashed onto the arm of a sofa. Her head slammed into the wall behind the furniture. Falling back onto the sofa, facing Bishop, eyes wide, she cried, "My God, what have you –" That's as far as she got.

Expressionless, eyes fastened on Roberta, Bishop withdrew a small plastic container from his suit coat pocket, placed the syringe and needle into it and returned it to his pocket. "To be truthful, Mrs. Wilson, while this wasn't part of the original plan, it does simplify things, at least for me. They'll find your note with its apology for all the lives you and your savage friends have taken."

Roberta's hands, then her arms began to twitch, the man in front of her, though already vastly overweight, took on the shape of a bloated, suit-covered balloon, floating before her eyes as he moved in front of her. Her body felt as though it was twisting, upper torso moving in one direction, hips and legs in another. No control.

She shook her head, trying to overcome the spinning dizziness that had enveloped her brain, her thoughts unable to make sense out of what was happening. Almost immediately, her breathing became shallower and shallower, her stomach churning as though a whirlpool was spinning inside. The burning, unstoppable flow and stench of vomit moved up her esophagus, through her mouth and nostrils, choking her before spilling out onto her lap, her hands, the sofa and the floor beneath her feet.

Bishop wrinkled his nose and looked away from the sight and acrid smell of vomit. He hadn't thought something like that would happen, the sheer nastiness of it, but then, if that was one of the effects, so be it.

All Roberta could think of with any clarity was, *God, please* .... Even the words *help me* refused to register. Everything, the twitch, the twisting, her legs and neck, her entire body went stiff. Her mouth, open as wide as possible, tried to suck air into her lungs, but it wasn't happening. She could feel the beat of her heart slowing. The last thing she saw was balloon man shrinking away into the darkness until he was no more.

Bishop waited for a moment, divorcing himself from the

death he'd created, the lifeless body that lay in front of him. Instead, he mentally pictured Roberta as she'd stood in the open doorway, admiring what had been a truly beautiful woman and imagining what he could have done with and to her.

After several minutes passed, he took a deep breath to avoid the odor of stomach acids and mostly undigested food, moved closer to Roberta's body and placed two-fingers against her throat in search of a pulse. Finding none, he went about preparing a scene he had already envisioned. The only sound in the apartment was the tune he whistled. Something vaguely remembered from a Disney movie as a boy, something about seven dwarfs whistling and singing while on their way to work.

* * *

We talked, watched part of a Denver Bronco and Cincinnati Bengals game rerun on the NFL channel until Gladys, having checked her watch every few minutes, said, "She should have called back by now. Let me try again."

The only response was Roberta's recorded voice on her answer machine giving her number and offer to return the call as soon as possible. Another five minutes, and Gladys made a second call, only to receive the same recording. "Matt, that's not like Roberta. Something's wrong."

"Where does she live?"

"Not far. She's got an apartment at The Homestead at Wilmore Plaza in Cherry Creek North. We can take I-25. This time of night, fifteen, twenty minutes at most."

We both grabbed jackets, Gladys her wallet, smart phone and car keys to an aging Ford Escape, and took the elevator down to the parking garage. Once on the Interstate, I looked up The Homestead on Gladys's Blackberry. From what I could tell, pretty nice digs.

The introductory description read: *Welcome to The Homestead at Wilmore Plaza, located in the heart of Cherry Creek*

North, one of Denver's premier neighborhoods. All 32 apartments have walk-out balconies that showcase Denver's picturesque skyline. A mere stone's throw away lies a vibrant neighborhood just outside your door and some of the best dining and shopping options in the state.

By the time I finished all the come-live-the-lifestyle information about the Homestead and Cherry Creek North, we were there. There was a four-digit security code required to enter the building which, rifling through her wallet, Gladys found and punched into the key pad. A buzzing sound and we were in the entrance foyer adorned with pictures of Denver's skyline, both night and day, each from a different perspective. Positioned at various locations were several fake, gold-leaved Aspen trees with surrounding plantings to simulate the great outdoors. Soft music played in the background.

We took the elevator to the ninth floor, walked halfway down a lengthy, thickly carpeted hallway and rang the doorbell at Roberta's apartment. No footsteps, no, "I'm coming," from the other side of the door.

Another ringing of the doorbell accompanied with the overly loud use of a brass door knocker gave the same results. The sound of the door knocker did, however, cause a door across the hall to open and a woman to peak out.

"Would you know if Roberta Wilson is at home?" Gladys asked.

"Roberta Pine Woman, the Indian woman you mean? The one whose picture's been on TV about those murders? Don't really know her, but wish she'd move."

"Yes, but the TV people –"

"Haven't seen her." The neighbor's face disappeared, and the door closed followed by the clicking sound of a lock being set.

Gladys immediately pulled out her car key ring, selected a key and started to unlock Roberta's door.

"No lock picks this time, huh"? I asked in a teasing manner. With a soft yet nervous laugh, she said, "No. We've shared each other's keys for a while."

She inserted the key and turned it counterclockwise. A sudden frown etched its way across her face at the lack of a *click*. "It's not locked. She wouldn't do that, leave it unlocked."

I reached for the brass door knob. "Let me." We changed places, and I turned the knob, pushed inward, took two steps into a small entrance way and froze. "Damn!"

Pushing past me, Gladys's response was definitely more restrained. There was no scream, the vocal response normally expressed by an actress in the movies or on TV, a reaction to seeing something unthinkable. It was a hushed, "Oh no, Roberta."

Her right hand automatically made the sign of the cross accompanied by a whispered, "In the name of the Father, and the Son and of the Holy Spirit. Amen."

Chapter 33

I supposed it was Gladys's CIA training that checked her emotions, demanding calm rather than a vocal or tearful outburst. For me, however, unexpectedly finding death has always been an emotional moment, one that, having experienced on numerous occasions, I still find difficult to accept. Especially for someone I know.

My initial thought was, *Murder!* Instinctively wanting to show my masculinity and impulse to protect the weaker sex, I said, "Stay here. Whoever did this might still be here." As I was later to learn, it would be Gladys who would be, if not actually protecting me, leading the two of us to safety and ultimate survival.

I stepped forward, careful not to touch anything, my body automatically tensed in case I found an intruder. Seeing nothing I could use as a weapon I doubled my fists and did a quick check of each room in the apartment. Fortunately, there was no one to be found. When I returned to the living room, Gladys had shut the door to keep people passing along the hallway from looking in and was talking to a 911 operator.

Until then I kept the sight of Roberta limited to my peripheral vision, but there was no putting it off. Roberta was sitting on a sofa, her head bent forward at an odd angle, a purplish bruise on her forehead. Blood and gray matter were scattered on the cushion and wall behind her. Her long black hair, her beautiful black hair was caught against the spread of drying blood from an exit wound at the top of her head.

The lower jaw of her mouth, drooped open, was stained with blood. Bending slightly and going with the angle of her head, as best I could see without touching, her incisor teeth, both upper and lower at the front of her mouth, were cracked where the barrel of a weapon had been placed at the time it was fired. A revolver lay haphazardly in her right hand, resting in her lap where the hand and weapon had fallen. Oddly enough, both dried on her hand and beneath on her lap was a fair amount of vomit. There were several pieces of meat, yellow corn and carrots, the digestive process having only started. Despite the blood, I could see the remains of regurgitation on her lips and in her nostrils.

"No way," I said, shaking my head.

Gladys, having moved to my side, asked, "What do you mean?"

"You said she met with Brave Wolf and Long Bow this afternoon with their lawyer. Plans apparently made to fight the accusations, plans with which she seemed pleased. Apparently, a successful meeting. If so, why kill herself now? And didn't you say she had just finished eating when you called?

"Wouldn't think if you were going to commit suicide, you'd waste time satisfying your appetite. Takes a lot of thinking and anguish before taking your own life." I automatically shook my head. "Something's not right."

It was less than ten minutes before we heard heavy knocking at the door and the shout, "Police. Open the door."

"Coming," Gladys called back. Turning, she hurried to the door and opened it. "Gladys Knight. I'm the one who called 911." She stepped back to stand beside me.

The group, two uniforms and one plain clothes officer, entered the small entrance way and stopped, quickly surveying Gladys and me before looking past us at what I considered to be a crime scene. The one in plain clothes was a woman, black, about five-four, five-five, straight black hair swept back into a bun, attractive. She was in navy blue slacks, white blouse mostly hidden by the same color navy blue Eisenhower-type jacket. A small caliber semiautomatic was holstered at her side. She reminded me of a younger Chief Kay, minus the baby bulge.

The two uniforms, one obviously Hispanic, the other white,

moved slightly to the side, giving separation in case we were really the bad guys and armed.

The woman held up a badge encased in a leather foldout. "Sergeant Sally Springer, Denver Police Department, Homicide, District Three. Anyone else here besides you?"

"Only the deceased," I answered.

To the two uniforms she ordered, "Check the other rooms."

"Already did." I said. "Nobody there."

Staring at me, she said to the uniforms, "Do it anyway," a line of annoyance in her voice, her facial expression letting me know she was running the show. The uniforms glared at me for a moment until she placed a hand on the weapon at her side and said, "I'm good." Once assured, they nodded, gave me the collective evil eye that told me, *move-and-we'll-kill-you* and split up, going in different directions into the rest of the apartment.

Trying to look past us, the Sergeant asked, "You know the deceased?"

Gladys answered, "Yes," as we stepped apart to allow the Sergeant a full view of the room.

She paused a moment, her eyes zeroing in on Roberta on the sofa. I thought I saw her throat constrict in a silent gulp, which seemed strange for someone in homicide, but she quickly recovered and looked in my direction. "Have you touched anything?"

"Yes, the door knob when we entered and a knob on a closet door in her bedroom. You'll probably find my prints on both knobs."

"The deceased's name?"

Gladys said, "I gave it to the 911 operator."

"Give it to me again."

Gladys gave her both the Wilson and Pine Woman names, explaining the reason for each.

Turning to me, the Sergeant asked, "You are?"

"Matt Berkeley."

"Photo ID," followed by a nod toward Gladys, "You also,

ma'am."

I nodded over my shoulder and reached back for my wallet, at the same time adding, "Wallet, back pocket." Didn't want her thinking I was going for a weapon. Once I retrieved the wallet, I handed her my Florida driver's license and my now useless picture military ID card, supposedly saved for nostalgia purposes.

She took them both, looked them over, spent a moment with my old military ID before saying, "Navy. Card's expired. You a Commander?"

"Was. Got too old. They told me to go home."

She handed both cards back. "Me too, Navy. Second Class, Gunners Mate. Did some shore patrol work stationed in Norfolk, Virginia. Liked it, thought I could do better on the outside. Law enforcement."

"Looks like you did. Thank you for your service."

She nodded and said, "You also."

Taking Gladys's Colorado driver's license, she looked it over, comparing the photo to Gladys's face before saying, "Almost time to renew."

"Just got a reminder notice."

Stepping back a foot of two so she could talk to both of us, she asked, "What are you two doing here?"

I left it up to Gladys to explain our relationship with Roberta. I added the part about our work with the Jefferson County Sheriff's Department over the recent killings in the Deer Creek Canyon area. My explanation also touched on Roberta's involvement, past and present, including the recently, in my mind, bogus evidence.

Pointing at Roberta and looking away just as quickly, Sergeant Springer said, "Hard to tell from the damage to her face, but from what you're telling me, she's the one whose picture's been on the front page of the papers and on TV about those Deer Creek killings. She and three or four men, one of them already dead. Right?"

I answered, "Yes, but as I said there are those of us who believe the accusations are false, a frame job to cover the real source behind the killings."

As soon as the two uniforms returned with their, "All clear," announcement, the Latino's hands now covered by latex gloves, gave the Sergeant an envelope. "Suicide note inside. Typed, no signature. Found it on a table in a small office with a computer and printer."

With the two officers' attention now riveted on Gladys and me, the Sergeant made a call, her first words being, "Lieutenant, she's the one. Although it looks like suicide, you need to get over here. I'll call for CSU downtown soon as I hang up. And you might want to let Commander Wallace know. This one could make the front page, big time."

When she hung up, I asked, "CSU. Crime Scene Unit, I understand, but you talked to a lieutenant and mentioned a Commander Wallace. Who are they?"

She held up her hand for silence while she contacted the CSU people, gave them a quick breakdown of the situation as she moved past, stopping at the coffee table. Ending the call, she stood for a moment, taking in the scene before her: Roberta, blood, bone and brain matter on the wall, the revolver in Roberta's hand. While doing so, she answered, "Lieutenant O'Connell, my boss, heads up District Three Investigations. Commander Wallace, the District Three Commander."

She turned, held up the envelope with the supposed suicide note inside, and said, "With the note, the revolver in her hand and after what I've read in the newspaper and heard on TV, strong possibility she decided the best way out was to take her own life."

I shook my head. "Don't think so. Tell her about your phone call, Gladys."

Gladys described the call which Roberta took after eating dinner, the information passed concerning her meeting with two of the Indian Commission members and their lawyer concerning the accusations and the doorbell interruption. Especially the fact that

Roberta was to call back after taking care of whoever was at the door. "When she failed to call, I tried to call her several times with no answer. That's when we decided to come over."

As we both answered her questions, Sergeant Springer took notes in what I called an op-event notebook until a tall, gangly man, middle aged with red hair opened the door and walked in.

"What's happening, Sergeant?" With that, he abruptly stopped, looked first at Gladys and me before immediately moving across the room and concentrating on Roberta. "At first glance, I agree. It looks like suicide. Any evidence it's not?"

"That's the way I see it, Lieutenant, plus we've got what appears to be a suicide note." The Sergeant walked to the Lieutenant's side. She nodded over her shoulder at Gladys and me, introducing us to Lieutenant O'Connell before saying, "Mr. Berkeley doesn't think so."

"And what makes you an authority in such matters, Mr. Berkeley?" O'Connell asked, turning back in my direction, a raised eyebrow indicating he doubted I knew shit about dead bodies and how they got that way.

"Without going into detail, while it wasn't of my choosing, I've found myself part of these kinds of situations before." I briefly described my past security work with the federally funded archaeological agency, sometime consultant to police departments in Florida and South Carolina, the most recent being the Deer Creek Canyon murders with Chief Kay Pierson-Sanders in Jefferson County. "She can verify the latter information."

He didn't look particularly impressed, but said, "Okay, without disturbing anything on the body or elsewhere in the room, why not suicide?"

Moving between the two uniforms as close as possible to Roberta and using my right index finger as a pointer, I said, "First, the revolver – a thirty-eight caliber from what I can tell – was fired with what we're led to believe was Roberta's right hand since it's still in that hand.

Based on meetings I've had with Roberta, I remember her

favoring her left hand." I looked at Gladys. "Correct?"

"Yes, she wrote with her left hand, held coffee cups in her left hand, everything left handed. The left hand was her dominant hand. I admit I didn't know she owned a gun. She didn't like guns. It was a gun that killed her husband."

I continued. "Second, she had just finished eating when Gladys first called. Both hands and the revolver are resting on the vomit in her lap. The hands are covered in dried vomit. When you throw up, do you normally keep your hands on your lap *or* do you run for the bathroom or the kitchen sink as fast as you can when you feel it coming on? She appears to have sat there the whole time.

"Other than where it's resting on the vomit in her hand, the gun is mostly clean. That indicates to me she was sick, was unable to move and threw up before the gun was placed in her hand and fired."

At this point, I wasn't going to be held back. "Check her lips, what you can see of them, and, what little you can see of her fingers, the nails, both hands. Bluish colored. Indicates some kind or poison or drug. Hopefully toxicology should be able to tell."

"I know for a fact she did not take drugs," Gladys said most emphatically as she moved to my side and pointed toward Roberta's throat. "With her head bent to the side, you can see scratches and redness on the front and left side of her throat. It appears there was pressure against the throat as though something or somebody was forcibly holding her. From the rear I would think."

She bent over slightly and pointed toward Roberta's left hand. "Finger nails on her index and middle fingers, partially torn. Typical defensive injury. I think she was struggling with whatever was against her throat, probably an arm. Caught her when her back was turned."

Sergeant Springer shook her head and gave a short, disbelieving laugh. "I suppose you're like him." She nodded in my direction. "Police experience and whatever."

Gladys looked at me and smiled. "Guess I should advertise in the paper." Back to the Sergeant, she said, "Hate to disappoint you, but no police experience as such. CIA for twenty-three years. Covert operations. Romanticized as black ops in movies, TV and in spy novels. I've seen dead bodies in places you never want to go." That created a subdued silence within the room.

Getting back to the subject, I said, "I'm sure you'll find gunpowder residue on her hand, but I don't believe she's the force behind pulling the trigger.

"I think you'll also find she was given something, either forced to drink or injected, powerful enough to incapacitate or even kill, before the gun was put in her mouth. Medical examiner should check her body for a needle puncture. More than likely in a muscle. Would have been more of a struggle if he or she had taken the time to find a vein.

"And yes, the bullet's in the wall board behind her head. Your CSU people might find its location questionable, based on the position of her head and the trajectory of the round after it exited to top of her skull. That is, if she fired the weapon herself. I'm just saying."

O'Connell grunted, still only half believing our observations regardless of the obvious physical evidence. "You two are a regular crime scene unit, aren't you? We'll see what our CSU and forensics people have to say when they get here. In the meantime, Sergeant, get all the information we'll need from these two as well as the victim's next of kin if they know."

"Family or what's left of it is in Wyoming," Gladys responded. "I'll have to get it from the office and call you. You have a card?" she asked the Sergeant.

"By the way, Sergeant," I said, "the men pictured with Mrs. Wilson in the newspapers and on TV related to the Deer Creek Canyon killings, if Mrs. Wilson was murdered, which I firmly believe, they could also be in danger. As a safety precaution, I strongly recommend you check on them." I gave her the names, including John's name.

Lieutenant O'Connell looked surprised. "*The* John Nabhe you're talking about? I know him. Helped us once in a narcotics case involving a couple of Indian kids. I didn't know he was implicated in Deer Creek thing. Guess I don't read the papers."

"So they're saying without proof. He's a personal friend and the reason I'm in Colorado. I've been trying to reach him since early this evening, but no joy. I'll keep trying."

The Lieutenant motioned to the two uniforms. "Once the Sergeant gets what she needs, escort these two down and out of the building, then start knocking on doors to see if anybody's seen or heard anything unusual."

Looking at Gladys and me, this was followed by, "And the two of you, tomorrow morning, ten o'clock, District Three Substation on South University. I've still got questions."

"Count on it," I replied.

Once in the car, Gladys said, "You're right. If this can happen to Roberta, it can happen to the others."

"I'll keep trying to reach John. What about Brave Wolf and Long Bow? In case the Sergeant doesn't, we need to warn them."

"The office. I have my key. Roberta's got the phone numbers, e-mail and home addresses of all the Commission members on an old fashion rolodex."

"I only hope we're not too late."

Gladys gave me a quick glance as she headed back to the Interstate and north to the office in downtown Denver. "We've got the rest of the night, but this time, if we find something suspicious, you're the one calling nine-one-one."

"You're so good to me."

Chapter 34

What we'd originally planned as a quiet evening sipping wine on the balcony followed by an amorous ending, resulted in a sleepless night for both of us. After arriving at Gladys's office and getting Brave Wolf's and Long Bow's phone numbers from Roberta's rolodex, we tried to call several times, both landline and mobile numbers without success. The same with John. No matter how many times, I was never able to get through to him.

Gladys was able to get back in touch with Sergeant Springer by going through the DPD's District Three's Substation, alerted her what we'd found, which was nothing, and provided her with all the contact numbers and addresses.

At my insistence, we did, however, go to John's condominium over near Chessman Park. Once there, it was what I expected – doors locked and no John. We doubled back to Gladys's place and got there shortly after three in the morning.

By the time we got to bed, tossed and turned, both agonizing over what we'd just gone through, dressed and ate some toast and an oversized omelet, it felt like I'd had at most five minutes sleep by the time we arrived at the District Three Station House for our command performance.

The building stood out from the rest of the more residentially oriented neighborhood. In front sat a large, white metallic-looking piece of modernistic art, the design of which made absolutely no sense to me. Of more interest was the multi-level pane-glass entrance. It reminded me of the prow of a ship. The rest of the building, however, was nothing more than a standard-looking office structure without any distinctive personality. Or maybe it was the lack of sleep causing me to cast a jaundiced eye.

We met around a large table in a well-appointed conference room, walls covered in award plaques, framed citations and color photographs of numerous officers in uniform. The only depressing aspect was a silver plaque mounted on highly burnished wood with the names of officers who had been killed in the line of duty. Neither Lieutenant O'Connell, Sergeant Springer nor the District Commander Mary Wallace who apparently arrived at the crime scene after we left, looked any more bright-eyed and bushy-tailed than we did.

After we were introduced to Wallace, a fortyish looking woman, blond, extremely fit looking and in full dress uniform as though headed to some kind of formal ceremony, it was the Lieutenant who broke the ice.

"It appears as though the two of you were right. The CSU people as well as Dr. Oswald, our Chief Deputy Coroner, a forensic pathologist, said after you left, they tend to agree your analysis of the crime scene. Based on what they determined, regardless of the typed suicide note, Mrs. Wilson was murdered. While we'll have to wait for the toxicology report, Dr. Oswald feels strongly that, as you said, she was injected with a massive dose of a currently unidentified drug that completely disabled her."

The Lieutenant opened a file folder and, before starting to read, said, "Sergeant Springer, your notes. I'll follow along with the written report."

The Sergeant flipped through several pages in her notebook and replied, "Per Dr. Oswald, two of the examples of drugs he gave were fentanyl, an opioid pain reliever used before and after surgery and ketamine, a fast-acting anesthetic used in human surgery and big time in veterinary surgery."

She paused a moment, looked around and admitted, "Big time, my words," before continuing. "Both fast acting and can be injected in liquid form. Found a reddish area in a neck muscle at the base of the skull. Looks like a hypodermic needle pierced the skin for introduction of an intramuscular drug. Can tell better during autopsy. Drug to be IDed by toxicology." She ended with, "That's all I have so far as any drug use."

Gladys's eyes focused down on the surface of the table. I

couldn't tell if they were tearing or not. I took hold of her hand and squeezed to let her know I was there for whatever she needed.

Finally, she raised her head and said, "We tried to reach Vincent Brave Wolf and Doctor Long Bow but were not successful. Since John Nabhe and Matt are such good friends, we went to his condominium on the way home, but no response. We did not attempt to get in."

I followed with, "Tried to call his mobile number again, twice last night, but no joy. This morning before we came over, but this time, the only answer was the number was unavailable."

Commander Wallace entered the conversation for the first time. "While we also have not been able to contact Mr. Nabhe, I'm afraid we have some bad news concerning the other two.

"Doctor Long Bow apparently received an emergency call from the University of Colorado Hospital while you four were at Mrs. Wilson's apartment. That's what his cell phone tells us. On the way, he was broadsided by one of the city's large garbage trucks, which according to two witnesses, ran a stop sign.

"The doctor's car rolled, and he was killed. The truck was stolen from one of the waste management's garages and the driver left the scene, disappearing into one of the Hispanic neighborhoods off East Colfax. The thing is, U.C. Health has no record of the call being made."

All I could say was, "They killed him, whoever *they* are."

The Commander continued. "Unfortunately, that's not all. Shortly after midnight, our people entered Mr. Brave Wolf's home and found him dead. Carbon monoxide. We had Excel Energy people in there this morning for a preliminary inspection. The heat exchanger was in good condition, but they found the venting system that carries carbon monoxide outside was blocked with rags. His CO alarms – two of them – were unplugged from their wall outlets and batteries removed.

"At this moment and in each case, that of Mrs. Wilson, Dr. Long Bow and Mr. Brave Wolf, our determination is that they were victims of very methodically planned homicides. The first to look like a suicide, the latter two rather clumsily done to appear as accidents."

Commander Wallace pushed back from the table and stood. "I have a ceremony to attend at City Hall, but for your information, since each death occurred in different police districts and appear to be related, we're turning everything over to our Major Crimes Division downtown. I believe Lieutenant O'Connell also has some additional information for you. Regret we couldn't have met under better circumstances." With that, she was gone.

The Lieutenant carried on. "We did enter Mr. Nahbe's condo unit, but he wasn't there. No sign he'd been there for the last day or so. As to what the Commander was referring, based on what you told me last evening, this morning, in advance of our meeting, I contacted Undersheriff Vasquez in Jefferson County. He verified that the two of you have been helpful during the Deer Creek case.

"He also said that you, with one of their deputies, provided certain evidence during a recent meeting. Since they've been unable to corroborate that evidence, they still consider the Deer Creek case to be closed. He was, to put it mildly, emphatic about that. Though he didn't say, I got the impression he wanted me to relay that to you this morning."

Gladys and I looked at each other. I could tell she was as frustrated and disappointed as I was. Without voicing my opinion, I shook my head, looked at my watch and said, "John's law office should be open. Let me check with his secretary. Maybe she knows something."

I stepped outside the room and gave the office a call, listened, and returned to the conference room. "His secretary said he's in Pueblo. They talked to him this morning, alive and well. Working with one of the power-generating companies down there, fighting some sort of Energy Department declaration.

"His car with his smart phone in it was stolen yesterday. The car was found last night, but the phone and some sunglasses were gone. That's why he didn't answer my calls. Said he was returning to Denver today. I asked to have him call as soon as he got back."

As we walked through the parking lot to the car, Gladys asked, "Where do we go from here? We can't just let this drop, especially after Roberta's death."

"I don't know, but I agree, there's no turning back, not now. Wait 'til we talk with John. Since a possible grand jury hangs over his head, he's still got a major interest in this thing. If we can keep him alive, that is. We might also want to include Deputy Innes. Wouldn't hurt to have an ex-army sniper watching our back."

Chapter 35

We met John later that evening at a restaurant called The Fresh Fish Company, just north of the Denver Tech Center, not far from Gladys's condo. Since it was a slow night with more customers gathered around the bar than in the normal dining rooms, we asked for and were taken to a small area used for private parties, giving us the opportunity to talk without being overheard. Deputy Ralph Innes arrived a few minutes later, still wearing that day's working uniform, showing no outward evidence of his wounded shoulder.

During before-dinner drinks, rather than immediately getting into the details of our evening in Roberta's apartment, John related his tale of woe while in Pueblo, slightly more than a hundred miles south of Denver. Rather than fly, he'd driven down in his pickup truck which was stolen later that night from his hotel's parking lot. He'd forgotten his smart phone and left it on charge in the truck. Making things worse was the damage done at the end of a police chase when the truck crashed through the city's historic River Walk and into the Arkansas River.

To quote John, he said, "Can you believe it? The thief apparently opened the door, got out of the truck, waded across the river which couldn't have been more than two feet deep, and walked away with my sunglasses and iPhone. I guess the cops didn't want to get their feet wet."

I thought he was going to cry as he described his year-old Nissan Titan pickup truck, recently repaired from the bullet-hole damage, and its condition once it was pulled out of the river to be impounded as evidence if they could catch the thief.

He went on to explain, "The reason I was in Pueblo in the first place, my law firm's client has two, coal-fired electrical generating stations that are to be replaced by plants fueled by natural gas. The Department of Energy, in its wisdom, is on the brink of denying the changeover in favor of remaining with coal for so-called national security interests. Of course, the company is fighting the action, their argument being that natural gas is as plentiful if not more so than coal, environmentally cleaner and cost less for the consumer. Go figure."

Dinner itself was primarily a time for eating and small talk until, over after-dinner coffee Gladys said, "It's time, John. I know you and Roberta were close. In addition to being on the Commission together, you helped her through some really bad patches, especially when her husband was killed and brought home for burial. We'll try to spare you as much of the details of what happened last night as we can, but you really need to know where things stand."

After discussing Roberta's death, the Denver police and the deaths of the other two Indian Commission members, Innes told how we learned about Mr. B and his relationship with Lundgren, including the shootout with the Chinese and his wounded shoulder, a flesh wound, healing, no problems.

Along with a second round of coffee, all this was followed with our conclusion concerning the identity of the mysterious Mr. B, his likely relationship with the Chinese and the Jefferson County Sheriff's refusal to follow up on the evidence.

To this latter information, Innes shook his head and cursed. "I knew damn well they wouldn't. If only we could have kept those papers from Lundgren's safe. Damn it!"

Gladys finished by saying, "I left word with Sergeant Springer that, when they get Roberta's autopsy and CSU reports, especially toxicology, I'd appreciate a call. Any time, day or night.

"Matt and I firmly believe there will be definitive evidence determining whether it was suicide or homicide, including toxicology results."

I ended by apologizing to John. "I'm sorry we've kept you out of the loop. It was because of the grand jury thing and of course, District Attorney Bishop's potential involvement if the jury is convened in the First Judicial District. We honestly didn't want to place you in any kind of additional legal jeopardy."

Gladys's Blackberry chirped like a mixed chorus of birds. She grabbed her purse, took out the phone and answered, "Gladys Knight."

There was a pause as she listened before saying, "I'm not at home, Sergeant. Mr. Berkeley and I have just finished dinner at The Fresh Fish Company on East Hampden. If you could come here rather than my condo, I'd appreciate it. We're in a private room, no one around. We'll buy you a cup of coffee or whatever."

Another pause before, "I really appreciate that. Look forward to seeing you."

"Sergeant Springer. Is she coming here?" I asked.

Gladys nodded. "Fifteen to twenty minutes."

"I assume she's going to tell us what's in the reports."

"I'd better go," John said. "If she knows I'm one of the so called accused in the Deer Creek case, she's not going to like me being here."

He stood, took out his wallet and tossed a fifty and a bunch of twenties on the table. "Ralph's and my dinner. Look, I appreciate all you've done, but regardless of what this sergeant tells you, what are we going to do next? Closer to home, what am *I* going to do? I can't just sit around counting Navajo beads while you two stick your necks out on my behalf."

Deputy Innes added, "Same here. I shouldn't be here. If Chief Kay finds out, she'll have my you-know-what. She'll think I'm plotting against her and the Department. I'm lucky she hasn't already fired me."

John looked at me, I looked at Gladys and as usual, she gave a short laugh and immediately said, "I know, it may sound stupid, but since the Sheriff's people won't do anything, somebody has to."

"So?" was my response.

"What?" was John's and Innes's equally quizzical

responses.

By way of letting the suspense build, Gladys took a long sip from her coffee cup and finally said, "Confront Mr. B."

Innes held up his hands, palms out. "Whoa up. You're getting out of my league."

John started to laugh, took a deep breath and said, "You've got to be kidding. Bishop, the District Attorney?"

"The same," she answered. "If he's really our Mr. B, you can bet your – not to offend your delicate sensibilities – your asses he's the one behind the supposed evidence against you, Roberta and the others. You can bet it again he's the one behind Roberta's, Brave Wolfe's and Dr. Long Bow's deaths. Why? I can't answer that question, but the only way we can find out is to face the man."

It was time for me to add my two cents worth. "I see where you're going, but it can't be John who confronts him." I nodded toward Innes. "It would mean Ralph's job if he was to go up against him." Back to Gladys, I said, "You, me, okay, but we need to figure a way to get him on neutral ground."

"Why?" she asked. "We go to his office, a place and at a time he would never expect. If nothing else, corner him and see what happens. First, however, we need to do a little more research on Bishop, his family, his weaknesses, anything we can use. You with me?"

"I'm in," John said. "Tell me what I can do, and it's done."

"Research," she said. "Your law office. You can do more than I can."

"Done."

Innes said, "Don't know what I can do, but if you need me, call."

"We will," I said, "and to be honest, before this is over, I'm pretty sure your particular talents are going to be exactly what we need."

Gladys looked at me. "You agree with what I'm saying?"

"Sweetheart, I agree with anything you want to do."

After John and the Deputy left and more coffee, it was

another ten minutes before a waitress led Sergeant Springer to the room where we were sitting.

"Can I get you anything?" the waitress asked the Sergeant.

"Coffee, black." As the waitress left, she added with a chuckle, "Like me." She took a seat across the table from us and, without hesitating, pulled out her notebook and flipped about halfway through. "I couldn't bring the reports, but I made notes on some of the more pertinent items."

Waiting until the waitress placed the cup of coffee before her and left, she said, "Without going into great detail, use of the right hand versus the preferred left hand in holding the revolver, the trajectory of the round when it exited the crown of her head and its position in the wallboard, the bruising on her throat and several other aspects indicate she was murdered."

"Other aspects?" Gladys asked.

"The weapon. Like you told us, she had no record of ever purchasing a revolver or any other weapon. Additionally, the serial number had been ground down, but we were able to recover it. Used in a robbery several years ago. The perpetrator is currently behind bars."

"Toxicology?" I asked.

"If you recall in my notes this morning, Dr. Oswald stated, based on the condition of her skin, the vomit in her lap and the discoloring at her feet and hands, it appeared she had been injected with something like fentanyl or ketamine. Based on that, he narrowed their initial examination to those two drugs before looking for anything else."

The Sergeant took a sip of her coffee before continuing. "Fentanyl. You wouldn't believe the amount." She looked at her notes. "According to toxicology and Doctor Oswald, our forensic pathologist, when it's used in surgery, on humans, that is, the amount is usually not more than fifty to two hundred micrograms if the patent is breathing on their own, three hundred to thirty-five hundred micrograms if breathing is assisted. Remember, I said micrograms.

"Mrs. Wilson was injected with at least three milligrams. That's equal to…" again looking at her notes, she went on, "…equal to three *million* micrograms. Can you believe it? The Doctor said that pharmaceutical grade fentanyl is fifty to one hundred times more potent than morphine.

"It must have hit her before she took her first step. She was more than likely dead or definitely on the way before the shot was fired. And yes, the autopsy verified the reddish area in the muscle at the back of her neck was where a hypodermic needle recently pierced the skin."

"While it may be a horrible thing to say," Gladys acknowledged, "in Roberta's case, murder makes more sense. It also gives greater credence to Brave Wolf's and Long Bow's deaths being planned to coincide with Roberta's."

She exhaled a long sigh of both frustration and sorrow before saying, "This leaves us with the two questions. One, why kill the three of them if there is sufficient evidence to bring them before a grand jury and potentially send them to trial, and two, will they still try to kill John Nabhe, the odd man out?" She shook her head. "It doesn't make sense."

We thanked Sergeant Springer for keeping us informed and asked her to relay our appreciation to both Commander Wallace and Lieutenant O'Connell. After she was gone, we switched to Jameson on the rocks, something more accommodating to our mood than coffee. We spent until the restaurant was ready to close discussing our forthcoming confrontation with Mr. District Attorney Christopher Warren Bishop.

We didn't know then that, before it was over, part of the job concerning Bishop might be done for us. That would be the good part. Unfortunately, there were several other things about to happen, somewhat like one of those 'make-my-day' things. Unfortunately, it would be with Gladys and me on the wrong end of the gun barrel. Not a good place to be.

Chapter 36

District Attorney Christopher Warren Bishop's five-bedroom brick ranch was in one of the more affluent enclaves within the City of Golden. A neighborhood aptly named Vista Estates was situated high atop the east side of Lookout Mountain. The home offered unobstructed views of Golden's downtown, north Denver and its several northern suburbs. Farther on was the beginning of Colorado's eastern plains and the tepee-styled Denver International Airport.

The home was really too large for the man, his wife long gone, deservedly dead for her adulterous ways, a son God only knew where in Europe and, most important of all, his stepdaughter, Riley in the ALS Medical Treatment Center in San Francisco.

Eight o'clock, the sun well up in the east, as Bishop often said to his staff, another day, another challenge. And this day was no different. As he was walking through the kitchen and about to open the door to the garage, his land-line telephone rang. The kitchen's phone was located next to the door. He took the phone from its perch and said, "District Attorney Bishop."

There was a moment of silence before he heard the now familiar female voice of Doctor Sun Xiaolin. "You disobeyed, Mr. B. You disobeyed." This was followed by a resounding *click*.

Bishop slammed the phone back into its cradle and shouted at the phone, "You Bitch! You can't threaten me. I'm the one who's gotten you this far." Hands shaking, he lit his third cigarette of the morning and again muttered, "You god dammed bitch!" and headed out the door.

Still cursing to himself, he shook his head as he backed the big Buick LaCrosse out of the driveway and started his morning drive down Lookout Mountain Road to the D.A.'s office in the

Jefferson County Government complex. The phone call did nothing more than fortify the plans that had been running through his mind. They included his daughter, selling the Vista Estates house and his place in the mountains and move to San Francisco, breaking free of Dr. Sun Xiaolin and her people. These thoughts merged into those concerning the last two days.

Disobeyed, hell, he thought. In a sense, he was proud of himself. He feared the evidence against the four Indians, evidence provided by Dr. Sun, was too weak, too circumstantial and would not stand up against grand jury scrutiny. He would look like a fool. Who the hell was she to know the evidentiary laws of the State of Colorado better than him?

That had forced his hand, ending the problem sooner than later, leaving the evidence hanging in the wind. Neither provable nor disprovable so far as the public was concerned – a dead case. The world already knew the Sheriff's people had found and disposed of the killer, a mentally disturbed man with hair covering his body.

What had the Sheriff said? "Case closed." That was the end of it.

Rather than use Sun's people who had botched the job at Lundgren's home, their stupidity forced him to use his own people, two of his long-time informants, to retrieve the original papers and destroy them. As soon as he had time, he promised himself, he would destroy the copies.

The two, a man and a woman, brought him the money they'd found in the safe, just under ten thousand dollars. Due to his magnanimous nature – he'd always liked that description when referring to himself – he told them to keep the money as a token of his appreciation.

As for the Indians, Brave Wolf and Long Bow, the medical doctor, he once again had taken the reins and used people he could trust. Former deputies, dirtied by their on- and off-duty actions over the years in Douglas County, now working on the edge of the law. Men he'd protected for future use as he'd done with James

Lundgren, men who owed him.

A smile crossed his face. He chuckled at the thought of the Indian woman. He couldn't remember her Native American name. Pine Wood, Pine Tree, Pine something. She should have stuck with Wilson, much simpler. He'd wondered beforehand if he could go through with the plan since he'd never killed a fellow human. On second thought, his wife, but that was different, the cheating slut. That time, he might as well have been chopping off the head of a poisonous snake.

But with the Wilson woman, no hate, no vengeance, he found he'd enjoyed the process, holding the power of life and death over another person who'd done him no harm. Bishop lit his fourth cigarette of the morning using an old Colorado Sheriff's Association lighter and inhaled deeply.

Three down, one to go, he thought, exhaling the smoke toward a crack in the window. He corrected himself. No, two to go, that damn John Nahbe *and* the man named Berkeley who Sun said was a potential danger, both wild cards. Except for them, perfect.

Though he'd now lost the element of surprise, as soon as he knew where to find them, he'd have them taken care of like the others. That is, unless he'd already left for San Francisco and a new life. Maybe open a law practice, catering to all the wealthy Silicon Valley geeks.

Deep in thought, he failed to notice the black, crew-sized Toyota Tundra pickup truck behind him. A truck with a menacing looking bush guard wrapped around its massive front grill. He was past Lookout Mountain Park and the Buffalo Bill Museum and was nearing the last of four switchbacks on his downward journey when he saw the pickup truck in his rearview mirror. It suddenly gained speed as he approached the final sharp curve. Its bush guard loomed larger and larger until it covered the Buick's entire rear window.

He stamped out his cigarette in a portable ashtray mounted on the dash and straightened the rearview mirror for a better view of the driver. "What the hell's he —"

His words were cut off by the jarring thud of the bush guard against the Buick's rear bumper. The impact forced him back into the seat, straightening his arms out in front of him, delaying his normal actions by a split second. He tried to make the left turn into the switchback, but the truck stayed with him, pushing, pushing.

He whipped the steering wheel to the left, but it was too late. The screech of tires when he stomped on the brake pedal tore at his ears, only slightly less than the terrifying sound of his own involuntary scream.

The Buick crashed through the guardrail, both driver and passenger-side air bags immediately deploying in an explosion of white powder, momentarily blinding him, side airbags erupting as the car tumbled and rolled several hundred feet down the mountain side. It hit the bottom of a narrow gulch, upside down against a line of pine trees. It lay there for a moment. Dirt, loosened rocks and broken scrub oak limbs cascaded down on the car's underside.

Bishop hung suspended by his seat belt and shoulder strap. Alive or dead, he wasn't sure until he heard a loud hiss an instant before the car exploded in a ball of flame. The blast immediately torched trees and surrounding brush into a wildfire that would take firefighting crews two days to extinguish. Until then, District Attorney Christopher Warren Bishop's whereabouts would remain unknown.

* * *

It was the day following our dinner meeting with John and Deputy Innes and the later meeting with Sergeant Springer concerning Roberta's autopsy, a little after two o'clock in the afternoon, that we were able to piece it all together. Between Gladys and John and through their various contacts, we formed an interesting and totally revealing biography of the fifty-five-year-old District Attorney.

It seemed that, when he was much younger before coming

to Colorado, there were accusations of sexual relations with a sixteen-year old girl when he taught American Civics classes in Cook County, Illinois, charges made by her parents. Though there was no physical evidence and refusals by the girl to admit to the relationship, he was suspended and later fired by the County Board of Education when rumors of other flirtations with underage girls began to surface.

There seemed to be a blank period in his life while getting a law degree from the University of Illinois until later when he married divorcee Sophia Louise Fountain from Colorado Springs, Colorado. A stunningly beautiful socialite several years older than him, she brought to the marriage a young daughter named Riley.

While we already knew of his time as Town Attorney for the city of Castle Rock down in Douglas County, what we didn't know was the specifics of his troubles with the local police and County Sheriff: Unauthorized use of county and city property and funds as well as interfering in a case involving two of the Sheriff's deputies accused of using excessive force on a racially mixed couple.

Later as Chief Deputy District Attorney for the Eighteenth Judicial District, coinciding with the time of Lundgren's incident, there were issues relating to illegal use of Judicial District funds for personal gain, much like when he was in Castle Rock. The charges were dismissed for lack of evidence and closed to public scrutiny by the court. This latter tidbit learned from one of John's lawyer friends.

In his personal life, his secret gambling addiction; the questionable murder of Bishop's wife, Sofia, a woman socially known for her promiscuity; his estranged son, Jamie and his disgraceful record at the University of Colorado, now somewhere in Europe.

What proved to be even more important was his beloved twenty-eight-year-old stepdaughter, Riley, who he had raised since his marriage to and following the ultimate demise of Sofia, stricken with ALS – Amyotrophic Lateral Sclerosis or its nonmedical name, Lou Gehrig's Disease. So young and talented from what could be determined, the daughter every man would want. She was under continuing treatment at the ALS Medical Treatment Center in San Francisco as part of their ongoing research program.

What was particularly intriguing about this was information Tom Granger was able to ferret out in a few hours through his FBI connections, apparently without any kind of warrant. Whether his methods were legal or not, I frankly didn't give a damn. For the past two years, monthly payments of one hundred thousand dollars had been transferred from the China America West Bank, San Francisco to the United Bank of California, also in San Francisco. Thirty-five thousand of that automatically transferred each month to the medical center for stepdaughter Riley's treatment. The electronic money trail wound its way back to an account registered in the name of the China Rare Earth Group LTD, Beijing, China, a state-owned corporation.

Not sure why, just a feeling Gladys and I shared, but time to confront the man seemed to be running out. Once all the information provided what we considered to be a relatively complete picture of Bishop's character and his past activities, we couldn't wait any longer. To get to Bishop's office before it closed for the day, Gladys's aging Ford Escape broke every speed limit between her place in Greenwood Village and Bishop's office on the Jefferson County Government Campus in the Town of Golden.

The small sign on the drive leading to the parking lot and glass-fronted brick building read *Jefferson County District Attorney*. The same information plus Bishop's name and counties within the First Judicial District was printed on one side of the double glass doors along with a notice on the other side that firearms and weapons were prohibited in the building.

The building itself had a concrete patio leading away from the entrance, partially covered with a four-story concrete block, open-air design that seemed a waste of tax payer money. But what did I know? As they say, beauty is in the eyes of the beholder.

A youngish woman, possibly in her late twenties, petit in

size, neatly dressed and a dark hair style that was heavy on top and one side, basically shaved on the other side, was standing behind a counter in the wide-open lobby area. She appeared to be clearing a desk of paperwork behind the counter in preparation of closing for the day.

When she looked up, she said, "It's almost five o'clock, and most of our people have already gone. Did you have an appointment with someone? Some do have after-hours appointments for important cases."

I shook my head. "No, but we were hoping to see District Attorney Bishop."

Gladys quickly explained, "We have information we think is vital to the possible grand jury concerning four Native Americans and the Deer Creek Canyon murders."

The woman started to speak. "There's one of Mr. Bishop's deputies still here, but –"

I interrupted. "No, ma'am. What we've learned is for Mr. Bishop, only."

She hesitated a moment as an overly stout but nicely dressed woman in slacks and a tweed gray blazer came out of a hallway. The woman smiled and nodded in our direction, went directly to an elevator, pressed the UP button and entered once the door opened. When the door closed and the elevator started moving to an upper floor, the young woman said in a near whisper, "The District Attorney hasn't come in at all today."

She looked around to make sure no one was near the entrance hall as though what she was going to say was top secret. "We tried his home phone and his mobile, but only got a recording on the home phone, no answer on his mobile. Since we keep a key to his house in case of emergencies, the Chief Deputy sent one of the investigators up there. House is on Lookout Mountain. Took a while for him to get there. Fire trucks, people fighting a wild fire down in one of the gulches. Mr. Bishop wasn't there, and his car was gone.

"He has a vacation home outside of Evergreen on some

mountain I think, but no landline. He only uses his mobile when he's up there. He seems to have been under a lot of strain for the last several days. He might be there and wanted some time to himself, but it's unlike him not to tell us. He was supposed to be in court today, but one of the other prosecutors took his place. Sorry."

"Maybe tomorrow," Gladys said. "Thanks for your help. Do hope Mr. Bishop's okay."

"We do, too."

Once outside the building walking to the car, Gladys said, "John gave me Bishop's home address on Lookout Mountain and the address of his second home in Evergreen. Want to take a look on our own?"

"Why not? At this point, we've got nothing to lose. Now or after dark?"

"I was thinking after dark. I'm also thinking if he lets the office people have a key to his home, I strongly doubt he keeps anything there that might incriminate him with the Chinese or anybody else. The vacation home outside of Evergreen sounds more likely."

The couple of small pine trees outside the building were starting to bend with a northwest wind that had picked up while we were inside. The wind brought with it a heavy layer of clouds and a chill that promised to turn bitterly cold in the next few hours.

There was also the smell of smoke in the air. Looking westward toward what Gladys pointed out to be Lookout Mountain, there was a line of smoke billowing up and, caught on the wind, bending in our direction.

"Wonder if that's the fire the woman was talking about?"

"Could be," Gladys answered.

While I was turned toward the mountain, a sharp gust of wind hit me face on, causing me to zip up my windbreaker and wrap my arms around myself. "Hey, that's like down from Alaska. I need a heavier jacket than what I brought with me if we're going on the prowl tonight."

"You should have known better."

"Thought I did. This one's lined, but –"

"This is Colorado and today's the first of November. Fact, I sense snow in the air. There's a Macy's and an L.L. Bean store not far from the condo. We'll get you a jacket and pickup something special from home before we tackle our little adventure. If there's time, there's a lovely restaurant in Evergreen, Willow Creek Restaurant, overlooking Evergreen Lake. We can get something there to fortify ourselves."

Gladys had roused my curiosity. "You said 'get something special from home.' What does that mean?"

"You'll see."

Chapter 37

That something special Gladys talked about came from a hidden space recessed in one wall of her master-sized bathroom. It was somewhat like a built-in medicine cabinet only deeper, wider, made of steel and hidden by a small marble-topped vanity, the kind without a sink. Above the vanity was a large, gold-framed mirror. You might could call it a makeup table.

"There's a place on the side of the vanity to grab hold. Once you find it, pull and slide the vanity out this way." She drew a clockwise half circle with her hand and index finger to demonstrate the path the cabinet would take.

While I couldn't see any rollers, I followed her lead and used one hand to feel the flat side of the vanity. Finding a small indentation, a handhold large enough to insert the tips of four fingers, I did as she said. My fingers felt a latch click, more of a feel thing than hearing. The vanity swung away from the wall as smooth as silk.

Gladys stepped past where I stood, stooped and worked the tumbler lock on the front of a safe pushed flat into the wall. When the final number was entered, she turned the handle and opened the door. A small light came on inside the safe. Once done, she straightened and stepped back for me to see her hidden treasures.

All I could say was, "You have got to be kidding! A nice little paralegal like you with an armory like that?"

She chuckled. "One bought last year, the others from my days with the Company. One of those mine, three my husbands. It took a lot to satisfy him."

"They didn't ask for them back?"

"There are ways to doctor the books when necessary."

Laughing, I shook my head and asked, "I'm glad you're on

my side. What do you recommend?"

The inner walls of the relatively shallow safe were lined with gray felt. Strategically placed were felt-covered hooks long enough to hang five handguns, all semiautomatics, different makes and models. I was pretty familiar with a fair number of weapons and started to pick one, stopped by her saying, "Any except the Sig Sauer P-229. That's the one I bought. Compact and fits my hand better than any of the rest. Nine-millimeter Luger bullets, magazine holds ten rounds."

Talk about black ops, they should be asking her how many she's killed, not me.

Putting that thought aside, I studied the four remaining pistols: Two Berettas, an M9 and a 96A1; an H&K 45 caliber and a nine-millimeter Glock 19 Compact with a sound/flash suppressor protruding from the barrel's muzzle. Looking closely, I could see that each weapon already contained a magazine, presumably fully packed and ready for action. Below the pistols on a shelf were additional magazines and boxes of ammunition.

"An extra magazine for each weapon," Gladys said. "And yes, all registered with the Greenwood Village Police Department. I fire them regularly at the Cherry Creek Gun Club and clean them afterwards."

"You're proficient with each of them?"

"Not really. The Sig Saur and the Glock, but I prefer the P-229."

"I'll take the Glock minus the silencer. I'll put the silencer in my pocket in case we need it. The magazine looks like it holds fifteen rounds. I'll take an extra mag."

She nodded, but before she said anything else, I hit her with, "Before we go looking for Bishop with these things, I'd like to hear why we're arming ourselves for World War Three."

"Why?" she asked. "We were blindsided at Lundgren's house. I'm not going to let that happen again. If we think there's something incriminating at the D.A.'s place in the mountains, involving not only him but others, you better believe somebody else is thinking the same thing. That is, if that somebody hasn't already been there. Namely somebody who speaks Chinese."

I humbled myself by saying, "You've got a point." At that moment I spied a knife positioned just above the handguns. "Where the hell did you get that?"

She laughed. "Long story. From a friend a couple of years back. Said if I ever went back to my old job, I might find a use for it. I never went back. Meant to return it, but he died in a skydiving accident."

"I can tell you've kept some interesting company over the years." She didn't respond.

It was the large version of a Duane Dieter's Master of Defense CQD knife, no longer in production. Once used by our Special Forces, it's equipped with a three and three-quarter inch black, carbon steel retractable blade. Looks somewhat like a blunt-nosed single-edge switch blade with the blade retracted and fits easily in a side pocket. It also has a glass breaker at the front end for use when the blade is enclosed in the aluminum handle. In short, a deadly weapon when properly used.

"Had one several years back when I was on the search for a Russian work of art in Paris."

Gladys asked, "Paris, when you were on the run from the French police, and the CIA helped you get out of the country?" She asked this with a sly, partly stifled laugh and one of those derisive, raised upper-lip looks on her face.

In return, I gave her the best nonchalant shrug-of-my-shoulders I could muster. "Yeah, pretty much. Unless somebody's found it, it's somewhere at the bottom of the River Seine with a nine-millimeter Beretta used against the bad guys." I nodded toward the knife. "You mind?"

"Be my guest. If nothing else, the glass breaker thing might come in handy."

I lifted the knife from its hooks and gently slid my thumb along the blade edge to gauge its sharpness. It was as I expected. I knew from experience the knife would do the job for which it was designed.

Though the CQD knife is not really made for throwing, to find the center of gravity, I laid the open knife across my outstretched index finger and slowly adjusted its position until it reached balance. I'd once seen it thrown, accurately and with the desired effect, but to be honest, I was never good at throwing knives, regardless if that was made for or not. God forbid I'd find Gladys and myself in the kind of extreme situation where I'd have to throw the thing.

Unfortunately, time caught up with us, negating dinner overlooking the lake in Evergreen. Once Gladys put together a couple of ham sandwiches and a thermos of hot coffee to take on our nighttime adventure, it was dark, the temperature below freezing and snowflakes flying, driven by an increasingly brutal wind.

In my new L.L. Bean down jacket with a lined hood and armed for bear, I'm sure I looked like the Michelin Man, only in dark green. I was, however, warm and that's what counted. As we left the condo, I asked, "Sure you know how to get there?"

With the windshield wipers on high, swishing away the snow, the blurry whiteness of the flakes made even worse by the headlights, she answered, "Based on what John told me, through Morrison, up state road seventy-four to Evergreen, hopefully before it freezes over and becomes impassable.

"Once in town, we take Highway 73, turn on Buffalo Park Road for a mile or so past the first entrance to Alderfer/Three Sisters Park. Right onto South Lemasters Road which intersects with Buffalo Creek Road. Bishop's place according to John is on Buffalo Creek."

"Rattling off all those roads, you sound like you might know the area?"

"To the park, yes, but I haven't gone past the park's main entrance. I've hiked Three Sisters quite a few times. The Three Sisters are three small mountains close together, each just under eight thousand feet in elevation with over fifteen miles of trails.

The park's trail map shows an unmarked entrance into the park at the intersection of Lemasters and Buffalo Creek. No parking, just a foot path through the park's fence line. I passed it on one of my hikes but paid little attention."

Once Gladys gave me the directions, I made a phone call to Deputy Ralph Innes. It took several rings for him to answer, but when he did, I told him what we were doing, where we were going, including Bishop's Buffalo Creek Road address. Most importantly, we could use him to cover our backs if we ran into any opposition. Example: Lundgren's house and the Chinese shooters.

He explained he was at Genesee Park off Interstate 70 on a carjacking case. As soon as he was free, he'd take the Evergreen Parkway. And yes, he knew the area around Evergreen and would meet us at Bishop's, even if he had to rent a team of flying reindeer to get through the snow. His last words were, "Although I'll be the invisible man, this I don't want to miss."

The road past Morrison wound around one curve after another into the mountains, past two small villages where there were already Colorado Department of Transportation snow plows and deicing trucks standing by. Nothing like Colorado in the fall.

It took us another thirty to forty minutes to Evergreen and along the back roads before we passed the entrance to the Three Sisters Park. It was another five minutes to the turnoff onto Lemasters Road past the Park's overflow parking lot and onto the crunch-of-snow-and- gravel up Buffalo Creek Road.

I barely saw the narrow entrance into Three Sisters Park Gladys had mentioned. As we turned at the intersection of the two roads, I caught it in the sweep of our headlights through the windswept snow. It was nothing more than a four-foot wide brake in a barbed wire fence, the path marked by two wooden posts.

Gladys rattled off the house number and said, "I've got to watch the road. See if you can spot the house."

My assignment was easier said than done. No mailboxes since mail boxes with numbers were set up as a cluster arrangement back at the intersection. Only fence posts with an occasional number, some not at all that I could see. Homes, some almost palatial, some little more than fancy log cabins, seemed to be a good hundred yards or more apart and separated by large stands of ponderosa pines.

We covered the entire road, turned around and headed back toward the intersection with Lemasters when I said, "Got it." It was the third house up from the intersection, partially rusted metal numbers on a post at the end of a short, snow-covered drive.

Since we were coming to confront Bishop, not burglarize him in the dark of night, Gladys turned onto the driveway, headlamps on low. They provided light enough through the falling snow to illuminate the front of a wood frame, two-story house with a two-car garage and a peaked roof over the main part of the house. Except for one area in front, the exterior was a dark color, the exact color hard to tell through the falling snow.

A yellowish porch light was on, positioned at the side of the front door. Two large picture windows stretched across a narrow porch, neither with blinds drawn. Two much smaller and narrower windows occupied space immediately above their big brothers. There were no lights on inside the home.

We got out of the car, the snow-borne wind immediately tugging at my coat, and tramped through the snow to a narrow, covered porch to the front door and rang the doorbell. We waited, rang again and a third time, but no response.

Was Bishop there? Asleep? Not there? Had we screwed up by not first going to his Lookout Mountain home? Since it was past ten o'clock going on eleven, if he was inside, asleep seemed to be the best answer.

I moved to my right to the first of the two picture windows, took out a flashlight, a small Surefire LED law enforcement light given to me several years ago by the Jacksonville, Florida Sheriff's Department, and thumbed the on/off switch. The beam bit sharply through the glass and into the darkness of what was obviously a family room. "Interesting."

"What?"

"Too orderly for a single man unless he's got some kind of fetish for neatness."

Magazines were stacked in perfect order with a book on a table in front of a sofa. A set of clean whiskey glasses and a bottle of Glenfiddich single malt sat on a silver tray beneath a shaded lamp on a side table. The oak-stained hardwood floor literally gleamed in the light; furniture like new.

A large seascape painting depicting a rocky coastline braced against a surging sea hung above a fireplace mantle, the fireplace cold and apparently unused for some time. Cord wood stacked neatly in a brass-colored container to one side. Continuing toward the rear of the family room was a small dining area and then a doorway, most likely leading to the kitchen.

"Maybe he has a cleaning company come in periodically."

Gladys moved to my side in front of the second window, also turning on a flashlight. After swinging the beam around the room, she pointed it upward and moved the beam around.

"Stairs and a loft overhead with a door at each end. Bedrooms and bathrooms more than likely. You're right, and too neat for anybody to have torn up the place looking for something, at least something like we're looking for."

"Either the guy's asleep, been drinking too much to hear the doorbell, or he's not here."

The snow by this time was really coming down, or more accurately, a horizontal flight path, driven by the northwesterly wind, the wind so strong we had to yell at each other. Swooping down from what Gladys called nearby Elephant Butte, it created a constant thrashing sound as it whipped through pine trees that surrounded the house. Quite honestly, the pines were a plus. The stands so close, we couldn't see lights from any of the nearby homes. Hopefully, neither could they see our flashlights.

Moving across the small porch to the side of the house, I said, "Since you apparently didn't bring your lock picks and before we break in, I'm going to check to see if there's a back door and if by chance it's unlocked."

"What am I supposed to do?" Gladys called back. "Wait here until I become a piece of snow sculpture? As my grandfather up in Estes Park used to say, there'll be no days like that. I'm coming with you."

Off we went, around the side of the house, the ground already over-the-ankle deep in snow. As we went, we removed the screens and tested each window along the way, but all locked. Same at the rear of the house as well as a sliding glass door leading from an awning-covered, wooden deck into the kitchen, the snow-covered awning flapping in the wind. Again, all locked. Since the sliding door was too thick for me to break, it was going to be a kitchen window.

That is, until Gladys called, "Over here," and motioned with her flashlight. "There's a basement window, two of them. I didn't see them at first. There're practically hidden by window wells sunk into the ground and covered by metal grates.

"There's an escape ladder inside one of them. About five to six feet deep down to the bottom edge of the window. I'm going down. If we've got to break a window to get in, this one will be less noticeable."

As she dropped from the deck to the ground, removed a metal grate and prepared to go down the ladder inside the window well, I handed her the closed CQD knife and said, "Carbide glass breaker at the front of the handle. Use it like you were trying to break out your car window."

She took the knife between her upper and lower teeth and started down. I heard a grunt followed by, "Window's locked." Two hard strikes of the glass breaker against the panes and the sound of shattering glass rose up from the well. With the continuing cracking and crunching of glass, I supposed she was using the closed knife to work her way around the frame to remove as much of the glass shards as possible.

"Going in," she called. "I can either open the kitchen door or you can come down. If coming down, watch out for broken glass." There was a moment of silence until she made her way through the window. I could see the beam of her flashlight circling the room. "Fully furnished, a bedroom and half bath."

In case Bishop was there, I didn't want her going through the house without me. "Coming down."

I waited a moment, listening for anything that might sound like a security alarm, but if there was, I couldn't hear it. As I wormed my way down into the well and through the narrow window opening into the room, my sleeve caught on a piece of remaining glass protruding from the window frame, showing some of the jacket's insulation. "Son of a bitch!" I muttered as I stepped down on the top of a single bed beneath the window, literally bouncing my way to the carpeted floor.

With a quick sweep of the flashlight, I saw what one would classify as normal bedroom furniture, a small TV on top of a chest of drawers, matching bedside tables and lamps, all covered with a layer of dust as if the room was seldom used or cleaned. Some inexpensively framed pictures of horses were mounted on beige colored, moisture-treated cinder block walls, a single, much larger one on a separate wall. There were several other items in the room, including an equestrian design on the bed spread that said whoever had once used the room liked horses.

"Let's see if the master of the house is here for a late-night chat. If not, we start searching the bedrooms and work our way down."

Using only our flashlights, we very quietly made our way up a set of carpeted wooden steps into the kitchen, through the family room, up to the loft and to the first bedroom. Empty, no furniture, no pictures on the wall, no clothes in the closet. The attached bathroom was the same, cabinets, linen closet and medicine cabinet all empty. Not surprising since the man had no family living with him. The second bedroom and bath showed habitation, but no Mr. B.

Gladys said, "My fault. Guess we should have gone to his Lookout Mountain home, but while we're here, we might as well look for whatever we can find."

From there, we started our search opening drawers, raising the mattress under which Gladys could take a quick look, behind furniture and pictures on the wall, evidence where the carpeting had been cut to hide something beneath the floorboards. Nothing! The same results in the bathroom.

The loft contained a couple of pictures on two of the walls, a sofa, two comfy looking arm chairs, small end tables, all facing a flat screen, forty-inch TV with two small Bose speakers sitting on a large entertainment center.

Through the entertainment center's glass doors, we could see additional pieces of electronic equipment: a tuner amplifier, a separate CD player and what appeared to be a Blu-ray disc player. We started with the center, checked each piece of equipment, but again, nothing. Under seat cushions, behind pictures, behind the TV, the same: *Nada, nicht, niente,* each word liberally translated to mean zero, zilch.

The family room and kitchen gave us the same results. "Damn it! I still believe you were right," I said to Gladys. "With the DA's office people having a key to his home in Golden, if there's anything, it's got to be here. Let's do the basement. If not there, we hit the Lookout Mountain place, that is, if the roads have been plowed to head back down the mountains."

Gladys looked at her watch. "Ten after twelve. Maybe you should call Deputy Innes and tell him not to waste his time."

I tried to call. "Busy. Let's do the basement, and I'll try again."

Since we were below ground and the room's lights not visible to the outside, we switched on a ceiling light to save the batteries in our flashlights. I took the half bath, Gladys started with the rest of the room. I even lifted the top off the toilet as I'd done upstairs, hoping to find the proverbial waterproof pouch loaded with incriminating papers, but it wasn't to be.

Back in the main room, I said, "I'm afraid this is becoming a fool's errand. What have you *not* covered?"

"Everything but the pictures on the wall." She started with an arrangement of four pictures, each frame maybe eight by ten inches or slightly larger, checking both the wall where masonry screws had been drilled and the backs of the pictures, her fingers methodically moving around each frame's backing in search of anything raised behind the backing.

I did the same with a much larger picture on the back wall, at least four by five feet in size, a color print showing a herd of wild horses galloping across the plains toward a line of snowcapped mountains. I took the picture down from the wall and laid it face down on the bed.

The wall behind showed only a shadowed discoloration of where the picture had hung. As Gladys was doing, I started moving my fingers over the backing. Immediately, I felt the outline of first one something, then another and another until I told Gladys, "Need the knife."

Once she handed me the knife, I pushed the safety button and the blade popped out. I ran the knife's spear-point blade around the edges of the backing. Snagging one edge, I pulled the backing away and there they were. "Got 'em!"

Folding the blade back into its handle, I slipped it into my jacket and gathered up each sheet of paper. Some I handed to Gladys for her review.

The first I looked at were the copies of the Lundgren letter, newspaper clipping and thumb drive which I assumed contained the nighttime thermographic photographs we'd seen. Other papers concerned at least two other deputies from the Douglas County Sheriff's Department plus several threatening letters to four other people. "Good stuff. Son of a bitch was blackmailing more than Lundgren. What've you got?"

"Enough to put Mr. B away for a life time. Some in Chinese, others in English. Could be the translations. Obtaining the land, regardless of what he had to do to get it. Two formal documents under the heading of the **China Rare Earth Group LTD and signed by a** Chén Liang, Director of Rare Earth Minerals

Advanced Research. For services rendered, it mentions a transfer of one hundred thousand dollars a month to be transferred from the China America West Bank, San Francisco to the United Bank of California."

She looked at me and added, "Exactly what your FBI friend found. Couple of other things here I didn't open, but I think it's time to put this stuff together and get out of here."

"I'm game."

Gladys handed me her papers, and with the ones I had, I pressed them into a three-way fold and put them into my jacket's inside pocket.

We were at the top of the steps leading to the kitchen and had just opened the door when we heard the click of a lock and felt a rush of cold wind barreling into and through the house. This was followed by a woman's voice speaking in Chinese. It sounded like she was giving orders.

A moment of silence and then in English, "I know you're here. If you've found the papers, give them to me and I'll let you go."

Chapter 38

I eased the door shut and silently mouthed to the woman's offer, "Like hell you will." At the same time, I jabbed my thumb back toward the basement and whispered to Gladys, "The window." The door knob required a key to lock on the kitchen side, a finger twist on the basement side. Backwards I thought at first, but most likely because of the bedroom in the basement.

I turned the twist and followed Gladys down the steps. I knew we didn't have much time, but better than trusting an unknown voice and hanging around to be killed.

Naturally with my luck, I ripped the other arm of my jacket on the broken glass still hanging from the window frame, but that was the least of my worries. Once out, we ran along the side of the house and across the road, obviously leaving foot prints in the deepening snow.

Once across and into the woods, we looked back to the front of the house. Gladys's SUV was blocked in by what appeared to be a large pickup truck, behind the truck a sedan. Both dark colored in appearance, or the best we could tell with only the front porch light dimly visible through the snow. Though the windows were somewhat fogged over, we could make out someone sitting in the sedan's driver seat, the motor running, exhaust swirling up into the wind from the tail pipe.

"Not good," Gladys said, catching her breath following the dash across the road.

"Idea?"

"The Three Sisters. I know the park. I know the trails."

With the sound of shouts seeping up from the broken basement window and through the window well, there sure as hell was no reason to wait. "Let's go."

Moving as quickly as we could through the snow and blasts of wind, we cut through the trees and across open areas in front of two houses, both darkened for the night, before we reached the intersection with Lemasters Road. Both the intersection and the foot path entrance into Three Sisters Park were illuminated by a street lamp next to the lengthy mailbox cluster I'd earlier seen. I thought about shooting out the light, but decided the sound of gunfire would only make it easier for them to know where we were.

Without hesitating, we broke from the trees and darted across the road to the park entrance. As fast as we ran through the lighted intersection, I imagined with each step a barrage of bullets slamming into my back and wished then I'd gone ahead and shot out the light. If the woman and whoever was with her had found the picture in the basement with its backing cut out, she knew we had the papers. Papers they wanted, and sure as hell weren't going to let us live once they had them.

Following Gladys's lead, I crunched my way along what must have been a trail leading through a snow-covered meadow to a massive rock structure. Any other time it would have been a veritable winter wonderland, but right now, it felt more like a killing field.

Half way there, I took a quick look back and could barely make out four dark figures running across the lighted road, following our footsteps. "Move out, Gladys. Company's coming."

"Fast as I can," she huffed over her shoulder.

Suddenly, there was a bright flash of light that reached across the sky, jagged streaks of lightning beneath the clouds. They followed the direction of the snow, lighting up the meadow and surrounding area. It momentarily outlined a massive, tree-covered outcropping of rock in front of us, some four or five hundred feet in elevation above the surrounding area. The lightning was quickly followed by a loud crash of thunder.

"It's snowing, Gladys, not raining," I shouted. "What that hell was that?"

"Thunder snow!" Gladys yelled over her shoulder. "Keep going, the rock formation up ahead. I'll explain later." Caught on the wind, her words were barely audible. "Crevices, places to hide and shoot. Our best chance."

Our only chance was what I knew she meant. Another blast of lightning. It was like an explosion of blinding white covering a great section of the sky, closer than the last. It sent out what seemed a thousand streaks beneath the clouds, some stretching out parallel to the earth, some bending downward in our direction. The rolling thunder and the smell of hot, instantly mixed nitrogen and oxygen swept past on the wind and snow, but we kept moving toward the base of the rocks. I also knew, if the flashes of lightning allowed us to view our surroundings, those following us could do the same, *us* being their target of the moment.

We heard the rapid *pow, pow, pow* of gunfire from somewhere behind us, but we kept running, or more like trotting. Lifting one's feet free of six to eight inches of snow and through even deeper snow drifts with each step does not allow for either swiftness or agility.

Gladys suddenly turned left at a trail sign at the base of the outcrop, barely visible in the snow. I followed along a boulder-and treelined trail leading upwards through great stands of ponderosa pine, getting higher and higher to a point where the sound of wind through the trees was almost like the invisible swirl of a tornado. It sometimes masked the increasing number of thunder snow volleys. Thank God Gladys knew where she was going.

Gladys stopped. When I caught up with her, she pointed. "Up there."

Our eyes having adjusted reasonably well to the night and falling snow, we climbed between giant boulders, slipping and grabbing our way in and out of rock crevices, finally getting to a point where we were fairly well hidden, both from below and, so we thought, from above. The location also provided an adequate view of the trail we'd just left in case they found we had to respond. If they were following our tracks, we knew that was inevitable.

We waited, catching our breath, until we saw movement along the trail and a small light being flicked on and off at quick intervals. Undoubtedly to follow our tracks. This was followed periodically by a brief flash of lightning and thunder.

"Two," Gladys whispered in my ear.

"I saw four crossing the intersection, "I whispered back.

The two, barely visible figures stopped where our footsteps turned up from the trail. The light was switched on, this time staying on, revealing our footprints, giving me time to see each was armed with an assault rifle. One man pointed his rifle at our foot prints and up in our direction. He spoke and the light went out.

"Chinese QBZ Ninety-five's," Gladys whispered.

I didn't have time to mentally question how the hell she knew what kind of weapons they were when the first flash and rattle of gunfire started. We ducked behind the rocks, making ourselves as small as possible, at the same time flinching with each chink of bullets ricocheting off nearby boulders. It seemed like hundreds of rounds were fired, but it couldn't have been more than twenty or thirty per weapon.

At the first break in the gunfire, I raised myself to a point between two rocks with the Glock. Gladys did the same with her Sig Sauer through a small open space hidden by a shrub. We both took aim, Gladys at the human form on the left, me at the form on the right. It was as if we were reading each other's mind.

She said, "Go."

We both fired at the same time, two rounds per outline, chest to head high. Only one cried out, but both fell in a lump of heavy clothing. Their weapons, hot from firing, sent up slips of steam from the snow.

Gladys edged over to my side. "Two down, two to go," she whispered. "I'm going around to the other side of the outcrop to see if I can spot them."

I tried to stop her. "No, damn it, we'll –" She was gone. "For Christ's sake, Gladys, we…" but I was speaking to the wind.

* * *

Gladys made her way over rocks and around pine trees.

Eyes now acclimated to the night, she searched for movement. The sound of her footsteps through the snow was covered by the wind and the thunder snow as its flashes and accompanying cannonades of deep-throated growls moved steadily off from northwest to southeast. Within minutes, she reached a location looking out over the snow-covered meadow she and Matt had earlier crossed. The snow fall had begun to diminish and visibility had definitely increased.

She looked toward the sky and realized the moving clouds were reflecting the lights of Evergreen from the other side of the mountains, casting a ghostly glow over the meadow. Movement! At first the muscles of her body went rigid, but she quickly realized it was a small gang of elk walking along the tree line across the meadow off to her left.

She started back when suddenly she heard a man's voice, Chinese, not more than two feet behind her. She instinctively knew he was holding a weapon, pointed at her back. She also knew enough Chinese to know what he was saying. She laid the Sig Saur P-229 on a rock, turned and said in Mandarin dialect, "I do not have the papers."

The man appeared startled, hearing his own language from this strange American woman. His momentary hesitancy was enough for Gladys to swing to the left and, at the same time lash out with her right foot. The curve of the foot caught the outside of his left knee.

The blow crushed the lateral collateral ligament into the articular cartilage, dislocated the thigh bone from the tibia and tore the anterior cruciate ligament. Crying out in pain, he automatically bent and reached for his knee.

At the same time, Gladys grabbed the wrist of his gun hand, twisted and slammed the back of the hand hard against a large boulder. The impact crushed and dislocated the eight bones of the carpus, virtually freezing the interior nerves of the hand. The pistol dropped harmlessly away.

As he tried to rise and shout for help, she sledge-hammered

the base of his breast bone with her fist. It cracked the tail of the bone and forced the air from his lungs, almost doubling him in half. With the neck exposed above his jacket collar, she brought the lower edge of the fist down hard against the first and second cervical vertebrae just below the skull's occipital bone, compressing and bruising the spinal cord to the point that he dropped like a rock, headfirst into the snow. His forehead struck the side of the boulder that had damaged his hand. The force of his body weight and impact of his skull against the boulder snapped his head back with a sharp crack.

Gladys stood for a moment, silent, catching her breath and observing the body at her feet. Was he dead or alive? She bent to one knee and felt for a pulse at the side of his throat. She counted one Mississippi, two Mississippi, three Mississippi… to what she considered to be twenty seconds, but felt nothing.

She'd only killed in the same manner once before, in Amsterdam to save an informant. She didn't like it, but as then, she had done it to save a life. In this case, her own.

Briefly turning on her flashlight, she found the man's pistol in the snow, a Chinese QSZ-92 semi-automatic, put it in her jacket pocket and retrieved the Sig Sauer from the top of the rock where she'd placed it. She took a final look around in case she might see some evidence of the fourth man. When she didn't, she started back in Matt's direction, the snow storm now little more than intermittent flurries, the wind quieted to no more than a strong breeze.

* * *

After Gladys made her way off to my left, the snow had all but stopped as I skirted around the rocks to my right, keeping the trail below in view as best I could, the Glock off safety and ready to fire. My head jerked around when, out of the periphery of my vision, a wisp of dark against the snow ran across the trail, something small on four legs. Something like a fox, I reasoned.

That incident told me how skittish I'd become.

I returned to our original position as Gladys rounded one of the rocks, at first little more than a shadow. I stopped, went into firing position as did the shadow.

"Gladys?"

"Matt?"

With a great sigh of relieve, I lowered the Glock. She lowered the Sig and, at the same time, ran forward and wrapped her arms around me.

My arms went around her just as tightly. God, I was glad to see her. "We almost did their work for them," I said, holding her tight. Letting go, I asked, "Anything happen?"

"Three down, one to go," she said. "Tell you about it later. We need to keep moving. The trail leads up and around through the woods to a Park and Recreation District headquarters. At least it'll be warm."

A rock fell from somewhere above and a voice in reasonably good English called down, "You go nowhere."

Gladys and I both raised our weapons. Automatic gun fire split the air above our heads, causing both of us to duck. When we looked up, we could see the man's silhouette against the grayish white of clouds as they were driven by the higher winds across the sky.

"Guns, put them down. I could kill you now, but Doctor wants papers you found behind picture, papers not damaged. She knows who you are. Wants Berkeley man alive. The woman makes little difference."

"Why him?" Gladys angrily asked. "Why should he live and not me? I know as much as he does." She touched my arm and inched away from me, pushing the Sig Sauer through the snow with her foot while increasing the distance, giving at least one of us the opportunity to fight back and possibly survive.

"Do not play fool," he shouted. "His trip to Washington, his talk with FBI man. She needs to know. Who has papers?"

"She does," I shouted back.

Simultaneously, Gladys shouted, "He does, but I know as much as him. Why should he get to live if I don't? To hell with that."

I heard the man laugh. He was apparently enjoying himself at our willingness to sacrifice the other in order to live.

"Let's make a deal," I offered.

"No deal. I do what Doctor Sun orders. If woman has papers, give to Berkeley man, *now*!"

Buying time, I asked, "Who is Doctor Sun? The woman we heard in Bishop's house?"

"Doctor Sun, leader and maker of plan. Enough."

I heard the click of something against metal as he raised the assault weapon and swung it in our direction. The rifle itself was quickly lost in the darkness of his silhouette.

"I am very good shot. She die, shoot Berkeley man in shoulder, great pain, but still walk to see Doctor Sun. Waste time. No more talk."

I sensed the shifting of the weapon in Gladys's direction. "No-o-o-o," I cried and threw myself in her direction. My weight knocked her over and pinned her to the ground, my body covering her as two shots rang out.

I lay there. I'd been shot before, twice, knew how it felt. Those times, both shoulder and thigh, respectfully, the feeling like somebody hit me with a baseball bat. Each time there was no immediate pain for what seemed like the first minute or so until suddenly, an acetylene torch turned on, burning a hole all the way through my body. This time, still no impact, no pain, no fire, but everything was black. Was I dead? Hell of a way to go without getting a shot at the bastard.

"Open your eyes, Matt," Gladys wheezed, trying to take a deep breath from the impact of my body. "We're both alive. It appears the cavalry just arrived."

A familiar voice called up from the trail below. "Mr. Berkeley, Ms. Knight, you alright?"

"Yeah," I shouted as I pushed myself off Gladys and asked

her, "You okay?"

"Probably a little bruised, but thanks for thinking of me."

"I think I love you."

"Funny, but I think I'm feeling the same for you." She reached up and gave me a quick kiss. "I also think maybe when we get home, you'll have to do a close body check for all those bruises you gave me."

"My pleasure."

The crunch of boots on snow, a quick, "Damn it," when he slipped on some loose rocks hidden beneath the snow and the clunk of gun metal against a rock alerted us to Deputy Ralph Innes. "I told you I'd get here as fast as I could."

I couldn't help but laugh. "I'd appreciate it, if there's ever a next time, you'd use faster reindeer. But how'd you find us?"

He laughed. "Went by Bishop's house, car and a truck in the driveway, front door open but nobody there. Sound of gun fire can go for miles out here, and you and the bad guys left a trail in the snow like a herd of horses going into the park."

It was Gladys who immediately caught the truck and car thing. Looking at me, she cursed, "Damn it! The man in the sedan, he was the driver. That means this Doctor Sun woman's gone."

Without asking, Innes started up over some rocks above us. "Need to check to see what happened to our shooter."

"Think he's dead?" Gladys asked, both of us looking up where the man once stood. The snow clouds had pushed farther to the southeast. The only things we could see was the outline of Innes as he clambered over the rocks, the tops of pine trees off to the side, their limbs weighted with snow and a host of stars sparkling in and out of what scattered clouds still existed.

In answer to Gladys's question, Innes called back over his shoulder, "When I shoot a man, he's dead."

Chapter 39

It was a week later that, based on what I referred to as a "special invitation" from the Jefferson County Sheriff's Department, Gladys, Deputy Ralph Innes and I found ourselves seated at the conference table in Chief Kay's office. Before me was a brown folder containing copies of papers which Gladys and I, legally or otherwise, had taken from District Attorney Christopher Warren Bishop's vacation home on that highly memorable dark and stormy night. They were organized by the alphabetical names of individuals our Mr. B had blackmailed. Each set of papers were in chronological order according to the various events surrounding the person whose life, rightly or wrongly, had been so manipulated. Other papers more directly concerned Bishop himself.

Across the table were Chief Kay, Undersheriff Vasquez and Doctor Wong. Since Sheriff Donnie Ferguson had refused to attend, it became obvious this was not to be a complimentary award ceremony. From the looks on their faces, I assumed they were going to be both judge and jury in our now well publicized adventure. In fact, they hadn't even offered us coffee, water or anything else. Simply a very rude, "Sit."

It was Vasquez who spoke first. "As you know, District Attorney Bishop was found dead, burned to death, his car accidently having plunged off Lookout Mountain Road into Chimney Gulch. The car exploded, causing a wild fire which took a little more than two days to put out. Once the fire passed the point of the accident –"

I cut him off. "I doubt it was an accident."

"Proof?"

"I don't have any, but I think you do."

"Don't get smart, Berkeley. I'm at the end of my patience with you."

I refused to let Vasquez push me around. I'd come too far

for that. "You impounded a black pickup truck from in front of Bishop's home outside of Evergreen."

"Goddamn it, how the hell do you know that?"

Staring him eyeball to eyeball, I refused to answer, but pushed the point even further with, "It has a black bush guard over the grill. I understand there's silver paint where the guard hit something. I also understand Bishop's car was a silver-colored Buick. You should know by now the kind of people he was dealing with. Getting the proof is your job, not mine. Talk to your forensics people, to Felicia Gonzales, and they'll tell you."

His face livid with anger, he shouted, "Goddamn you, Berkeley, I'll see you –"

Chief Kay jumped in, cutting him off. "Undersheriff, please. We're all tired of anything and everything to do with the case, but you have to admit, Mr. Berkley and Ms. Knight have been extremely helpful, at least until they decided to go rogue."

She shot an evil eye and a raised eyebrow at Innes. "Not so sure about you, young man."

With a sigh of frustration, Vasquez sat back in his chair. A frown and sideways glance at Chief Kay showed his dislike for her speaking in our defense. "Continuing, the District Attorney met his death on the day that you, Mr. Berkeley and you, Ms. Knight, so blatantly went to his office to confront him using unsubstantiated information, primarily that which you generated on your own."

I butted in with, "Much of which we'd already shared with you and on which you refused to act."

Unfazed and once again, leaning forward and glaring at me, he went on. "Unknown to any of us, it turns out he was already dead at that time. Within hours, you broke into his Evergreen home, vandalized the place and with Deputy Innes's help, killed four men, men who –"

Again, I interrupted. "Men who were probably the one's that pushed Bishop off the mountain. Men who were trying kill Gladys and me to get the papers which we took from Bishop's house. Papers that will explain a helluva lot more about the Deer

Creek killings than you wanted to know, but we'll get to that once you decide to stop berating us."

"Stop it, you two," Wong ordered. "Since I've been involved throughout, I was invited to this meeting to hear Mr. Berkeley's and Ms. Knights stories about what happened that night at Bishop's home and in Three Sisters Park. Right or wrong, there's been enough conjecture in the media. Let them speak."

Knowing Wong wasn't under his control, Vasquez huffed, once again sat back in his chair, arms crossed and said, "Do it."

I looked and nodded at Gladys. "Gladys, you first."

Gladys reviewed our last meeting with the three sitting across the table, the results of her research relative to Bishop and the Sheriff's Department subsequent refusal to investigate. I took up with what we now knew was fake evidence concerning Roberta Wilson, aka Pine Woman, John and the other two members of the Indian Commission. As for the murder of Roberta, Long Bow and Brave Wolf, I explained the forensic evidence in each case shared with us by the Denver Police Department.

Gladys followed with our time at Bishop's home, including finding the papers in the back of the galloping horses' picture, the intruders and in Three Sister's park. Innes explained why he was there and the death of the fourth killer.

Following a number of pointed questions, Chief Kay said, "On the ten o'clock news last evening, KCNC Four I believe it was, there was the mention of incriminating papers taken from the District Attorney's home." She nodded toward the folder in front of me. "Is that what you have in that folder, Mr. Berkeley, the one's Ms. Knight spoke about?"

Ah well, no more *Matt,* back to Mr. Berkeley. I looked at Gladys and chuckled. "How times change," I said, before looking back to Chief Kay. "Yes, ma'am."

I slid the folder across the table. "Copies of copies plus a thumb drive with some very interesting photographs of your Captain Lundgren. Those copies are the sum of what we found between the picture Gladys mentioned and its backing. Everything to do with Lundgren, two former deputies from Douglas County and a number of other past and present employees of Jefferson, Arapahoe and Denver counties he was blackmailing to do things for him. Makes for interesting reading.

"What's best is in the two envelopes in the folder. One contains correspondence, written on paper and by e-mail, between Bishop and a person named Chén Liang, a man I believe. One letter discusses money to be provided by a company called China Rare Earth Group LTD. Money used to finance Bishop's daughter's medical care in California. It also discusses obtaining the Deer Creek Canyon land before the current Administration makes a final decision about rare earth elements.

"The second envelope contains the fabricated evidence in the Deer Creek Murders against John, Roberta and the other two men in addition to the already dead Samuel Hataali. It portrays them and the Denver American Indian Commission as responsible for the killings in an attempt to rid the Deer Creek area of property owners who they considered having desecrated sacred land.

"Their actions and motive were supposedly distinct from those of the British company trying to also buy the homes in Canyon Creek Estates. As of this morning's news, the company has further distanced themselves from any association with the Commission or the named individuals. Unfortunately, no one seems to be able to reach their representatives for further comment.

Taking a deep breath, I ended with, "Gladys and I contend that this company, Ralston World Wide Entertainment, is nothing more than a front for the Chinese government in an attempt to tie up the land."

"What do you mean," Doctor Wong asked.

"We tried to tell you and Chief Kay, and later the Undersheriff, about our visit with the Colorado Geological Survey. At the time, although we suspected, we weren't sure of the Ralston company's true objective which we now know was to keep U.S. companies from mining potential deposits of Bastnäsite for their various rare elements, militarily and domestically valuable to our country. By doing so, it would aid the Chinese to maintain their international monopoly on rare earths. There are others who agree with that thought, but that's a problem well above your pay grade."

"Is that all," Vasquez asked, shaking his head, visibly disturbed with what had been said.

"Not quite," Gladys answered. "In the second envelope Matt discussed, the one Chief Kay is opening right now, there's a short, hand-written note signed by a Doctor Sun Xiaolin. We believe it's the Doctor Sun – Sun pronounced 'Soon' by one of her men who tried to kill us – a woman whose voice we heard at Bishop's home. The man followed her name with words like 'leader and maker of the plan.' During my time in Hong Kong, Xiaolin was and I'm sure is still a common given name for females, in this case, Sun being the surname. Doctor Wong?"

"That's correct."

"Again, is that all?" Vasquez asked, continuing to show his impatience.

"Unless either of you have questions," I said.

"That being the case," Vasquez continued, "if you have other copies of these papers, I'm advising you to turn them over to us, immediately."

With as much sarcasm as I could put into a short laugh, I said, "I thought you might say that. Yes, we did make several other copies of the entire package, and no, we're not going to turn them over."

"If you don't, I'll put you –"

"Damn it, Vasquez, you'll put us where? Under the jail? This is bigger than you people. We gave you the opportunity to go further, explained the national implications of the case and recommended you investigate Bishop for his part in the scheme, but you said no."

I stopped and took a deep breath. Vasquez started to speak again, but I held up the palms of both hands and said, "I'm not through. As I told you before, I was in Washington a few weeks back and discussed everything with a friend of mine in the FBI's

Counterintelligence Directorate. At his request, a copy of the package has been sent to him. Gladys forwarded copies to contacts she has in the CIA's Intelligence and Analysis Division, and State Department's East Asian and Pacific Affairs. I'm sure they'll make certain the papers get to the right people."

Gladys picked up with, "As for what we kept, we've mailed them to someone who, if you try to take action against us, will provide every page plus the original evidence we gave to you to the national television networks, the *Washington Post, New York Times, Chicago Tribune, Los Angeles Times* and for local consumption, the *Denver Post*. All of it hinting at a local political cover-up concerning the D.A. Not good for Jefferson County, the Sheriff or the two of you." As she spoke the word *you*, she alternately pointed an index finger at Chief Kay and Vasquez.

Chief Kay tried to say, "But I didn't –"

"That's enough, Chief," Vasquez ordered.

"One more thing before we leave," I said. "If it hadn't been for Deputy Innes and his willingness to pursue the case with us, his mother and sister could have been assassinated and Gladys and I would definitely be dead. He is one of the good guys, and we'd hate to see anything happen to his career." I was sure, based on the tone of my voice and the pointed look I gave each of them, Vasquez and Chief Kay knew what we could and would do. I stood, followed by Gladys.

We both shook Innes's hand and said in our own words but with the same meaning, "Thank you for all you've done and for protecting our backs."

As we opened the door to leave, I turned and admitted, "Actually, up to a point, it was a pleasure working with each of you." Just before closing the door, I added, "The best of everything for your new son, Chief Kay.

"And Doctor Wong, take care the next time you go caving. As you've told us, bat droppings and those beetle things can really do a number on you."

He smiled and waved a friendly good-by. "Thanks, Matt.

I'll remember that."
    Closing the door behind us, we walked out of the building.

Chapter 40

Despite the loss of Roberta and the two other members of the Indian Commission, we decided it was time to have a celebration, at least a small one. Just John, Deputy Ralph Innes, Gladys, me and a couple of the Commission members who could make it. Gladys was at the supermarket buying some good, wholesome party food, the kind with lots of cholesterol, sodium, sugar, saturated fat and anything else that's bad for the human body but positively delicious to the taste buds. Following that was to be a quick stop at the neighborhood wine, beer and booze store for a couple of six-packs of Breckenridge Avalanche Amber Ale, Coors Light and Killian's Irish Red. For those with more refined tastes, a couple of bottles each of Jameson Irish Whiskey and a bottle of Glenmorangie Single Malt Scotch.

Back at Gladys's condo with a kitchen of Viking stainless steel appliances dedicated to good food and an off-white tile floor easy to clean, I was spicing up a crock of baked beans with plenty of chopped onions and sorghum molasses. Finished with that came the slicing and dicing of potatoes using my mom's greatest potato salad recipe, or as best I could recall.

Since Gladys had an eclectic collection of CDs – classical, Broadway and motion-picture-sound tracks – I had Prokofiev's Symphony Number Seven playing from the entertainment center in the living room. While my singing can be compared with that of a prehistoric pterodactyl squawk – think *Jurassic Park* – I was instead attempting to hum along with a particularly beautiful melody which surfaced periodically throughout the symphony.

Life was beginning to look a lot better until I heard my name called. The words were slow and deliberate. "Mr. Berkeley. You are Mr. Berkeley, are you not?"

With the music still sifting through my brain, the voice didn't register at first until suddenly, that same voice did an emergency ascent from the depths of my memory banks. *I know you are in here. If you've found the papers, give them to us and I'll let you go.*

I whirled around and saw a woman standing in the doorway to the kitchen. Her head was tilted as though to form a question mark with her body. She was only slightly shorter than me, a solid build and dressed in a light gray pants suit, the collar of a charcoal gray and white blouse showing just above the jacket. Long, midnight black hair, not unattractive, but a face that was hard, uncompromising with eyes that shot daggers through me.

The most impressive thing about her was the semiautomatic pistol in her right hand, one similar if not the same as the Chinese QSZ-92 semiautomatic Gladys took from the man in Three Sisters Park.

Naturally my initial reaction was to ask, "How did you get in here?" As soon as the words escaped from my mouth, I realized it really didn't make a damn bit of difference how she got in. What was important was she was here and the weapon she held in her hand.

"Dumb question. You must be Dr. Sun, Dr. Sun Xiaolin. Your name was in Bishop's papers. You were at Bishop's house in the mountains. Your men tried to kill us."

Her laugh was soft, yet tinged with bitterness. "A pity they did not succeed. It would have made my life much simpler. Your meeting with Mr. Granger of the FBI and information you've provided has created many complications."

"Sounds like you have an inside informant, but regardless of what I've provided to the FBI or anybody else, you're here to kill me."

"Yes. Your actions have been most troublesome, in particular, for me. My government does not look favorably on failure. At least I will die with the knowledge that I have eliminated you and your female friend." She raised the gun and pointed it at my chest.

I quickly raised my hand as if asking permission to speak. "Before you shoot, at least answer two questions which have bothered me during this entire affair."

"What is that?"

"First, why kill Bishop? I know it was your people who did it."

"He disobeyed my orders."

Having spent a lot of years in the Navy and knowing orders had to be followed, all I could say was, "Fair enough, and second, why didn't Ralston Worldwide Entertainment, as well as your other fake companies in the other states, try to get the mineral rights along with the land you were trying to buy?"

She laughed softly. "Come now, Mr. Berkeley. That would have raised even more questions than simply purchasing the land, the land's use in each case having nothing to do with mining or drilling for minerals. I would have thought, you of all –"

Dr. Sun jerked her head toward the living room as she and I heard Gladys call, "Matt, the front door was unlocked. Is there any –"

From that moment on, it was as if everything happened in nanosecond time. I cut her off by yelling, "Get out, Gladys. Get out."

I switched the potato dicing-and-slicing knife in my hand from handle to blade and threw it with all my strength at Dr. Sun in an attempt to distract her. With that, I started to duck behind the granite-topped island at which I'd been working.

At the same time, Sun's pistol fired, twice. On the way down, I felt something punch me in the top of my left shoulder, twisting me around as I went down. I remember grunting, "Son of a bitch!"

Simultaneously I heard a scream, followed by what I assumed was cursing in Chinese. Had I miraculously hit the woman with the knife?

More shots in my direction, round after round, an unending

barrage fired with apparent frustration and anger. Each bullet ricocheted off the granite counter top and shattered the hand-painted tile splash board above and behind the glass-topped stove. I stopped counting at ten.

The shooting stopped with a loud *click* as quickly as it had begun. With the left shoulder of my sky-blue shirt beginning to turn a dark red and fire starting to burn down my arm and into my chest, I lifted myself up with my right arm to standing position.

Dr. Sun was pulling the knife from her thigh as Gladys flew through the doorway, screaming, "Bitch!" and slammed into Sun, sending both to the floor. Sun's pistol skidded across the tile floor and disappeared through a narrow opening beneath the stove.

Sun, larger than Gladys, managed to force her way on top of Gladys and with the knife she pulled from her thigh, stabbed down at Gladys's neck. Gladys jerked her head to the side. The blade missed the throat, but took off the lobe of Gladys's ear before striking the tile floor, snapping off at least a half inch of the blade's point.

Before Sun could strike again with the knife still in her hand, Gladys slapped both of Sun's ears with the flat palms of her hands, forcing tremendous pressure against the ear drums and a cry of pain from the woman.

I stood as fast as I could and swung around the side of the island. Using my right arm and hand, I grabbed a fist full of the woman's below-the-shoulder-length black hair and yanked her backwards. She let out a howl, filling the air with Chinese curses, arms flailing with that damn knife.

With me still holding on to her hair, to my amazement, using one arm and both feet, she twisted her body around like a cat snagged on the end of a dangling rope, pushed forward and swept the broken end of the knife at my midsection.

The knife sliced through the front of my shirt and carved a line through the skin across my abdominal muscles. No real pain at first, but I could feel a wide line of blood seeping down into my undershorts and to my legs. With only the one good arm, my left shoulder and arm hurting like hell, I let go of her hair and grabbed my stomach. Bad move.

She got to her feet, not as fast as she had been, but then I saw why. The inside of her left pants leg and the crotch area of her slacks were dark red, almost black, soaked with blood. I didn't know if it was my imagination or not, but it looked like blood pulsing against the material of her slacks where she'd pulled the knife from her thigh. Had I hit an artery, and was she bleeding out? If so, it damn well wasn't fast enough.

Teeth clinched with determination, mumbling words I couldn't understand, Sun came at me, both of us leaving a trail of blood behind, the knife blade swinging back and forth, closer and closer. My backward progress came to an abrupt stop when my back slammed against the cupboard door, the knife only inches from my stomach.

A shadow from beneath the bank of overhead lights, a yowl that sounded like an Indian war cry and Gladys flew through the air, feet first. Both feet caught Sun in the back of one knee. The blow forced the knee out into a horizontal V shape in my direction. The weight of the woman's body settled backwards in a crushing thump on the floor, the damaged leg super extended at a 180° angle beneath the woman's body. The knife skittered across the floor out of reach.

Despite Sun's scream of pain, Gladys deliberately stomped the ankle of her other leg, tearing tendons and separating the leg bones from the ankle bone. Except for moans and tortured curses piercing our ears, there was no way Dr. Sun was going to cause any more damage to either of us.

"I'm calling nine-one-one," Gladys said. "We need to get you to the hospital."

I slid my backside down against the cupboard door into a sitting position, keeping pressure on the cut across my stomach. "I'll live, but first, my knife must've hit the woman's femoral artery in her thigh. She's bleeding out. Grab some towels. Give me one for my stomach and use one for a tourniquet around her upper thigh. Then call nine-one-one. As much as I dislike doing it, we need to save her for Tom Granger and his FBI playmates.

Chapter 41

It was later that night when I awoke – close to midnight from what I was told. My brain and entire body felt like it was coated with fuzz, washed out like I'd been on a two-day drunk. Everything was hazy, as though looking through a frosted glass. Actually, all I could make out was a wall and curtains, the curtains wrapping around me on what appeared to be a continuous rod covering two sides of the room. On the wall was a plastic board, different entries, some checked off with a black marker, some not. Beneath was a roller-type table holding clip boards and various papers.

A machine at the side of the bed *bleep-bleep-bleeped* every few minutes when something around my arm swelled, tightened and gradually loosened. What was behind me didn't really enter my mind. Past the curtains, however, there was a lot of loud talking that sounded like so much gibberish. It was hard to concentrate, to focus on any one thing. I knew there were things I had to do, but I wasn't sure at the moment what they were.

I saw the outlines of what I thought to be human figures moving around me, shifting pillows beneath my head, adding a blanket to my feet. In addition to their soft murmurings which I couldn't make out because of the outside noises, the pair of images, both wearing light blue scrubs, moved in and out of my gradually improving eyesight.

Something I did hit on was two, relatively clear plastic bags hanging on an IV pole a foot or so above my right shoulder. Two tubes ran down from the bags to separate ports on what looked like a hypodermic affair mounted on the back of my wrist. From the looks of it, I would have sworn it had at least six yards of opaque tape holding everything down.

"Where am I?" I asked a light blue scrub who was adjusting something under one of the bags hanging on the pole. Even my voice sounded as though it was forcing its way through a layer of gravel, my throat dry and scratchy.

"You're in recovery after what they said was very successful surgery. Would you like some water?"

I gave a slight nod. "Cold, ice, please."

As she left for the water, I asked the other scrub who, it finally dawned on me, had to be a nurse, "What's... what's that thing on the back of my wrist? Some kind of needle thing?"

She chuckled, answering, "It's called a cannula, and yes, a kind of needle thing, only slightly larger."

I shifted my eyes up toward the two bags hanging on the pole, a slow drip, drip, drip flowing from each bag into their respective tubes. "And you're pumping what into me?"

"Good things," she answered, her voice sweet, assuring as though explaining the sprinkling of fairy dust on a child to stop the pain of a skinned knee or elbow.

I suppose at that point I *was* pretty child-like. "What kind of *good things* are they?" I wanted to answer my own question with *fairy dust*, but held back.

"A saline solution to keep you hydrated and an antibiotic just in case of infection from the bullet wound and the cut across your lower abdomen."

"That's nice, but we need to take the needle out and help me up. I need to get dressed."

"Why is that?" She placed a hand on my shoulder as though to hole me back.

Along with the two drip bags, the cannula thing and the machine going *bleep-bleep-bleep,* from somewhere back in the fuzz of my mind, I had been picturing the Intracoastal Waterway flowing south, or was it north? The pier, my paint-scarred L. L. Bean two-seater canoe and an oak tree limb sticking up through a hole in the roof above my beautiful back porch and kitchen. Everything vivid, as much as the room around me.

"I've got to get on my roof down in..." I had to think a moment before the word surfaced. "... my roof down in Florida. Make sure they fix it right."

"It might be best if you wait a few days before you go to Florida and climb up on your roof," she said, a sympathetic smile on her face. "You wouldn't want to do anything to tear the stitches in your tummy and shoulder."

Things were beginning to get clearer: surgery, stitches, tummy, shoulder. Lots of blood on the floor, Gladys with blood running down the side of her face from ear to jaw line, the woman, a Chinese woman crying and moaning in front of me, blood pooling beneath her legs.

I tried to move, at first surprised there was no pain, gradually realizing it had to be anesthesia hanging on after surgery. At that moment, I said to myself, "Thanks, God, for anesthesia."

I did, however, feel a kind of pressure around my midsection, like a wide belt of tape stretched taut across my lower abdomen. Slowly, gingerly, using the hand with the taped-on canula, I held the sheet and blanket up as best I could. Without raising my head, I looked down. And there it was – tape. Glancing to my left, my shoulder looked like it was covered in a cast. It kept me from moving my arm, like the time as a kid when I popped my wrist falling out of a tree.

I nodded approval to her suggestion to wait on the roof, the visions of my house fading from the present. "You're probably right," I agreed, immediately thinking, *Where the hell did the roof thing come from? I'm in a frigging recovery room after surgery, at least that's what they're saying.* "Not a smart thing to do."

I nodded toward my stomach and continued with, "I remember the knife cut, but the bullet wound. What did it do?"

"The doctor will explain in detail when he visits."

The second nurse pushed the curtain aside, entered with the ice water and tilted my head up slightly from the pillows so I could get a bent straw into my mouth. I sucked and God, the water and its coldness felt so good.

My thirst momentarily quenched, my mind finally accepted reality, where I was and what had happened. With that, I said, "Thanks, but a question. There was a lady, Gladys Knight. She okay?"

"Ask her yourself. You have two visitors, a Ms. Knight and a Mr. Na…"

I finished the name for her. "Nabhe, good looking guy and a great looking woman."

The nurse bent over close to my ear. "About the man, you can say that again. If I wasn't married…" She let the final words drift into silence, but the sly smile on her face gave away the meaning.

"Yeah, good looking guy and he's single." We both laughed.

The other nurse said, "We'll leave you for a short visit, but not too long."

"Hi, sailor," Gladys said as the curtain separating the room from the passage way parted. "The surgeons, two of them, said you'd probably live another ten to twenty years."

I couldn't help but smile. With my vision getting better, I reached out and touched Gladys's hand. "Only if you'll be there with me."

Another voice, John Nabhe's, warned from the end of the bed. "Gladys, if I know the guy, he's delirious. Don't believe a word he says."

"Don't listen to him," I argued.

Gladys prodded me in the thigh. "You'd better damn well be serious, or you'll be spending a lot more time in the hospital than you planned."

My vision had cleared to the point that I saw Gladys's left ear wrapped in gauze and tape.

"Your ear!"

"Dr. Sun's work. Part of my ear lobe – *lobule* being the correct anatomical terminology so I've learned – it's missing. Will you still love me?"

With my voice, as croaky as it was, I said, "Sweetheart, as the old song says, 'I'm gonna love you, like nobody's loved you, come rain or come shine. High as a mountain, –'"

"Knock it off, Berkeley," John said with a groan. "Sinatra you're not."

"Hush, John," Gladys warned. "I don't care if he can carry a tune or not." Taking my hand in hers, she said, "As Lynn Anderson sang, 'I want the whole wide world to know you're my man.' So there." As she leaned over, whatever lyrics might have followed disappeared in a kiss which was definitely the best thing that happened to me in the last twenty-four hours.

Her song followed with, "Now, to business. Although I'm not family... not yet anyway..." she smiled, one eyebrow raised as though in question.

"Are you proposing?" I asked.

She ignored my question, continuing, "Your two surgeons met with me following your surgery. While you did need a pint of blood, the wound in your stomach area was basically superficial and should heal without any problems. The bullet wound in your shoulder, however, was a little more complex."

"Complex? Like what?"

"The bullet nicked the underside of the scapula or shoulder blade only a millimeter or two from where it connects with the humerus, the arm bone. To quote her, 'It did a number on your deltoid muscle.' Even with a lot of rehab, the shoulder may never be one hundred percent, but she did say you were lucky."

"Better than being dead," I said. "Anything on Doctor... What's her name? I'm still a little groggy up here." I tapped to the side of my head with the hand carrying the cannula or whatever the hell you call it.

"Dr. Sun Xiaolin," Gladys supplied.

John said, "I met and talked briefly with a Sergeant Sally Springer with the Denver Police Department down stairs. She finally connected my face with my name. I helped her people some years back on an American Indian case concerning drugs."

For the thousandth time, I thought, *who the hell doesn't he know?*

"She said she knew the two of you. Told me after X pints of blood and many hours of surgery, the Sun woman's in intensive care in critical but stable condition. And Matt, Sally's working with your friend Granger. Gladys got his number from a card in your wallet. He flew in from Washington this evening.

"He's got people from the Denver FBI office standing guard outside the doctor's room. Gladys and I talked briefly with him. He said he'd see you tomorrow morning." John ended with, "While she did some damage, you guys must've really put her through a wringer."

"What I did to the woman you'd better believe was a fluke, but Gladys is the one who delivered the knockout punch." To Gladys I added, "That was one hell of blow you gave the woman's knee. I remember you literally flew through the air to get her. I don't know whether I heard it or felt it, but thinking back, I'd swear there was a distinct snap of bones, ligaments or something."

Gladys laughed. "I was really aiming for the middle of her back to break her spine, but I slipped in all the blood and ended up hitting the back of the knee."

I took her hand and pulled her down for a kiss. Once finished, I said, "Like Joe Namath once said, 'When you win, nothing hurts.' Knee or back, lucky for me."

She laughed again. "Luck or not, I have to tell you I'm really good at taking out knees."

"How's that?" John asked.

"I'll tell you both sometime, but for now, just take my word. As for my semi-proposal, Mr. Mathew W. Berkeley, what's the answer?"

"I'm good, but for a honeymoon and winter coming, we've got to get back down to Florida. I've got a two-seater canoe you're gonna love."

THE END

ABOUT THE AUTHOR

William Kerr, whose naval career spanned 25 years of ship and shore commands, including liaison to the United States Congress on behalf of the Deputy Chief of Naval Operations (Logistics), retired at the rank of Captain before starting his writing career. Kerr is the author of the best-selling series of action/suspense novels featuring Matt Berkeley, former Navy Special Warfare officer and security expert in the field of archeology. Originally from Mississippi and Florida, Kerr lives with his wife in Highlands Ranch, Colorado.

Made in the USA
Coppell, TX
09 November 2019